'Tho I Be Mute

Heather Miller

'Tho I Be Mute

First Edition: April 2021

Printed in the United States of America

10 9 8 7 6 5 4 3 2 1

ISBN 13: 978-1-948035-75-0 Paperback
ISBN 13: 978-1-948035-76-7 eBook

Published by Defiance Press and Publishing, LLC

Bulk orders of this book may be obtained by contacting Defiance Press and Publishing, LLC. www.defiancepress.com.

Public Relations Dept. – Defiance Press & Publishing, LLC
281-581-9300
pr@defiancepress.com

Defiance Press & Publishing, LLC
281-581-9300
info@defiancepress.com

CONTENTS

October Hills

I look upon the purple hills
That rise in steps to yonder peaks,
And all my soul their silence thrills
And to my heart their beauty speaks.

What now to me the jars of life,
Its petty cares, its harder throes?
The hills are free from toil and strife,
And clasp me in their deep repose.

They soothe the pain within my breast
No power but theirs could ever reach,
They emblem that eternal rest
We cannot compass in our speech.

From far I feel their secret charm—
From far they shed their healing balm,
And lost to sense of grief or harm
I plunge within their pulseless calm.

How full of peace and strength they stand,
Self-poised and conscious of their weight!
We rise with them, that silent band,
Above the wrecks of Time or Fate;

For, mounting from their depths unseen,
Their spirit pierces upward, far,
A soaring pyramid serene,
And lifts us where the angels are.

I would not lose this scene of rest,
Nor shall its dreamy joy depart;
Upon my soul it is imprest,
And pictured in my inmost heart.

–John Rollin Ridge 1827-1867

CHAPTER 1

Daughter of the Sun

Clarinda Ridge

October 1856

Near Rome, Georgia

Murky green light escaped the branches above me through their canopy of last leaves. Ever-changing sunlight illuminated the path as I rose beneath the forest shadows. Red hair, gifted from my mother, reflected the beams in ultraviolet luminescence. Wearing a fringed, old coat of goat hide, my back became the canvas for this painting of light, seeping through the wispy branches of oak. Retrieving a small bag at my side, I opened it and placed my treasure: moonflower blossom, leaves, and vine. Cinching the satchel tight, I looped its leather ties through my belt.

Hickory trees towered my petite frame as I crossed the creek with ancient knowledge, gained from many moonlit crossings through this, my last home in the forested mountain valley. Moccasin-covered feet paddled through the light and shadow, following the path of the rabbit, the deer, skittering in quick bursts before me. My feet glided unencumbered above the ground.

Golden streams of light faded to hues of blue while storm clouds fronted their way into the sanctity of my quiet. Thunder in the distance woke the owl. His eyes opened, startled wide and golden. I stopped and held his gaze. Mind to mind, I acknowledged the owl's warning of the storm's approach this upcoming night. I turned forward to proceed home but stopped, in awe, mistrusting my vision.

Translucent against the grassy distance, Papa appeared, dressed in our people's regalia; gray and black feathers adorned his buckskins. He reached for me. I feared running to him meant he might dim, disappear. Remembering his warmth, I watched him with my child's eyes and followed his stained hands, pointing to the owl's mighty talons grasping the top branch.

Papa's spirit walked to me, free of limp and cane. Once beside me, he pantomimed his bedtime story of the woman who married the owl, one he'd told me hundreds of times.

Papa's legend was just for me, one he didn't share with my brothers or sisters. He began then as he did now, with arms stretched wide, like wings. In human form, the owl husband provided only insignificant creatures for his new wife to eat. Once learning his secret, the new wife released him from his marriage vow. He transformed back to his bird form and flew to the utmost branches. Although she shunned him, he watched her, protected her while she remained on Earth.

Papa's spirit laughed at his tale again tonight, as he had many nights before, touching my cheeks and eyelids with a feather's softness. His hands signed,

"Don't marry the owl, Moonbeam. No one is smart enough for you."

Papa's spirit rose to the heavens, although his smell remained, air tinted with pine sap and fresh ink, black pepper and saddle leather.

In Papa's absence, my eyes met the owl as his attention shifted from protection to the hunt. He angled his head to the east and focused on the ground. His wings spread aside to dive, talons extended in silent might. His prey was lost to me after his descending swoop into the earth-littering brush. Owl attacked a sound, a rattle not reaching my ears.

Changing light from approaching clouds reminded me of my task.

Proceeding to the edge of the valley, I slowed my pace and emerged from the dense forest to sense the rising charge. Hair on my arms lifted. Static traveled up from the ground and down from the air to connect through me. At this distance, lightning-filled clouds arced in blinding brightness, turning the sky's gray-blues into hues of momentary purple. As I turned away, the heavens shook in long, slow vibrations of thunder following each incandescent crescent of light. Wind blew the storm to me. With attuned eyes, I followed its fate, shaming the clouds for snuffing emerging night's stars.

With deliberate steps, I crossed the high grasses bordering my secluded valley. I waded through, like stepping in knee-deep water. Behind me, the suffocated, dusky sunlight faded as the approaching wind swarmed me. Like bees knocked from a hive, wind blew my coat away from my frame, filling and blowing it outward like blazing flames from the first fire. Loose red hair atop my head wound and twisted into an unformed crown woven by wind's skillful hand. I tempted the same current to raise me to the Nightland, to Skili, to Honey, to Papa, to Momma.

Nearby, rabbits and squirrels ceased to scurry and burrowed for cover; birds hid their heads under their wings, preparing for the tumultuous night. Nature braced itself for the rain and wind, quiet and still. I knew this storm. Grandmother told me the story of the Brothers of Thunder: one brother wild, the other tame as they played ball in the sky, shaking the earth below. They were the sons of *Selu*, born from the corn, and *Kanati*, the hunter.

I pushed open the deer horn handle and stepped up slabs of slanted wood on their stone foundation to the awaiting calm of my single-room cabin. Aromas from herbs of summer's last color blew from the sudden atmospheric change, filling the air with fragrances of plantain, jewelweed, yellow root, sassafras. These herbs were necessary for my work. Dried to death, these medicines healed the sick, both slave and Cherokee alike. My grandmother taught me, Papa's mother. She trained me to watch the plant, to understand the root, to respect the illness, to administer the remedy. If the Great Spirit sent disease to take man or woman from the Earth, no intervention would prevail.

Digaleni, my sleeping redbone coonhound, sprawled beside my door with his hind legs stretched behind him. He opened one eye in acknowledgment as I pushed the door closed against the intrusive wind. I set the large, wooden latch swung from a nail in the wall. Outside, imminent rain turned the leaves of the sturdy oak downside up as the storm charged upon the land. Beneath my feet, the floor trembled.

I made this desk and its awaiting chair from driftwood flowing down the Oostanaula River near here. Lying open was my plant journal, homemade with brittle parchment of brown and gray, covered with goat hide. Edges and corners, bent and faded, were worn lighter than the cover itself. This volume contained secrets from the forest: pressed in life, preserved in death, and sketched with homemade ink from walnut shells and rusty nails. My journals contained the lessons learned from a life of sight; so many, they hid the floor. I pressed the moonflower between its blank pages. Captured this evening before the storm, this young blossom was open and full. Now, the bloom slept in perpetual night. Alive, the moonflower opened its petals only at midnight. Ground in mortar, pummeled by pestle, these blooms stopped life short. Flowers brought illness, tremors, visions, death. Some warriors fought with pistols, some with tomahawks; my weapons were not forged but grown. As if a warning against such weighty thoughts, the wooden planks renewed their rumblings.

From the closed book, I reached for the emerging ribbon marking my page. Frayed from age, the green velvet ribbon slid between my thumb and finger, still soft on one side and silken on the other. Momma's image collected behind my eyes, dressed in the ribbon's same shade. From my memory, Momma appeared youthful, her red hair holding green ribbons in braided locks against blossoming white skin. Papa called Momma *Dh Ani*, his strawberry.

Opening my eyes, I reached for an older volume, one overflowing with scribed and sheathed memories. I traced my hands over Papa’s script in Cherokee syllabary and English letters. My lessons began before my feet met the end of the chair. Papa sat me on his lap, writing questions, asking for my answers in one language and then another. As I grew taller, he stood behind me, running his hands through my hair as I practiced. His notes became longer as my child’s scrawling script became smaller, each question more important and complex than the last. I turned each page where his hands had been. What would he write to me now? If I could only craft another answer.

Subsequent pages showed Momma’s small script in words, love behind drawings of flowers and herbs. “To my Moonbeam,” headed each rendering. No matter how tall I became, Momma addressed me the same. She’d write, “God made you from the sun and sent you to the Moon, who loved so bright.” This drawing held a moonflower, like the one I pulled from the ground. I bent to the words and rested my head. Momma’s breast returned my embrace.

Thunder shook the oak tree’s limbs, sheltering my cabin. Through the cracked glass, blue lightning cast a shadow on the floor, white man’s silhouette in a brimmed hat, black against the grain of the floor. I feared this sign, a warning of dangerous strangers. Cold rushed through me. The shape disappeared as fast as it revealed itself. White men still tempted, taking more than a single life could offer: Home, Heritage, Legacy, and Legend.

Storm clouds stole the last daylight while I removed my coat. In the sudden darkness, my hand reached for the cold pewter candle holder, topped with beeswax stick and wick. Carrying it to the wood-burning stove near the window, I pulled a twig from a thin broom, its usefulness long forgotten, and removed a switch, touching it to an ember in the banked fire. Smoke billowed into the cabin from the stove’s door. The switch sparked. I torched the candlewick in its man-made rest and returned to the wood-burning stove, dragging the chair behind me—the tree’s extension of my hand. Opening the stove door and loading the iron beast with oak, wood smoked, ignited. This weather premeditated more of its kind: a harsh, blowing fall that doused and chilled the bones of those left outside under tonight's storm's revenge.

I removed my leather shoes and woolen socks, stretching out my legs near the fire. *Digaleni* stirred and stood, expecting the stove's radiant heat. He stretched his hind legs, extending his hindquarters high as his ears weighed his head low. He slunk for a scratch behind his namesake—*Digaleni*, ears in English—and sank low in front of the stove. I propped my feet atop his shoulder blades, both of us content to remain for the upcoming hours of this full moon's rebellious storm.

Anxious rain pelted the roof with innumerable drops. Water collected in an old iron pot from a small hole in the roof where the oak's branches grew through weaker boards. Neither limb nor rain intruded, was only a welcomed, accustomed guest. Like two people sitting with their backs together, my home and oak tree held one another upright.

I grabbed a spool and my hoop from Momma's sewing box beside my chair. Using my teeth to separate a strand, I licked the thread to make it straight and held the needle steady to weave the cotton thread through the eye. With the muslin-covered hoop angled in my lap, I stitched from practice and skill. With continued minute and deliberate gestures, a border formed with each stitch. Then, with keen eyes, I rethreaded the needle. This time, instead of thread, I used a strand of my hair, licking the end before threading the eye.

From here, I sewed with my eyes closed, each stitch guided by touch alone. The door rattled against the wind. Not hearing, I sewed one petal of the incomplete moonflower. *I must complete this task tonight*. Opening my eyes, I saw the shape of the full bloom, filling with my hair, sewn by my fingers. I continued to the next.

Digaleni stood with a slow-rumbled woof to the door while I sewed and prayed to the Great Spirit for an hour longer. The rain beat and blew. With one last elaborate pull and knot, the poisonous moonflower was complete but starkly different from the one between the pages. It contrasted in color from the bloom, as do I, with my blood from two nations.

From exhaustion, the rain ceased its tantrum. The moon looked peacefully again upon the Earth. While the Thunder Brother, the one that lost the game, growled and rumbled with resignation from the far side of the mountain. I moved to my bed and dreamt of bird spirits who lost their wings and transformed into great white snakes.

Daylight found my eyes in the eastern sky's morning haze. It turned colder. *Digaleni* pawed beside the door as I rubbed my eyes against the day's masked sun. I moved first to sit and then to stand and walked to lift the latch. *Digaleni* bounded down the steps and pawed at the grassy ground. I could not see what he sought. Then, his body contorted and limped away, darkened within my standing shadow. He fell on his side, curled, and did not move again. With hurried steps, I reached for him. The rattler struck, jaws spread wide, clamping onto my outstretched forearm. I gasped with escaping breath—soundless.

Poison seeped into my blood. My eyes clouded as I fell. My body spilled down the stairs. The snake slithered across my tousled strands into the grass. Having completed his quest, he rattled in triumph. Continuous ticks pulsed in time with my failing heart. Owl's wings shuttered, and he flew northward.

CHAPTER 2

All That I Have Ever Had Is Yours

John Ridge

November 1818–1820

Cornwall, Connecticut

Little on our long-distance travels from Cherokee Nation Territory to Connecticut held my attention as much as the pocket watch in the window of Riggs and Brother Emporium in Philadelphia. I stood, mesmerized by brass and silver, circles and chains, illustrating man's mechanical genius. Lock and key opened the mechanism, splitting the case into symmetrical sections. Brass gears and copper springs unwound with pressured precision. Inside, the face was white with Roman numerals surrounding the dial. Black hands marked hours and minutes in minutiae. Man's engineering made real the abstract concept of time, measured by pulsing ticks.

Staring through the glass beside me was Dr. Dempsey, my chaperone, who advised against the expense. "The cost is impressive, John; it is a gentleman's watch." My glare's intention was distinct as he began his wielding retraction. "Not to say that you will not be a gentleman one day when you finish your education, but you are yet just a young man of fifteen." He implied no Cherokee should own such an expensive possession.

With sarcasm, I refuted his warning. "In my youth, does time not pass in the same manner as it passes at your age? Do all men not answer to the same thrift use of minutes, hours, and days?" He did not engage in my philosophy or the insult to his advancing age.

"The cost will take most of your remaining travel money." He attempted to deter me with guilt. "I would have to loan to you for the remainder of our trip."

"It would not be for long. Father enabled you to sign a draft from the New York bank fund for contingencies, should a need arise." This purchase was no contingency—not one my father could have foreseen. Nevertheless, if Father were here, he would recognize my desire and intention—impulsive but imperative. I imagined the watch resting inside the pocket of my waistcoat, hoarding hours, but seen by others as an outward sign of my family's class. How was my desire any different from my father's love of an excellent horse? The watch would show others that I am a man for this age, progressive. Had I explained this to Father, he would see the watch in the same manner I did.

"Vanity," Dempsey claimed sin.

I claimed hypocrisy. "If that is so, why am I asked to dress this way," I gestured to my cravat, "instead of my buckskins and moccasins? Even my stockings are silk under these boots."

"Damn it, John." His stretch into profanity and his concession let me know I won the debate. He rang the bell inside the store and made the purchase. It became my accustomed humiliation to be unable to make the purchase myself. Rapt attention held me to the shopkeeper's hands. Through the glass, I watched the merchant wrap the watch inside the crinkling paper as he placed it in a box adorned with golden filigree. This timepiece would be my constant, weighted reminder to make opportunities of time.

Long days later, we approached Cornwall, Connecticut, from the south. From the coach windows, the village introduced itself with stables and sawmills to accommodate the apparent logging trade. Many sheep grazed in the valley of Colt's Foot Mountain, supplying the wool mill with its need for raw materials. Hamlets of family farms surrounded First Church, not only in location but also in my impressions of the pious lifestyle of its parishioners. Wooden fence posts and rails divided Cornwall, where at home, Cherokee land overlapped and provided for an entire people.

The Academy of the Foreign Mission schoolhouse sat among bare cedar trees and hemlocks this blustery fall of November 1818. The school building was a gambrel-roofed, two-story structure with a chimney on one end and weather vane on the other, acting as bookends. Next to our classroom, a winter garden grew purple-leafed kale and hearty cabbage. A bare maple stood alone in the yard. With it, I sympathized, separate yet under constant surveillance—naked. Unimpressive in appearance, this academy was where I hoped to gain insight into history and English, more advanced than my previous schools at Spring Place and Brainerd. Here, I must endure the constant watchful eye of Cornwall's residents: my teachers.

Reminiscent of the original 'city on the hill,' the Foreign Mission School was primarily for religious instruction, training future missionaries whose intent would be to convert the 'savages.' I understood the whites' faith; the Great Spirit had many names. Therefore, I would be contrite, but full conversion was not my intention. I did not plan to become a missionary, but a lawyer, a politician. It was what my people needed. I would leave it to the Great Spirit to guide the Cherokee to salvation.

Dr. Dempsey interrupted my observations with reminders of my father's expectations and guidelines for my behavior. To say these reminders were absent from my attention would imply his words were irrelevant. Still, Dempsey's lecture was unnecessary. "We are here, John. Let us make our introductions," concluding his sermon from the coach. We crossed the worn path, with Dempsey leading and I following behind him as these crutches slowed my walk.

Upon entering, smells of recent peat fires and old books struck me. Sheer numbers of texts bordered the log walls of the schoolroom. The spines on the shelves wrapped around home-crafted tables and straight-backed chairs set for study and meals. A small fire burned in the hearth, and candles lit this day of clouds. As we entered, students, grouped in pairs, hovered over what appeared to be books of prayer. Students took turns reading in English, various verses absent of context and translated them into the languages of their homelands—missionary school indeed. The Bible taught me many things from the stories whites esteemed, including what it means to be a man. Although I would never be a Sampson or King David, my English name was John. My Cherokee name, *Skahtlelohskee*, the mockingbird.

Reverend Herman Daggett, principal of the school and teacher, introduced me to my fellow students. "Your arrival pleases us, John Ridge. The Lord has directed your steps. God guided your journey, not just to save you but the many you will advise. May I introduce you to your fellow students?"

He recited their names, and I acknowledged them with courtesy, not knowing the full extent of English spoken in the room. Students stood upon introduction, dressed in clean, black homespun coats. Some were from islands far to the west; some traveled here across the Pacific Ocean from China; some were from countries in India and the Middle East; and to my surprise, there were three white students. There were Choctaws and Abnaki Indians and Cherokee, including my father's brother's son. He adopted the name Elias Boudinot while living away from our homeland, naming himself after a missionary who enthralled him with passionate prose. To me, though, he was my brother and cousin, Buck Wattie.

After the others were dismissed for afternoon chores, we embraced as brothers should. He spoke in Cherokee, inquiring of his father's health and mine in sequence, and received news of their strength and successes. After assuring him of our mothers' continued good health, Buck wanted a report of the crops and surpluses from the year's harvest. He asked whether I had ridden his horse. Buck was my truest friend, cognizant of my past illnesses of lungs and hip when I was thirteen, just as I was aware of his propensity for abstractions and distractions.

Near home, at Spring Place Mission School, I asked questions our teachers found insufficient knowledge to answer. Elias told stories, erupting the class with roars of laughter from tall tales and epic journeys. We compensated for one another's inadequacies.

"You will like it here," he remarked in Cherokee, assuring me of the arrangement of which I had no choice, but welcomed the same. *"I am glad to see you, Skahtlelohskee."*

"I have missed you, brother. All send their affections." With that, he held me at arm's length and switched tongues.

"You are taller." Our eyes were parallel, more so than memory recalled.

"So are you, Elias." Since he changed to English, I did as well.

"I am too big to climb trees anymore, John. But, I'm still a stargazer."

"No doubt of that." I grinned, remembering our time hiding aloft in dark limbs, revealed momentarily from the yellow beams of intermittently zinging fireflies.

When we were boys, dressed in buckskins breeches, bare-chested in the humid, summer heat, we climbed aloft in the black oaks at night and looked above us to "the place where the dog ran." It was a tale among our people that an old couple saw a mystical dog stealing and eating their ground cornmeal. As the beast consumed their livelihood, they banged rattles and beat drums to scare him away. When the dog ran in fear, he jumped into the sky, spilling cornmeal from his mouth, creating the stars.

"I am learning trigonometry now: the triangles of the sky. Earth rotates, but constellations never change. Makes for sleepy mornings after nights spent in study."

"'… it is the star to every wandering bark whose worth's unknown, although his height be taken,'" I quoted.

Elias puzzled, and I held my breath while he searched through memorized verse. "Byron?" he guessed.

"Not current—older. Shakespeare. Mapping is your quest; quoting it is mine."

His smile grew. "John, you appear so fine in your waistcoat, compared to my humble clothes. I must appear a pauper to you. Our teachers expect us to show devotion to God in the humility of our outward appearance, reflecting our inward devotion." His quoted expression was one of repetitious memory and not necessarily his opinion. "You look as a princely gentleman should, with watch and chain."

"To me, Elias, you dress in wisdom. I will consider your advice."

One of our fellow students opened the door. He stood in the gray brightness, causing our eyes to squint at the sudden change. "You should." The stranger eavesdropped on our conversation.

"John, this is Samuel, from near Cornwall. Samuel, this is my cousin, John Ridge."

He strode into our privacy with the absent grace of adolescence—feet too large for his height, hands slung from gangly arms. His shoulders slumped while cocking his head. "This is not Yale; best to remember where you are." In three, wide strides, he reached the fireside in the schoolroom, grabbed a burlap sack near the corner, and left, leaving the door open as an invitation to chores he and the others had begun.

Elias and I looked at one another. "Perhaps you should only wear your watch to chapel on Sundays," and Elias walked through the open door. I remained, lit by a candle flame, alone.

Elias and I would grow taller here, in the knowledge of white living, experiencing it for ourselves. Seeing him again brought peace to my anxious thoughts. Elias saw my watch as a flourish while I viewed my watch as a symbol, a chained and sheathed reminder of how whites viewed time: once obtained, lost eternally. To Cherokee, time seasoned in cyclical growth: seed to stalk, tassel to harvest, seed corn to earth. While here, my time would mix in gears of copper, encompassed in a casing of silver, ticking away until we could return home and be of use.

My habits of days lay scripted on parchment with countless split quills. Impudent comments from Samuel, and those who followed him, marked the months, a year of dismal routine and studious composition. The only interruption was Samuel's condescending attitude and trickery. His ridicule only brought my sympathy.

Elias told me Samuel's parents died. His parents were murdered, his mother by his father's hand, and his father by the noose. For his unfortunate youth, I pitied him. However, I found empathy difficult, as I spent my childhood in the loving care of two parents, who found joy in one another's company. My parents' greatest care ensured my sister and I would recognize their affection in our education, even if that meant sending us to school miles from home. However, in Samuel's life, little brought him contentment. Perhaps, as an orphan, he was placed in an Indian school and resented that fact. In a state of constant anger, he appointed himself judge and jury of others. It became difficult to ignore his insidious intent and find some rationale for his behavior.

Many days we read aloud. Samuel stumbled and mumbled over his compositions, no doubt because of his poor penmanship and lack of attention to spelling. To any task, his choice was sarcasm and boastful laughter. He strode proudly to the front of the classroom at each task's beginning, but by its end, flushed red, felt assaulted after the other students snickered. One of the strongest of us, he would criticize me for my inability to work outside, even though it was my ailment and not my choice prohibiting it. He mocked me for any mispronunciation, although there were few; he mocked me for any mistake in arithmetic, although his proofs lacked evidence; he mocked me for my slower pace, although his feet crossed distances, unaware of where his feet led.

In November of 1819, Reverend Daggett asked me to attend him after our evening meal. I studied my memory, questioning every potential purpose for this invitation. The probable cause was my inability to ignore Samuel's continual rudeness. My answer to Samuel's constant criticism came last Sunday after chapel.

One of the first snows of winter covered Cornwall the previous Saturday night, and the morning after, I anticipated injury with each crutching step. Elias carried our Bibles as we crossed icy ground, hidden beneath layers of snow. Samuel turned to us from his position ahead and plodded back to our twosome. He entered my space with unfounded anger and rude indiscretion.

"So when you leave, will your Father 'slaughter the fatted calf' for you, Ridge? Will he kill it with his bow and arrow?" Disdain dripped like icicles from his open mouth.

I replied to his white eyes, standing as tall as I could. "Yes, he will. However, I am the son who remains behind."

"I doubt that." He reached for my fob chain, close enough to smell steamy breath. Our eyes found one another's, steeped in bravado and courage. I grabbed his wrist. Minutes passed. His eyes wavered, and he released the chain. Once he did so, I reluctantly stepped back, knowing I could not best him, even on a day with minor pain. His bulk overpowered me with muscled stupidity.

Elias perceived Samuel's threat, stepping between us, perpendicular, encouraging distance with his open palm on the lapel of my coat.

"What a feast it will be, John, when we arrive home again." Elias sought not an altercation but would act as my second, if necessary. Samuel snuffed through his nose, thinking, for once. Unknown to me what made him change his mind, he turned his body first and stared at us over his bulky shoulder, choosing to walk away.

Elias matched Samuel in height but not weight. Elias could best him in speed and dodge his blows if Samuel sought that fight this day. After he left, Elias exhaled the tension Samuel's presence lent us.

"Thank you, brother." Samuel was too far to hear my words. But, standing behind us was Reverend Daggett, who nodded and continued passing, crunching the snow-crusted ground.

"Gentlemen," he said without making eye contact with me or Elias.

"Good day, Reverend Daggett," Elias and I spoke in near unison. Perhaps Samuel's retreat was due to the Reverend's watchful and judgmental eye.

After the Reverend passed, Elias said, "I hate the rogue." He unclenched his fist and shook the tense muscles in his hand as if he used them to some violent end. "Your father, my uncle, same man. What do you think my uncle would have said?"

"All that I've ever had is yours." It took no time to imagine his words.

New snow fell earlier today, and I found myself ascending the path to Reverend Daggett's residence. I walked slowly along the uneven ground, shielded by ice puddles, warning me from underneath their cracked surfaces. I passed the lone maple who whispered a reminder: The Cherokee were wrong, no matter their righteous intention.

Reverend Daggett's broad desktop hid under the weight of criss-crossed stacks of paper with no discernable organization. On his desk sat broken quills, dried inkwells, and dog-eared books, open upside down, one atop another. Teacups on saucers, empty to varying degrees of consumption, wedged into nooks left by narrower books on his shelves. For someone who presented himself as a man of letters, I could not rationalize this appearance. One's ability to find a passage or correspondence deceived any comprehension.

He invited me to sit, clearing phlegm from his throat. In my nervousness, my crutch fell to the floor with a crash. We both shuddered at the sound of the crutch against the polished wood floor.

After, he cleared his throat, asserting his authority; his eyes glared above the rim of his spectacles with directness. "John, I asked you here to give you something but also to make a request."

At least, he would arrive at the point in haste. I doubted my father would travel so far this time to punish any behavior that Reverend Daggett conveyed to him in a letter. Concern stirred in my stomach, unabated by the tightness of the staunch collar and buttoned waistcoat.

"Yes, sir?"

"First, my request … This academy's funding is not such that we can afford more than our present allotments. Our future is not as secure as we might like. Therefore, I am drafting a petition to the government to fund our noble and Christian pursuits here."

This conversation replaced anticipated scorn with lofting confidence. I was confused.

"I do not understand. How can I be of service?" I asked.

"I want you to begin a draft of a letter to President-Elect Monroe. The People's House re-elected him, even though New Hampshire's Congressman Plumer voted against him for no other reason than to keep Adams' record of an unopposed second term."

"I was aware of President Monroe's good fortune, yes. What issues would you like me to address in this correspondence?" I inquired, fearing I might need to tell mistruths to encourage the United States to support such a singular endeavor—the good of the many before the good of the heathen masses.

"Write to him about your people's struggles and successes. Write about how you find your instruction here as it relates to those at home. Just keep it short." He leaned back in his chair, pulled off his spectacles, and placed his fingers like a temple at the steeple at his mouth, covering broken teeth.

"It is an honor I accept, sir. Thank you for trusting me with the task."

"John, there is little doubt, to any that ask, you are one of our brightest students. You have a great capacity for language and philosophy." His words seemed to lighten his expression and his memory. "Philosophy … onto the gift."

"The gift was in the honor of your request, sir. I deserve no other." My father's dictates for my behavior were ever-present in my mind. *Contrition and integrity,* I thought.

"Nonsense." He brushed aside my gratitude and dug through

volumes on his desk, sifting and shifting one year for another. "Ahh, here it is." He handed me a small book, hard-covered and blue with a gold-embossed cover. My eyes accepted it before my hands, and I opened it to study the title page.

"Hamlet, Prince of Denmark, written by William Shakespeare," I read aloud. "I know some of his poetry, but I have never read his theatrical works."

"It is a story of a son whose father, the king, was murdered. Hamlet, away at school, returns home for his father's funeral to find his mother married to his uncle, who took the throne. Hamlet must decide whether revenge for his father's murder or passivity and patience should be his recourse for the machinations against his family." Daggett spoke as if this prince had a choice between honor and salvation. After his summary, I knew honor was the course of dutiful sons; eternal soul be damned—family duty above all else.

"I will begin it today, sir. In all sincerity, thank you for the gifts."

He stood and pulled his black vest lower to hide its rise. His hand sought unfilled desk space to stabilize a walk hindered by legs spent too long seated. He helped me stand with a handshake, expelled another cough, crouched against his ample belly, and stooped and to hand me the fallen crutch.

"We shall discuss both after you have finished the tale and the draft for President Monroe."

"Absolutely, sir." He escorted me from his study, turning the gilded knob of polished brass.

Samuel slumped in a straight-backed chair in the foyer; booted feet sprawled askew in nonchalance, blocking my path. It would seem Samuel was next in line to speak to the headmaster. Reverend Daggett kicked Samuel's boots with scorn to move his idle feet.

In January of 1819, Reverend Daggett's quest for funding continued. Elias was chosen to greet a heavily-accented, wealthy merchant from Liverpool, who visited our academy for intelligent Indians. Elias told me they discussed complex questions of navigation.

Constellations bantered about Reverend Daggett's white plastered walls, and sophisticated answers settled into fibers of musty, sapphire rugs. Impressed with Elias' intelligence, this baron sent 1,500 florins to supply the school's needs. Arrogant with victory, Reverend Daggett gained money and prestige, although Jesus, his Savior, might question his motivation for notoriety.

In our bedroom, the single fireplace held few remaining embers, and our stock of wood remained sparse. Outside, snow barricaded and sealed closed the windows. Ten wood-framed beds covered in single, military wool blankets dampened the snoring. Once the accustomed sounds began, I read by a single candle's light of the Danish prince's substantial loss. It was not a text I could engage quickly for enjoyment. Rather, with the missing syllables and meter, it became a lengthy walk in an unknown wood. Challenging yes, impossible no.

Father's eagle feathers were the same as Hamlet's father's crown: "… so excellent a king." Hamlet's father must have been a noble man, who loved his son by sending him to school in Wittenberg, like my own. My father was too stubborn to fall; he was legendary, a warrior who walked on mountaintops, the Ridge.

On this January night, with no wood remaining to burn, I burrowed under my blanket deep. With constant visions of the ghosts of home, I blew out the flame on the spent candle, hearing my voice recite Hamlet's question, "Must I remember?"

I closed my eyes and heard my Father's Cherokee words, "*All that I have ever had is yours.*" Sustained only by their warmth, my shivering increased until sleep finally begged, "*What dreams may come?*"

CHAPTER 3

Knitting Socks

Sarah "Sally" Bird Northrup

January 1821

Cornwall, Connecticut

The stillness of evening brought continued snow. Jane, our family's housekeeper, lit candles in the parlor and dining room as the clock over the mantle struck six. The fire popped and sizzled, illuminating my view with warmth, seeping through the air with firelight. Father had not returned from the Foreign Mission School where he was steward, and Mother remained upstairs in her room occupied with dressing for dinner. Chilled, I sat alone in the front room, expecting any minute the sound of my father's boots from the foyer knocking free the stubborn snow. Outside, wide flakes of heaping white mounted in billowing curves quilted from another day's accumulation.

Mother would remark that I should occupy myself with more productive tasks. Beside my chair, the sewing box overflowed with skeins and spools; holey socks needed darning, and a half-crafted shawl remained unfinished for Mother, a gift I intended for last Christmas. Instead, I stared down the sidewalk, avoiding the tasks. My eyes wandered, unfocused, dancing like the hearth fire's irregular light, dreaming of waiting buds and blooms under those drifts and mounds in my garden. Do Tulips dream while asleep under a blanket of winter snow? Do Roses whisper to one another not to wake black-eyed Susan? To me, my flowers were trusted friends away at school, returning each summer.

Distracted by my musings, hidden behind blowing snow, a lantern turned up the walk. Two students held a muslin stretcher aloft, walking beside two other men, one with Papa's broad gait. They reached the door before I could do so.

"Sally!" Father called me from the entryway as he and Dr. Samuel Gold preceded the stretcher to the parlor fireplace under the resuming chiming clock. "Get your coat and light a fire in the sick room."

"We must warm him; his condition worsens in these dastardly Connecticut winters." Dr. Gold insisted with the quick tempo of a man raised under military banners.

Their conversation skipped any introduction for my benefit. Father remarked with affirmation, "He is unwell. In this state, we cannot send him home to his family. He might not survive the extensive trip southward in a carriage. He must stay here where we can care for him; it is the Christian thing to do." Father looked at Dr. Gold with half-closed lids, squinted from seriousness, as the two students lowered the student to the floor. Father's eyes remained on Dr. Gold, but his voice addressed the standing students. "That will be all. Elias, you and Samuel return to your room. We will let you know about your cousin's condition in the morning."

The student bent low and whispered something inaudible to the blanket. Then, he stood tall, acknowledged my father and Dr. Gold with a solitary nod to each, and left without his boots making a sound on the hardwood floor.

Frozen by my chair, my balance shifted. The mass lay wrapped in a single, gray wool blanket covered in speckled snowflakes. His hair, black and tousled, remained free of the blanket enveloping him. Seconds before, the rug dressed the floor in colors of ruby and gold amaranth, raised in a textured, dense plush. Now, the floor lay covered in steel-hued wool, mounding around the patient. He was reminiscent of an oil painting, snow-capped mountains with broad swaths of indiscernible, sapphire-tinted, gray fog.

"Please, Sally. Do what I asked of you."

Father startled me from my frozen gaze. "Yes, sir," I spoke the words from habit.

My feet led through the parlor to the closet beside puddles of melting snow. I pulled on my hood and wrapped my cloak. When I turned around, Mother's eyes peered at me from the crest of our staircase. Similar to mine of pale blue, her eyes questioned mine. Through our glances and expressions, inaudible conversations lilted back and forth along the banister. From landing to landing, she read my wide-eyed concern and nervousness. In response, she replied with a tilt of her head at the unknown, questioning whether her intervention was necessary. My look unlocked her anxiousness, like unseen, muted footsteps surprising one into an irrational, jolting shiver. After our exchange, she pulled the handkerchief from its home in her pocket, held it to her mouth, grabbed the rail to descend, and added additional worry to the already tense parlor.

The key with the yellow tassel hung beside the kitchen door. Grabbing it, I scurried out of the kitchen, pushed by waves of white. The single-roomed shelter behind our house was where sick students, who found a need, came to stay near the kitchen for soup, bread, and bed, undisturbed and isolated during illness' confinement. Darkness greeted me with smells of stale ash from burnt-down fires. I scolded myself for the forgotten flame. With slow steps from memory, I wove left to avoid the bed frame. Flint and steel resided on the mantle. Gathering by touch alone, I built a nest of splintered kindling left intentionally on the hearthstone. Fingertips numb, I scuffed it and lit a dim spark. I fed the minuscule fire shaved pieces of wood, one at a time, until I could see where I was.

In the growing light, my thoughts returned to the ill student in the parlor. I closed my eyes holding empathy for his pain. He was so quiet and still. What illness brought him to our home tonight? My thoughts returned to flames licking the wood. Absentmindedly, I replaced flint and striker, paying little heed to the dusty mantle. My eyes never left the flames, and my thoughts never left the boy.

Only one thin quilt dressed the sunken mattress, made from old curtains and fabric, patch-worked together. I would bring another, for the patient lay snow-covered and wet from its melting.

As I opened the door to return to the principle house, Father and Dr. Gold met me in the doorway, assisting the pupil to walk. They carried most of his weight on their shoulders. He barely opened his eyes. When I stepped aside, looking from the wool trailing behind him, I saw him, shrouded by waves of black hair. His face grimaced with a weary protest against the movement. Melted snow reformed on his blanket from the journey through the short space between our home and the sick room. Father and Dr. Gold easily lifted his weight up the single stair and across the scant distance, placing him on the bed with awkward, unbending grace.

"Sally, bring him some soup. Go calm your mother," Papa remarked in haste while Dr. Gold assisted the student to turn on the edge of the bed, removing unbuckled boots.

"I will," I said.

There was no response.

I did as I was told. Entering our home again, crossing to the arched entryway of the parlor, Mother interrupted my pace. "Sarah? Is that you?"

"Yes, Mother. Is that boy very sick? Will he be all right?"

"Only the Lord knows, my dear. He has an affliction in his hip, cough, fever. Your father said tonight's storm aggravated his rheumatism. We must warm him to ease his suffering. John must not move too much."

His name was John.

"Do you mind if I take him the soup and sit with him to keep the fire burning?"

"You have a kind heart, my dear." Mother absentmindedly said this same phrase, many times each day to Jane, Papa, Mrs. Gold from chapel. She turned herself away from the fire with an abrupt redress. "What about your dinner tonight? It seems as if our home is in an uproar." However, in the next heartbeat, she spoke her presiding concern aloud. "I must write to John's family of his worsening condition." Her voice carried motherly intuition.

It was not me she sought to nurture; it was her reputation and that of my father's at the school. Several years ago, another student became ill and passed away. Both Papa's care and her own might come into question if another student were to lose his life.

"I'm not hungry, Mother." My words flew around her, blown like dandelion seeds. Her unspoken worry overpowered my timid voice. I left her standing there, gazing at flames, and contemplating the fate of the dark-headed, dark-eyed student who disturbed her evening.

I went to my summer-dreaming chair and took my yarn and needles from the basket. Punishments for running up the stairs forgotten, I grabbed a quilt from the chest in our guest room and ran down again. This time, I grabbed Father's lantern on the way through the kitchen.

Arms already full, Jane handed me a tin canister of soup and a spoon wrapped in a napkin. Jane did not express indifference to the emergency, but her face held a disappointed droop. Her dinner, prepared and steaming, would be late, if eaten at all.

I told her, anticipating her thoughts. "Let everyone get settled, and I'm sure Dr. Gold and Papa will dine."

Jane was a creature born and reared in her habits.

I crossed to the sick room, stepping in my Papa's embedded footprints. I struggled to knock, balancing the provisions in my arms. As Father and Dr. Gold spoke in mumbled tones, I re-entered, pretending not to hear what they were saying.

"Tonight, just try to keep him warm. I will return tomorrow morning and check on the degree of his pain. Laudanum will allow him to rest. Send for me if you find yourself concerned. In this condition,

I cannot say whether he will ever see his native country again." My heart broke at his words, and I closed my eyes after hearing them.

I knew Dr. Gold to be a skilled physician. He took care of Mother well last fall when her fever exceeded control, and her throat would not allow her to swallow. He was a kind man with kind eyes, although he continuously spoke in a staccato, making me think I'd wronged him somehow.

"Is there nothing more you can do for him?" I said. Both men looked at me as if it were inappropriate for me to have spoken.

No one answered as I watched the snow on the patient's mountain of wool melt, and his body shivered, intending to turn snow's white flecks invisible.

Father attempted to redirect Dr. Gold's apparent gall at my question. "Sally, assist John and stack wood on the fire to warm this room? Come in the house then; it would be improper for you to stay."

"Mother sent me to sit with him. She began a letter of concern to his parents."

Papa coughed at Mother's granted permission. Dr. Gold gestured as if he would protest, but the patient interrupted him.

"No," he commanded, with resonance. His face grimaced at the word, and a groan escaped his lips as he shifted on the bed. Dr. Gold took a cloth from the things in my arms, wet it outside in the snow, and folded it, placing it on his patient's fevered forehead.

Father and Dr. Gold left without adding a word, but their lasting gaze over the bed spoke of their worry about John's life. Before the latch on the door caught, stillness overcrowded the space, driven inside with the patient's singular syllable, slamming the door adamantly behind itself.

The soup tin and lantern handle clinked against their metal housings as I placed them on the bedside table. From against the wall, I moved a chair and sat beside the bed. My hood dropped to my shoulders, wet with icy water's weight.

"Your name is John?" I inquired.

"Ye-es," he said, breaking the word into two syllables.

"I'm Sarah. Papa's the only one who calls me Sally." He looked through me. His eyes were teary, glassy, red, and his skin russet brown and olive. Like a witness to the forest at night, his face reminded me of hickory trees, still but alert. In his suffering, he looked older than me. He was one of the Cherokee students I heard speak at chapel. Papa boasted of his accomplishments with the Cherokee pupils.

"Would you like soup?" I asked him, offering a spoon and napkin, but he did not answer. Painful eyelids drooped from medicine's elixir, and he curled into himself towards the window. He became taciturn and still once he shifted.

Resigned to silence, I needed to move. With the temperature in the room barely above freezing, I left on my cloak, retrieving the blanket from the floor. I dressed the gray wool covering him. It was forward of me, but I tucked the blankets around his feet. I spun to face the fireplace, stacked more logs crosshatched onto the fire, and then resumed my seat in the straight-backed chair. I could do little for him but keep watch through the night and alert my parents if he stopped breathing.

Draped across his body lay my grandmother's quilt, patched teal-blue squares and triangles, forming the shape of dove birds flying against a white sky. At his shoulders, the crumpled wings spread and stretched high as they soared down his form. From the extended slope along his hip, birds ascended higher only to land again and nestle at his feet. Noah's peace flew to awaiting land.

John's breathing echoed in pace with my own. I pulled the needles and yarn to begin a sock. Clicking my needles, I accompanied snow blowing against the windowpane. No further words interrupted the song, but my silent prayers soared heavenward. *Lord, please place your healing hands upon John tonight and each dawn to come.* With reassurances from the book of James: "Prayers of faith shall save the sick, and the Lord shall raise him up; and if he has committed sins, they shall be forgiven him."

Yarn pulled free from the ball as I wrapped my needles in loops.

When I was hurt, a song my mother sang came to mind, one I hummed to myself, only thinking the words.

May the road rise to meet you … The ballad pitched with an ascending tone, only to glide lower, mirroring the phrase. *May the wind be at your back ...* I inhaled. *May the sunshine ...* My phrase broke as the pitch extended, *warm upon your face.* I repeated the tune's melody as I knitted the sock's rim. My tempo increased, *May the rain fall softly on your fields ...* The tune fell to resolve the chord, *and until we meet again, may you keep safe, in the gentle …* humming through, resuming my previous pace, twisting my needles, *loving arms of God.*

I hummed the chorus twice and followed through the square heel to the connecting bridge of the tune. Words rose in my throat, "For everything, there is a season … a time for laughter, a time for tears and pain." I paused the song at the tricky switch in fold and pattern for the heel. Once complete, I resumed the verse, *"In all things God is near, always guiding your way."*

Not wishing to wake him, I kept my voice low. I could hardly hear myself. However, I feared he awoke as he rolled over onto his back. His face lulled to the side, and thick hair fell back across his forehead, parting down the middle to reveal his face. He had full lips, defined high cheekbones, a straight nose, and underneath, no stubble of mustache whiskers. He was handsome.

The pillow cradled his head. I took the cloth back outside to wet it again and placed it on his forehead. He jolted from the cold. When he stopped moving, my incomplete song began again, as did my knitting. Not looking at my hands, I hummed the last line of the chorus, forgetting where I ended, trusting my memory. *May you keep safe, in the gentle, loving arms of God.* I reinforced the toe and sealed the sock closed.

I started on its mate as time passed, and the moon's light shifted his seat to one beyond the window frame. The lantern burned low. When my hands ached and my own eyes sought to close, I left both socks on John's bed. I crunched through settled snow behind our house, making new footprints, humming the tune, and prayed for healing dawn.

CHAPTER 4

Aloud

Sarah Bird Northrup

Spring 1821

Cornwall, Connecticut

John's condition continued to plague him even after spending February in New Haven, accepting Doctor Gold's recommendation. Although his fever abated, he still used crutches to move short distances. During these months, unable to attend classes, I sat beside John while Mother assisted Father with other students' needs.

During our time, we became accustomed companions. John asked me to bring him books authored by ancient Romans on rhetoric and language. He read orations of Cicero and Plato's philosophy. His papers sprawled around his sickbed like a folded fan, marking the full picture of his study simultaneously. He completed a full-page, blew it dry, and then scratched through thoughts he had just donned in permanent ink. John was a man of letters.

Often, we read in silence together, although my small text of Psalms seemed far less daunting than his ancient texts. I stared at sequenced letters forming words, absent of context, while his words animated his ever-changing face.

For days and days, I watched him and made assumptions about

what his expressions meant. John gasped as if a chapter shocked him. He shook his head with disagreement or tilted to the right if he read something curious or some original expression. He pulled the text closer, finding the author passionate instead of droll with exposition. His golden eyes tightened or relaxed, depending upon whether he agreed or disagreed with each successive sentence. Scowl-wrinkling dents in his forehead implied he quarreled with the author's assumptions. Perhaps, he rifled through the texts like imaginary desk drawers, searching for a lost key. I saw a questioning determination in his spectrum of expressions, like seeking a friend in a crowd of tall heads and recognizing no one familiar. Absent of any acquaintance, he saddened in disappointment, which must have pained him as profoundly and endlessly as the ache in his hip.

Early in April, I placed my gardening trowel inside the watering can beside his door and proceeded to remove my dingy apron and soil-ground gloves. I knocked and turned the knob to enter with hasty familiarity instead of appropriate patience. Surprising me, another student opened the door, dressed formally in a black coat and linen white shirt and tie. At my sudden appearance, he covered his surprise with a cheerful grin and bowed to me with such formality. Rushed to leave earthy articles behind, I curtsied, realizing my interruption.

"I'm sorry. I will come back later if John has any needs."

The unfamiliar student stopped my retreat. "Miss Northrup, I presume? It is a pleasure to meet you. John has spoken …" John coughed, glancing up to him, and the gentleman shifted. "My name is Elias Boudinot. I am John's cousin." I remembered he was one of the students who carried John on the stretcher.

I curtsied to him in return and said my name as a way of greeting, placing wisps of hair behind my cap.

"Miss Sarah, please come in," John spoke my Christian name. I pounded my boots to avoid traipsing hidden dirt on the floor.

Mr. Boudinot picked up the stack of books and papers from the chair beside John's bedside, inviting me to sit.

Mr. Boudinot announced, "John has written a letter, at Reverend Daggett's request, to President Monroe. He was reading it to me before you came."

"It is not good enough," John interjected and looked away, embarrassed.

"Compared to what, might I ask?" I should have thought before I spoke so freely. "I'm sorry."

"For what? It is a valid question." Elias' curious smirk was directed at John.

The letter's author considered us both and cleared his throat, convinced to share his work. "I rejoice that my dear nation now begins to peep into the privileges of civilization—that this great and generous government is favorable to them, and that ere long, Congress will give them the hand of strong fellowship—that they will encircle them in the arms of love, and adopt them into the fond embraces of the Union."

John stopped, looking to us for reassurance of the eloquence of his phrases. I was in awe, yet shy like my forget-me-not seeds, burrowing under the soil in shallow pots.

"Keep going," Mr. Boudinot encouraged.

John was a perfectionist. I sat, amazed at what I heard of the Cherokee's introduction into a new American life. John progressed down the page and read, "I left them about two years ago; when they were at work with the tools whites used—some possessed large farms; cattle, horses, hogs. Women were seen at the wheel, and the weaver's shuttle was in motion. How different is the condition of that part of my nation, who have been enticed by their foolish imagination, and particularly by the allurements of the white men, to remove to Arkansas."

Mr. Boudinot drew my attention, pacing between John's unused desk and the foot of the bed, with hands grasped in consternation behind his back. "With every correspondence, we must help this President remember his government's solution is not one at all."

"Yes," John replied.

This sentiment belonged to a previous conversation between them, one to which I had not been privy.

John continued, "The hunters are now in pursuit of game, in which employment we have reason to apprehend, they would have continued, or perhaps have sunk into oblivion, were it not that teachers have been sent to them by Christian benevolence."

In reaction, Mr. Boudinot lifted his head from his study of the floor. "Exactly." I did not know whether these words were an affirmation of the truth, but John relaxed after Mr. Boudinot's exhilaration and continued pacing.

"Are you ready for me to take it to Reverend Daggett?" Mr. Boudinot asked.

"Yes." John dipped his pen one last time and signed his name with a beautiful, sprawling flourish of his hand, scripting like a trout circling in shallow water, curving darts slanting to the right.

My presence unnecessary, I rose and stepped to the door to curtsy. "Thank you, gentlemen. I will leave you to your work. I'm sorry I hindered your task."

"What were you planting?" John mumbled. He looked at me, eyes stunning, golden, and clear. I caught his gaze and returned it. Seconds passed, and I pulled my eyes to Mr. Boudinot, who seemed to notice his cousin's stare. Bewildered by Mr. Boudinot's look, unable to move forward or fall backward, I remained in orbit, fixed by the gravity of John's gaze.

Mr. Boudinot answered, "No need, Miss Northrup. I will take this letter and John's other assignments back to school. I only stop by for a moment. Don't leave on my account." Awkwardly, we switched places, taking turns moving in the small room. He grabbed the books moved earlier and papers from John's nightstand, taking the letter from his hand, the one with fresh, dried ink.

"Oh, I brought this also," he said and handed John a small text of blue from inside his pocket. I watched as they moved with one another, glance and gesture answered without words. Two forces moved through the same space; I listened to their hands' rhythm and paper's flourish.

"Elias," John called to him, smiling at his cousin, "bring me Daggett's approval, or I will redraft it." Mr. Boudinot nodded and promptly exited, leaving the door open. Outside, the wind shifted; it would rain soon.

I closed the door to keep John's work where he organized it, and I sat in my chair again. "Forget-me-nots," I replied, wondering whether he remembered his question.

He didn't respond. I took the Psalms out of my pocket. Distracted, I read two unremembered verses before staring out the window beside his bed. In my mind, I replayed his voice reciting the letter, and I must have sighed.

"My father and mother do not speak English," he revealed, absent of any introduction, looking down at the quill in his hand.

I returned his gaze. "Do you find that difficult?"

"No. Others will." With his statement, his tone changed, and he stared straight ahead at the hearth. His eyes retreated from whatever he saw and looked out of the window.

Time ticked, but his phase did not alter. "Help them grow." It was all I resolved to say.

"I will have to speak for them all." He countered with exaggeration; although upon second thought, perhaps it wasn't.

To him, I imagined that his premonition seemed an earnest expectation.

I had no words to balance the weight of his thought. Never having strayed further than New Haven, there were things, worldly customs and conventions, I did not understand, let alone his Cherokee culture. His people lived so forefront in his mind. It seemed those I knew, the people of Cornwall, were selfish by comparison.

"To become a sovereign nation, the Cherokee must expand their beliefs beyond Nature's superstition and clan rules of justice." He bent the white feathers of a quill in his hand, touching the point against his opposing palm, one end soft and the other sharp by contrast.

"What is a clan?" The word seemed tribal and uncivilized.

"Family. Children and grandparents, cousins and parents following the mother's bloodline. They defend one another, care for one another. Clans are Wolf, *a-ni-wa-ya*, Deer, *a-ni-a-ha-wi*, Bird, *a-ni-tsi-s-qua*, Long Hair, *a-ni-gi-lo-hi*, Paint, *a-ni-wo-di*, Wild Potato, *a-ni-go-da-ge-wi*, Blue, *a-ni-sa-ho-ni*.

"Which do you belong?" I asked.

"My mother's clan is Deer."

Unimaginable to me, the Cherokee stood aside in my mind, absent of context. I understood John's intent to push his people into progression, but his concerns burnt hot, dissipating with noxious fumes at his reticence to convince them to change. He thought of the Cherokee as a family, one that the American government may force to sacrifice all they owned and travel to uncertain ground. John seemed defiant against that ever-present fear.

"The buffalo are gone. Deer and turkey soon will follow. Cherokee may starve if they do not make a choice." He broke the quill in half.

I decided to distract him from the thoughts pressing against him, thoughts that filled the ceiling like smoke from a closed damper above a roaring fire.

I inquired, "What is that?" I gestured to the book on his lap.

". . . a play, a tragedy. Reverend Daggett gave it to me."

"What is the matter of this tragedy?" I smiled, a poor attempt to be light-hearted.

"It is the tale of a betrayed prince." In hindsight, this might not distract him after all.

"Who betrays him?" I asked.

"All do, but his best friend. His uncle is a traitor, his mother is oblivious, and his woman lies to him. Her father purses him relentlessly."

"How does it end?" Closing my book of Psalms, I leaned my elbows on my knees, shortening the distance between us without leaving my chair.

"I do not yet know." He thought a second, "Shall I read some to you?"

I dismissed his offer. "I would not understand. By your marker, it appears you are nearly through."

"The words are poetry. You might be one to understand."

"How could you know that?" I spoke without thinking.

"Because you mumble the Psalms as you read when you sit here for hours." My cheeks flushed.

I thought him wrong, but he opened the book where his marker protruded and began at the top of the page.

> "'... They say the owl was a baker's daughter.
> Lord, we know what we are but not what we may be...'"

He interjected a summary. "This character, Ophelia, Hamlet's love, she has gone—" searching for the right word, "—feeble-minded." He inhaled deeply. "Hamlet killed her father by accident in his rage. She buried her father alone. In her grief, Ophelia lost her wits. Hamlet was sent away to England. Ophelia's brother, Laertes, was away in France."

"How sorrowful—dark and lonely," I said.

"Should I stop?" he inquired.

I shook my head no and resumed my empty stare out the window beside the door. John's voice was on my left, and it took all my hearing to catch his words. He continued.

> "'I hope all will be well. We must be patient.
> But I cannot choose but weep, to think that
> they should lay him in the cold ground.
> My brother shall know of it.
> And so, thank you for your good counsel.
> Come, my coach! Good night ladies, good night.
> Sweet ladies, good night, good night.'"

"She is speaking to people and things that are not there," John revealed with pity. Rain pelted the glass. He stopped; I waited. "Go on," I encouraged him to continue.

"This is too sad for this day of rain," John said.

His voice rooted me to the floor. "It is. But, I want to hear."

"Her brother returns," he said and flipped another page forward. Laertes, Ophelia's brother, rushes into the castle to tell the King he plans to avenge his father's murder by killing Hamlet. Then, Laertes sees his sister, so mad with grief.

"'... Oh rose of May,
Dear maid, kind sister, sweet Ophelia!
Oh heavens, is't possible a young maid's wits
Should be as mortal as a poor man's life?
Nature is fine in love, and where 'tis fine
It sends some precious instance of itself
After the thing it loves.'"

"Can her brother not console her? Ease her grief?" I interrupted.

"I do not know." He closed the book. "I will stop."

I heard the book's muffled close. "Please... don't," I said.

He opened the page again.

"'You must sing down, a-down, and you call
Him a-down. Oh, how the wheel becomes it!
It is the false steward that stole his master's daughter.'"

He coughed, clearing his throat. I heard him grab the glass from the bedside table to drink a sip of water. Rain fell harder as I pulled the handkerchief from my pocket. "Ophelia gives the dried weeds in her hands to the court ladies standing nearby.

"'There's rosemary, that's for...'"

"Remembrance," I whispered, sensing his gaze's intense and sudden pull, like standing too close to a fireplace, turning to warm one's still-shivering side.

"'Pray, love, remember. And there is pansies,
That's for...'"

"Thoughts." I broke through.

"'There's fennel for you,'"

"Victory," I spoke to the glass, my voice bounding back.

"'... and columbines,'"

"Reverence and faithfulness." I prayed, listening to Heaven.

"'There's rue for you, and here's some for me.'"

"Sorrow," I spoke through the window glass to the filling puddles on my worn path.

"'We may call it herb-grace Of Sundays.
Oh, you must wear your rue with a
Difference. There's a daisy...'"

He listened, testing whether my definition would follow. In my reflection, I imagined myself beside Ophelia's garden. Her tears pelted against the window in front of me. I inhaled and pulled my forehead from the cool glass. "Innocence." My answer found his eyes.

From memory, he recited,

"'I would give you some violets
But they withered all when my father died.'"

He closed the book. "Miss Sarah?"

He pulled me to him with my name. I sat on the bed by his feet.

"Violets mean love beyond time."

Embarrassed by my reaction, already having spoken too intimately, I sniffed back my thoughts, curtsied, and falsely smiled.

Leaving John, I gifted him no time to speak any further. I leaned against the outside of his closed-door and walked back to the kitchen, my face drenched and dripping.

Time waxed forward like the moon. John chose not to read to me anymore. We kept our conversation cordial to obvious topics when inclement weather forced us to walk from one corner of his room to the other. I described my garden's current blooms, the hearty green of unfolding purple hyacinth, sweetly fragrant in black-soiled beds of forgotten fall.

May sent warmth, enabling us to take longer walks, following the path of the blackberry's white buds bordering fences. He struggled, sighed, raising his arms off his crutches. To fill the time of each of his measured steps, I pulled weeds away from blackberry's thorny vines.

May brought pain more manageable. We stepped in slow progress to Kellogg's Mercantile, resting on a bench. Another student lumbered from the store's stairs, with hands full, one holding ax blade, the other gripping a menacing maul over his shoulder. His name was Samuel Meeks.

"Hello, Miss Sarah," he shouted to me. I waved and smiled at him with an absentminded gesture.

John watched me, sitting with his arms propped on his crutch handles, wrists dangling from the handholds. He squinted against the sun. "Do you know him well?" John's tone was sharp. I did not understand the reason for his aloofness.

"Only a little. He's not called me by my Christian name before."

"Hmm. Not sure I know you well enough to do so either." He stood, placing crutches under his arms, and led the way home. John paced faster than during our earlier trip. He was quieter, and his head hung low, eyes following the path he walked.

Once at his door, he turned around. "I'm sorry. I shouldn't have been so curt to you. Samuel and I are not friends, Miss Northrup."

I felt a distance grow when John called me my formal name.

"Samuel and I are merely acquaintances. You and I are friends." I wanted our ease renewed. "Call me Sarah. Please."

He smiled, and the tense mood shifted. "Sarah, my father is coming. I received a letter from him yesterday."

Having heard John speak so frequently of him, I looked forward to his arrival and my parent's reaction to Major Ridge.

John nodded and entered his room. Hesitant to close the door, he bowed his head, and I curtsied to fill the time.

Summer's heat eased, and drier air replaced humidity. John's father arrived, appointed a major from his service during the War of 1812. The Ridge made the nine hundred-mile journey to see his son, worried about never seeing him again. John's situation was no longer grave; however, his father left home months ago, when John's condition gave due cause for alarm.

With grandeur, the elegant carriage stopped in front of our home, pulled by four graceful horses. It was the largest hired carriage and team I had ever seen. His white-rimmed boots exited the carriage first, carrying their owner, as he made huge strides up to our front door. Unaccustomed to the flourish, my father gasped, revering Major Ridge's firm and war-like steps.

Father was Irish, and although a strong man, he was not tall. Years of comfortable living and disseminating tasks to others left him idler and stouter because of it. Major Ridge was exceedingly tall, standing far above the rest of us. Mother's indiscrete glances at the neighbors and their gaping stares from porch railings assured her to be the talk of the congregation for at least a month.

To me, Major Ridge's appearance and demeanor were impressive, intimidating—a chief standing so grand, I stood in his shade. A formidable man, broad-shouldered, draped in an elegant blue wool coat bordered with golden braid and buttons. John's father looked like a man weathered with southern heat, yet still sophisticated in this world not his own. Silver at the temples, his black hair, like John's, drew his chin high, counterweighted by the braid draping down his spine.

His voice was deep, sincere, as he spoke in beautiful but unfamiliar rhythms and stresses, full of rich N and L sounds slipping through long As and a pitched I vowel sound. He had a rich voice, resonant, like an oak tree hiding decades between its circles.

Accompanied by an interpreter, dwarfed beside Major Ridge, the young Cherokee spoke words in quick, rehearsed English, "Thank you, kind Steward, for taking such excellent care of my son."

Perhaps, Major Ridge felt stiff, awkward displaying his gratitude.

Perhaps, this formality was another display of wealth to show my parents he was quite a capable man. I watched the scene unfold, trying my best to be a young lady with manners.

"John is a most excellent student: intelligent and genteel. It has been our pleasure to care for him during his confinement. I know you will find him stronger with each passing day." My father assured him. "Welcome to our home."

For the first time, I saw my father uncomfortable in his own body. Intimidated and perhaps fearful, he took a step back from Major Ridge, covering his incalculable awkwardness with introductions, "May I present my wife, Mrs. Lydia Northrup." Mother curtsied with darting eyes to Major Ridge, his interpreter, while the neighbors came nearer, eager for a closer look.

While the interpreter spoke my father's words in Cherokee, I curtsied in greeting. Then, Major Ridge addressed me in as formal a way one could do, with a sweeping bow and gentle smile. He spoke in beautiful baritone rhythms.

"It is a great honor to be named Bird among my people. They are messengers that bring guidance from the One Who Makes Us All."

Embarrassed by the interpreter and Major Ridge's sentiment, all I could say was, "Thank you, Sir."

My father welcomed Major Ridge, who immediately requested to see John, inquiring about his current condition. I followed the company through our foyer but stopped at the foot of the stairs, waited for them to pass, and ascended to my room. Now was not the time for me to sit by John's bedside or to assist him on a morning walk around the house. His father needed assurances of his son's health, and there was little to do for either of them.

Major Ridge insisted he stay at the local inn rather than at our home. My mother invited him to dine here continuously, but he argued against the idea, citing that the inn was comfortable and his family had been enough of an intrusion. I do not know which scared her more, worry Major Ridge would say yes to her hospitable invitations to dinner or the ensuing gossip sure to follow if he had accepted. If Major Ridge supped at the inn, the choir women would accuse Mother of unchristian-like behavior. If he stayed, they would accuse her of the same.

Either way, Mother fought against understanding Major Ridge, even with his excellent interpreter; however, he must have understood her subtle snubs of superiority. She darted her eyes with evasion when he spoke, choosing instead to study the ceiling for dust. She moved to the other side of the room when he ducked under the arch to enter the parlor.

Mother was a Christian woman to those whose likeness mimicked her own, and she worried far too much about how others viewed her. She did her Christian duty to the students at the school, but unlike them, she considered herself saintly. I know I am naïve, but I believe God made us all, some in shades of dusk and some in shades of dawn. God placed us in the path of those He intended us to meet and those He meant for us to serve. With kindness, they returned the gift. John's friendship taught me that valuable lesson.

Father and Major Ridge found mutual respect during the two weeks he visited John and Cornwall. Each seemed to admire the candid manner of the other. Sometimes, though, their conversation became one difficult to hear.

"Surely, sir, the Cherokee people expect the government to keep their word," my father intoned with assumed assurance one afternoon.

The interpreter crooned my father's words to Major Ridge, who replied with a tone unmistakable in any language.

"White men ask us to learn their ways, their language, to accept their customs, their religion. I find it difficult to trust men whose greed for land exceeds their respect for mankind, red or white."

Pride must be an inherited trait.

Gossip ensued about the eloquent Cherokee father, whose outward wealth and inward integrity wrapped Cornwall in a fog of surprising interest and admiration. Major Ridge met Dr. Gold and thanked him for John's care and treatment with a gift of a Cherokee pipe carved from black stone, while Dr. Gold gave Major Ridge a small telescope. After hearing the tale, I knew the son would use the gift given to the father.

I looked in on John one time during his father's visit. I admit I missed our companionable silence. John used a single crutch now, and while we drifted slowly, he winced less as he moved more. He resigned himself to walk with a limp but wanted to do so without the crutch.

"I hate this stick of wood. A cane would be more refined, but this makes me appear weaker than I am." Frustrated John appeared today, which meant he would speak unedited. Secretly, it pleased me. The more irritated John became, the more he paced, and that was healing for his infirmity.

"You seem stronger today." Attempting encouragement, his insistence on a cane made me laugh. It would suit him and his pocket watch, making him more sophisticated than I already recognized him to be.

"May we sit a moment, Miss Sarah?"

"Of course." We found an iron bench out in the dusky evening light, even though the day was still bright enough to see the cerulean sky. The moon began his ascent, sharing the heavens with the sun. My reticence returned, interrupted by birds speaking in *hoos* and *whirls* in the overhanging tree, announcing our invasion into their privacy.

To break his vexation, I inquired, "Do you think in English or Cherokee? It must take twice the effort to translate every thought."

"My thoughts are in Cherokee. You are so observant. Cherokee is a beautiful language, defining our land in more specific terms than in English. Many words sound similar but with different accented syllables, meaning two different things. Single words can mean an entire English phrase."

"I understand," I replied, really not understanding at all. I was not sure why this conversation felt strained. We spoke freely for so long.

Now, every question and sentence preceded a season where neither of us knew what to say. My eyes evaded his and instead traced ivy's route up a poplar, tangled and dense with leaves masking the bark.

I remembered Major Ridge's introduction and his remarks about my name. For a more pleasant topic, I changed our conversation to one less likely to remind John of our differences.

"My middle name is Bird." I recited the story, often told by Mother. "I was born in December. The following spring, Mother rocked me on the porch in the morning light. She named me Sarah, with no middle name. A hummingbird buzzed close to us, with its spectrum wild and vibrant. Mother said the bird recognized me as family, with its curious hovering, so she called me Bird after that. At my baptism, she wrote the full name on my church record."

"Hummingbird, *Wa-le-la*."

I tried to imitate the sounds, but my attempt made him laugh.

"Try again," he encouraged.

"You'll just laugh at me … again," I shunned the embarrassment, although I'm sure he knew.

He laughed again without my second attempt.

He looked away for a time, leaning toward my shoulder but keeping his eyes on the darkening horizon. "My people think of hummingbirds as messengers. They fly so swift and keen to deliver medicine to those who would die without it." Within our sheltered privacy, his voice did not disturb the birds. Brushing black soles under the bench, John held a silent conversation with someone invisible to me. While shifting, he inhaled deeply and roused the courage to speak, losing it seconds later. What was wrong between us?

"I have seen you many times before we met here." He chose a different topic.

"Cornwall is a tiny village; it is easy to see others often," I answered.

"At church, Elias … we spoke before the congregation for the first time. You were younger, maybe thirteen years old. You looked through the window the entire time we spoke."

"I do that. I'm sorry," I admitted with sincerity.

"I know." Did he observe me as I did him? For someone so intelligent, I felt meek and silly.

"What did you say at the service? I do not remember." I confessed.

"It isn't important. The day is marked by the memory of your red hair curling from your bonnet."

His eyes spoke more than his words. His glance felt stronger than one recalling a simple observation. Embarrassed and flattered, my eyes sought my gloved hands. Without warning, he reached for my wrist with the back of his finger where my sleeve ended but before my glove began. He touched me with a feather's pressure, where my pulse pounded. Birds hushed their repeated complaints. We both watched the movement of his hand.

The following August, when baby birds found the strength to fly on their own, I found a gift, wrapped in a month's old newspaper, bound closed with string sitting beside our back door. I unwrapped it, knowing who delivered the carved hummingbird. Its artisan was no foreigner, no man less than any other. To me, he had become quite the opposite.

CHAPTER 5

Laundry

Sarah Bird Northrup

September 1821

Cornwall, Connecticut

Wood smoke lofted and seeped through my open window. I opened my eyes in the dark. Conscious but not awake, I knew to dress and take my post beside Jane, our housekeeper, to assist her with the laundry. At least I could spend the day in the sunshine instead of surrounded by the stifling smells of the house. Fall approached with golden light threading through maple's red leaves.

Awake, I swung my legs over the side of the bed, dragging my quilt like a queen's cape around my shoulders, and stepped into the moon's remaining glow through my window, trying to delay a moment longer this relentless day of chores. Cedar leaves rustled and scraped against the windowpanes, disturbing the birds in their nests. In reply to their fervent squeaks, I whispered, "Me too." Neither of us wanted to be awake before the morning star. Washing days began and ended the same way with the same light. Tonight, Jane, Mother, and I would be curt and tired.

I donned my housework dress of green and white and buttoned the bodice. My mirror's image reflected a girl's freckled face. I brushed and braided my red hair and wrapped it around itself at the nape of my neck, securing it with a ribbon of green. I tied my bonnet over my cap; it was not likely to stay in place atop my head, regardless.

Downstairs in the kitchen, Jane spooned a bowl of porridge and placed it on the white linen where she expected me to sit. Steam from the bowl was all I could see. "There's only porridge for breakfast today. Wash day," Jane remarked in a quick singsong. Her tone implied I was to eat quickly and carry the baskets of clothes and sheets outside. Jane was kind except on Mondays when we washed. Now she was chipper, but later she would be fussy for no particular reason. She preferred the indoors and her regimented timeline of baking bread and making beds. Perhaps it was that the sun burnt her skin, no matter the season. She was as pale as she was robust.

"Yes." Sarcasm hefted on my breath. It was not as if she needed to remind me. At sixteen, I helped with laundry since I was strong enough to move the dolly stick. Resigned, I took a bite and burnt my tongue, knowing better.

"With the wind beginning this early, it should be a pleasant drying day." She stepped back outside with her obvious premonition with arms hugging a basket containing garments collected from the school Saturday last. Five more sat eagerly beside the door. With so many clothes, she began earlier than usual. Our underclothes would be last in line for the lye and tallow.

Unable to taste, but with my mouth full of porridge, I mumbled, "Yes Jane," with as little attitude as I could muster, not to hasten her inevitable change in mood. Too hot to eat, I left the bowl with my spoon inside it, stuck permanently in its new home of porridge.

I carried one of the enormous baskets of garments seated beside the kitchen door out into the grass and sat on top, waiting for Jane to soap up the water in her large, iron boiling pot. In her black dress and bonnet, standing around the caldron mumbling under her breath, I half-expected the devils of Hell to rise. Instead, overpowering and instantaneous ammonia boiled away in wafting fumes. Sour and bitter smells served as our constant companions.

"Heap your seat in the pot, Sally Bird," Jane said.

So it began: the dropping of clothes, the agitation of the stick, Jane seating herself on her three-legged stool. She plopped her legs, one at a time, around a silver basin with her waiting washboard to scrub the first drowned victims from my pot. Clean laundry took four steps: douse, scrub, rinse, and hang. Repeat until shirts, shifts, and sheets masked barked lines of trees.

As the day progressed, we continued Monday's quiet laundry day. Mother joined us as the sun crept over the hill behind our house. Without her customary grace and stature, she stepped in front of the rinse tub, filling it from buckets set aside earlier. Mother's hand gripped the large paddle, smooth from weekly use, and stirred away soapy remnants. With one basket ready to hang on the line, Cornwall awoke with people beginning the routine of their daily lives. Some mimicked our ritual. Some hoed in garden beds. Some opened stores of flour and cloth. Some hunched over Bibles and English textbooks. While the sun traced its pattern across morning, routine made Cornwall ordinary and blessed, both at the same time.

The wind continued until late afternoon when I was the last to remain in the yard. At my feet, the final basket held wrung, twisted heaps mounded to overflowing. I dipped, grabbed a tangled sheet, and flipped it into the wind. Still hesitant to unroll, I tossed it two more times to unfurl its length. I secured it in place to dry, crossing the hem over the line. Mother reminded me to use the pegs on the sheets, so the crease would be at the seam rather than down the middle.

Later that afternoon, against the bright light, I squinted and found a walking silhouette against the sheeted walls, fluttering, stretching their wings to the lofting wind. The dark shadow's gait was slow but steady, rising on the left side, assisted by a single crutch. From the ground, the profile wore boots that clung to thin, tall legs. It wore a fitted, frock coat, casting the black outline of blousing sleeves and vest, whose buttons gave circular shape to adorn the torso's front. The silhouette's head rode atop its neck with stately grandeur, chin pronounced, and short, wavy hair brushed away from the forehead. John's gold eyes found me between hanging sheets, which fell in dense waves like white charm peonies held aloft against firm shrubbery.

With only a glance at him, I focused on my task. "You are earlier than usual." His shape was a few feet from me. I stretched from the waist, stepping down the line, and grabbed another peg. I avoided his gaze. His gravity made my arms heavier.

"Dr. Gold is coming by this afternoon, so I must be well," he said with a hint of tiredness likely caused by his walk from the wagon near the yard. He often spoke of his family's expansive farm, so I imagine him bored, sitting in class studying crop rotations when he wanted to read President Jefferson.

"Good." It was all I managed to say, mispronouncing the word with a clothes peg between my lips. I unfurled another sheet. If Dr. Gold was coming, that explained why Jane and Mother made their premature departure from the washboard and tub. I wonder why they chose not to tell me.

I paralleled the line, and John pantomimed my movement with a momentary delay. Pulling the peg from my mouth, I sighed and trapped the right end of the sheet, frustrated with my tired arms and endless work. Jane's mood was not the only one to sour this afternoon.

John sensed my temperament and looked at me inquisitively. "What's troubling you, Miss Sarah?"

"Nothing, just washing day." My impatience hid the truth. "Mother and Jane still think I am younger than I am."

"So, you're ready to fly the nest?" he asked with a measured pace and chuckled, thinking of something I found difficult to read from his expression.

"No, I just do not wish their constant reminders of things I do by habit." He did not deserve my tired curtness.

He hummed a single note and replied, "Since I have been from home, I have taken care of myself a great deal. As soon as I return, it is the same for me. My mother reminds me to cork the ink and to take off my boots before falling asleep. I can hear her say it now as if she stood here among the drying."

I stopped moving, and we saw one another in the absent space on the line. "You must miss home. Your mother and father wish for your return. Your father told me so when he was here."

"I miss them, but Elias eases some of my loneliness for home. He is my father's brother's son."

"Yes, I remember. He said so. He's your cousin?" Surely, John knew the word.

"Yes," he said. "We are as close as brothers, and his father is my father in many ways. Therefore, that is a better description. He plans to leave soon to attend Andover Theology School. Here, Elias has more friends than I do, but I am a better student. He is witty and personable. He is a wonderful storyteller, a skill I do not have."

John was saddened by Elias' pending departure. His expression brought lonely thoughts to my mind. Affirming what I already knew to be true, "… and you want to make people think. Your talents are a gift from God. It is a noble weight you seek to carry."

"It is why I was sent here: to study, to learn the ways of your lives. It is what our elders insist must happen. Jefferson warned the Cherokee to learn what it is to be American. My people must seek the education provided to us. Now, Cherokee land carries my people, but in the future, I fear we may have to learn to carry it on our backs."

"Made any discoveries … about us?"

"Mostly how hurried everyone seems, except you."

He paused mid-thought and followed me, speaking with a younger expression on his face, one more reminiscent of his age. He seemed to catch the memory of his home in the wind, squinting against the fading sun. "Light. I miss the light. I miss running my horse along the edge of the Oostanaula River in the morning's glow. I miss green haze above acres of grass bordered by trees as far as one can see. I miss council meetings with enormous fires under starry skies in autumn. Mountains and coves pebbled with spectrums of color… I miss …"

I interrupted his musings, changing the subject. "Have you slept with your boots on, John?" My mind held to what he'd said earlier; I covered my mouth with my hand, hiding my grin.

"Only when my mother cannot see me." He returned the smile I hid as I laughed louder than I meant to.

"Your cousin isn't the only student that makes others laugh. You do too. Why would anyone sleep with their boots on? I cannot imagine that comfortable at all."

Repeat: flip, flip again, pegs on the seam.

"It only happens when I'm tired from working the ferry or from the days in the orchards harvesting apples. I collapse on my bed and fall asleep. Mother wakes me and, seeing my transgression, reminds me again, 'Take your boots off before you sleep!'" He imitated her tone with higher pitches. "Staying awake to copy English verses, I wake at my desk, face marked with paper seams. Alas, boots remain. I slept with them on several nights last summer. There was something I needed to finish." With wit and a grin, he said, "Please, don't tell my mother."

"I promise; I won't." Then, remembering the images of his land, I said, "Forgive my interruption. Your home seems like Eden. Be faithful. I am …" wanting to add *in you,* but I feared the forwardness of the admission. The wind picked up the sheets and blew the cap from my head while branches of hair flew across my eyes, unwoven from my braided bun.

Courtesy compelled me to thank him. "The hummingbird, it is beautiful, and I'll always treasure it. You didn't have to do that for me. I imagine it took quite some time to make."

"Oh no." His comment piqued my interest. "It was for Jane." He lied with a mocked gasp at our buxom housekeeper. I smiled and dropped my head, knowing. So did he, as he tilted his head around the damp sheet.

Not ready to return to the drying, he studied me, recognizing the patterns of my motions, and bent to meet me at my peg bucket, which must have caused him pain. We reached for the pegs, not collecting any at all. Instead, he rose first, taking my hand and helping me to stand. It was I who was accustomed to helping him, not the inverse.

"I have another gift, one I hope you'll accept. Months ago, I asked Father to uproot them and pack them in his trunk. Come with me?" I didn't want him to let go, but he did first and led me to his door. I remained outside.

"Close your eyes." He rummaged through his trunk and returned. With a tilt to one of his eyebrows, I protested but indulged him.

"That's silly. What is it?"

"Close your eyes." He whispered with a sweeter persuasion, soft, like ornamental violet leaves.

Once I did so, he picked up my hand, turned it palm up, and placed the weight. He guided my other hand and put it on top, trapping both inside his own. The canvas was scratchy and not bulky. Shapes inside promised more.

"Imagine the deepest green cove near a river, rocky ground, with steep ridges and falling water. Through winding vines, leaves, and brush, its green stalk stands tall, with no stem leaves, reaching a foot tall. Three leaves unroll from the bud, larger than a warrior's hands to protect the tiny bloom."

I still had my eyes closed. "What color?"

"Some are white, and some, deep maroon. Three petals on petite blooms, each with green spindles shooting from their black center." I could feel his breath.

"Their name?" I asked, hoping to keep him close, for one more moment.

"Trillium or Sweet Beth."

"I've never seen any before." From my touch, the bulbs had dried tops. Like lilies, these fit in the cup of my curved palm. There were two alike inside.

"They don't grow here, only on the Blue Ridge Mountains." His warmth kept the sun's light at bay.

"When?" I was unmovable.

"March. Maybe April." His hair touched my forehead.

I opened my eyes. He stood above me, smelling of wood smoke, deep earth, black pepper, and ink.

"Let me know before you bury them." He watched my lips.

"Why?" Sharing breath, I barely said the word.

"Elias and I need to go fishing first." He closed his eyes, pulling his body back, letting sunlight stand in as a delayed chaperone.

"Why?" He gestured back to my basket across the yard.

"Because we will bury fish underneath them, so they'll grow taller."

I forced my feet to follow him back to my basket, leaving the bag hidden in my palms. Once arriving, he bowed his head and reaffirmed his crutch under his arm. Before he left, he took a finger to the side of my face, tracing the hair away from my freckles. The breeze blew it back.

"Does the wind mean to blow you away?" he asked.

"I hope not." I wanted to say something more important. Words parched my throat.

He whispered words only his Cherokee wind understood.

"What does it mean?" I meant to say, *please don't go*, but I forgot the words.

Without speaking another sound in Cherokee or English, he replied with his expression asquint in a rising smile. As he walked away, he turned back to run his free hand through his hair. Whether out of nervousness or frustration, my words and his response remained unspoken. I opened the bag to inspect the bulbs. Inside, John had written a note.

I looked back to our house for Mother or Jane, Dr. Gold or Father. No one watched. With sheets as my sheltering friends, I opened the folded paper. In elegant, scrawling script, it read,

Sarah Bird,

Your voice never leaves me. Next to me or absent, the sound of it wraps around me, sustaining me. I cannot take my mind away from you. Watch for the candle. Meet me by the river.

John

Tossing my head over my shoulder, I looked toward the house where no one sought me at all.

CHAPTER 6

Black Coats

Clarinda Ridge

October 1856

Near Rome, Georgia

After the full Harvest Moon, nights filled with chills and shivers, like a warrior's threat, discovered true in the dawn. Summer and fall argued, fighting nightly skirmishes with weapons of wind and falling rain. Each evening, Sun threw her hands to the sky and retreated sullenly into dusk. She returned each morning, knowing she could not stay. Each day, she grew more distant, like returning home, a familiar stranger.

The earth remembered my hands, although her memory faded. This land was Cherokee's Eden, given by our Heavenly Father, the Great Spirit. Once the great serpent, *Uktena,* came, white men followed, overtaking and owning these mountains and valleys. Paler farms replaced Cherokee roots, not with corn harvests but with inky signatures on paper. White men's quills stung with the Devil's forked tongue.

My heritage, my grandpa, earned his name, the Man Who Walks on Mountaintops, on the southern tip of the Blue Mountains. He knew the land by sight, the rivers by touch. He lived within their bounty, returned to them after battle, grew from them his family and farm, found solace breathing their familiar smells—vast expanses connected to arched horizons like his shoulders. Mountains bent low, watching dizzying streams and silty rivers: the Oostanaula, the Coosawattee, the Conasauga, and the Chattahoochee. Grandpa and Papa protected their homeland, their nation's people, as long as they were able. They failed. Their names forced tears along the path where they cried. They paid the debt for their signatures in full, bleeding and dying from red hands they tried to free.

Left behind for so long, Momma and I lived together in silence. She lost her heartbeat for the last twenty years of her life after Ross' war party murdered Papa. She fell mute after, her heart's sounds absent. Papa took its beating with him to Heaven, to the Nightland.

During the last full Snow Moon, 1856, Momma's lungs swelled and filled. Her skin turned gray, the same shade as her silver hair. No earthly cure could ground a spirit destined to fly to the Great Fire. Earth cannot heal soul wounds.

Rollin, my brother, brought me here after she passed, brought me home, although he could not stay. After Momma's funeral last winter, he asked if I wanted to return, knowing my answer before he finished the question. We packed my books in Momma's hummingbird box and left the house in my adopted brother's care. His roots spread there, entwined around corn stalks and wheat fields. The land in Arkansas belonged to Waccoli now.

Rollin and I traveled by train, south across Arkansas, east through Mississippi and Tennessee, to Georgia. Upon these same roads, many Cherokees' bare feet sunk through mud during the coldest winter of 1838 and 1839. Images of rickety wooden wagons, long boats on muddy water, snow covering shallow graves haunted me. Rollin and I retrieved and renewed their tears during our return. To any that asked questions of our faces, our skin answered, appearing white. No one called us savages or said we could not stay.

Home. One of my earliest memories was riding high on Papa's shoulders through drying laundry. Rollin was still a baby, propped in a basket at Momma's feet. Holding my toes with one hand, Papa handed me clothes pegs with his other. After Momma hung the sheet, I leaned down from above him and placed them on the line. It is a memory, so ordinary, but thinking of my earliest self, it is the moment forefront in my mind. It was a rare moment, one not filled with all of my brothers and sisters. I am the oldest of eight: Rollin, Susan, Herman, Aeneas, Waccoli, Andrew, and Flora.

Momma told me a little more of her and Papa's courtship, only what she called 'the days where they talked,' as much of their time was spent watched by the Northrup housekeeper, Jane, Grandmother Northrup, or Dr. Gold. While Father lived and healed behind Mother's childhood house, their later conversations took place in remembered looks and courteous bows to one another. They found themselves separated by chores, classes, and church pews until he lit the candle.

In Connecticut, Father and Uncle Elias wore black coats, called so during their school years by townsfolk, attaching their attire to their presumed missionary occupation. The Northrups and Reverend Daggett invited them to dinner parties and social gatherings. Their lives became a conversation piece, a living demonstration of God's efforts and Christian doxology, educating them to enter decent American society. They found themselves accepted, well-liked by this small fraction of America.

Reverend Daggett requested Uncle Elias and Papa present a mock Cherokee council meeting in their native tongue. Performed after Sunday's sermon for Cornwall's residents, they sat tall in the minister and choirmaster's chairs, angled toward one another. Cornwall must have imagined them adorned in feathered headdresses and been quite disappointed after arriving at services in student dress. With broad gestures, they emulated a disagreement and concession, a treaty party.

Put on display like wooden puppets, another contorted their movements; however, the humiliating play's unintelligible lines became their own. Uncle Elias told me once that they debated which dessert to sample after their speeches from among the many delicacies brought by Cornwall's wives and daughters. However, to Cornwall's Episcopalian elite, surely Papa and Uncle Elias spoke of noble things: Moses coming down from the mountaintop with God's commandments carved in stone, laws meant to halt the Israelites' worship of idols, converting the ignorant and savage masses to civilization and humility.

Instead, Papa and Uncle Elias debated a treaty to decide whether to enjoy Harriet Gold's blackberry cobbler or Momma's lemon cake. When recanting the story, Uncle Elias said they ate cobbler; Papa disagreed entirely with his recollection.

After the service, Harriet Gold, who later married Uncle Elias, bounced between her sisters, attracting a throng of following admirers. Uncle Elias stood behind a tree devising a hidden stickball game with the other Indian students until she walked near them. Once seeing her, Uncle Elias left the group to decide for themselves who would be on each team and followed Harriet Gold to complement her fine baking.

Momma's cake plate held only remaining crumbs as scores of farmer's sons, even the burly Samuel, sought my mother's attention. Grandmother Northrup looked on with an approving grin or a deterring scowl after each young man greeted her daughter.

Momma talked of that day, how Papa's black coat and silver watch chain made him the most handsome student among the boys with sheep's oil absorbed into their calico reds. No one else spoke to her of faraway mountain coves holding ruby-colored lilies or read Shakespeare aloud.

I imagine Papa heard his own voice behind Hamlet's soliloquies. Although he wasn't the Danish prince; he became the murdered king. My brother wore Hamlet's princely crown. In 1847, unable to subdue his need for revenge, Rollin shot Judge Kell, a Ross man. Kell stole Rollin's horse and castrated it. Kell was the man who slit Papa's throat in 1839. After the ensuing argument, Rollin shot him. Fearing further retribution and finding a sudden desire to mine California gold, Rollin ran, taking Aeneas and Waccoli with him. Momma knew he must go to stay alive. Rollin inherited Papa's fire along with his voice.

Banished because of blood revenge, the three rode west. Rollin sat atop his Appaloosa gelding, leading my brothers to distant, rolling waters through crooked places.

CHAPTER 7

Rolling Waters through Crooked Places

John Ridge

October 1822

Cornwall, Connecticut

Time at the Foreign Mission School was quickly ending, and I needed to forge decisions that would either bend me or break me. I completed all the coursework I could do here. It would not be long before I ventured home to the uproars and angry tones of men, brooding, hunched over papers strewn across expensive, mirrored tabletops. I recognized these present moments as the last of my youth, for traveling home meant I must use the worthy education to argue in English, loud enough to be heard among insults left unsaid. Jefferson predicted, "In time, you will be as we are. You will become one people with us; your blood will mix with ours and will spread with ours over this great land." It was time to build Jefferson's new America and the conflict it would surely bring. This choice would change all that I was—all we could be. With that knowledge, I welcomed it.

I placed the candle in my window and hoped Sarah would see it. It was five o'clock in the afternoon, no time for wasting wax, but I could not meet her after dark, unchaperoned. Once lit, I stood as a silent sentry, gazing at her upstairs window. Within a short time, my candle's reflection found its twin in her upstairs room, framed by the curtains of Sarah's beautiful vibrancy: the reds of her hummingbird hair, the sapphire covering her breast mirrored in the color of her eyes, the lines of her frame blousing with new woman's curves.

Extinguishing mine, I waited for the sound of the rear door to the Northrup house to open and close. Pacing through several minutes, I opened and crossed my threshold, not knowing entirely what I would say to her. There were many things to explain and a few words in English to articulate them with the righteousness they deserved.

By then, Dr. Gold permitted me to ride a horse borrowed from the Northrup stable. According to the rules, foreign students could venture within two miles of the Northrup home and neighboring school. The river was a small distance away from that invisible barrier, and I hoped the ride would be easier than the walk. Sarah would more than likely arrive before I could, regardless, on foot or horseback. I detoured to the stable, saddled the horse, and began the short distance downhill to where the Housatonic River bent near the border to the Northrup property.

If only I were a poet. She sat alone in blue. Her slender frame was seated upon a stump near the water's edge. In her line of sight, the tumult of the river flounced over rock and crest, revealing the underlying topography. Summer's splendor framed her, and the last smells of honeysuckle nectar filled the air. Sensing me, she turned. In profile, she smiled, one I did not deserve after a month of little conversation. I stopped a distance away to dismount onto higher ground. Pulling my crutch from the saddle strap, I crossed the distance.

No language held the right words. I knelt beside her and followed her gaze, interrupted by the sounds of the water where her transfixion fell.

I do not know why this memory felt appropriate; however, I told her, "When I was a child, I would strip my clothes and wade through waters like these with my cane gig to catch crawfish. If Father sought me, it was where he began his search."

She found my eyes. She always did.

"I wonder where the water has been and what it sees as it travels downstream. I wonder how long it will flow before it turns into summer's humidity. It does not matter, though." Her image dissipated like the water.

She disregarded her thoughts as those of a child, but her vision reminded me of my task. I stood, propping on our shared stump, and offered her my arm, which she took. We walked beside the water, where sand mixed with the soil. I leaned to her instead of that crutch, forgotten, not feeling the need for anything but her to sustain me. Her arm in mine silenced any remaining doubt.

She stopped us in a shaded clearing near the bank. I do not know why she hesitated, but I followed.

"Sarah, can you hear me above these rolling waters?"

She replied with brief tension in the muscle of her arm but did not let go. Then, she articulated the same fear occupying my thoughts for weeks.

"Your schooling is complete. You've studied all you can here."

"True." Would she want me to stay? I questioned myself without intonation, asking for more than any single answer she could give.

"It is pointless for you to remain. It will sadden me when you leave. You have become ..." She looked to the water cresting white over rock and fallen limb. Sunlight blinded against her white skin, radiating from the side I could not see. She didn't finish her thought.

"Sarah, when I arrived here, I wanted to blend. I wanted to wear the clothes of your people. I bought my watch to show I was equal to, better than, what others assumed about me. I thought if I carried myself as white, others would see me as such."

She opened her mouth to speak, but I continued. I needed to voice this to her.

"I thought if I were to marry, it should be a woman from your world. Doing so might allow me entrance into the freedom promised by America. I am a second-generation American Cherokee; I see the world through two sets of eyes."

She pulled her arm away.

"Let me speak," I stopped her movement, "please?" Her eyes drifted from me as if I betrayed her loyalty, even as I vowed to love her for the rest of my days. "You gave so much to me. I knew what I thought before was a selfish desire, one that couldn't hear the needs of anyone else."

If I sought what I wanted, fear of retribution and punishment to her consumed me. It is not something I could ask her to endure. Would she endure it, though? "You taught me I was wrong. I waited for the Great Spirit, God, to guide me to a partner who trusted me, forgave my impatience, and helped me recognize my selfishness. I am so very grateful to Him for sending you." Clearing my throat to free my request, it came from me, more implied than stated. "Sarah, I fear the consent I seek will never be given."

She slid both of her hands down my arm and wrapped both around mine, where they belonged. Her chest rose, and mine fell in the extended time it took her thoughts to choose words. She rallied her courage to speak.

"There are no other words to say. No refusals or denials from anyone would change anything."

"Our world is loud, Sarah. People will say I have ruined you." I worried.

"You have, although not in the same way that rules their gossip. You live in my heart. There's no room for another," she confessed.

"And you, in mine." Understanding what she meant, I had to proceed now, or what courage I had would lose itself in ramblings of forsaken love—how I would fight to have her. Neither of which either of us would want. Instead, I told her my concerns rather than filling her mind with illusions, misleading her into an untrue perception of our sweet but bitter situation.

I began with the tale of the letters sent and received during this last month. I tried to show her my intentions, hoping to maintain her trust and propose to her a choice. With solemn tones, I told her of my battle between my head and my heart and the latter's victory.

"Last month, your mother's entrance to my room was full of sincerity, although her knock was unusual at that hour of the evening. Offering her admittance to the room and your chair, I sat on my bed to address her as she greeted me. With sudden frankness, your mother began."

"Dr. Gold said you could ride again. I know that must please you."

"It does. It has been a long time since I've had the freedom to travel even the shortest distances we are allowed to go alone."

"Dr. Gold told us you appear not quite yourself."

"I have kept abreast of my studies. I do not know what he asks of me."

"Well, we want to know that you feel well, John."

"I'm content and as blessed as I could hope to be, under the circumstances." Gesturing to my leg, I asked myself why she was here.

"Is anything troubling you?"

Through my silence, my reply resonated as loud as if I shouted.

"John, while you've been at school these past few years, I have tried to treat you as your own mother might. Please, tell me what troubles you. Perhaps, I can help solve whatever problem that causes you to remain …" She sought the right word. I thought she might say weak, but her adjective surprised me. "… restless."

"That is not what I thought you might say."

Now, I doubted her nurturing sentiment. We sat in anxious silence. I ran my hand through my hair so many times, a reaction to her effrontery. I heard my watch tick.

With resignation at her expected shame with my disquieting revelation, I walked over to the desk and pulled from the single drawer three bound letters. Handing them to her, I resumed my seat to watch her eyes.

My father's brother, Wattie's voice, came to my mind. Surrounded by known and unknown sounds in the forest, Wattie's eyes replicated fire's light while telling stories. One particular story was of a man's fight with two wolves inside him. One wolf had a mild temperament, serene and humble, while the other wolf paced with restlessness and cruelty. Whichever wolf was fed triumphed in battle.

Tonight, I fed the angry wolf and flung my crutch across the room, hoping to cease her incessant intrusion. The sound made her jolt. With determination, she remained seated and opened the first.

Son,

Missionary Buttrick read your letter and will pen this response. First, my fervent prayer is you are healing and well.

As to your request, I must decline. Come home. Meet and speak to some girls in your native tongue, Chief's daughters from Wild Potato or Wolf clans; they understand our people and can make a proper wife for you. Go hunting; take a deer to her family. She would understand you far more than this girl you desire could. Miss Northrup cannot be a wife to you; both of you live on opposite banks to a wide river. In her white manners and ways, she would feel superior to the ways of those who would surround her. It would place you in a position to deny those who need you, choosing instead to suffer under the desires of the one you married. Waters between each of you roar between opposite banks. I believe, through the rushing sounds, you would not hear one other's voice.

I can only imagine my words will not content you. You have always sought the difficult path, son. Choose now the wiser and straighter distance. Come home to us to sit at the head of our table.

With love,
Mother

I informed Mrs. Northrup, upon her closing the first, "Arguing with my mother with quill in ink is as pointless as doing so in person, but I felt her concerns deserved an answer, so I sent a second appeal. That is not the exact letter, but one of my last drafts."

Mrs. Northrup held open the second page with shaking hands.

Dearest Mother,

I feel renewed in my body but am still unwell. You do not understand the depth of my affection for Sarah. Please reconsider.

To heal my pain, she offered serenity to my restlessness. In the exchange, I found her remarkable. Her patience is endless with my moods and discourses, whether or not she understands their origins. She reads my silence, and when I speak, she hears my words, concerns, fears. My temperamental demands should not seek her pity. If she accepts my proposal, as my wife, her kindness will add strength to my voice, unraveling my quiet like a watered rope. She frees me from bindings, those of my creation, with her curiosity.

She is beautiful, eyes the color of the sky during the orchard harvest, and hair as red as apples, ripe on our orchard's trees. Her limbs will not break with weight—withstanding.

She does not yet understand how I feel, as I am awaiting your consent before speaking to her and her family. I must tell her how we might surpass the condemnation we will receive from white and perhaps Cherokee alike. She deserves to know how trouble may befall us both for this passion. More than that, she deserves a choice. To deny her voice would be dishonorable. Many dictate her life now. How could I do so and love her at the same time?

Father met her and her parents, and all seemed on amicable terms. They are good people, blessed in God's graces. Sarah is devoted—a true Sarah in patience and piety. She, too, will give birth to a new Nation.

I can only say again that in the time Sarah and I have spent together as I heal, she has given me trust. Because of her gift, she is my choice. This marriage will make two peoples one, and your grandsons will become elders to a new world, where Cherokee thrive beside our white brethren. Mother, reconsider and trust me in this choice, one that will guide me the rest of my days.

Your son,

John

Her hand covered her mouth. Mrs. Northrup whispered but spat with each consonant, "You love her then? With such passion and earnestness that you would disobey your parent's wishes?" She measured my character against her own perceptions of right and wrong, white and red.

"No, I could never disobey, but I thought to be more explicit in my appeal. The month's time between sending my renewed request and my mother's reply was the longest of my life. Father would abide by her decision, and asking a third time was a risk I could not take.

Where I come from, mothers are creators, life-givers, and because of that, they decide the fates of families. Knowing this, I struggled to put into words what I felt, knowing my choice might disappoint her. With fervor, I drafted that letter until there were no blank pages left to begin again, still feeling the inadequacy of the words. I expected Mother's second refusal would be longer than her first. Only time can change her seasons."

With that, she opened the third, reading the fewest words Mother ever recited.

Son,

You may speak with her and her parents. Ensure their consent. My fear is that you will row upstream your entire life. Be sure she chooses this life. I trust your choice.

Mother

Sarah's mother refolded the third, one that would force her to change if her daughter agreed. Mrs. Northrup stood, returned the letters to my hand, and trailed silent indignation behind her, wafting from the hem of her dress.

After recalling the memories of conversing with her mother, the Housatonic rushed louder through Sarah's reticence. She let go of my hand. Every fear, imagined, real, concerning this moment heaved to my throat. She walked to the water's edge and knelt. In prayer or sadness, I could not know. With measured strides of my limp, I stood behind her, listening. I had a month to consider the effect of my decision; she had minutes to make a choice.

She removed each tan glove to reveal bare hands. Those slender, freckled hands became my constellations in restless nights. Without a notion as to the significance to my people, she went to water, doused her hands in the lapping, and rose, leaving her gloves alone in the sand.

I needed her to speak, but she stopped short of a declaration. Instead, she recited Ezekiel, "John, should I, like Ruth, sleep at your feet? 'Wherever thou goest, I will go. Your people shall become my people.'"

I breathed and knew our choice was made—a blanket to cover us both. In pursuit of our happiness, we walked where we began, on the same side of the river, arms woven together. She leaned to me, guarded by witnessing trees, hushed by the volume of rolling waters. Her resolve reminded me of God's promise in Isaiah, "I will go before you and make the crooked places straight." Our decision made, the goodly men and women of Cornwall would not put us asunder.

CHAPTER 8

Love and Longing

Sarah Bird Northrup

October 1822–June 1823

Cornwall and New Haven, Connecticut

Dinner tonight would be the longest of my life. Mother must have sensed in my blissful return home that John had spoken his wishes. By shunning him, I could save her from ridicule and blame of impropriety. I did no such thing. Her sensational reaction frightened me if she confronted me with John's request. I needed time to know how to proceed.

I removed my bonnet and met my Mother and Father standing in the hall, murmuring with audible distress. Mother snatched the bonnet from my hands.

With an elevated pitch and lacking any courtesy, she asked, "Do you love John?" Her affront, so direct, stung like a stern slap.

Mother's abruptness contained no preamble, and I imagined her anxiety multiplied ten-fold. Father walked to our minor-keyed duet and stopped the music with his conductor's baton, swiping with curt directness. I do not know who was to cease singing; I'd spoken no word. Measures upon measures of rests, I waited.

Then, borrowing John's courage, I said, "Yes. I do."

The dam broke.

"This cannot be," she exclaimed, distressing in Old Testament fervor, holding her dainty handkerchief to her mouth, a lace pyramid in her clenched hand. "You will go to your grandparent's house." No question, just the commanding order from Mother's almighty voice.

"We must send him home." With five words, Father exited the stage with the deliberate strides of a man seeking solitude, forgetting his hat.

Silenced, fearing the pointlessness of any debate, I walked to my room, heaving each boot to climb each stair. Turning the familiar handle, I refastened the latch with my back, exhausted. In the dark, I sat at my dressing table; my reflection stared at the unlit candle in the window. Earlier, its wick lit joy, but hours later, wax turned cold with regret at my departure. No flame could sustain through unspoken words. I lost tomorrow.

At daybreak, they packed me in a carriage. Absent of choice, I left the shopkeepers of Cornwall, horses to pasture, flocks of sheep, the cedar tree by my window, my parents full of spit and fury, and my John.

Escorted by Reverend Clark, my parent's hope was that the day spent in the hired carriage with the Godly man might help me see my error. I am sure Mother trusted him and his presumed confidentiality. With that knowledge, I spoke little.

Watching the terrain change on our southern mission to New Haven, my will dissolved more with each passing mile. I worried about what my parents might say to John in my absence. Would he abandon his proposal, anticipating reprisal? There were no words to say that might halt anyone's course. I prayed as the road wound south, baptizing it anew with dripping cheeks.

We arrived on Friday to exclamations from Grandmother of the wonderful time we would have together at dinners and parties. I wanted none of it but smiled at the sight of her and hugged Grandpa Abel.

Days waned on, and I strolled through the black iron-gated border of roses, fragrant but bringing little happiness in the present. I often embroidered, sewing clumps of Bizzy Lizzy flowers, but my French knots pulled straight through, unraveling from behind the hoop. Grandpa came through the room, blocking my light. I smelled him behind me: wood shavings and soil. His slim stature, hunched with age, still held his salt and pepper hair higher than most men. He stared over my shoulder as I failed two more times.

"Give up," he said. "Sew an X right there and call it finished."

"That isn't how it is done, Grandpa."

"Who cares how it's done? Go about it a different way, but just finish it. Follow through. Don't leave things incomplete."

Grandpa understood people's thoughts, discovered mine just as easily. Kissing my forehead, he recited, "I love you the most," with the sole purpose of raising my cheeks. He wandered away to find something to prune or build. He was always in some state of construction or deconstruction, depending upon the season.

My appetite left me, as did restful sleep. I found joy difficult but faked a weak smile to those recent acquaintances Grandmother invited for tea. I wrote to John a single letter inquiring about his health, giving him my new address and signing it, *"Yours, S.B.N."* Afraid to say more, it was pointless to maintain an attachment he might have dissolved. Each afternoon, with no post, every room darkened, lifting smells of stains on the floor and dust from the ceiling, converging in a confused and brackish middle. While time sped forward in Cornwall, it unwound incomplete in New Haven. I was never in the room to catch the dongs from the chiming clock. The sound seemed more distant with each spinning hour, no matter how many times Grandpa wound the spring.

As dramatic as my thoughts ran, there seemed to be a new weakness beginning in my chest, resounding outwards. On a Thursday, with the post, some forward movement of time arrived, sealed with wax, scripted with ink on paper.

May 1823

My Dearest Sarah,

The longer I am away from you and Connecticut, the shorter my temper. Ink dries before I can finish each sentence, and as you well know, that is uncommon for me. My heart is weaker, my tones somber, and I find myself bitter at our absent goodbye. Every candle reignites your memory.

I asked our Wise Man to pray for our coming marriage. After days of ritual, he assured me our roots would grow well together, a blessing for our union. His revelation assisted in my pleas to Mother to sanctify this marriage.

Once she meets you, she will call you daughter. Fear not. I have described you to her as spring rain, sunshine that warms corn husks tasseled for harvesting, autumn blue and cloudless skies, like the hyacinth you described to me, 'through a landscape of forgotten fall.' I remember every word. Our fragmented courtship, only a single chapter.

Proposals and debates. I continue to study American law. Father tries to keep my mind engaged in the ongoing treaty process with the U.S. Government. My voice is part of the Cherokee appeal; however, I fear my translations will fall on ears that are too young to hear or too old to listen. However, talks in phases sleep better than nightmares from speed. There has been enough bloodshed on our land disguised as water meant for Cherokee to drink. I fear it tainted water, unclean.

These talks will be a crux for my people and cause a great bend in our roots, as there may be no place to escape the thickening of the geographical noose. Our land is who we are. Without it, we lose more than negotiations. We lose peaceful rest.

Upon my return, Father renewed my acquaintance with John Ross, a man born of a Scottish father and a Cherokee mother. He speaks on our behalf at great meetings with white Senators and

Representatives from Georgia. He has often been at our dinner table since my return and has similar views as Father and myself as to the path for peace. We are fluent together. How I have longed for the sounds of my native language spoken by many Cherokee, all with one voice.

Sarah, please forgive my melancholy mood. Before my return home, your parents and I agreed if I could return to Cornwall and walk without crutches, they would grant their consent. I imagine they assumed the moment an improbability. Nonetheless, it is a negotiation I will win. Expectations to stroll beside you, your arm in mine, reminds me to walk with unassisted swiftness. As for Ross and his companionship and confidence, I have been grateful. It has eased the burden of the miles of separation between us.

Let me assure you the pain is less. Mother has resumed her regimen of herbs. These walks through the fields of grain have been medicinal for my hip as I continue to heal. Your family was correct, Sarah, I mean to marry you, but I must do so standing tall. Until then, the memory of your voice must be enough to subdue my hunger to hear it.

With love and longing,
John

After reading, I sought escape from the antiquated furniture, holding scents reminiscent of their age and attitudes. I stepped outside at the close of the day, seeing the front garden. Columbines stopped me, both of us confined and landscaped. Purple and white buds spilled haphazardly onto the nearby sidewalk, while their stems remain rooted behind iron.

I bristled, hearing imagined thoughts of Father's cryptic words to John. "How will you support her if you cannot farm, cannot work?" Although, what my Father meant was that my mother would not survive the shame of a daughter married to a Cherokee husband. John would not provide with his hands; he would do so with words. Words, a year ago, my father was proud to call one of his greatest successes. All I could do was wait across the distance. I missed John's temper, his thoughts, his voice most of all.

Just breathe. When I inhaled, my head spun, and my ears rang with a piercing pitch so high, unceasing. My world slowed and blurred, and I fell. My hand caught the pocket of my apron. Beside John's letter was the hummingbird. Grandfather carried me inside.

When I woke, the clock chimed six. I was in my bed, and a doctor stood beside me, holding my wrist.

"She isn't eating." The doctor assumed. "Her color is too sallow."

I caught snatches of their conversation and fell asleep again, dreaming of a hummingbird batting her wings against an unnatural cage.

"Consumption …" the doctor said.

It was more than a word. His tone implied genuine fear.

In sleep, I dreamt of unmoving and patient wings. My heartbeat pounded. From my perspective, I looked with eyes inside the bars, a gilded cage aloft on a brass hook.

Waking again, I listened as the clock struck eight. Grandmother sat by my bedside, holding my hand, while Grandpa Abel sat in the comfortable chair across the room. He scolded her, "You've been trying to take her mind from him, and all it has done is make her remember him more."

In glimpses, I watched her pursed lips reply to him. "Pointless," she said. My closed eyelids followed; moments grown from my memory chimed with the hours on the clock.

"Dangerous," I heard Grandpa, understanding him but not seeing him.

"Home." I woke. The clock rang nine chimes.

Once I could take soup and not sleep throughout the day, we rode for Cornwall. Grandpa sat in the coach beside me. Grandmother's gloves grasped and unfolded as she smacked her lips, passing the time in audible and unceasing sighs. Leather seats seeped scents of polish and wax mixed with Grandpa's pipe smoke. Sunlight mixed their scents in my memory, etched in olfactory permanence. Wildflowers comforted me as I prayed for God's interceding action. Peace came in the smoke from Grandpa Abel's pipe tobacco, smoky and savory. I remembered his words, as steadfast and firm as he smelled. Grandpa advised me to finish what I began. With newfound resolve, I vowed to trust and wait for John.

CHAPTER 9

Stained, Staying, and Standing

John Ridge, *Skahtlelohskee*

May–October 1823

Cherokee Nation Territory

Like black hornblende woven through granite, ink stains covered my Apollo finger from its tip to the first joint. I signed the letter, and after examining it, recalled the many times my hand appeared this stained. With the ability to foretell his destiny, Apollo, son of Zeus, knew what he would become. Leaning back into my chair, I realized my gifts were barren. Powerless to control my life, time lapsed in excess as news traveled slowly. Once fate's judgment reached me, my destiny lay imprisoned instead of freed. Grasping for choice and control with stained hands, I wrote my thoughts to her.

A loud voice from the bottom of the stairs drove me from my seat. I stood and crossed the hall to listen from the landing. Beneath me, Ross read in English, and Father's presence manifested from his questions and audible sighs. I followed the sound of his breathing and ascended the stairs to greet Ross' English scattering through Father's Cherokee, like a whirlwind of sand and dust. Apollo rose next to his own father's Great Spirit; I would descend to Earth to receive the news with my own.

"I rode as soon as I read it. The paper's dated late February." Ross remarked while Father circled with his hands behind his back. The unknown hung in the air, denser than turpentine vapors.

"*No one should be negotiating.*" Father's finality was impenetrable.

Ross spoke to me as I limped to their duo, holding the stair rail. His breath carried sincerity. But rather than flourish words, he spoke successive phrases without pause. "John, the court has ruled that land occupied by Indians cannot be purchased unless agencies of the United States negotiate the sale."

After Ross' full stop, Father crossed between us, stepping into the open doorway facing blinding sunlight. His shoulders hid the years, miles, people carried upon his back, darkening the light in the space. Father picked up his pipe from the table beside the door, packed the tobacco, and placed the thin end between his lips, unlit. Ross and I stared, glancing between his squinting silhouette and the wider-eyed floor. We waited for him to shift and listened for his advice.

"Ross, John, I'll meet you both at the stable." He freed the light held as he looked to the horizon and stepped off the porch. My eyes strained to resolve the daylight emerging and emanating from his absence.

"We must think of how this could benefit our people. At least now we know there is only one negotiator, instead of Whites persuading Cherokee on fringe land to sell without the U.S. Commissioner's consent."

"That is true, John."

Ross passed to the porch, and I grabbed my crutch left beside the door.

"Leave it," he remarked when seeing me stop.

As we turned, the view behind the house cleared, and I walked behind my friend. Ross was taller than I and more solidly built. His physique was one of a bull, stout and square. His hair was lighter and grew grayer at his temples, his years, ten or fifteen more than mine. His heavy-booted feet progressed first; his face filled more with the hair of whites, but eyes of Cherokee brown armed the deep forest of his face. Elected and held in high regard by all, Ross was one of us in heart and mind, even though his ancestors crossed salty seas, watering down his blood.

The path smelled rich in black soil and deep roots, dense with foxglove and spiderwort bordering the house. On the horizon, there was a patchwork of squares: corn high, boarded by plentiful wheat bending to gusts of warm air, tense with summer's heat.

Father instructed me to saddle my horse and Ross to mount as he rode ahead, turning to parallel the river behind the house to the river ferry.

Father never rushed to lead. When he noticed us both beside him, he spoke.

"*Time spent being present ...*" Father remarked between piped lips.

Ross changed the subject in his mother's tongue, albeit slow with incorrect verb tenses, "*The negotiations will be in October at the new Council House at New Town. We must be of one mind as we begin the speech.*"

"You know my mind and that of my son's." I did not need to talk; our thoughts were one and the same on this matter. We would not sell.

"... and I agree. Will you act as Speaker to the Council?" Ross knew Father's acceptance without asking, but in respect, his inquiry was due.

"Yes. John will turn my words to those of the whites."

"I am honored," I remarked with sincerity. Trusted with the distinction to perform as linkster and secretary, my father placed his integrity in my hands, to speak on his behalf to those yet determined as friend or foe. For his confidence, I was grateful. Ross and Father debated and discussed tactics as we traveled and wound through trees. I listened but found myself lost in remembering—a time before my pain grew—passing a familiar field of clover.

I saw images from my past, Buck's story at the council when we were ten-years-old. Buck, my cousin, Elias, my friend—same man.

Sparks flew from a fire near where I sat beside Vann while Buck recanted our tale to the Cherokee huddled around the circle. Buck, the storyteller among us, found flourish and exaggeration more common than the stars in his sky. He told how we'd tracked hoof prints for four days on foot.

Buck's shadow grew with ascending embers beside the fire, highlighting his face. His arms imitated his words.

"Skahtlelohskee's bark quiver was full of sacred, sourwood arrows, sharp with flint strapped across his back, and his longbow, strung in yucca, stood tall in his hand. I carried the knife at my side. We wound through trees, zigzagging, making a fresh path. I led, while Vann crept behind Skahtlelohskee, all three with silent feet." Our faces were smeared with mud and dirt; our buckskins ground black at our knees.

"Hickory trees opened into a small clearing where we crouched low to the ground, side by side, and sat on our heels to wait. Clover grew here; the buck had to come and go from this field. Hoof prints, repeated, crisscrossed in dry mud, pressed earlier while making wet impressions.

Through the trees on the opposite end of the field, we could see movement, where before, none had been. The big-bodied buck raised his weighty head to taste the air for intruders on his protected land but sensed no one. Then, the deer bent again to savor the green clover, smashing the small plants in his jaw."

Vann whispered beside me, "*The story sounds so much better when Buck tells it."*

"I know. Shhh."

Buck continued, lowering his voice to mimic our character's words from memory.

"Vann said to Skahtlelohskee, 'I will go around to the far side of the field and push him to you. Then, he will be closer.'

Skahtlelohskee warned him to stay with us. 'You will get lost or hurt alone.' Vann knocked him off his heels and told him to stop acting like a baby."

With snickers of those sitting around the fire, Vann shoved me for dramatic effect.

Buck continued as the crowd's laughter faded. *"Skahtlelohskee moved so slowly to nock his arrow and take aim at the moving grass. He raised and stood, moving only small inches in long time. His fingers became weak with the long draw he held within the frame of shade.*

From behind the deer, Vann's chest slipped behind the bark, and the buck raised his antlerless head to turn broadside. Skahtlelohskee stood full and released fletching, shaft, and arrow, and it flew straight into the deer, behind its shoulder, with a thumped intrusion into fur."

The crowd cheered me, and I hid my embarrassed blush behind Vann's back. My teeth displayed a full grin.

"Skahtlelohskee ran for the deer and knelt, fletching protruding from the buck's summer red coat. He prayed thanks to the Great Spirit for the meat, the pelt, the hooves. He looked to the woods for his friend, who alerted the deer and assisted in the hunt. But Vann no longer stood where he had seconds before."

Mothers cocked their heads with curiosity and squeezed their young ones close.

Buck changed sides of the fire and pantomimed to accompany his words. "*With my knife, I removed the deer's guts to free the meat and make it lighter to drag back home. Distracted, Skahtlelohskee stepped over the deer's head and walked into young, bristling pines and elder, saw-leaved oaks. Skahtlelohskee crossed left, looked right, listened, and found his friend whimpering. Vann's eyes were wide with silent fear. He lay on the ground bleeding from the bite of a great snake."*

Buck stretched the animal's name to terrorizing heights and held his hands in front of him, mimicking the animal's coiled attack. The crowd gasped and shook their heads in disbelief. Vann had recovered; he sat there now in plain sight.

"Skahtlelohskee called to me as I sliced the hamstrings, 'Buck, Vann is bitten, and he isn't arguing. He's pale.'

I left the deer and ran to see Skahtlelohskee hunched over him, looking at the two tears of blood easing from Vann's leg.

Skahtlelohskee said, 'Give me your knife and gourd.' I wiped the deer's blood from the blade on my buckskins and passed the buck-horn handle to him. He cut between the two bites, and Vann yelped as Skahtlelohskee squeezed the blood into the ground seven times.

'Give him your water,' Skahtlelohskee said. Then, he kicked and searched the surrounding plants, looking on the ground for healing leaves, stemless, the broad-leaved plantain.

'Shh,' I warned Skahtlelohskee, 'Listen for the snake, watch. He may still be close.'

Finding the plant he sought and not finding the snake, he pulled it from its home, handing me a leaf. He told me to chew and did the same. Once we mashed the healing leaves, he packed the bitter mush into the hole in Vann's leg. He took more leaves to cover the wound, packing mud around it to keep the bandage in place. He gave another to Vann to chew and swallow."

Vann moaned with his recollection of the pain, as did others listening who had not experienced it.

Elias didn't wait for their worry to ease. *"I said, 'We cannot carry both—deer and Vann.'*

Skahtlelohskee decided we would leave the meat and carry our friend on our backs. Vann's blood dripped from his leg onto the forest floor while we made our way home."

Buck sat beside us then, with flame reflecting on our smiles. Cheers and nods of the crowd rewarded our trio.

Interrupting our laughter, I looked up to see Medicine Man's shoes and skins blocking the fire's light. Voices fell to hushed whispers. He reached out his hand and said, "*Skahtlelohskee, come.*"

He asked me to remove my shirt. He said I was to be painted for my knowledge of the forest—for valuing my friend's life over the meat and the kill. The painting's design would be of the root, so I would remember that standing together, healing one another's wounds was most important to Cherokee.

Elias' story drifted through the campfire's fog, returning me to the present through Father's smoky exhales as he rode in front of me. As I touched the painting again, our horses circled back for home. With the image on my chest, my destiny sketched in blue, curving lines, stretching to water's unseen source, my heart.

I could not recall Ross and Father's words, but I caught their conversation's essence. My memory and Father's lesson mirrored one another: A united people were never alone. Fear was misguided as we thrived among the healing plants obtained from the Mother. Bounty grew freely around us.

October 1823 came, and with it, unfamiliar men stood around a similar fire's light. We dressed in our best frock coats to attend the council meeting, knowing whites would be in attendance. Father rode his beloved horse, Priest, and mine, a wide Appaloosa stud named *Salali,* ironically 'squirrel' in Cherokee. We rode west, and Ross joined our band. Elias and Vann were already present in New Town. Others would follow as they could, converging from the four hours' ride, traveling on hope alone.

Joseph McMinn, an agent from the United States, was a fat man with a beard of red and yellow and black with an indistinguishable pattern. His chins bellowed from his neck in abundance, constricted by his cravat. Ross began and spoke of Cherokee improvements to governance, diligence of missionary school education, hard work rewarded in successful land improvements, and the Savior's guidance to religious conversion of many Cherokee. McMinn sat near the Chiefs' white bench, a place of honor, with his hand under his hairy chin. Disengaged, his head faced Ross, as his hands shook—thinking the distance too far, too cool to strike.

Georgia's Commissioner Campbell paced while talking too much. His words slipped from his mouth with finesse but lacked integrity. His interests were his only concern: white settlers inhabiting Cherokee land. It was as if Ross' words flew around Campbell, who never appeared to understand our complaints of white squatters and illicit treaties.

To him, Cherokee would never be a part of America. He said we must move west of the Mississippi into an unknown land. However, I heard his distress hidden behind golden temptations and found myself resistant to his assumption that he had enough money to purchase Cherokee Nation.

As they talked, I had the first opportunity to acquaint myself with the manner of the proceedings, acting as interpreter and secretary. Each party's demands must be in writing and passed to Vann or me to transcribe and file for reference. Agent McMinn and Commissioner Campbell's intended to divide our leaders, to convince us to bend with Creek Nation's pliability.

We held fast, even after they claimed just and longstanding claims against Cherokee lands with quotations from old treaties out of context. They tried tones of anger to turn us to fear; they tried gentle, brilliant eloquence, strongly backed by sizable sums of money. We stood firm in our resolve; we valued the lives of our people and the land those people tilled, more than coins of gold from the bureaucratic purses of the state of Georgia. We saw little worth in the disengaged commissioner from a nation that did not recognize the sovereignty of our own.

A week later, Chief McIntosh arrived with six of the other Creek chiefs. He was equal to my father in rank and status, leading the Lower Creek people. While Ross bored McMinn, the two-faced man welcomed McIntosh.

"Beloved Brother," McMinn said as a greeting. My stomach flipped at his words.

McIntosh was broad and well-fed, draped in a red and white plaid tartan lined in yellow silk and a Muskogee Creek crown plumed behind his ample head with a red-tipped feather. Those accompanying him were traditionally dressed in skins and furs covering buckskin breeks. McIntosh's warriors circled around him with premeditation. Warriors smirked as if some plan, built in private, once made public would serve their masked purpose. I knew McIntosh thought to sell Creek's land to the government, ensuring his power in the white world and funding his people for their journey west. I feared his ambition stemmed only from personal greed.

Talking stopped for a time while the men stepped closer to the fire, exchanging strained pleasantries. No one spoke directly of what I anticipated: Muskogee Creeks had already bitten Campbell's treacherous bait. Campbell banked with the knowledge of his strategy's success manipulating the Creek. His assumption was, by applying the same tactics, the day would conclude with Cherokee signatures.

Chief McIntosh preached to us. "The white man is growing. He wants our lands; he will buy them now. By and by, he will take them, and the little band of people, poor and despised, will be left to wander without homes and to be beaten like dogs."

I listened to his words, translated them, comprehending his hidden fright, sensing Cherokee's apprehension to his resignation to coin. McIntosh was a legless chief, fighting on horseback from behind volley after volley of warriors. Seeking allies, his schemes lay in wait under his mix of tartan and feathers.

On the last evening, Ross stood before aged Chief Pathkiller and handed me a letter. I read the words aloud. In very broken English, McIntosh's letter offered Ross a bribe of two thousand dollars should Ross concur with the Creeks, agreeing to a new treaty, selling Cherokee fertile land to the state. The truth spoken; we must hear it.

Silencing murmurs and gasps, Father stood and spoke alongside Pathkiller, his trusted council, and dying friend. Indiscernible chatter ceased when Father stepped closer to the fire. Featherlike light sealed his words, ancient and binding.

"As the speaker for the Cherokee Nation, I now address the Honorable Council...." I repeated his words in English. He spoke of the 'sacred trust,' we hold for those not present, Cherokee and Creek in homesteads who farm and hunt, who weave and rear children, those who sit at home, unknowing the words passed tonight. Father said McIntosh betrayed the trust of those who allowed him to speak on their behalf.

"'I cast him behind me. I now divest him of trust. I do not pretend to extend this disgrace in his own Nation. He is at liberty to retire in peace and resort to the bosom of his family, to spend his sorrows and revive his wounded spirit. He has been the concern of my warmest friendship and still carries my sympathies with him.'" Father waited for my translation and turned his back to McIntosh.

In disgrace, the Creek mounted their horses and rode with impressive speed into the night, humiliation tainting the dust green flying from behind their horse's shoes. At that pace, the horses would die of exhaustion. Rightful fear of Cherokee retribution would double on foot.

To all present and hearing, Father vowed *"... not one more foot of land" would be sold.* Mighty Zeus had spoken.

From my viewpoint, Creek dishonesty gave credibility to the honest negotiations of the Cherokee. The commissioners observed our integrity, understanding Father's view of McIntosh's immoral behavior. Although, they left in haste with bribe money still bulging from their saddlebags. The commissioners fled with words of gratitude, but side-eyed looks emanated their disappointed disfavor to our united front. They failed. And from that failure, we were victorious, for however brief a time that achievement might hold.

The meeting ended a month after it began. I sat exhausted. My right hand covered in ink ached from interminable nights of scribbling and re-dipping my quill to write another request and transcribe its refusal. Ross stood near me, undid the tie at his neck, as father turned to us both, *"We must go to Washington and go now. Time has come."*

Time had come, and my fate appeared to me, scribed on stained hands. In Washington, *I, Skahtlelohskee, would stand for the sacred trust of my friends and brothers and bear their weight, suffering no pain at all.*

CHAPTER 10

Knocking

Sarah Bird Northrup

January 1824

Cornwall, Connecticut

During the last few nights, a recurring nightmare lurked behind my lids. I stood facing a crowd of strangers shrouded in pale winter's light, escorted through arms of frigid gales. Without a home, without a husband, I walked beside other unknown women; women dressed in beaten colors bordered by ragged hems, shuffling in mass. Snow wrapped, they protected loved ones with guiding hands and bent arms. One girl tried to keep an old dog close, prodding his snout, directing him with a stick. An old, hunch-backed woman faced the ground. Mothers struggled to carry babies in their arms, all crying but mute, perpetually moving. I stopped and stood still among them, as one of them. I tried to speak, but words escaped soundlessly in my breath's steam.

I reached for a sleeping child, but my hand became translucent and passed through the baby unfelt. Without purpose, I felt compelled forward to where no one knew. Anxious and ill-equipped, I moved with frantic steps and isolated gestures. A part of these women, we journeyed together. I looked behind me, in front of me, eyes seeking familiarity and orientation, with none found. Not only was I alone, but they shunned me. In unresolved dread, abandonment held my hand through blinding snow. And panic from the sightless night was coming fast.

Unsettled, I awoke in the dark from the visions within the nightmare. Once my eyes opened, I thought about why these women and children would make this exodus to unknown places, pushed by the will of unseen enemies. Villains in this dream were not monsters with horns and malice; instead, quiet played the antagonist. My dream remained, and I lay haunted by feelings instead of spirits.

Sunlight rose and spilled through the bottom corners of curtained windows. Jane knocked and entered my door. I rolled away, binding my time in blankets.

"Sarah, time to wake for the day." Jane bustled, trying to ease the pall of morning. She filled the basin with water to wash and laid out petticoat, pockets, skirt, stockings, overlay dress, and shoes from the wardrobe. All I could feel was tangible guilt for the luxuries draped across the end of my bed. The dream shadowed me, anchored me in solitude and shame, shame for warmth. Still, the fears of those women lingered. Abandoned together, in distress together, together in the agony of each step, we were lost to nowhere certain.

Since my return from New Haven, Jane's footsteps were quieter. Brief and chosen, her murmurs talked around me yet were more emphatic.

"Would you like my help?" Jane inquired.

"No, Jane. I will be fine."

"Dress, my dear. Your mother and father left for school. Harriet will be by to take you into town today."

"I did not forget."

Jane nodded and retreated, clicking the door's latch closed behind her rolling exit.

After returning from my grandparent's home, my parents worried I contracted consumption, and soon, it would force them to quarantine me away. I had not inhaled that awful disease. The coughing never came. I found peace alone in my room. I ate again. In New Haven, eating was not a conscious choice. Without motivation, I continued to rise, with little to look forward to and little to do. It had been two months since I last had words from John. Tears turned into empty gestures in moments of absentia among those who claimed to love me. With my outward calm, my parents relaxed their worry.

Arriving today was Harriet Gold, my friend from childhood and one of eleven children born to Colonel Benjamin Gold and his wife. Harriet was one of those girls who talked incessantly but said little. She enjoyed laughter, but it unwound in triteness. Her purpose was to pray thanks to God for her abundance, but she resisted hearing the troubles of souls surrounding her. She did not care for others, only talked of the need to do so. She did not feed those who were hungry, only prayed God would provide for their needs. She was a woman of great belief with little practice.

Together, we would while away an hour in Kellogg's Mercantile browsing fabric. She would talk of patterns and ribbons, and I would trail behind her, listening with half-attention. Interested in nothing, this momentary distraction from home served Harriet's purposes of helping those less fortunate, counting myself among the ranks.

Before long, Harriet entered and met me in the foyer, hurrying me through cloak and bonnet. We walked arm in arm along patted down dirt on the side of the road, smiling at others who sought outings as a distraction. It had not rained or snowed in several days, and the roads were not wet, nor were they dusty. Leaves and remnants of snow guarded edges of flowerbeds with protective blankets. While the temperature was brisk, today's wind was mild. Distant clouds did not hide the sun. Through town, a beautiful rig led by parallel horses pulled down Bolton Hill Road and turned left toward the inn. I wondered who expected such fine company. My days of meeting strangers were at an end; everyone was family by blood or marriage in the entire population of Cornwall.

The bell rang as we entered the store, and Mrs. Kellogg met us, inquiring about our needs. She did not look like she belonged in Cornwall. Mrs. Kellogg had the thickest hair of any woman in town, cascading brown curls around her face. She dressed in royal colors, jeweled, with never a stitch out of place. As the finest seamstress in town, I awed at her craft. Her beauty taught me envy.

"Excellent day, ladies. Can I help cut you some dress fabric?"

Harriet responded with mock surprise, "How could you have known?"

"If I didn't notice Harriet, Mr. Kellogg might send me to the back of the store." She winked at each of us.

"Good day, Mrs. Kellogg," With polite distance, I responded, lacking Harriet's abrupt, informal courtesy.

"Sarah, so nice to see you out." Mrs. Kellogg's implication was nothing but concern. In truth, she was interested in why I'd spent months in New Haven. Well, let her wonder, I thought to myself. No one knew of my attachment to John, save my parents, Jane, and my grandparents. Father decided it was no one's business, and he commanded us to hold our tongues.

"Mrs. Kellogg, may I see the new purple satin you told me about last Sunday after services?" Harriet's distraction and Mrs. Kellogg's potential sale lured both from my presence.

"Of course," Mrs. Kellogg preened, "right this way."

People crowded into the confines of Kellogg's General Store. Children in shoes too big climbed under tables laden with bolts of multicolored gingham and calico. They were playing with invisible muskets braced on their shoulders, aiming and ducking, pretending to die in horrific ways, while their mothers strolled casually through the aisles. Underfoot of those present, the children hid with few able to stop them.

One boy, in particular, eight or nine years old, attacked his younger brother. With his legs weighing his victim's arms, he pretended to unsheathe a large knife and scalp his enemy on the floor. It alarmed me in every way, and I could not stay, nor could I pull my eyes from the scene of pretended slaughter. These children knew nothing of politics and injury, infirmity, or death. Truth be told, neither did I.

Harriet glanced at me and then to Mrs. Kellogg and chatted away, expecting poor weather and difficulties with upcoming travel. I backed into a spectrum of racked ribbons lining the wall, trying to find some air and compose myself. I recognized my overreaction. By doing so, it forced me to slow my breathing. The children panicked me, and nothing comforted.

I found my way around benches and shelves to Harriet, dodging the injured along the way, avoiding the stretched tongue of the victim on the floor.

"I'm stepping outside for some cooler air, Harriet," I called, interrupting her conversation. Mrs. Kellogg felt the softness of some exquisite purple satin, stocked for June weddings. Most gowns took months to create. My anxiousness renewed. Far too much took place in this overwhelming space. Mrs. Kellogg turned a pitying glance at me and returned to her admiration of the amethyst sheen and potential sale. To my knowledge, Harriet was not marrying anytime soon. Unfortunately, neither was I.

Harriet appeared not in any rush. I rang the bell a second time in exit and stepped into January's morning with sunlight's deceiving warmth bordering the awning.

Mr. Kellogg and Mr. Copeland stood on the divided porch, opposite the stairs. Steam from their coffee cups mixed with their breath as they spoke, unnoticed by anyone, save myself.

"See that carriage pass by earlier?" Mr. Copeland remarked.

"I did. You don't think that rich Cherokee is back, do you? He has no reason to come since his son left and good riddance. That school attempts to spread the Word, just wishing missionaries would go to the heathens instead of bringing them here among us good, Christian people. It isn't safe." Mr. Kellogg's commentary was one my Father countered at select opportunities, in the right company.

"No matter, even with education, those Indians are savage killers."

The victim and murderer must be Copeland's children. Mr.

Copeland sought to advance Mr. Kellogg's opinion of him by agreeing with the rude remarks, shifting distaste for the students into slander.

"Well, I won't turn away their money. Their kind never seemed suited for proper society. No matter their education, naked and wild Indians murder women and children. No cravats or pocket watches will ever change those instincts. They shouldn't even pretend to be what we are, God's people." Kellogg confirmed Copeland's opinion. Confident, both men boosted pride within themselves after dismissing and lowering John, Elias, and the entirety of the original people who saved the settlers only a century ago.

Unable to catch my breath, I turned my back and coughed while Harriet whisked through the door. She heard the last words of their conversation. No one within hearing distance would disagree, so they spoke carelessly. She glanced at me, to Mr. Copeland and Mr. Kellogg on the other side of the porch. She stepped into the aroma of their bigotry, hanging in the air with thick heat only hatred could produce.

"Gentlemen, how are you this fine January day?"

"Fine, Miss Gold. And you?"

"I'm feeling God's grace upon me and choosing to turn the other cheek to what I just heard spewing from your mouths. Your words sound more savage to me, far more ignorant than any of the students." With that, she looped her arm through mine and escorted me down the stairs into the brimming sun. Her hand shook, so I covered it with my own. We crossed the street, unaware of crossing horse or buggy or any walking soul that might pass us accidentally.

Once on the street for home, Harriet hushed, a volume unusual for her. "Never in my life have I spoken to anyone like that." Harriet looked over her shoulder and took a deep breath. No one followed us.

"I'm jealous of your candor, Harriet. Wish I was so bold. To remark as you did, I would have to replay an incident for hours, and I still would not find the right words."

"May we go back to your house? I'd like to share something with you." Harriet remarked.

Intrigued and chilled, I replied, "Jane might make us tea. What do you say?"

"Delighted is what I say." Harriet beamed with her secret.

We crossed up the stairs and into the foyer, removing scarves and bonnets as we entered Mother's parlor. Here, two chairs awaited us by the fireplace. Harriet sat in one, removing her gloves and rubbing her hands together on her lap.

"Sarah, are we alone?" Harriet asked.

"Jane is around somewhere, but Mother and Father are at the school. I'm not expecting anyone." That realization both hurt and relieved me.

"First, you must understand, I did not expect this, but find it glorious and Heaven-sent. You must not breathe a word of this to anyone. You will understand, because of the student who stayed here so long. Was he nice?"

"Who?" John's memory distracted me, entering the room in stunning retrospection. Why did I have to remember his eloquent words? Forgetting him was the last thing I wanted to do.

"The boy who stayed here with your family." Harriet clarified, eager to speak her news.

"Yes. I did not spend as much time with him as I would have liked." Not a lie.

She stood, and her skirt brushed dangerously close to the fire. Giddy from happiness, she turned, absent-minded.

"I just have to tell someone."

"All right," I reassured her, but her introduction only made me uncomfortable, expecting trouble with the secret's inevitable reveal.

"I received a letter last month from a student who attended the school. He went to seminary in Andover but has since traveled home because he became ill, a severity of the stomach. Did you ever meet Elias Boudinot?"

"Only a few times." She could not learn what transpired between Mr. Boudinot and me as we cared for John, nor the genuine reason for my months away. She thought my absence was because of illness, thanks to my embarrassed mother and her choir of gossips.

"He wrote to me, and I am so taken with him. I responded. Posted last week. No one knows, and you cannot tell a soul." She sat again, seeking confirmation and my approval. Her hands reached out, grasping mine.

"I will not speak a word. But how could your affections build so much for him after one letter? He isn't here any longer."

"I know," she sighed. "I remembered how handsome and funny he was; he walked into any conversation adding delightful wit. His smile astounded me then—still does when I imagine it. I did not think he noticed me."

"Was there something he asked of you?"

"No, he just remarked about how he 'sees me when he connects constellations.' Don't you think that is a lovely turn of phrase?"

Thinking of some of the most honest and poetic words read from John months ago, I agreed with her.

"Girls, you are home? Are you frozen stiff?" Jane curtsied under the archway, interrupting our confidences. "I'll make us tea." With hope for an invitation, Jane returned to her kingdom in the kitchen.

Harriet sat again beside the fireplace, unable to stop smiling, while my face wafted towards the fire. The weighty sensation behind my eyes pressed, as waters do, rising from deep underground.

She said what I never expected. "That is why I couldn't pass by Mr. Kellogg and Mr. Copeland without saying something. Elias isn't here, but I wanted to stand for him, regardless."

Harriet's words suspended in mid-air. In the years we knew one another, her notions of right and wrong took passive action, but now, she strengthened in her newfound affection for John's cousin. Perhaps lack of opportunity dictated her actions and not her character. I was sorry to have unkindly judged her.

Jane answered the door, responding to a knock I did not hear. Thanking the post carrier, she walked to the archway, flipping through a newspaper and several letters. Stopping at the bottom of the stack, Jane held a note. She looked to me, grimacing with brief indecision, weighing her options and their repercussions.

"What is it, Jane?" I asked.

She debated, breathing deeply but immediately exhaling the air. Her face held her faithfulness as she returned to me and extended a letter between her blunt-nailed fingertips. Harriet and I rose. The penmanship on the address was familiar, not in its frequency, but in repeated readings of the same hand.

"Thank you," I remarked. No matter what it said, at least it was some word.

Jane curtsied and left us two to talk through our confidences alone.

"I ought to share some things with you too, Harriet. Lock my words in your heart. Father has forbidden me to share this story with anyone."

She took her seat again, interested by my secretive remark and curious about the letter I held. The thin parchment in my hand took away my ability to reveal the beginning before knowing my story's end. I had to open it now.

I ran my finger to lift the seal and unfolded it. The letter contained only one sentence:

My Sarah,

I will never leave this town again without you, Sarah Bird Northrup Ridge.

Yours,
John

The letter rested in my lap while tears overflowed from their significant source. Drops pushed upward, not falling from rain's loneliness. "Harriet, I am …"

Before I could tell her, we heard a quiet knocking at the door. Impatient, Jane sighed at the constant interruption, passed by the arched frame, and answered the door a second time. Harriet and I followed behind her, the letter still clasped in my hand. When Jane opened the door, John stood there alone.

From the momentary glance he gave me, his skin was darker and hair longer, not that any of that mattered. He was taller and stronger, filling his clothes more man than boy. He appeared complete, healthy, and well. He entered without invitation, removing his hat.

With little care to decorum, he crossed the foyer and kissed me. Hands free of crutches, he held my teary cheeks and smiled into my own.

"I've waited my entire life to kiss you." My waiting ended.

Jane stood there with the door as open as her mouth, aghast at John's impropriety. Harriet held her hand to cover her surprise and vicarious glee.

I broke the moment and spoke to my friend, "Harriet, this is my John."

With effort, he pulled his gaze from me and said, "Pleasure to renew your acquaintance, Miss Gold. Good to see you again, Miss Jane. Do you know when Mr. and Mrs. Northrup might arrive home?"

CHAPTER 11

Storm

Clarinda Ridge

October 1856

Near Rome, Georgia

Legacy. Papa kept a journal written in Cherokee syllabary. The entry dated November of 1823 held a lined smudge from his pinky, smearing an angry stream of words. He wrote of the Cherokee delegation's trip to Washington to meet with Calhoun, the Secretary of War. During the talks, Grandpa and Papa, along with John Ross, vowed not to sell our homeland, no matter how many elegant dinners were served or the amount of money suggested at the bottom of each treaty proposal. Continual questions and ignored offers angered both sides of the debate.

Afterward, Papa traveled to Philadelphia, meeting his friend Vann on a speaking tour. Joining the exhibitions for a time, Papa spoke to full churches, engaging the crowds and offering them his forgiveness. America discriminated against the Cherokee Nation, against all Indians. Whether they sought his offered forgiveness was another question entirely.

Then, he traveled alone to Cornwall to marry Momma. Forced to concede and permit the marriage by their agreement, my Grandparents suffered brewing rumors. Some said Grandmother Northrup wooed

Papa for her daughter; some hinted that my Grandfather Northrup lost his sanity and deserted his family. None of the rumors were true. No one could imagine two people whose skin color and backgrounds so different could find any blossom of love.

So foreign, so disgraceful to the town's shallow minds, Cornwall sought allies instead of Papa's forgiveness. The town's initial friendship with him turned bitter. They found few who acknowledged them with more than whispers and stares at their assumed disgrace and shame. Ministers who once shook Papa's hand now denounced him in public. Momma held her head high while Papa's turned red with flames. Whispers and denials stirred his smoke like an unattended fire in the woods. One ember found the wind and sought fuel outside its rocky boundary.

Regardless, ministers read wedding banns during Sunday services. Dr. Gold invited my parents to sit beside his family in their pew as an outward sign of solidarity while editorials banished and condemned their union. Published in Litchfield's newspaper, *The American Eagle*, in black and white, slander condemned their marriage and blamed the school. Editorial rage and discrimination could not have been more evident if printed in red ink.

No one gave them credit for their rebuttal, sent and printed in the *Eagle* as an explanation and response to the hatred. To them, recognition mattered not at all. She loved all of him, and he adored his "white girl fair." Finding shelter in one another, they weathered Cornwall's storm. From what I have seen of this world, some would shiver and soak rather than admit fault, take off their coats, and come inside.

CHAPTER 12

My White Girl Fair

Sarah Bird Northrup

January 1824

Cornwall, Connecticut

Father entered our house past dark, his black cloak dotted with snow. Without pause, he stopped one-step short of the first stair. "Lydia . . ." he called and entered the parlor, pale, hunched over his boots. In an instant, he appeared gray, older.

John moved from his chair to encourage Papa to sit by the fire. I helped him ease from his coat but stopped at the sleeve. A copy of Litchfield's *American Eagle* held in his hand prevented me. John took the paper.

Reading the front-page heading, John discerned the relevant page and cleared his throat. He walked away, scanning the article. "'The affliction, mortification, and disgrace of the young woman, who is only about sixteen years old, will, it is believed on examination be found to be the fruit of the missionary spirit, and caused by the conduct of the clergymen at that place and its vicinity, and those who superintend the school. And though we shrink from recording the name of the female thus throwing herself into the arms of an Indian, yet, we hesitate not to name those believed to be immediately the cause of the unnatural connection.'"

John rolled the paper and smacked the end table with the folded sheets, dismissing the paper to unfurl on the floor. He faced the snow-crusted window, arms crossed, rigid, and spoke no more. The tension in the room incensed. Bitter smells of hatred cut through the familiar smells of home.

My words pressed against an imaginary barrier John placed between us, "What this man thinks does not matter," I said, but John's tacit stance told me my undertaking was unsuccessful.

Father's voice sliced, "Yes, it does. Reverend Daggett will request my resignation. Your mother and I will be run from town."

I crossed to the point of our triangle, stood between my weary father and angry fiancé, and picked up the paper again, finding the most worn page. I continued.

"'… and the relatives of the girl, or the people of Cornwall, or the public at large, who feel indignant at the transaction, some of whom have said that the girl ought to be publicly whipped, the Indian hung, and the mother drown'd, will do well to trace the thing to its true cause, and see whether the men above named or their system, are not the authors of the transaction as a new kind of missionary machinery.'" With that, I sat, alone.

In lingering silence, Mother's footfalls appeared louder with her pervasive nervousness seeping along the floor like valley fog. She stopped, looked at us, a fated constellation in her parlor. She recognized the cause of our disturbance, the newspaper in my hand. Expecting the remarks, her aggression focused on John. "You knew this would happen, and yet you still pursued this marriage." Her lips pierced taught, and her words were curt and crisp.

"I love your daughter, Mrs. Northrup. Our happiness is tied together in unmistakable ways. I am no different from who I was two years ago when you treated me as a son, begged me to tell you how I felt. I feared this trouble for Sarah and your family." His voice rose louder with each sentence, and his gaze never left the window's reflection of evening snow. John's resentment and my Father's fear pivoted into Mother's palpable anger. I alone sought resolution.

Reading further into the article, I said, "Why did this editor call me, 'a squaw'?"

"Sarah," John scolded the sound of the word on my tongue.

"It is time I spoke." Affirmed, I stood and shocked all those breathing air in the room.

Appearing from the hall, eavesdropping, Jane crossed to answer a hasty knock at the door. She opened it for Colonel Benjamin Gold, Harriet's father, who held a copy of the *Eagle*. He nodded to Mother and me, addressing John's back with a look of apology.

Father rose with Colonel Gold's presence. "Northrup, we will not let it stand. We will demand a retraction. These accusations are base fabrications."

"They will not print any retraction," I interrupted, assuming Father's similar expectation. "Although, I appreciate your kindness in defense of John and me and my family."

Grandpa Abel, the man who loved me the most, said, "… to finish, to complete what I started." Compelled to honor his lesson, I addressed my father and mother, walking to place my back parallel to John's.

"I will marry John, no matter what this editor, or Cornwall, or Litchfield County, or the entirety of Connecticut have to say about it." I raised my exasperated voice and shocked my Father and Mother into an affront unwitnessed in my lifetime. "I'm seventeen. We will leave, Mother, and marry at John's home if you wish." My remarks surprised John, pulling his gaze from his studied uncertainty to me. "Some cruel words and evil intentions of the *American Eagle* or a written decree from President Monroe will not deter me."

Concern and anger shook and broke, running to separate corners of the house. Colonel Gold and Father retreated to his study. In her room, Mother sought refuge in her Bible and prayed for deliverance, and John and I remained.

With a deep breath, John turned to me and breached the quiet left in the wake of my parent's hasty departure. He meant to calm me, but there was no need. I was not angry, only determined, evident by the purse to my lips and the set of my chin.

He wrapped his arms around me and put his head atop of my own. "There is a story of a Seminole captured by the Cherokee. Injured, he needed time to heal before facing his sentence from the Cherokee Chief. The daughter of the Chief nursed him, taking care of him as few others sought to his needs. He fell in love with her and her with him. Knowing she could not stay in her village because her clansmen might kill her Seminole lover, she vowed to run away with him. Before she left, she took with her a white rose as a memento of her home."

"Were they able to escape?" I asked.

"Yes. That is why the Cherokee white rose blooms over our homeland, all the way south to Seminole land."

I stepped out of his reach, breaking his embrace. "Do not treat me as though I am a child soothed by bedtime stories of flowers and happy endings. You've never treated me so before."

"I'm not; I would never. The rose traveled far and made new roots. You will too, Sarah." For someone so assured, his voice faltered. "I fear you will change your mind."

"When my parents sent me away, and you left for home, Grandmother made it her goal to introduce me to every available man in town. She bought me two dresses, fans, bonnets. I meant nothing more than a plucked flower displayed in a crystal vase, purposefully attractive. Men dropped their cards, seeking to engage me in conversation. I didn't want to attend any of the gatherings."

I sighed and continued, "Parents expect their well-bred daughters to bloom. Mother sent me there in the first place to find an eligible man to marry—anyone that was not you. It was dishonest, pretending to be interested.

There was one particular dinner where Grandmother introduced me to a printer's son, new neighbors who owned and published the *Connecticut Centennial* newspaper. His family was cordial enough, although he stared at me throughout dinner. I did not understand why;

I barely spoke during the meal. Archibald Cooper was a pale man, blonde hair, blue eyes, dressed in finery. After the dinner I did not taste, his father retired to my Grandfather's study. Instead of following the men, he followed Grandmother to the parlor. He and his mother talked with Grandmother, thanking her for the meal. He sat beside me on the settee. His presence forced conversation." I inhaled as if my entire body could hold air.

"What did he say?" John interrupted, concerned about where my story might end, but he did not reach for me. He did not force my explanation but listened. John knew I had more to say, but I needed to say it unassisted.

"Mr. Cooper asked me questions about a world I don't yet know. He spoke of current news in America: a slave rebellion in South Carolina and of the new statehood of Missouri. He spoke about uncharted Florida territory and Cherokee removal from Tennessee, Georgia, and North Carolina. I questioned his accuracy."

"Before I came to you, I met with the Secretary of War in Washington City translating for my father. That was the exact topic of conversation."

His accomplishments had begun, yet he was still mine: sincere, honorable, intelligent, and full of pride. I inquired, "How could the government force your people to go?"

"Georgia wants our land. To keep our home, we must either integrate into the white culture or emigrate west of the Mississippi River. By leading conversations about Cherokee Christianity and education, and our men taking to the fields instead of the woods, one would think it would satisfy America." John remarked that the meeting was bitter and dividing, not one seeking neutrality or compromise.

"Mr. Cooper believed the Cherokee had no say in the matter. Is that true?"

"We will argue the issue through the courts if we must. I drafted an argument for Ross before I left Washington. Cherokee people remained the original inhabitants of the land. The government must recognize the sovereignty of any country within the limits of its territory. "It is...," he struggled to tame his thoughts, "already occupied." I assumed John would need the determination to surpass the rising covet of his opposition.

"My questions to Mr. Cooper, of what he assumed as a certainty, affronted him. Mr. Cooper expected my faithfulness where there was none. I could never agree with him, although he appeared to worry more that I was the sort of girl who asked questions. I watched his mother nod in certainty. My grandmother claimed ignorance and quoted scripture, a dogma to guide our honest government. And I..."

As I spoke, I understood my dream. Speaking to John helped me recognize the significance of those women who could not see beyond the distance of choices made by their husbands. They could only imagine better lives; they did not know by choice. So, they walked.

With newfound understanding, I said, "I am not well-educated, even though Father makes his living teaching and taking care of others, he never felt it proper for me to read more than my Bible or to write much more than simple correspondence. I was to learn to do daily tasks: sewing, cleaning, attending church, cooking for the school. He and Mother appreciated my quiet manner. Both assumed I would marry some farmer and learn to be a farmer's wife, give them grandsons, and live an ordinary life beside them." With that realization said aloud, I sat and absentmindedly stared at nothing, seeing more than I had in my life.

"You will be a farmer's wife, Sarah, granted it is a big farm. You'll also be a lawyer's wife. There is nothing wrong with you; they disapprove of me. If I were white, your parents would share their elation with everyone. Never would they attempt to prevent our marriage. With my departure, your parents hoped time and distance would end what we barely began. Now, though, you must see the danger and risk of becoming my wife. I cannot blame your parents for their reservations, nor can I argue against them. I would never force upon you a choice only you could know, but I am fervent in my will to be your husband."

"I want to be spoken to, John. When I ask you a question, you've never failed to answer while not making me appear ridiculous for the asking."

"Then, it is good Cherokee men seek partners, not servants. Our culture shares the harvest with all, instead of biting with jealousy at those who grew the corn."

He knelt without pain at my feet. "You've never made me feel alone, Sarah. You've sat beside me, never allowing it. When I was at home, I was lonely in ways I never understood before coming here. I missed you, not your family, or school, or living as white—you."

"It has been a long two years." Courage seeped from me; my stores were empty from my time in solitude.

"An eternity." His honest eyes no longer held anger.

The *Eagle's* accusations grazed in valleys, shaded by mountains of assumption and misunderstanding. Our connection was to one another's character, not to one another's culture. I understood John's silences, and he valued my thoughts, complete together. I stood with a realization of what we could do.

"John, I have an idea. It may help us deter those who would seek to stop us. I need you to help me, though. Would you?" I grabbed the candle flickering on the mantle, and he took my other hand in his.

I rushed him through the hallway, past the stairs, across Jane's kitchen, and grabbed the key with the yellow tassel. It was a quiet space, one where I spent many hours with John, a room I loved. We both guarded the candle's light as we traveled the last steps.

Shuffling through the door, John knelt to begin lighting a fire while I stood beside the desk, lighting one candle from another.

"I remember that chair, the most uncomfortable in this house," he commented as I sat and retrieved paper and pencil from the single drawer.

"I sat in it all night when I first met you, a frigid night, too," I said, shivering.

"I pretended to be asleep to hear you sing." He struck flint to steel.

"You didn't." Embarrassed, I was sure my cheeks were pink, not from the cold.

He smirked with a foxlike grin and changed the subject. "Our winters are bitter too but do not linger. I cannot wait for you to see our land in the spring."

"Tell me …"

John took a position unlike any I had ever seen him do. He sat on his heels, knees bent, with his back to me as he lit the kindling for a fire.

"My parent's home has an awning where vines twist and gather. In April, we picnic underneath it and pull cherries for dessert. Wild geranium grows there too, and coral belle of such color. The house is narrow, built of rough-hewn logs. The orchards surround the house, extending to the river. At night, water's sounds remind us we are never alone."

He laughed then, remembering. "By the bank, Father, Elias, and I built a canoe out of a fallen log when we were old enough to use sharp tools. It was small, not well balanced, but ours. Anyone who wanted to use the canoe helped in its making. Once the tree fell, we knew we had to begin, so the bark would be easier to remove. Elias sharpened one end, and I the other, while talking of future adventures far away from the safety of home. It was a symbol of granted freedom, or so we assumed at the time. Elias talked more than he helped, so he didn't hesitate when I told him he had to row on the maiden voyage.

Once Father was content with the fire, we burned the top surface and along the bottom to make it flat. We ate deer jerky until late in the evening, guarding the fire, packing mud on the sides to guide the flame. Elias' father, Wattie, brought us bear grease to make it waterproof as a gift for our diligence. The lesson was not one of canoe building but was a father's lesson in patience. I need to make another to remind myself." John chuckled again, much needed after the revelations of the evening.

Upon the parchment, I wrote as he continued:

Come with me, my white girl fair
O, come where Mobile's sources flow
With me, my Indian blanket share,
And share with me my bark canoe;
We'll build our cabin in the wild,
Beneath the forest's lofty shade,
With log on logs transversely piled
And barks on barks obliquely laid.

Seeing my quick script, John stood and read the words behind me. I looked to him, "We might help them understand more by giving them some of what they seek, twisting their words more towards the sun." I replied. "At least, it might make me feel better."

"So, you haven't changed your mind?" With a smile, finding some secretive way to fight the article's cruelty, John added to the verse. He stole the soft quill from my hand and dipped it in ink:

O come with me, my white girl fair,
Come seek with me the southern clime,
and dwell with me securely there,
for there, my arm shall round thee twine;
The olive is thy favorite hue,
But sweet to me thy lily face;
O, sweet to both, when both shall view
These colors mingled in our race.

He returned the quill, kissing me at the exchange. "Your turn," he said with a grin from one side of his mouth. He untied the cravat at his neck, went back to the fireplace, and sat on his heels. Watching the tilt of his head and the thickness of his hair, I knew I could live with this man's honesty for the rest of my life.

At that moment, I realized John's anticipation of our arrival at his home was tangible for both of us. With the stressors of judgment here, I wondered whether I might face the same from the Cherokee. He reassured me this would not be the case. I worried about meeting his mother.

"On your land, in your culture, what does a Cherokee man do when he wishes to marry a Cherokee woman?" Why hadn't I asked before now?

He turned his head and stood, leaning against the hearth to assist his rise. His head towered mine. "After I secured permission from your Mother and mine, I would go hunting and kill a deer and bring the meat to your door. If you cooked it for me and in exchange gave me corn, then we would marry."

"That's all?"

"Yes, that is all. Wives and mothers allow marriages. Most of the time, married couples move to the wife's land. If a wife decides she doesn't want to be married any longer, she takes her husband's tools and places them outside the door to their home."

I touched his face, bringing him closer. "So, if I didn't want to be married to you any longer, I should put your ink well with all your parchment on the porch?"

At that, he laughed. "Exactly, and the law books, although you might need some help to take them outside. That would make it official. I hope you have no need to do so, Sarah." He kissed my palm, entrapping it with his free hand.

Then come with me, my white girl fair,
And thou a hunter's bride shall be;
For thee, I'll chase the roebuck there,
And thou shall dress the feast for me:
O, wild and sweet our feast shall be,
The feast of love and joy is ours,
Then come, my white girl fair, with me,
O, come and bless my sylvan bowers.

An hour later, the fire roared, and our verse, completed. John walked familiar circles on the floor. "How shall we sign it? Should we put our names?" I inquired.

"No. If people knew, we might face further threats. Think of a pseudonym."

"A what?"

"Choose a man's name, or the paper won't print it. Choose a name from the Bible, someone who gave decrees."

I wrote *Silas* on the line under the last of our verse.

With that, he turned the paper to himself and wrote,

"*MacAlpine*. Let's make him Scottish. I'll post it tomorrow."

CHAPTER 13

Hearth and Home, Happiness and Hope

Sarah Bird Northrup Ridge

January 27, 1824

Cornwall, Connecticut

John slid the ring over my knuckle. Amethyst gems circled a white pearl set in gold, a violet on my left hand. My eyes rose from our hands when he leaned over and whispered in my ear. "May I chase you through the heavens for eternity?" Blush painted across my cheeks, like the sun's elegant gown at dusk.

Harriet was the first to meet us in the receiving line after the ceremony. She placed her hands in mine and pulled me to the window beside the fireplace. She whispered, "I have not spoken to you much since John's arrival. I was working on this, and I wanted you to have it." In my hand, she placed a handkerchief embroidered with a scripted H. "The H is my wish for a safe home, warm hearth, long health, happiness, and hope for you and John." Embroidered with violet thread, the handkerchief was impeccably stitched on white linen.

"Thank you, Harriet. It is a treasure." Honored, I took a breath after the sincerity behind her blessing. We were leaving shortly, and this gift might be my only memento of Harriet. "I hope to see you again," I leaned to her and placed my mouth beside her ear, "… riding beside Cousin Elias, somewhat south of here. Ask him about his horse."

"I can't ride!" she spoke out loud and blushed.

"Neither can I. Perhaps we both will learn." I encouraged her.

John stepped between us, placing me behind him. Everyone's attention, except Harriet's and my own, focused outside the sizeable rectangular glass, where a throng of men walked towards the house from the street. Mr. Kellogg was one of them. I could tell from his fine clothes. Others hid their faces behind large brimmed hats or rags tied around their faces. Some held mauls, some pitchforks, some carried stones. Their strides were wide. Mr. Kellogg held a lit torch, although the mantle clock struck 11:00 in the morning.

Framed behind glass, our appearance stopped the men's raised voices. A single man shouted, "Come out, Ridge."

John edged me into the corner as Colonel Gold exchanged places with his daughter. Gold shouted, "He will not. You are too late anyway, Kellogg. They are already husband and wife."

"Then, she will be a widow. Send him, or we will burn you out!" Once one man spoke, others shouted indiscernible insults amidst profanity, drowning with their fervor. We stood, blind and deaf to their next actions, while their intent was cloudless. The mob grew more populated from behind.

With an increasing clamor, Father opened the billows door beside the fireplace and pulled a rectangular box. Inside were two flintlock pistols, anciently effective. Father handed John one pistol and carried the other one himself. Apparently, this was a wedding provision the men prepared. Mother seemed to know, although I am sure she foresaw no need, predicting no eruption to this extreme. Father ordered our sparse guests to exit the house through the kitchen, all doing so without hesitation. Harriet nodded to me, to her father, and rushed her mother to the back of the house.

John packed the lead ball in front of scentless gunpowder.

Jane tried to escort Mother from the room, but she would not budge. She stilled, stoic from fear but determined to be in the right. Adamant, her house might burn around her before she would budge from the rug. She grabbed our family's Bible, clutching it to her chest, protecting unknown names of unknown grandchildren yet to be conceived or born.

"Go, Jane," I whispered, and she hesitantly retreated through her haven, the kitchen, to leave the five of us to our fate.

Gold bellowed from the window, dodging behind curtains. "Why don't you put down the stones and torch? Your anger is unnecessary. This is none of your concern." He finished with a command, learned from years motivating soldiers with his voice.

John aimed his pistol, looking down the barrel, resting it on his other arm to steady his aim. Gold held his hand, encouraging delay. This sight was so foreign to me. John knew how to handle guns; I just had never seen him with violence in his hands.

Outside, the men stepped around the cedar tree, dividing their ranks only to regroup on the other side, now feet from the house. In my line of sight, one man tossed a granite stone in the air, only to catch it again and repeat his toss. A familiar voice shouted, "You've always thought you were better than us, Ridge, with your fancy clothes and your father's money. Gold, Ridge is a savage, endangering Miss Sarah, stealing her from Cornwall. She should be with one of us, not married to bear his half-breed children." At that declaration, the voice launched the stone, shattering the parlor's window glass.

The stone ceased its moving in the middle of the floor, spraying a crashing array of shards and slivers too tiny to be seen. John blocked the spray, facing my mother to shield her eyes from injury. She screamed and felt the day's frost swirl around her like an icy veil. John and I looked across our temporary distance as we both recognized Samuel's voice, identifying the brutish ignorance bellowing from the yard.

"Come out, Ridge, and we will leave the Northrups alone. You're only marrying her because she's white. You think it'll get you somewhere. It won't." Samuel's voice was bitter and jealous, deep and sarcastic.

"He's hated me from the moment I arrived—before meeting you."

John mouthed the words quietly beside Mother's breathing and wails. Father did not retreat as I thought he might; instead, he took John's place beside the window, masked only by curtains and angular glass. Following the rock, wind and cold forced itself into the safest place I had ever known. Uncharacteristically, the curtains blew into the room.

Colonel Gold took charge and whispered, "Northrup, go upstairs. They will think there are more of us if they compelled us to return fire."

Father answered with only a nod.

"We may have no choice." Gold's words forced my mother's acceptance. Her breathing became rapid, driven so by panic.

Father stopped short of the staircase. "John, take the women from here before they fire the house." I will never forget his words. Father's command exchanged doubt with trust in my new husband.

My father came back to Mother and kissed her forehead. No one else moved while the rumblings increased outside. Unspoken commands stretched from one man to another while Mother and I interpreted our protector's gestures.

John broke the reticence. "The longer we delay, they will surround the house if they haven't already. We must decide. Stay or run; fight or flight. I may not keep up with you. I am well, but I do not think I could outrun an angry mob. If I go outside, they may leave. If they light the house, we will have no other choice."

Mother shocked the room, "They cannot have you, John."

Then, as quickly, Father walked away from her to ascend the staircase across the hall. The conversation ended with plans agreed upon, albeit not discussed aloud.

Trapped, Gold threw his voice outside the fragmented glass, encouraging the mob's delay, hoping for wiser choices made by angry men. "Be reasonable, do the Christian thing. Sarah made her choice. God has blessed their union. It is over."

"When Ridge swings from this tree, it will be over." The image made me nauseous.

"Don't walk out the door to them… you cannot." No words would stop him if he chose to protect us with his sacrifice.

"I will if I must." One of John's hands held a weapon; the other held onto me.

Gold countered the mob again, "If you care for Sarah, why would you want her hurt? There are women here. Think about their safety."

Mother whispered, "How will we escape?" Her faith kept her rooted to the ground while fright encouraged her to flee.

Without warning, window glass fell above us. A lead ball from Father's pistol split the cedar tree trunk's bark, hitting above Samuel's head. The house shuddered with the pistol's report.

The piercing blast shocked me to speech. We had only one alternative. "We won't escape. Could we hide in the root cellar?"

"If they think we left, they might not fire the house." John understood me.

"And, if they think we are hiding?" Mother questioned.

"They might burn it around us," John spoke the truth.

In a second, my mother's face accepted her ill-placed blame levied on John. Her shoulders slumped, and her head dipped, recognizing her fault, contributing to the sinful part of a town, whose piety elevated their perception of themselves.

Colonel Gold approved of the plan. "I will get your husband, Mrs. Northrup. I promise. John, take the women below ground."

Colonel Gold surveyed the grounds once more before leaving the room and assured John with a nod, affirming the mob was organizing the split into two separate hordes, thinning into lines to encircle the house.

Walking behind us, John rushed us to the kitchen and checked for men through the back door's window. "I don't see anyone yet."

I opened the root cellar's door on the floor and encouraged Mother to descend the narrow staircase. She clutched her Bible to her chest as she crossed into the dank dark. John pushed open the back door joining me by the stairs.

"Why open the door for them?" His action confused me.

"If they think we've fled, they may leave to search for us in the woods." We descended with a backward pull on the rope behind us, closing the hidden door made from the kitchen floor.

Boots and echoes buffered the shouting. Huddled together, our breathing escaped invisibly. The air smelled stale, old. Onions and dirt mixed and burned, watering my eyes. Darkness squeezed me tight. My ears pierced a sound only I could hear. My lungs pushed against my stays, not allowing me to expand my lungs. My heart pounded in my throat. I reached to my chest, attempting to slow my heart. My fingers tingled. My feet were weighted with unaccustomed gravity. My eyes searched for a focal point, any light in this cave. Nearly fainting, my lids compelled to close. Noise escaped my lips with gasps of unfound air.

John turned me, so my head rested on his chest. One of his hands reached behind my back and unbraided the bun at the nape of my neck. He ran his fingers through the strands, pulling every pin free. All I could smell was him. John could not speak to comfort me in the confined space, but he dissolved the tension with the pressure of his hand. His smell reminded my heart he was still here.

This gamble meant our lives and the lives of my father and Colonel Gold upstairs. Doors slammed; feet ran, but no gunshots sounded. The ceiling dampened the clamor. After several silent minutes, John ran his hand down my arm and maneuvered to climb the steps, pistol first. Light spilled from the doorway before John could reach it. Father let the air flow.

"Hurry, they think we've fled to the river. Get to the rig. We leave for Litchfield now."

We ascended into the light and hurried across the open yard to the waiting carriage, packed earlier for our journey. Time no longer allowed delay. John trailed mother and me, watching the woods. Colonel Gold and Father hitched up the team.

Behind wood, leather, and glass, we held despair with clenched fists. John covered my hands with his. Harriet's handkerchief remained balled in my fist. He gripped the loaded pistol in his other hand. He did not feel cold at all, while I tingled as if I thawed from ice.

As soon as we pulled down Bolton Hill Road, a single man on a horse pursued the carriage. The rider shortened the distance. It was Samuel. He unsheathed his pistol, aimed, and shot, missing the coach. After the smoke cleared, our four horses paced faster than Samuel's single horse. With no chance to reload, he turned back toward town.

John spoke with angry fragments, "… accursed, frowned upon by the meanest peasant, they are the scum of the earth, sacred in comparison to me, a son of nature.… educated, modest and polite, yet I am an Indian.… stupid and illiterate white men will disdain and triumph over me."

No one knew how to answer him. The man I loved fought an invisible battle in his mind, one he could not negotiate or reconcile. He perceived our hiding and running as necessary but a loss to a greater war. His anger held our tongues.

Mother broke first as she held onto the sides of the carriage to steady herself, "John, I owe you a debt of gratitude." Her voice began with vigor but ended with humility.

"I'm so sorry, Mother. I know you and Father have sacrificed, may sacrifice even more in the future for John and me."

"John is one of my children now, in my eyes and the eyes of my God." Mother's reply was sincere and heartfelt. She cried, and I moved seats to hold her.

John ran his hand through his hair and looked outside the carriage's windows to assure himself no one followed us.

"Words, John," I said. "Let hope dictate your words." We hid this day so he, that we, could fight a war against those who chose to frighten, to hurt those different from themselves. In my imagination, I saw a future of men who would attempt to steal the accomplishments, possessions, homes of John's people as trophies from an inevitable war.

There was no time for my regret or any reminiscence at leaving Cornwall. Amidst rings and vows, rocks and root cellars, rushing wind seared my ears, propelling us away from danger and onward to warmer climes. Our coach twisted free from the claws of Colt's Foot Mountain as it waved an absent fare-thee-well, surrounded by barns full of ignorant sheep.

After leaving my parents in Goshen, a tearful goodbye ensued. I did not say much until we reached Litchfield, late in the afternoon. Since we were alone, he wrapped his arm through mine, trying to ease me. There seemed no warm air, only oppressive cold. After a time, he talked of warm places and warm rooms with open windows and cool breezes. I thawed inside with his affectionate calm.

We took a single-engine steamboat from Litchfield to New York City, where there were more people than horses. Houses bordered the street with no space in between. Black carriages speckled the city. We were not there long enough to observe much, although I noticed people never stopped moving, and there was a noticeable lack of trees. Some buildings reached over three stories tall, all painted in similar fabricated and muted shades. Disembodied voices on the street spoke so many languages and dialects; there was no hope of discovering their conversations. It provided us safe passage.

John and I both stopped and moved aside to watch wealthy travelers in elaborate hats stride by in colors I had no words to name. Dockworkers and porters hauled trunks. Cargo passed in wagons full to the brim. Men with guns guarded the unknown contents of crates. Immigrants carried children on their shoulders, held safely aloft by fathers gripping with scarred hands over small, block-toed boots.

We ate at an inn near Liberty Street by the docks and sat beside the windows while porters transferred our trunks to the *Robert Fulton,* scheduled to leave at seven that evening. John remarked about the ease of the trip so far, considering the month. With the wind, we might make Charleston sooner than our tickets indicated.

"The fare was so expensive," I remarked.

"Before I left for Washington City, and for you, I earned a sum translating at our council meeting with leaders from the state of Georgia and the Creek Nation, who live south of our land. This Creek chief believes selling now would ensure his place in the white world. He has a Scottish name, after his white father."

John continued with disdain, "Chief McIntosh said, in essence, Cherokee must sell now or face the wrath of the white man and have our land stolen with no recompense. *My father and I disagreed with him in sharp words, and the meeting ended with our backs turned against him."*

John drifted to a place in his mind, one I had no ability to follow, remembering in a language I did not speak. I coughed when the waiter brought our dinner. Sounds of other diners and aromas of roast beef reminded him where we were. He shook his head, freeing himself of the memory.

John had the table manners of a man born in England. His sophistication melted into this place, this world, far more than I did. Plates steamed, and I was too hungry to wait. He continued while I prayed and listened. John explained complicated issues in clean lines. He took a month's debates and conversations to words I could discern meaning. In doing so, he opened the door and allowed me into his world.

As we ate, John told me more of McIntosh. He was the son of a Creek mother and Scottish father and married two women, one Creek and the other Cherokee. His oldest son, Chilly, was illiterate in written English. John seemed to have little respect for the son or his father.

"A man married to two women? It isn't God's way," I said.

"Don't even think about it, Sarah." He shook his head and looked back at the last bite on his plate.

"The King shall not have multiple wives for himself, lest he turn his heart away." I resorted to scripture, trying to restore his good humor but also to hear his response.

"The McIntosh Creeks are less civilized than the Cherokee Ridges. How could I ever turn my heart away from you or the decree of the God that made you? This King's heart is full and overflowing."

The couple beside us turned at his remark. The woman rolled her eyes, snubbing our intimate conversation.

After her stare, I remarked, "John, someone might overhear."

He ate the last bite and continued. "You said, 'I do,' so, I will say whatever I want to my wife, in front of all of New York, New England, or President Monroe for that matter." He paused and reminded me, "You said it first."

"How could I argue?" I gave him my upper hand.

"You can't." He took the hand I offered, kissing the ring under my glove. "Your ring …"

"The violets, the candle you lit, all you." I suddenly felt shy.

"What about me?" His head borrowed the tilt of a mockingbird's, one calling to his mate, waiting for the returned song.

"The amethysts, grand and independent." He slid his hand down mine, holding my fingertips until the last second.

"And the pearl?" He stood and came to the back of my chair to speak away from listening ears.

My voice followed in his direction, "Resolved, determined."

"Hmm." With his hands behind me on the chair, I stood, braiding my ring back through the crook in his arm.

"Perhaps it is me who chases you through the heavens, and not the inverse," I said.

"I'm on your hand. You found me." He needed to say nothing more.

We left money for the meal and collected ourselves for the distance ahead. Arm in arm, we wove through crowds of travelers and families, all moving in different directions. Linked together, we darted left and right. Once clear of carriages and passengers, I asked how to say what he was doing for his father and the Cherokee chiefs. "How would you describe your profession in Cherokee?"

"*Ditiyohihi.*" He breathed after the word's completion, extending its meaning.

By now, I understood one Cherokee word defined entire English phrases, so I asked. "What does it mean in English?"

"One who repeatedly argues, on purpose, and with a purpose …" His remark was laden with weighty pride.

I responded under my breath for his ears alone, "… except with your wife. Don't argue with her," I said, continuing his lengthy definition.

He promised not to, reiterated my last phrase with a serious tone. His humor and matter-of-fact-ness amused me. "I cannot imagine it. Will there be a need to argue with me?"

At that, he chuckled, thinking of future disagreements and future resolutions he did not share. "If we argue, you'll begin and end it. I have not the power to argue with you." He turned his head to whisper in my ear, "… even if you were wrong. Your eyes distract me. I find myself unable to think." He held up his hand and said, "If you are unhappy with me, I promise to end the quarrel without ever raising my voice." No one ever described me as smart before that day.

"What if I wanted to argue with you?" I said louder than I meant. John must have thought my question rhetorical, as he did not answer. He gave me the pleasure of his lopsided grin and walked us onto the planks that led us to the ship's deck.

"Because I would be right," and he kissed me, "and you'd be shouting to the walls." There he was, the man whose lofty pride reminded me to keep him close and grounded. I found no evidence as to why he chose me.

"Before you ask, never would I leave you. If we argue and I am reticent, it is because I will be listening, keeping my mouth closed, until you stopped talking and apologized."

My laughter held no longer, no matter who heard our smiles.

Our passage ended in Charleston, South Carolina, nine days of circling a deck holding eighteen other souls with ours. We ate hardtack and jerky during the day while dinner was some type of soup. Each night, the only discernible flavor was salt, no matter the variety of meat swimming inside. Not the fine fare of New York, but it did not matter.

The coast crept closer, navigating the ship like a secret escort. Gray cargo holds and docks from New England's shoreline shifted to greens and browns of winter grasses and pine trees of significant height bordering sands the color of cream in coffee.

Gender separated the ship's hold where we were to sleep. Men slept on one side of the steam engine and women on the other. It would be impossible to stay together. The sleeping quarters felt too confined with damp air and the irredeemable habits of unknown women. On our first evening in the Atlantic, we crept behind wooden crates and found a nook to the side. Where the full moon hid his eyes, we claimed the reach as our own.

With my back to his chest, we slept, olive and white wrapped in seamlessness. John said he preferred it and never complained. Timid to leave his side, he was reluctant to leave mine.

It rained only once, a misty, two-day stretch of water-soaked cloaks and slippery decks. The last night, we exchanged places. He curled on his good side, with his head in my lap. I covered his head in my hands, bending his hair in the opposite direction. His breathing told me he was asleep.

I stared at stars peeking around rain clouds. He mumbled, "Above him were seraphim, each with six wings. My doom is sealed; I am a sinner. One of those in a foul-mouthed race. I have looked upon the Lord of Heaven's armies and been so afraid."

I bent to his ear, not knowing whether he talked while asleep or quoted scripture wide awake. "Now that I have touched your lips, you are forgiven." His lips revealed their master awake.

He inched forward, propping himself on his palms to raise and find my eyes in the dark. His voice exhaled more air than words.

"Whom shall I send as a messenger to my people? Who will go?" He undid the ribbons of the bow on my bonnet and pulled the hat from me. Propped, on one hand, his other hand traveled along my scalp, widening his fingers to unbraid my hair, dripping collected drops from the mist in the air.

"Send me," I replied with air borrowed from his lungs.

We both slept, seamlessly wrapped in one another as strongly as God's protection.

CHAPTER 14

There's Room at the Inn

John and Sarah Ridge

February 1824

Charleston, South Carolina

Sarah

Darkness and rain brought a misty fog over the water. With the sun's heat and light, morning broke through. Each day we traveled was warmer, like April in Cornwall. Although I was filthy, I lifted my face to the sun's light fully as we stretched into the Charleston shoreline. After eight nights of sleeping on the deck, dressed and wrapped in coats and blankets to stave off cold nights, I embraced unfamiliar freedom. Unaccustomed to solid ground, I rocked, unsteady, once we disembarked the ship. Charleston bustled, rich with travelers and boats, smelling of salty fish and people's odors, a stark contrast to the sea air.

We booked passage with a momentary stay at a local inn to change clothes, wash, and eat something not boiled in a pot. The stagecoach would drive us inland to Dorchester County, South Carolina, where we would stop for two days. John said this was one coach of many on the longest stretch of our journey. I wore the new blue traveling dress my grandmother bought me but left my hair long. John wound the ends behind me as we passed vast acres of grasses patched with puddles of black water he called a swamp. John reported they were inhabited by poisonous snakes and large-shelled turtles.

Our coach driver was stout, while his partner was a rail-thin man. Both were intoxicated. The driver hoisted our trunks and baggage on top of the coach, greeted us, and declared his name to be Charlie. Once we embarked, he sang a sad song about a woman, "Black Was the Color of My True Love's Hair." He sobbed and sniffed through many miles, concluding only to begin again and stopping only once to blow his nose. John imitated Charlie's sobs and whispered one word into my ear, "Red," every time Charlie reached the chorus.

The smaller driver, Davie, carried a pistol and called random animals' names as we passed. It took great restraint not to burst with laughter each time Charlie began again, singing and crying with Davie's wild interjections, driving the song's tempo with the unpredictable shouts of "red-tailed hawks" and "deer."

Charlie belched and forgot his black-haired lass, turning his love to America. He sang *To Anacreon in Heaven,* but with lyrics unknown to me. The patriotic ballad gave homage to the battles fought to give birth to our infant nation, "*… at the twilight's last gleaming*." Charlie and Davie bellowed to the listening alligators, described to me as long green reptiles with short legs and a mouth full of ferocious teeth. Alligators were a sight I relished in their absence.

The singing lessened the tension between two other female passengers: inseparable sisters, Penelope and Pamela, traveling to Augusta to visit their mother, Mrs. Betty. They sat in contrasting colors of calico fabric: Penelope in purple and Pamela in red. Their hats were mismatched, inverse colors of their dresses. Large plumes bounced, in turn, as each sister spoke. Davie announced another deer and distracted Charlie from his tunes for a time while reopening a recent conversation between the sisters, paused only for our benefit. Twins, the two women discussed ways to keep deer away from a particular peach tree outside their shared home.

"Urinating on pillows and wrapping the peach trees in them will not keep the deer away," Penelope remarked, reinstating the lengthy discussion abandoned earlier in their journey.

Pamela sighed, insisting her solution to peach thievery would, "… look like snow." It was clear Pamela thought a great deal of the matter.

Penelope just *tisked*, "Well, it smells like sh …"

Charlie sang a note outside of his accustomed range as we bounced again, "*… rocket's red glare, the bombs bursting in air.*" He did not reach the pitch he intended, and his voice broke like a teenage boy's. He coughed to hide his embarrassment.

John confirmed Pamela's opinion. "Although unsightly, deer would indeed seek a less fragrant variety of tree from which to steal fruit."

We tried to remain neutral, hoping the sisters would not resort to violence to win the day, although John's comment gave credibility to only one side of the claim.

"See, he agrees with me." Pamela sat back against the seat, smug with the victory.

"No, he doesn't. He agrees it is ugly, and people will talk about what a looney woman you have become in your old age."

"We are exactly the same age," Pamela reminded her angry sister.

"I'm four minutes older, as you are well aware, making me wise and you silly. Wouldn't you agree, Madame?"

Penelope sought an ally and forced me into their discussion.

I asked, "Does the tree face the front street, or is it hidden behind the house?" It seemed a pertinent question.

"It is centered from our front door," Penelope exclaimed, staring at Pamela's animated and appalled reflection.

"Then, perhaps, I would not choose the pillows." I hesitated, unsure whether my contradiction would spawn a physical altercation. John grabbed my waist, not to silence me, but to protect me from whatever dangers might fly into our world from bouncing carriage wheels or disagreeable sisters.

"Ha! A woman raised with decorum and manners," Penelope commented, feeling vindicated by my advice.

"Maybe you could use scented handkerchiefs?" I said.

Both Penelope and Pamela said, "Hmph," simultaneously, stared at one another, crossed their arms, and looked out opposite windows.

Amidst patriotism and sharp-tongued banter, we disembarked at the Koger house, seated from the road on the flattest and most bare ten acres I had ever seen.

Charlie introduced our innkeepers as Joseph Koger, Jr. and Mary Murray Koger, who greeted us, knowing the coach's schedule better than Charlie could recount between his melodious commitments to America.

"Mary and Joseph?" I giggled at our innkeeper's names.

Mr. Koger said, "There's room at the inn, folks." He had a long, gray beard and silver hair that curled up around the collar of his open, green calico shirt. Although I am sure Mrs. Koger was a superb cook, Mr. Koger was as thin as a sapling stripped of leaves in the winter. He laughed at his joke and bent forward with his perceived humor.

Mrs. Koger remarked with her hands on wide hips. "He says that to everyone," she retorted to his back, rolling her eyes. "You aren't funny anymore." Her focus returned to her guests, "Supper's ready; y'all hungry?" She entered the house sideways, so all of her would fit through the open door.

Penelope and Pamela passed the threshold first, trying to enter at the same time.

"Ladies first," Penelope said, leaving Pamela behind on the porch.

I looked to John and whispered, "Y'all?" while John subdued his laughter into my sleeve.

The Federalist-style house boasted two stories of small but comfortable rooms, full of mementos of lost lives and children grown and gone. A child's shoe sat on the mantle next to dried flowers and strings of orange slices draped to scent the room. In the foyer, John took my bonnet and coat from me as he took his coat to the hook near the front door. He removed his cravat and undid the neck of his shirt. He sat at the table relaxed, blending into this family fare. The immense table fed far more than the eight in our party, including our patriotic coach drivers.

Mr. Koger took the lid off the pot and inhaled the steam seeping from carrots, potatoes, and a large, baked chicken with raised legs. Then, he sat at the head of the table, preparing his silverware and napkin in his shirt front.

Only then did Mrs. Koger take her seat beside him. We bowed our heads as Mr. Koger prayed in gratitude for the well-prepared meal. Our host included safety and guidance for our travels to far-away destinations.

I wished I remembered dinner specifically, but I stared at my bountiful plate the entire meal and missed much of the conversation, hearing only scrapes of pewter on china. I only stopped eating to breathe. John nodded at me to look at the sisters across the table. Miss Penelope took half of Miss Pamela's biscuit. Immediately following, Miss Pamela stole a chicken leg off Miss Penelope's plate. I assumed they robbed one another all the time, based on the lack of reaction from either sister.

"So nice to see a woman eating. However, you are too thin, Mrs. Ridge. How long have you two been married? Neither of you looks old enough." I did not respond until John touched my leg. Mrs. Ridge was not a name I had grown accustomed to hearing. Mrs. Koger did not appear to judge me, only poked with her thoughts to encourage me to fill my plate again.

John answered for us both, "We married two weeks ago and left after the ceremony on this journey. This is Sarah, and I am John." Mrs. Koger reached for her husband and touched his arm to stop his eating.

"Well, call us Mary and Joe then. How sweet for the two of you. Where y'all from?"

John then looked to me to respond, and I said, "Connecticut, Mrs. Mary. John's family lives west of here. We are traveling there to stay."

Mr. Joe interrupted by tapping his fork on the table linen. Holding tines aloft, he said with boisterous tones, "Hear that state has the best roads in the Union."

"That they do, Mr. Joe." I thought about the unseen bruising I would have when arriving at John's home. If the rest of the trip were like the second leg of our journey, I would be purple and yellow for weeks.

Mrs. Mary shushed him, not wanting to talk about roads. Instead, she changed the subject. "Joe and I married in December of 1812. Best decision I ever made. We must celebrate your nuptials then. I'll get the pie."

The sisters looked up from their empty plates and stared at one another, both with bubbling curiosity under the crust like Mrs. Mary's dessert.

John leaned back in his chair, smiled his one-sided grin, and felt compelled to ask, "What kind of pie, Mrs. Mary?"

She shouted back as she exited the dining room to her kitchen, "Peach." Laughter John and I held for miles spewed into the room and found its freedom.

After dinner, Mary and I left the company in the dining room and adjacent parlor to clear the table. She seemed grateful for my help, and I did not care to sit any longer after the coach ride. I stretched from stillness and stiffness.

"Have many more miles to travel?" she asked me as she set water to boil in the swinging pot above her fireplace. Heat and steam in the room weighted the space.

"I have no idea. We are going to Cherokee territory, to John's family near the mountains." She said nothing of John's complexion, and I hoped her Christian sensibilities and kindness might overwhelm any prejudice she held towards his people.

"Love doesn't choose according to man's rules, but according to God's will." She spoke with sincerity.

I breathed relief. "I agree, Mrs. Mary, but the Christians at my home didn't seem to understand that parable." My mind flashed to torches of fire, shattering glass, dank cellars.

She walked to the pot and stuck her finger in steaming water, approving the temperature. Without drawing her hand back, she grabbed a cloth to lift the pot from its hook, hoisting it with both hands. Into a basin under the darkening window, she doused the used plates and forks with liquid steam and settled the pot back home on an iron hook that swung away from the still-raging fire.

She submerged her hands into the scalding water as if the pot held water freshly drawn from her spring. She washed, and I dried, stacking clean dishes on a preparation table in the center of the room. Simple chores, something so normal, so easy, stretched my body in familiar ways.

"Would you like a bath, Sarah? I would be happy to put more water to warm you. No need to walk to the cold springhouse in the dark. I have a washtub you are more than welcome to use."

"Thank you, Mrs. Mary. I appreciate your kindness. We've been traveling for days, and I feel each mile on my skin."

"I will put you and John in the small room on the first floor and move the tub in there."

After her offer, she stepped from her back door to gather an enormous bag made of animal hide, holding gallons of water. It would have been too heavy for me to heave by myself, but she seemed to lift it without care and refilled the iron pot above the fire, hipping the handle and sliding the pot back in place. Her hands never rested from constant tasks.

"Thank you. The stairs might cause John difficulty. He has some stiffness in his hip." Comfortable enough, I confirmed what she already assumed.

"That's too bad. My knees crackle and cause such a ruckus every time I climb those steep stairs each night. I figure I should just cuddle up to Joe instead of coming back down them again each morning."

We both chuckled, her at her body's age and infirmity, me at her word choice. We relaxed with one another and moved through her kitchen as if we'd done so for ages.

John

Sarah disappeared with Mrs. Mary for an hour as the carriage drivers settled the horses for the night and brought in our traveling bags. Those bags belonging to Miss Penelope and Miss Pamela were individually larger than the traveling bag Sarah packed for us before leaving Cornwall. It was quiet in the house, so much so, Mr. Joe fell asleep in his overused armchair. His snoring was so loud I thought the house walls might cave inward as he inhaled. I read the local paper beside the window, although all it contained were weather predictions, local church announcements, and advertisements for various items of household trumpery.

Mrs. Mary passed through the room with her candle and woke Joe by jostling his arm with a brisk gesture. He reared back in his chair, startling himself awake with her prodding and his snorting. He took her hand with no words to me, the only one remaining in the room.

Mrs. Mary spoke from the top of the staircase. "John, you and Sarah are in a room beside the kitchen. Your bag is already in there. Spring house is in the back for you to wash up. Just follow through to the kitchen fireplace and go through the door on the right. I put on an extra blanket in case you two get cold." Mrs. Mary giggled while Mr. Joe cleared his throat and shook his head.

"Thank you, Mrs. Mary." I refolded the newspaper back into its original shape and returned it to my seat.

Invited by the amber light streaming from a tiny crack of the door, candlelight cascaded and widened as I approached, following the beam of manmade moonlight. I sought my Sarah with creaking steps on the planked wooden floor. My feet followed the lighter wood, sanded smooth from the repeated sleepy shuffles of Mrs. Mary and weary travelers. With the steamer trip and coach travel south, tonight was our first night as husband and wife. I waited three years to wake, to find her face in the dark, to feel her breath before opening my eyes.

The door made no sound when I placed my palm against the

wood, widening the candle's light. She didn't know I stood behind her. The stretching flame cast her shadow with elongated and exaggerated lines, darker than the pale walls, a canvas for her silhouette. She bent to refill the small basin in her hand, pouring steaming water from above her head and down her hair, lying flat against her paleness. Her hair stretched, hiding her skin from my view, crimson against her bare shoulder and translucent shift.

I shut the door with my back. She startled as the latch caught, and her sudden glance found me. She did not hide but remained statuesque, like Aphrodite in marble. I walked behind her, no longer having to envision her subtle color and the curved expanses of her skin. Water slid down her arm to reveal her shoulder, stemming from her thin neck, traveling to the roundness of her breast beside her raised arm. Her skin was a cream-colored sky dotted in freckled constellations, except for scraping scars on her right shoulder. I traced the limbs of each one with my finger. She did not shudder; she did not move.

Water stepped off her shoulder in irregular rhythms, returning to pool near her silhouetted calves in the washtub. She stood mute as I questioned her thoughts. I questioned my own. To answer my unspoken plea, she leaned against my hand and shared the scars' origin.

"When I was eight years old, I climbed my cedar tree to find a robin's nest. I reached high, testing my weight on the branches. I listened to the birds for weeks, hearing their hungry squeaks as their mother flew in and out of the nest with worms. Injury never entered my mind. When I neared the nest, as tall as my bedroom window, I slipped on wet leaves and fell to the ground."

I could not speak, not while she did so freely, so unguarded. Her voice was as beautiful a sound as the sight of the rest of her. The English word 'beautiful'—weak. Her essence—*Uwoduhi*.

"My body was too big to reach the robins, even in childhood. I no longer belonged there. I lost my grip, gasped, seeing branches blur and leaves distort and darken. My shoulders, my arms, my head slowed the inevitable fall, but I could not stop the drop. I did not cry;

it happened too quickly. As I fell, I realized I would never reach the birds. I would no longer try. The climb terrified me more. Both left scars—scars outside from the gashes—scars inside from my fear."

As she spoke, I traced the scars' paths with my finger, intersecting where the largest gash healed. With her age and growth, new skin stretched paler against the skin's surrounding pattern. My touch slid to her hips, pulling her against me. I needed all of her under my hands.

Steam rolled from her feet, and her shift clung to her in ways I only imagined in my mind. Her unguarded moments since we met—her stepping off the dock in Charleston in the sunlight, her perching on the stump by the river lost in the rapids, her pacing between rows of laundry drying in the wind, her reciting the meanings of the flowers in Ophelia's garden, her telling me her name. Her honesty and beauty enchanted every desire I held, every memory of her, bewitched into this one.

"You had to fall before you could fly." Words didn't seem enough.

After hearing, she rolled her head into my neck, seeking my body to counter her weight. I felt her breath. Her eyes followed the motion of her own feet as she turned to face me, winding her leg around my own. Her eyes traveled up my body, reaching my shirt, pulling the hem over my head and down my arm. She pressed her body to my bare chest, tracing my lines with her hands, memorizing them in her mind. Her eyes told me she understood by sight the contrast in our color, and with her touch, the sameness of our design.

Our eyes stopped at our lips; our chests weighed against one another.

"How badly were you hurt?" I spoke to her waiting mouth.

"Everything went black." She stopped speaking as our lips sealed, moved, pursued, exchanging from our lungs the steam rising from her feet. Her divinity seared my fingertips.

I undid the ribbon of her shift, unsealing the linen from her skin to float in the washtub. I whispered to her, "*Adanvdo*, Spirit," unable to separate mine from her own. She peeled her wet skin from me; her hands balanced on my shoulders to ease her step to the floor. Water dropped while her height shrunk to one more familiar.

She saw the drawing on my chest, blue tattooed lines, roots stemming from their source underground. I expected her response to be one of repulsion. Instead, she touched her lips to the pattern emblazoned on my skin, and my spine arched at her lips' warming contact.

Without decision, my body twisted into hers. I wound her crimson hair around my fingers, pulling her head to the cradle of my arm. Her hands wove up my back, grasping with embrace and opening again, pulling me nearer to her in what seemed like impossible proximity. Instinct ruled me.

In between inhaled kisses, I asked, "Do you think me a heathen?"

In between her body's exhales, she said, "Do you think me flawed?"

Neither was true. We intertwined our bodies, following where our souls, our spirits joined, ancient and binding, to fly.

CHAPTER 15

Asking the Right Questions

John Ridge

February 1824

Cherokee Nation Territory

The longer we spent together on this never-ending journey, the more I discerned Sarah's rainbow of expressions. Focusing on the quiet crux between her eyes, I watched her study the passing still-life paintings of barren fields with bristly brown stalks standing above red-clay mud. Roof-high firewood stacks leaned against ramshackle log cabins with ill-mudded seams barely able to block the night wind's intrusion.

Sarah forced me to read her thoughts for much of the last stretch of road on our long journey. She lived inside her mind a great deal. Poverty—her thought so apparent to me—evident in dirty soles of red, shoeless boys playing stickball in the yard, and long-haired girls carrying water in gourds, slung heavy with the leather straps behind their necks.

We filled several miles coughing the smoke from fires set by families burning their fields to fertilize the soil for spring planting. She inquired as to the purpose but did not delve deeper into that subject or any other. Instead, her mind spun outwards, trying to wind fate's spring too soon. She concentrated our unknown future into existence, one she could plan and predict. As she thought, I memorized the squint to her eyes, the sound of her anxious sighs, the slight shake to her head.

We sat across from one another with my feet crossed at the ankles, making a cradle for her own. After leaving the Koger's, we barely slept and had not bathed or eaten a relaxed meal in a week. Coaches traveled from early morning until past dark, and our bodies struggled as drivers completed stops to gather post and eat brief meals. We slept separately, taking turns to lean on one another with a company of travelers heading west, but had scarce time for private conversation.

Today though, we were alone on this twenty-mile stretch near New Town. Soon, familiar roads leaned in to say, 'Follow me; I know the way home.' Her pensive mood contemplated the blue-hazed mountains ahead. How grand her thoughts must have run while my feet took smaller steps—how her hair parted on the side and swept into a rose at the top of her spine, gold mixed in auburn with shorter strands curling away at the base of her tapered neck. Unseen collarbones, her tapering waist expanding at her hips, the dents in the muscle at the base of her spine, valleys of definition down her outer thighs, the paleness of her calves, the shape of her toenails.

Without preface, overreacting, she startled. "John, I've not been taught how to ride. I did not need to learn. In Cornwall, anywhere I would go, I walked." Sarah revealed this to me as if it were some abysmal secret.

The need to make her laugh, to pull her from worry, became a compelling force and stretching me to comedy. I scowled, changed my voice, pretending to be older and wiser, "Hmm, so you are thinking about what your new life will be like. I was trying to think through what must be on your mind, speculating the cause for each expression in your sky eyes. I assumed it was unpleasant, based on that crease, right there." Undeterred, she lost the complement.

"Will you teach me?" she asked from worry, trying to solve a problem that didn't exist.

Most Cherokee rode horses from birth until death. It will be one of many discoveries lying in wait for her.

"To ride? No. I couldn't." Father would want to teach her.

"Why ever not?" she scoffed at my refusal.

"You don't have to learn unless you want to do so. My wife can choose and ride in carriages if she wishes." I enjoyed the taste of the word 'wife' on my tongue, no matter how many times I used it.

"I've only ridden in carriages, but I imagine that isn't the way things will need to be once we arrive. I hope never to ride in another coach again. How does your mother ride?"

"She rides bareback and astride, but you are not her, and that is the best wedding gift you've given me. I love her, but she respects the old ways, so change is difficult. This journey has been so trying for you, for me too. We will be there soon enough, and you will see. Proper or not, ride how you are safest if you choose to learn."

"So, you will not teach me?" she asked, not reacting to my comment about her freedom.

"No, my father will." She heard that.

"Why would your father want to teach me to ride?" Did she think he would ignore her?

"Because he loves horses so much; but will love you more. My father's horse is his prized possession if a man can own a horse. In his case, I believe the opposite is true. His horse's name is *Atuyasdodi,* which means Priest because the stallion bows his head so frequently in prayer." Talk of horses was a distraction, but the unknown might not frighten her anymore if she asked the right questions. I needed her to ask, to tell me her thoughts.

"I am concerned I will break some rule I do not understand or do something foolish to cause an upset I do not intend. I worry about not being able to speak with your mother and father. What will we do?"

"Trust me. No one will allow that to happen. In time, you will understand. There are those here that speak English, too, albeit broken, and they mostly use commands. You will find your way. Most things are the same; people are the same, Sarah. Our customs are not so far stretched from yours; only their words are unfamiliar."

"Tell me," she insisted while stifling a yawn.

I sought to ease her rather than worry her. I pulled my feet from under hers and crossed sides. Her gaze followed my movement, and she eased closer to the window to allow me space on the leather bench beside her.

"The whippoorwill sings at dusk; katydids chirped masked behind bushes. To you, the sounds are trilling flutes and repeated chords on a harpsichord. To me, they are unseen friends singing from the Nightland. You hear both; you always have. You heard me."

"So, it is solemn John today?"

"What do you mean?" I removed my hat and rested my head against the seat. She gazed at me, stopping my movements, understanding more than I planned to reveal.

"Sometimes you talk like you're reading to me, reciting words you've learned, ideas you share. Other times you speak as if you are a hickory tree above the forest, silent but so very alive against the sky. When you are angry, your spirit is mute like the moon, and it makes me worry."

"You'll never cease the search to find me, Sarah." Her eyes penetrated deep into mine, without intention, only from habit. I needed her touch and wound her arm around mine.

"Beside the Housatonic, you took my arm the first time, and I never grow tired of it. Please never stop."

"Never," she promised.

She sagged her weight and thoughts against my side, trusting me.

"What will be the same?" she inquired, finally.

She wanted to learn. I hoped not only to compare the differences but to discover the subtle commonalities. She reminded me of that purpose, not that I had forgotten.

"Well, we do what your family does in Connecticut; we farm our gardens and take care of those who need us. Women read, sew, spin, wash clothes, cook, make butter, milk cows, and harvest orchards along with their husbands and brothers. Some of us ride to neighboring villages to trade skins; we write letters to family members far away … or to argue with ignorant politicians. Some missionaries teach Cherokee children throughout the territory and hold services close by."

I changed the subject to draw an analogy, illustrating my meaning. "That day at the shore, why did you take off your gloves and rinse your hands in the water?" I am sure, in her mind, one had nothing to do with the other.

She looked at me then, or rather through me, and gave me her gifted smile. A calm washed through her as though she had doused herself again at the water's edge.

The crease disappeared between her eyes as she revealed, "I felt the need to start over and be clean of the person I was, so I could be something entirely different, with you."

She dismissed her serious thoughts. "Perhaps, that makes little sense? Perhaps, it was foolish."

"No, not foolish at all. To me, what you did was *amayiditatiyi.* It means to go to water and wash, not submerge, just douse your hands. Cherokee live near rivers; rushing waters bring the holiness of purification we revere. Christianity believes in the same thing by the ceremony of baptism. Perhaps that is what we should call you, *amayiditatiyi.* Or, we might call you sock maker. I'm not sure which one would be more apt."

She laughed at the jest made at her expense. "You won't call me Sarah anymore?"

"I will, although it might sound different when others say it. '*Say ge'* is how many will pronounce it."

She closed her eyes, and the coach's cabin chilled. "How do you say your real name, John?

"*Skahtlelohskee,* the mockingbird."

"So, we are both birds, then?" she said sleepily and nestled into my neck.

"It would seem. I told you my name once before, knowing you would not understand. I think I realized you would be my wife and me your husband even then. Although, I think we have it backward from nature."

"What do you mean?" Her lips pronounced the words, but her question was barely audible.

"In most species, the male is more colorful than the female." I took a strand of her hair, separating the strands between my thumb and finger.

"No, John. You are more colorful; you know all the words." She smiled and fell asleep with the same expression on her face.

Rain fell, turning cold in the warm air of the morning. Later in the afternoon, when the sun peered through its gray guardians, I stopped the coachman along a desolate stretch where farms and homesteads were sparse. The ground stretched wide, a flat riverbed. The two-room council house stood, anchored by perpendicular outbuildings, open on both sides, and several log houses with accompanying corncribs, wells, and smokehouses. The land surrounding the buildings was brush and forest, where the Coosawattee and Conasauga Rivers intersected nearby.

"Sarah, wake up. I want to show this place to you." She stirred and looked up at me with sleepy eyes. I took her freckles in my hands, thumbs gracing her cheekbones, and kissed her ancient beauty, feeling her natural animation respond to my touch.

"Where are we?" she said.

"New Town, the future capital of the Cherokee Nation. Come. See."

I opened the coach door for her. Taking advantage of the time to rest, our driver checked the horse's shoes and patted their necks. Sarah followed. She walked two steps behind me as I hurried through daydreams, escorting her through the lights of imaginary oil lamps on the street only I could see.

"The log cabin is for clerks, and this is the council building."

Further, I walked to what must appear to her as just a vast expanse, but I explained. "Along here, the Council plans to stake out one hundred lots for homes and construct an Academy for Cherokee Children, filled with books contributed from all over the world." I stopped where the principle building was to be, looking into my vision. "Forty by forty-foot square, spouting four chimneys and eight fireplaces, the finest glass windows." She caught up with me, stood beside me, trying to see the same. "This is to be a southern Baltimore. At the center of town, a museum will fill with artifacts from past and future triumphs of the Cherokee Nation."

I took her hand and walked further down the imaginary street to a grassy opening, cleared with four-level stone stacks marking the perimeter.

"What will be here, John?"

"The newspaper printing office—Elias' idea. With the new syllabary, the Cherokee will read news, send in editorials. Cherokee will come together, near and far, spreading information, laws, education. Father is planning to order the press from Boston once the treasury holds the funds."

"What is a syllabary?" Sarah asked as the word was foreign to white and Cherokee alike.

At her question, I smiled, reaching in pride at my people's grand accomplishment. "My father's cousin, George Guess, has created a written language. Most Cherokee call him Sequoyah. He smokes incessantly and wears a red turban, requiring no ceremony to do so. He is quite a novelty. Nevertheless, he has done it; he has made a book with letters for each syllable spoken—eighty-six different consonants and vowel sounds. With these learned, Cherokee can become literate in their native tongue, preserving our ways, our stories, our lives."

"What an undertaking." She tilted her head, stretching sore muscles. "Did the council approve it? Are you sure people will take the time to learn it?" Sarah's questions were the same many asked on this ground months before.

"You and I will be a part of it. How can the government say we are uneducated when Sequoyah has developed a way for all Cherokee to read across the miles, for America to follow our accomplishments? His wife burned his first drafts."

"Why ever would she do that?" Sarah inquired, appalled.

I wandered on. "Well, his fields had turned to weeds, and his village thought him insane, including his wife. She burned his manuscripts every time she found one."

"What convinced her he hadn't lost his mind?" She caught up to me with faster steps hidden under petticoats and skirts.

"Sequoyah asked her and some of his neighbors to make a speech. He transcribed their words and read their phrases back to them. After that, they appreciated his mastery of our language written on the page, the 'talking leaves.'"

"So would Elias' paper only be written in Cherokee syllabary?"

"There are enough Missionaries on Cherokee land to warrant English too. We want whites to read of Cherokee's diligence, work, and education. And now, there is an esteemed wife of a future Cherokee Legislative Council member to warrant English."

She blushed. "There may be another esteemed wife who might like to read the news in English too, especially if she marries the paper's editor."

"Harriet?" I guessed before Sarah revealed the name.

"Yes. Harriet has returned Elias' correspondence for quite a while."

"Hmm." I had not written to him to tell him what occurred when we left. My concern for my brother and his affection for Miss Gold squeezed my chest tight—like clenched hands holding green fruit, dripping sour juice. Resentment from my lingering anger stopped our conversation while neither Sarah nor I spoke any more about our departure from Cornwall.

We crossed further down the wide street, an expanse exceeding the present tickling knee-high weeds. "This is where Father plans to build the Cherokee Supreme Court."

I turned into her, weaving my arm around her corseted waist, rolling my forehead against hers. "A Federalist two-story, white with gray shutters. Maroon podiums for lawyers to present arguments before the council. Benches for witnesses and jury." I studied her blue eyes with my brown. "I read of a student at Harvard, Ralph Emerson was his name, who questioned whether the U.S. government was treating Indians with justice and humanity." Bending close to match our faces in height, my hands traced her slim arms with a molding grasp. I admitted with selfish adamancy, "I must speak to them; argue to them that they are not, not yet. Perhaps here, on these imaginary boards and stones, is where I will make my case. Can you see it?"

"I see you here," she said.

She stirred my confidence like walking along the river's edge lifts silt in thin, transparent water. It was not her place, but my future she saw, although her destiny lay behind a stubborn cloud line of her creation, shrouding the dawn. Hidden but moving, time and wind would force it to pass.

"I cannot do it without you. Even in your silence, you encourage me to ask the right questions, *Say ge.*" Would she ask, though? Our success hinged upon her ability and frankness to ask questions aloud, to speak openly with me, instead of spinning a weave in her mind of colors only she knew.

My parents taught me that marriage took intimate comfort, sharing unrehearsed questions and uncovering answers together. Her parents didn't model conversation, at least not in front of me. My impression was they held their marriage in secretive looks rather than discussions of questions and answers. It was all she knew.

Here in New Town, our marriage hinged upon my answers to her unspoken questions. The same was true of the Cherokees' lives. Both would pivot and widen if we asked aloud the right questions and sought union, trusting the Great Spirit, God, to reveal forthcoming answers in a language we could hear and comprehend.

CHAPTER 16

Osda, Good

Sarah Bird Northrup Ridge

Late February 1824

Cherokee Nation Territory

Naïve as I might be, I was ill-prepared for the view as the coach horses pivoted the last bend. From the windows, expansive farm land, green hills, and the forest opened to where a plantation manor stood angled against the road, warm and inviting. The day was bright and crisp, and my demeanor, the same. The home and property were more extensive and grander than those in Cornwall. The house was two-stories, built with aged logs holding windows reflecting afternoon's golden rays. There were three silent chimneys, while the one in the back spewed smoke from a kitchen fireplace. There were outbuildings, smokehouses, and a two-story side apartment next to the larger home.

When the carriage stopped, I hesitated and breathed the stale air one last time. John exited, leaving the door open, and extended his hand to guide my last step. We were here.

Atop an elegant and broad, spotted horse, Major Ridge met us at the carriage, more a farmer than a gentleman. As I watched him, I knew his true self belonged here. His horse swirled from around the house with mane flying. John's father touched the sky. With their matching black and white speckled hair, horse and man galloped in harmony. Major Ridge was as dignified as I remembered him to be, although instead of coat and necktie, he wore blue pants ribbed in colors in thin lines below his knees and an open shirt with a high collar; he was wrapped in a coat of tan skins extending to his knees and kept closed with a long red sash. His braid was missing, his hair more white, but it did not change how the man carried himself. Without the rider pulling the reins, his horse stopped with a squeeze of his thighs, and Major Ridge dismounted without his hands, swinging one leg, to root to the ground again. He crossed to meet us in wide, smiling strides.

He embraced his son with open then tight arms, absent of formality. Instead, their embrace was one of familiarity. At this moment, I saw John as a boy, scooped up to ride atop the shoulders of this giant from myth and legend. I saw them both in my mind's eye, dressed not for interaction with white's impending judgment, but dressed in tradition and ties.

All at once, I saw the son's respect for the father's many lessons mirrored the father's love for his son, hard-earned through discipline and struggle. Both seemed to recognize all that they were before, in all that they were now, standing in profile against a backdrop of amber light. John adopted the same admiration and affection he must have before, laughing atop the shoulders of the Ridge. For a moment, feeling voyeuristic and sinfully out of place, I must have appeared to be eavesdropping on a private relationship constructed of parallel memories, so foreign yet fascinating to me.

My parents loved me, but they did so with little touch. Both men breathed deep as their shoulders relaxed at their closeness, breathing in the same ancient Cherokee air, assured to sleep soundly tonight absent of worry for the other.

Major Ridge looked at me and cocked his head, and smiled the same smile John had when arriving in Cornwall. He welcomed me, while I still feared John's mysterious mother. Major Ridge was no longer intimidating, but his shadow darkened with protection. His stature did not overpower me as it once had. This time, his height wrapped me in the weight of a heavy blanket, reassuring. Major Ridge stepped beside his son and bowed to me as he had years before. I did not deserve such grandeur, but it was allotted to me, nonetheless.

He spoke to his son with mumbled tones that rose in inflection to conclude the sentence, and John nodded in return, agreeing to his father's request. Major Ridge took my hand with the gentleness one might take an infant's and turned back toward the house, wrapping my arm through his. He placed his opposite hand atop my own and reached full and prideful height as we began our promenade through the grass growing between broad and ancient trees. John followed close behind us with hands behind his back.

"It has been a long time ..." Major Ridge paused, looking to John over my head. John translated the vague and profound remark to me as we strode in steps small, uncommon for such a tall man, but allowing me a leisurely pace. We were in no hurry, it seemed. In English, his statement seemed incomplete.

My voice sounded distant in response, inquiring to his intent. John did not put my words into Cherokee, though, to my surprise. Major Ridge must understand more than I thought and chose not to voice English.

Major Ridge finished, *"... a long time since we've had a new sun to warm our family. I hope you will be at peace, at home, here."* In translation, John's words did not come with his own intonation, but a nobility, tilting them with a gravity different in my mind; the words were not his, but his father's.

How to respond to such beautiful language and weighty greetings? I should speak but wanted to do so with Major Ridge directly. I stopped walking in the shadow of an apple tree already hinting with budding green on its youthful branches. I thought to reach back for John's hand to encourage him to step beside us. Not knowing words to say that Major Ridge would understand, I wanted to reassure both that I thought of this place as home. I belonged wherever John was.

I never thought they would consider me a guest. Perhaps, that was my first error. I did not seek formality with lofty manners and the best china. I envied the connection between John and his father—an unbreakable attachment, without judgment and without distance.

"John, what is the word for 'home'?" My hands guided all of our hands together, olive and red framing white, a mass of grasps criss-crossed in shades. Both men answered me with parallel sounds and tempos, *"Owenvsv."* I mimicked the word, overcome by its reverence.

From the three stairs in the doorway, I saw John's mother, Susannah. She stopped, framed by darkness, wiping her hands on a white apron. She wore a calico dress with flowers in red and light blue and pulled her black hair from her face, nested in a white cap. She cupped a hand to her eyes, shielding them to see her son, and I, and her husband, standing in a triangle under the trees. I thought she might run to greet us, but she turned and reentered the house only to emerge again. Without an apron this time, she wrapped a red and white knitted shawl, crossing it over her arms as she stepped down the steps, lessening the distance between us.

As she grew closer, the respect these men held for this woman caused the wind to change, from small whips behind us to a breeze blowing from behind her into our faces. Her quick steps brought a force against our trio, and with it, both men stepped back, allowing Mother Susannah to step in front of me. Warmth lost from their hands was noticeable, and I cleared my throat in nervousness but did not retreat. When she reached us, her face found mine. I smiled; she did too. John had her eyes.

Her voice was slow, but she spoke in accented English as she examined my face without touching me. Then, her hands found my own. My thumbs felt the back of hers, wrinkled from years of scalding water and lye and knotted with age with concern for her husband and her sick and distant son. Thin-skinned from plunging into rocky dirt to harvest crops, calloused from sewing and weaving, this woman sustained this family. Her mind was quiet to me, while I found my own persistent with the constant inquiry whether I met or did not meet her expectations. I could not know what she thought as she examined my young, white hands.

"God be with you, *Say ge*." Speaking in recited and broken English, she returned her gaze to my face.

I responded at the same pace, "and also with you, Mother Susannah." I am not sure she understood my words, but her eyes opened wide, another expression I recognized from her son. It waylaid my nervousness temporarily. Time would reveal whether my fears were genuine or mere stories enriched by my imagination.

She looked to her son, and a tear came, just a single drop of joy at her renewal from seeing his face. I imagined every time he left and returned, her happiness doubled, as would mine. He would have to leave too soon. My joy at his future travels and returns home would be with similar solemnity. She touched his face with both hands and pulled his height lower so she could kiss his forehead. He bent to her, well-rehearsed from many trips home from schools far from her land.

"Are you well, my son? How is your hip? Crossing the land is difficult for you." She spoke her native tongue with faster rhythms.

John spoke to me alone, "She asked about my hip, but I don't want to talk about that, not when I am this hungry."

"*The pain is bearable, Mother. We are hungry and dirty and tired, but we are here."* He responded to her with a gesture to his leg and a wink to me. I assumed his meaning, trusting.

She embraced him then, took him in tow to the door of her home, and left the Ridge to escort me with the sunlight warming our backs. John stopped as he led his mother up the stairs, hesitating. She stopped, looked down at him from the top step, questioning without words. He returned her look but did not move. His pause was not one of manners but one of love and respect for me. I knew him well enough to know he did not want to go in without me as I did not wish to enter without him. We exchanged that understanding, meeting at the foot of the stairs. Between us, Major Ridge passed, breaking our concentrated gaze.

"It is as you told me so many times," I said into his ear.

"You did well, Sarah. With them …" he reassured.

"Did I?" I questioned it myself as I let the air blow from pursed lips, relaxing before we crossed the threshold.

After leaning back, he said, "Very well."

"She didn't say much." Worry crept into my tone again.

"Neither did you, but it was enough. It was exactly enough." His faith in me was all I needed to step.

The house was narrow and divided into rectangular rooms, unrevealed by the house's exterior. The entryway was brief, and to the left, opened a dining room framed with a fireplace with warming ovens built into the stonework. Sunlight streamed through glass in gold, lighting dust particles and a table set with china upon a white tablecloth. Rich aromas of stewed beef and carrots salted the air. Log walls were aged with aromas from repeatedly cooking the family's favorite stews. The house comforted while still keeping its distance, respecting the formality of greeting someone new.

My parent's home in Cornwall was never one where warmth was a word I would use to describe it. Instead, while my old home was comfortable, seeing John's home here, my house seemed pale by comparison. My eyes took in color everywhere, baskets beside the fireplace woven with thin lines in geometric patterns, purples and greens of dried flowers lofting from the floor of the second story above the table, matching the china pattern. New, early, yellow jonquils bounded from clay at the center of the table. Candles flickered in shadowed corners with dancing shadows on rough walls smelling of sap and stain.

Major Ridge gestured for his wife to sit, and then John and I followed from the other end of the table. Last, Major Ridge sat at the head of his table of plenty. He bowed his head in prayer without speaking, and John's mother spoke what I could only guess to be a prayer of thanksgiving to God for bringing her son home. I wonder whether she included me in her gratitude. My mother would never have led a prayer at dinner.

The family's formal etiquette was not what I was expecting. The table's fare was not what I was expecting. Unchipped china in swaths of greens and purples held patterns I had only seen in the finest shops in New Haven. Blacksmiths engraved the silvered cutlery with the family's 'R' on the handles in scripted font.

Although hungry, I took small bites of the stew and listened to exchanges of laughter and concern, each speaker in turn. John tried his best to include me in their conversations, but distant I remained, hearing summaries rather than each speaker's words as intended. Were they talking about me, recognizing I would not understand? Was John editing their judgment?

Mother Susannah interrupted my musings by passing a plate of cornbread glazed with honey. Sweet cornbread was succulent on my palate.

I took a deep breath and exhaled slowly. John stretched to reach for my hand atop the table and rubbed circles on its back. He reminded me to trust him, not hiding the gesture at all.

John spoke, "Father asked if you'd like to see our land tomorrow. Would you like to go?" Everyone stopped eating when he spoke English, waiting for me to respond, holding full spoons in the air.

I answered him with another question. "Are we walking?"

John laughed, but Major Ridge looked appalled, furrowed brows with pursed lips.

His answer did not surprise me. "Probably not."

"Did you tell him I couldn't ride?" I inquired with an embarrassed pull of my hand from under his, hiding both in my lap.

John leaned back in his chair. "Yes. He's pleased. He hasn't had someone to teach since Sollee was little. My sister is ten and quite the rider. I need to meet Elias for a while to update him on the situation in Cornwall, but I will follow."

"How will you find me?" I inquired, preparing myself for his witty retort.

"I will." Could he track us? Smell me in the air?

With dinner concluded, Mother Susannah escorted me to an adjacent room, closing the dining room doors. Comfortable and well lit, the furniture was golden, broad and plush, newer than what my parents owned. Two matching china vases sat on the heavy mantle, framing a wooden-framed clock chiming seven times. Heavy and elaborately colored draperies hung in red hues to frame the sunset's pallet in purples. Dry and warm from the fire, outside the wind whistled through tree limbs. I heard the outside door open. Sounds of footsteps crossed. John and his father must have stepped outside.

Mother Susannah's slight frame reached beside her sofa. She placed a piece of thick fabric on her lap, white deerskin, bleached, and in the shape of a diamond. She had shells in a small satchel beside her. Some were pearl, some tinged with blue. She draped the fabric over our laps and handed me her needle-keeper and thread from her sewing box. I laughed to myself, remembering what John said. 'We do the same things, just calling them unfamiliar names.' He was right, again. I would not tell him, though, not right away.

The implication was for me to join her. For several moments, I watched as she threaded her needle and strung beads and shells to attach to the skins, sewing them to the base. She paced her hands to stitch and gestured for me to follow her pattern. My eyes were so tired, and the fine work was slow, but I imitated her skill as she continued on her side. The fabric was thick, not one with which I was familiar. My thumbs were not yet calloused enough for this work. Her silence made me reluctant to speak, but I did so anyway.

"My mother taught me to sew. Most girls learn from their mothers, but I never mastered her embroidery skills of French knots. Every time I would try, the thread would unwind and pull through, and the knot would dissolve on the other side of the linen. It is something I need to practice." Barely a whisper was warranted as we shared the same space, and our hands worked in the same time, like two notes in a chord.

Outside, the door opened and shut again. I expected John to enter, but instead, I heard rising footfalls on the stairs and then heard nothing more. We continued, as Mother Susannah did not change her studied pace with the screech of door hinges. Not wanting to stop before the task was complete, only she could assure me the work was done. I must learn to finish things here on my own.

She handed me three more beads for the last of the pattern, and as I sewed, she finished her portion. She leaned against the back of the golden sofa and examined the work on her side of the piece by tugging gently on the adornments and measuring the distance between the patterns of shells with her knuckle. I had not thought to do that. I was only working from approximating the distance by sight.

I knotted from the back of the piece. With that, Mother Susannah took my portion and examined my work. With an anxious sigh, I waited for either approval or her blade to cut the stitches. I folded my hands together rather than have them shake in my lap and awaited the score for this minor task of needlework.

"… *osda,*" she remarked. A slow smile lit her eyes.

"Is it good?"

More affirmative this time, she repeated the same word. I took the word and her expression as confirmation that I did not embarrass myself with needle and knot.

So, I tried, "... *osda*," and returned the word back to her.

We held a silent celebration between the two of us. She would teach, and I would try, and we would find a way.

Later, I climbed the elegant staircase alone and followed the low railing to the only room with candlelight flickering, the last room on the left. When I cracked the door open, there were eight beautiful windows, side by side, trimmed and curtained in a sheer fabric that allowed the moonlight to pass and beam across the floor. A sizeable bed extended from the back corner. John's desk stood riddled with broken quills and inkstands left open, cluttering the shelf above the desk's slope. There was a trunk at the foot of the bed, propped open with books no longer contained within its shell. The room smelled of him, emblazoned again with his past in his present.

He curled on his good side atop woolen diamonds of red and blue. He was already asleep, breath silent, and I watched the rise and fall of his shirt. I laughed inside my heart at my husband's image, fully dressed, with his hands under his cheek like his childhood self still existed somewhere here.

Perhaps it was my nervousness at meeting John's parents, or perhaps I just felt relieved to be somewhere for more than a few hours. Perhaps the day's stresses had passed and made me weary. Perhaps, I felt overly emotional, but I did not stop myself from sitting beside him and bending to whisper in his ear. I did not intend to wake him, not at all.

"I love you." It was the first time I said so to him that I spoke the words to any listener. Words like that, told to sleeping heads and closed eyes are far easier than when one expects a response.

He rolled onto his back, opened one sleepy eye, and said, "*osda*," with arrogant affirmation.

I touched my hand down his face, closing the eye he opened. "Don't sleep with your boots on."

He smiled and sat up to grab me by the waist, shifting me to curl in front of him. I squealed, and afterward, we heard similar laughter lofting from downstairs.

It had been the longest day.

CHAPTER 17

In Strawberry Blossoms

John Ridge

February 1824

Cherokee Nation Territory

I could not approach them; the picturesque view stopped me. I whistled to stop my horse. Father and Sarah followed the Oostanaula and passed uphill to the ridge where the path led, sheltered by jagged rocks against curling leaves, still timid against frost's nightly abrasions. Wind gusts blew in from the west, forcing a spring storm, one I expected this evening.

I watched Sarah in green gingham perched atop a broad brown mare whose white legs mirrored Sarah's petticoats rising clear from her boots in the stirrups. Father taught her to ride astride. In the distance between us, I could follow the wind in her hair, flung back from her face, framing her against gradient sky.

Sarah's loose hair was her most stunning feature, and on this occasion, the sun put her on display, two stars replicating the other's glow. Her horse's canter was slow. Father on Priest neighbored her, staring ahead for anything that might disturb their cadence. Father studied her form to correct her hands from grasping the reins too rigidly or encouraging her to keep her knees above her ankles. It had been so long since he instructed me; I could not recall a similar lesson in posture.

Obviously, she proceeded well, as Father wandered the horses this far from home. This ride would tire her this evening.

He signaled to gain her attention, which she returned. In my awe, she kicked forward to begin a trot. She sat tall and balanced. The mare pulled ahead, distancing her from her professor. Out of character for Sarah, I did not recognize this assertiveness, although I appreciated that it slept within her. She took the lesson, making it more—brighter, as she constantly seemed to do. I felt guilty for not staying beside her today. With the language barrier, this lesson would be problematic. However, Father asked me last night to provide him and Mother both time, each in their own manner, to discover Sarah as I had found her. I wondered what conclusions the day's sun returned.

Sarah watched her hands grip the reins, glancing for Father's approval, which he undoubtedly gave. They set their descent back in a controlled walk, the mare behind Priest, taking the same path that lofted them to the ridge and let the horses steer them home. I dismounted, watching my horse graze during the time it took them to intercept me.

Father acknowledged me, but Sarah did not speak aloud or converse with her eyes. Immediately, I sensed her distance, so I mounted again and followed behind the two of them. We proceeded into the grove, propelled by the sounds of crunching leaves and horse clops and whinnies. What she was not saying echoed in my mind with constancy.

After arriving at the pasture stable an hour later, Father reached for her waist to support her dismount before I accompanied my horse to stall. She curtsied to him in gratitude for the day. Like any teacher, when the student found the correct sum or solved a teasing riddle, Father glowed with pride. Wordless, he strode away from the stable shadows. Confused and now consumed by my own questions, I urged her to reveal what she wasn't saying.

"Nothing is wrong, John. Nothing."

I did not accept her answer, not at all.

Sarah waited for me to dismount and remove the saddle. She studied my feet, not my face. She meandered, following the sun's light to the stable door. She remained eclipsed. Her hands pushed against her back, fingers spread downward to counter muscles' strain. She turned in the light and spoke her mind.

"Why didn't you tell me?" she said with her face dark in the distance of her gaze.

"What did I not tell you?" Had she not had enough time to find words for her question?

"About the slaves, John, about the slaves." My surface rippled with her disturbance.

She left me standing alone, tossing me back in her wake.

She entered our new apartment next to my parent's house and left the door open. We had not been in this space together yet today. It was a new place for us both. However, our first words here did not love; they were brackish and confused. This conversation brushed unfamiliar color against new and dark walls. I tried to approach her as I closed the door behind me, but my eyes needed a moment to adjust to the changing light. The room lay stagnant. I was blind to whatever tide built against me.

"This morning when I woke, you were gone." Her back was to me, arms crossed, holding her waist.

"I called on Elias this morning. He sends his greetings and looks forward to seeing you." Was she mad I left her? "I told you about it yesterday."

"I remember. A dark-skinned girl came in with clothes from my trunk to help me dress, ten-years-old at most. In my shock, there were no words to thank her for her help."

"She is Old Saul's daughter; her name is Honey. She works beside Mother most days."

"I met him, too. He was chopping wood outside of their cabin. Your father and I rode past many cabins like it today, some even up the ridge."

"There are twenty cabins. Father works thirty slaves, last I learned."

She stopped talking and fled the room. I did not know whether I should follow her. Something shifted, unfamiliar. Trepidation stirred, tainting the air. Rather than let it fester, I followed her.

"What thought entered your mind, choosing not to tell me?" She demanded.

I did not have an answer. Quietly, I sat and stretched out my hip, leaning on the other.

She continued in elevated pitches. "How could your family own another person? Other people? Knowing, as you do, the struggles of suffering judgment yourself? How is it possible that your family does the same to others?" She was tense, and her face became a younger version of her mother's.

After my lengthy pause, listening as she hurled questions, I answered; although, I should have edited my response. "Sarah, calm down. It is your people's way, not mine, who invented slavery. I have known nothing else. We all gain in the transaction: our care sustains and protects them. In exchange, they serve us and our land; planting crops or reaping the harvest would be impossible without them."

"It isn't my people who created this way of life." Her face flushed.

She denied what she interpreted as an insult to her own race—her own personal character. It was not meant as an accusation; it was factual. I continued, even though I feared flares by doing so.

"Whites recognize wealth and superiority, displayed by what one owns. We own slaves as an outward sign of that wealth." She understood that fact already.

"People are not meant to be tools used by others. It is unchristian." She spat judgment with consonance.

I stood, trying to delay this, and my leg faltered. I stepped behind the chair, leaning to it, raising my eyes to hers as she watched the patterns of my movement. She refused to hold my gaze.

"Who are you to judge us?" I knew I should not have said it the moment it left my lips.

She spoke before my question had time to pass in the air. "They had no choice in their situation. There are even others, others like you, who work and slave here." She opened her eyes wide, and her brows rose at her recognition of the irony.

"It was their choice. They sold themselves, preferring a life of servitude to one wallowing in starvation or drunk with whiskey," I said with indifference. "We reap what we sow."

She put her back to me and began rearranging the cushions on the sofa and bustling about the room, caged, making circles of frustration at her inability to get free. I saw it and didn't, all at the same time.

She stopped at the window and took her time, turning again to illuminate Honey's situation. "What choice does Honey have in her future? None, John. None whatsoever. She is just a child. She should play, climb trees, learn, not bound to me, not bound to you."

"You don't understand." How could I help her rationalize something so plain to me?

"Explain it to me then in all of your colorful words!" she shouted with exacerbated frustration and pleading hands stretched for answers. I did not know if it was possible to find any words to bring her skin back to a color I recognized. I said nothing at her outburst, resigned only to shake my head.

At that, she came to me in a straight line with untamed eyes lashing back with rebounding fear. I had never seen her in such a mess of beautiful temper.

She spoke through clenched teeth, "You're a hypocrite, pretending to be something, someone you aren't. By owning them, your family stands on top of the weary backs of others."

I raised my voice and grabbed her arms with heat generated by her insult. "And you are privileged and have never known a life without advantage." I sneered with pride. Sarcastic in what I interpreted as her apparent lack of comprehension, I continued, "You will be given even more privilege here, on their backs. Your life will be one of leisure, with no tasks you don't choose to do."

She shucked away from my hands. I was alone in the room as the door slammed shut and bounced open again with her adamant departure.

Leaning back in the chair, my stomach weighted with stones. I looked where she stirred dust in the room, each particle heavy with my burden. My watch ticked, and I listened to the seconds marking the space between us in growing acres. There were too many dangers for her in my wilderness. It took me time to realize she questioned her safety while inside, recognizing myself as the cause for her alarm. I shouldn't have touched her. Burns on my hands will never heal.

Time spun. I remained, recanting her tone, her exhales, her movements. In my harshness, I wanted to help her face a reality nature doesn't teach. Slavery was not represented in tree or animal; this was man's way. I was foolish to assume she knew. Her heart lay in her chest larger than any other part of her, and through her empathy, the understanding did not reach her mind. She saw what slavery took from Honey and Old Saul. In them, she recognized my reflection.

For a moment, that infuriated me. I would be no one's slave. Absent from lineage, absent from their homeland, a slave's only choice was to serve others. In her heart, she expected such nonexistent fairness. I was her example, how the world oppressed those perceived as ignorant, perceived as savage. Never did she envision me in labor to benefit another. Her opinion of me was nobler than I deserved. In her absence, I realized I had disappointed her. Infused with her perception, the image of my family's slaves appeared a moral weakness. Her heart was what she gave to me; as a result, I understood her sympathy from the pressure within my chest.

Time flashed forward. I knew what needed to be done. Sun fell. My worry grew exponentially with her stubborn absence. I stood with pain and moved with more, swollen from inside my chest, not my hip.

On horseback rather than on foot, I decided to cover the distance. I woke my sleeping horse, passing Old Saul in the stables after bedding them for the night. I stopped him as he crossed into the night.

In Cherokee, I inquired, *"Are you happy here, Saul?"*

He was lost in my question, snatching him from his thoughts, detaining him longer from his rest. Saul was not a friendly man but a loyal one.

Turning to me, he responded, anticipating my expectation. In English, he said, "Yes, sir?" With lingering inflection, he left me to walk to his daughter, Honey, and the waiting light from their cabin across the yard. I would reflect more on his answer later. I had to find Sarah. Everyone had their backs to me, or maybe it was I who turned my back to others. I did not understand which was true and had little time to reflect on the question's philosophy.

I stopped at the house to inquire whether she went to my parents, but she was not there. Father walked me outside and asked why she left. I did not have resolve in me to answer. He asked if I wanted his help, which I denied. I needed to find her myself.

"Follow the strawberry blossoms," he said with knowledge I did not have. It came from living, not studying.

The strawberry field was beyond the wheat and stretched where untouched vines wrapped wild trees. Preceding the fruit, white, strawberry blossoms grew, bordering on the east and west by cotton mounds, what would be the newest crop. In a month, planting would occupy the slaves' time incessantly.

"Sarah ..." I called out to the blossoms surrounding my horse's shoes and scanned the field, looking for movement under the sparse moonlight. Thunder rumbled in front of me; it would not be long before rain drenched me. I saw nothing.

I looked left and right between sprawling blooms and turned dirt mounds. Louder, I called, "Sarah ..."

Nothing.

Turning right to border the forest, I passed the field again, looking for her shape, any form light would allow. At the top of my voice, I roared, "Sarah."

Nothing.

The darkness of the forest scared me as it never had before; if she ventured into the woods, I might not find her.

I would be nothing—until she returned. She would have to find me and might not have the skill to do so. Not yet. She had not given herself time to learn her way home.

"Sarah …" I whispered, more sorry than I had ever been.

As I reached the end of the strawberry field's reach, where green met black fertile earth, I looked back to where I passed and recognized her or what I hoped was her, lying on the ground, curled into herself.

Was this something?

Her dress was the same color as the leaves' vines and the buds beneath her; her hair mimicking the color of the fruit these buds would bring.

I left my horse where he stood, dismounted, and stepped to her, following moonlight's reflection on white, strawberry blossoms.

I walked behind her, not the most cautious approach to ease her anger, fearing her fright at my approach. She had to know I was there, so I spoke first.

"I found you."

She did not respond. I stopped at her hushed shape, breaking her solitude. "Sarah." She didn't budge. "I needed time to consider what you said. I needed time to consider your perspective. If there is more you did not say, I want to listen. I hope you will tell me."

I stepped closer while her side shuddered at the curve of her hip, a momentary shiver from cold or tears, the movement too similar to determine. Her curves hovered in silhouette, reflecting only half the moon's light.

"I never considered how the slaves might affect you, and for that, I am sorry. I should have told you more." I stepped closer as she sat up, shrouded in tangled hair.

Her visage reminded me of the budding bravery in her. Without concentrating on the right words, I said, "I recognized your fire." She looked at me. Although I could not discern the expression on her face,

I sensed her gaze in the darkness. "You glowed on that ridge today." I looked in the direction of the memory, inching closer to her. "You did so again this afternoon, although the flame was hotter. The light was blue."

I reached her back and sat beside her but refrained from touching her. I held my hands still around my knees instead. Omniscient woods pulled my attention. "The slaves, they belong to my father. It would be dishonorable to question his judgment and ask him to free them. I imagine that appears a weak answer, but it is true, nonetheless. What we can do for them, we will. My family always has."

Thunder closed in on us, as she sensed, but still, she had not spoken or breathed loud enough to allow me into her solitary space. She would have to invite me into her thoughts, into her voice, into her hands.

She cleared her throat. "What you see as a privilege, I only see as my past. And I do understand, even though you assumed I would not."

With a memorized touch, she reached for me as words forced past her reticence.

"We all grow up with what we are given. I was wrong to assume you had any choice in the life you were born to either. I'm sorry. I didn't mean what I said." She took me to her, and her lips passed over mine, tasting salt from tears diluted with raindrops from the sky. Her feelings about our slaves would not change. Her love for me had not. We both were right.

"Come home?" I asked.

"No." Her voice pierced with another cry, as she would be weary no longer and crossed over me to wrap her arms under my shoulders and wrap her legs around my back. I held her, and we breathed together, facing opposite directions. The mountain pushed the thundercloud away, still soaking us with the edge of rain.

After a time, she asked, "Does my weight hurt you?"

"If it did, I would not say one word. You scared me, *Dh Ani*." She had become accustomed to me saying words she did not understand.

"As you did me." Her words resonated in depths, perceived from echoes in a bottomless well. She crawled her weight from me and helped me stand.

We did not rush to find my horse, walking slower than the remaining pats of rain dripping from tunneled leaves.

I mounted again, but not alone, and pulled her with my arm as she used the stirrup to climb and sit behind me, finding balance.

"Hmm," I said, remembering sleepless nights envisioning this exact future.

I reached for the reins. She peered over my shoulder. "You do that all the time, hum. Tell me."

"… to ride with you. I dreamt about it for months after you would leave me for the night and go to your room. In that time, I convinced myself this time would never happen."

"Hmm." She echoed my response, following my thoughts.

I laughed. "Do you know what blooms these are, *Dh Ani*?"

I nudged my horse faster as collected rain dripped through our hair, pooling our skin's salts to sting our eyes. I wrapped my free hand behind her.

"Hmm?"

"Strawberry blossoms, *Dh Ani*."

"Hmm, *Skahtlelohskee*." She said my name, recognizing her own.

CHAPTER 18

Skili

Clarinda Ridge

October 1856

Near Rome, Georgia

Throughout Momma and Papa's marriage, disagreements rarely survived the night. Their souls' forgiveness spanned years. Momma embroidered tiny, French knots, like dotted seeds intermingled among long red stitches, an embroidery of the strawberry fruit. Her artistry hung on the wall in their bedroom to remind them. God chose the family they were born to, but their souls chose one another. Souls fall to earth whole, perceived by others as shallow or wise. Those who recognized one another, remembered one another from before the fall, created legendary love.

After Papa's assassination, we lived in a constant state of fear. Momma couldn't protect us from further Cherokee revenge and moved us to Fayetteville, Arkansas, away from those who despised my family and our politics. However, some Cherokee families emigrated years before 1838. Many did not hate us. They wished us well, to harvest peace beside wheat and corn. *Skili's* family settled in the west years before we'd arrived.

In 1842, my seventeenth year, my spirit harkened back, knowing *Skili's* soul by heart.

Rain poured on the May morning when *Skili* ran to my parent's store in Honey Creek, asking for help for his father. Grandmother and I followed him to his family's cabin. His father's illness was severe, although his hair was still black. He clutched his thin chest and struggled for breath. Without words, Grandmother asked for my journal and turned to the page depicting the hawthorn, a tall shrub, with parsley leaves and white buds. Once I showed *Skili* the drawing, he took my hand to show me where many grew. Tea made from hawthorn bark and leaves slowed a rapid heart, slowed the pace of breathing.

We returned, arms full with bark, leaves, and buds. Grandmother took the herbs from us but closed the door. I assumed she barred us because we dripped from hair and hands, and our shoes were thick with mud. That night, *Skili's* father passed to Heaven, to the Nightland. *Skili* passed as well, from carefree son to protector, instantly becoming sole provider for his mother and sister.

Skili had little time to attend Miss Sophie's school. We often saw one another near the river as he fished or in the forest separating our farms. I watched for him in the trees as he climbed branches to hunt above the ground. Hidden amongst the foliage, his eyes turned to watch me gather herbs. Always aware, his presence was never secret to me, making little difference how bright or dim the sunlight.

In 1842, years later, *Skili* hunted for us and found me. He stood in Momma's open doorway, a thin, bare-chested Cherokee, draped with long, black hair covering his shoulders, tied away from piercing brown eyes with a band of white feathers. At first, she feared him, refusing to open the door. Then, with persistent gifts of corn and apples, squirrels and rabbits, she no longer dreaded his arrival but welcomed him. I skirted past Momma to take his hand before she could refuse permission.

We ran along the horse's path each summer evening under pink and purple-banded horizons, where sunlight burnt through feather-swathed clouds. Born from the Bird Clan, *Skili* called hawks from the skies above, spoke to them, and released the feathered predators to find new homes great distances away. His ability to tame the beasts earned him his name.

After the hawks flew, his kiss became his promise, *"As long as I am man, you will never want for affection. When I am no longer man, I will protect you from the Nightland."* We understood one another without spoken words.

I chose him. In time, Momma saw how similar we were and allowed our marriage. In his bark canoe, he rowed me home, parting the full moon's reflection floating on the surface of the river's waters.

Love and contentment filled our home although, *Skili* was no great hunter. No furs warmed our marriage bed. Outside, no skins stretched between trees, taut with sun's heat. No plentiful game filled our iron pot. However, each morning he kissed me in our doorway before the sun rose. But each evening, he returned with only two small animals' tails wrapped around his fists.

Curious as to why his hunting was so unsuccessful, I followed him. I tore my skin, my skirt, running behind him and hiding behind green vines. While my husband stopped at the edge of the cornfield, I hid, close to the forest boundary. There, he raised his arms to the sky, offering himself as a sacrifice to brimming dawn. There, he grasped his chest and collapsed, pressing the corn stalks flat with his weight.

I ran to him, shook him to wake. I placed my hands to his thin chest, his narrow neck. His eyes were black; *Skili's* stillness never altered.

Old was Skili's soul, although his thin body passed to the Nightland as a young man. No time remained to heal his heart's wound, the same as his father's. No time remained to speak to hawks at the close of day. No time remained to grieve the loss of our souls' brief reunion.

At this moment, sensing the rattlesnake's poison pulsing through my heart's last pulses, I knew *Skili* had kept his promise. My soul sensed *Skili's*, assuring me his was still there.

CHAPTER 19

Fearfully and Wonderfully Made

Sarah Bird Northrup Ridge

February 1824

Cherokee Nation Territory

It was quiet inside our house. Often, John and I have occupied the same space, not feeling any need to speak; it has been our accustomed way since we met. However, my parents were always in and out, or Jane's nosy and watchful bustling interrupted the quiet. Here, we fell into a contented silence, finding tasks to occupy our time, moving harmoniously through our days. Constant in my thoughts was worry our porcelain peace might shatter soon enough. Others would call John away for longer than just the day—to distant rooms full of men who would not trust him. For now, I enjoyed every quiet evening surrounded by the smells of him and home.

It was mid-afternoon when Honey knocked on our door and entered a second time. Her feet shuffled to me with timid steps. In her arms, she carried several letters. As she handed them to me, curtsied, and began to return to the sunlight, she brought in with her. She came to me each day since our arrival but had not spoken. I thanked her for her assistance dressing each day, but she would not reply or barely look at me. She curtsied before leaving the room, but I never heard her voice.

Today, she applied her courage and spoke, "These bees for Mista John." Her voice was a child's whisper. I watched her mouth form the words to be sure of understanding her.

Curtailing my surprise, I responded slowly on purpose. "Thank you. Would you stay for a while? We could have some tea." I did not want to scare her, but I hoped she would. Her hampered, high voice contrasted against her dialect, long and drawl, taking time with each English word.

She looked back to Mother Susannah's house, seeing through the walls, unsure of the right answer. She seemed not afraid of me but being late to complete her next task. From our brief interaction each day, I knew she fled rooms with speed.

I expected Honey's worry. "You'll be back to Mother Susannah in no time."

She stood near the edge of the sofa with eyes watching me but hid her gaze under mounds of hair twisted and tied in strips of multi-colored fabric, circles bounding all around her head.

"I'll prepare for our tea." Sugar might make her smile.

She followed to help and closed the door she left open. We stacked cup to saucer and pot to the tray. As we proceeded, I thought how she must have heard many reminders to close doors left open after each bustling entrance. If she imagined leaving again quickly, to her, there would be no need to close a door she was going to reopen.

Honey fidgeted, not knowing what to do. I, myself, had been scolded for fidgeting many times. I wondered if she thought she had done something wrong.

We returned to the sofa with the tea tray, and she sat this time, inching back, so her shoes dangled from the edge. I handed her a teacup full and dropped one small sugar chunk in so she could hear the plop. I filled my own cup and dropped a sugar piece in as I did hers. She blew away the steam, took a sip, and grimaced. Honey watched me drop in another sugar bit with the suspicion that it probably would not improve the taste.

"I brought yous da letters righ' away. Da Major sent me." Honey gave me the complete story of how the rider galloped to the house with a bag at his side but did not stay for even a drink of water. He handed them to Major Ridge, got back on his horse, and rode away. She seemed pleased I recognized her contribution to their prompt delivery.

"Thank you for bringing them; thank you for all of your help. I have appreciated each of your kindnesses every day. Your help dressing makes my mornings so much nicer."

She stretched her words as all children do, tying youthful perspective to her proud notion of her accomplishments. Based on her simple dress, I imagined she thought my clothes had too many skirts.

"I's good at knots, Mz Sarah. Mz Susannah says I's tying you up and help yous with all the skirts."

She took another sip of tea and tilted her head forward to dribble the sip back into the cup. It was Honey's compromise between will and manners. I dropped another cube in her cup. This time, I stirred it with the spoon.

"Mister John appreciates your care with his letters. I never expected such …" What might be the right word she might understand? "… quickness from someone so young."

"I thought I might bees in trouble, and dats is why yous asks me to sits still. Papa says I wiggle more than a fly caught between the light from the winders and da curtains."

"All girls wiggle too much. I was in trouble many times from my own Papa."

"Did you? Yous seem so proper, I didn't thank you would has evvveeer gots in no trouble."

I had to laugh. "I did, many times, for running up and down the stairs, and staring out of windows when I was supposed to be paying attention, and not finishing things my mother asked me to do. I preferred to be outside digging in my flowers."

"But yous so pretty? How could you ever gets in trouble? Did you ever haves to sits in da corner?" Obviously, she spoke from experience.

I thought back. "No, but when my Mother tired of my running, she made me write twenty times how I would not run up and down the stairs. It made my hand hurt, and I would get ink all over my fingers. And my maid, my friend, Jane, would scrub them in her tub with soap that made my skin crack."

She scowled and asked, "Why do Mister John always have da black splotches ons his hand? He in trouble?"

"No, he isn't in trouble." I subdued laughter. "Because he spends a lot of time writing letters, and the ink stains his fingers."

As she spoke of him, I saw him from the corner of my eye around the corner. Seeing us, he leaned against the wall out of her sight and smiled at us both. He listened, nodding for us to continue. He looked at his ink-stained hand when hearing Honey's comment and crossed it under his arm, out of visibility. His shirt sat open in the comforts of home, and his tousled hair stretched like branches from his head, from having run his hand through it many times. He sighed with his entire body.

She took a sip of her tea and finished the cup. "I's glad dat I's can't write. I's rather sits in da corner." She replied with indignation, tilting her chin. I understood. I would have preferred to sit in the corner rather than write. She was thinking all the while and indulged her youthful curiosity.

"I's never seen hairs like yours before." She remarked with the bluntness only children could use, with volume I no longer had to stretch to hear.

"My mother has the same color, although hers has gone white around the edges." I thought of my mother's hair, always bound and proper. I touched my own, hanging down my back. I thought of her disapproval nine-hundred miles away. Still, I hoped that there was a letter from her amongst John's correspondence. The lack of news from Connecticut distracted me. It seemed I was always waiting on letters.

I did not want Honey to think I forgot her, so I answered with similar astonishment. "And I have never seen hair like yours." At first, she seemed embarrassed until I said, "I love your colorful ties."

"Thank you, Mz Sarah. I dids it. Makes me feels like I's full of flowers to the top, and dat da bees will come and sits to makes da honey. Dat's what I's called, Honey."

John covered his smile, but I paid him no mind.

"I promise to find more colors for your blooms. I will save all I can for you."

She gently handed me her teacup and stood. With gratitude, she pulled one of her blooms away from its stem and handed it to me. Never could I refuse a flower made from Honey.

She curtsied, but this time I earned her smile and her eyes, the same brown as her name, rimmed in gold, lashes curling to touch the lids. She was so beautifully made.

She ran to the door. John ducked behind the wall, so she would not see him. In the afternoon light, she looked back to grin. Her blooms intensified in the sun as she skipped back to her chores at the house.

He stepped from behind the wall and came in his slender shape to stand above me, touching my face with the back of ink-stained fingers hidden moments before. He bent to kiss me as he grabbed the letters from the end table.

"Hmm. So you ran up and down the stairs?"

"Yes, a lot," I admitted with my eyes still closed.

"And you had to do lines?"

"Yes, a lot," I confessed, opening them.

"Trouble found me at my school in Spring Place when I was her age. So much so, Reverend Gambold, my teacher, wrote to my father. Apparently, I made the other children feel bad about themselves."

"Surely you weren't mean." I could see it but thought it doubtful.

He smiled, kneeling with some difficulty at my feet, but in his presence, there was a cool breeze.

"No, Vann was the mean one. I was just irritated with slow students who could not keep up with me. School bored me often. Father rode all afternoon, surprising me as soon as he received Reverend Gambold's letter. He scolded me, told me to behave, or he would take me from school. He did not want me to embarrass him or our family. He made me chop wood until the stack was higher than I was. I tried not to cry the entire time. He stood beside me with his arms crossed until I finished.

I tried to run away and come home. Instead, I should have continued to insult the other students. I didn't think of it at the time. Those days were before my illness, sending me to my bed for months."

I attempted to divert him from the memory, "Always the smartest one in the class?"

"Did you doubt?" His attention left me as he flipped through the letters Honey brought. In recalling her visit, he said, "She rarely speaks much, but you got her to talk. Here's one from Connecticut."

The letter had familiar penmanship, and I touched my hair.

He did not look at the letter as he handed it to me but stared in my face with a distant smile, seeing things there I did not see in my reflection. I gazed back at his golden eyes.

"Hmm." His smile pitched lower.

"What?" I asked after he put the remaining letters on the floor, kneeling but saying nothing.

He took my hands in his as he shared his thought. "I just thought what a caring mother you will be when we have children. I can see you sitting on the floor, babbling, teaching them."

"Them?" Were there to be many?

"While I'm on my knees, there's something I want to ask you."

I brushed his hair from his eyes, but it would not stay. It was longer, and while I did not mind, it needed cutting before he met with others on business.

"What is that?" I asked, focusing on the letter in my hand. He looked at my hands, flipping the letter over in my lap, and he reached to stop my fidgeting. He turned my attention as he spun the ring around my finger with the memory of placing it there.

"My mother has a request of both of us. Father thinks it might offend you, but mother insists. She thinks that is the reason … Well, it is her superstition, but one she still gives some merit, even after becoming a Christian."

"Ask me."

He cleared his throat and surprised me.

"I love you, Sarah. This spring, marry me again. Here, in her way? In our way?"

I could not answer immediately. I stuttered, trying to comprehend the idea and see it in my mind. "I wouldn't understand the words said over us or what to do."

"Mother will teach you, and I'll be right beside you. You do not have a clan. That may become an issue. We will work through it."

I did not understand what he meant.

He took a deep breath and let air escape with my name.

"Sarah, I'm asking on bended knee. Be my wife: again, still, tomorrow, eighty years from now? In the Nightland? In Heaven? Not just for my mother. Well, some for my mother. I do not want to remember only bitterness and fear when I think of the day you and I promised …"

A quick knock at the door interrupted John's thoughts, and we turned at the sound. Elias stuck his head inside. He had trouble getting in the door as he dropped books, spilling them as he made his way to the table. He looked wild from the neck up, with a wide grin and bushy hair that hung in a triangle onto his forehead, like the tail of his Cherokee namesake, Buck. Instead of white as the deer, his was black like obsidian rock.

Seeing us, he said, "I thought you already proposed." John and I both stood when he entered. Our untimely guest bowed to me with unnecessary courtesy, and from the weight in his arms, "Mrs. Ridge, it is a pleasure." It was something he said every time we met, after our introductions so long ago in John's sick room.

I countered in kind, "Mr. Boudinot, such a delight to see you again." I could not help but ask, "Have you received a letter from Harriet?" Vows and promises were on my mind.

He dumped his arms and bags on the table. "Harriet? Not in two months."

"I'm sure she is fine. Have you written to Colonel Gold?"

"Not yet, but I will. Maybe that is why she hasn't written." He'd thought of this already.

John interrupted, paralleling Elias at the table. He coughed with Elias' intrusion but gave instantaneous forgiveness. "What do you have, brother?"

"For the literary society, donated from my visit to Spring Place. I thought you'd like to read them first. I rode in and came straight here to unload them."

Books toppled over the table and slipped to the floor with a thud. Bindings held marks of abuse, beaten and aged, although it did not matter. John and Elias were eager to begin their quest to educate as many Cherokee who would learn. Their idea for a Cherokee Literary Society, to teach all things philosophical, formed in our living room with glasses of wine and fireplaces roaring with air from their lofty debates. When their conversations settled, blazing fires relaxed to embers. Through the walls in the bedroom, I fell asleep to their cadence. Hearing them exchange ideas back and forth in two languages was a tune where one could not recognize the song's verse, but the chorus was familiar.

We sorted Elias' collection at the same time. On the table and floor lay books of philosophy and collections of hymns. Stories with titles of distant places I never heard of and bound collections of poetry. The largest book took up half of the table, an atlas, and underneath that, laid a thin child's primer.

"*The Aeneid.*" John found next winter's reading.

"I'll go let Mother know you'll be staying for dinner." As I stepped away from our trio, I picked up a book from the floor. It was brown with gold embossing framing the edges. I dropped it on the top of the stack and left to follow Honey's skips across the yard. I would see if Mother Susannah needed any help, leaving behind the fraternity to stew over ancient wars and maps of the world.

I walked, looking into the waist-high grasses with my open palms brushing the seeded tops, thinking of John's request and the letter in my pocket.

John followed me, calling my name from the doorway. He squinted his eyes and rested his arm above his head to block the sunlight. "*Dh Ani,* my request?"

"I'll send you a note with my answer, Mr. Ridge." I smiled in coy reply. "If you wish, please ask Elias to stay the night before he rides home."

My wit dissipated to anxious worry. In this ceremony, would others think I was pretending to be something I was not? John must have felt the same coming to Connecticut.

I entered to find Mother Susannah praying. She sat in the dimness, with her palms open on a Bible she could not read. I awed at her faith. How distant she must feel—not able to read God's words when they sat open under her hands. Without trying to disturb her, I prayed beside her in her moment of solitude, asking God myself for His guidance.

In Heaven, there was peace. Worry and fear did not exist. However, I was not in Heaven. Among my new family, I felt nocturnal: awake while others were asleep or asleep while others rose. How would I manage our language barriers when John and Elias were away in Washington or Philadelphia? How could I accept my husband's culture with many beliefs so different from my own? My family was far away, reminded of such by my Mother's unopened judgment in my pocket. However, on this beautiful piece of earth, I was the one separate in appearance and voice, enclosed in a design of my choice, surrounded by unfamiliar sounds. Would their ways always be so foreign to me? Would they welcome me still when John left home, as they do in his presence? I questioned my place, the place I wanted, needed to be my new home.

Mother Susannah placed her Bible in my lap; her eyes closed in prayer. It sat open to the second book of Corinthians. I read aloud, knowing she could not read the words, but we would both hear God's promises just the same. "'We have the same spirit of faith,'" and I looked up to breathe, continuing, "'… for all things are for your sakes, that the abundant grace might, through the thanksgiving of many, rebound to the glory of God.'"

I was so grateful for where I was, just unsure of my role here. I had to trust I was where I needed to be, that God sent John to me and I to him as earthly gifts from Heaven. God reminded me to be thankful for the struggle now, no matter how lost or weary I might become. More of His many blessings would present.

I continued, "'… for which cause we faint not; but though our outward man perishes, yet it renews the inward man, day by day. For our light affliction, which is but a moment, worketh for us a far more exceeding and eternal weight of glory; while we look not at things which are seen, but at the things which are not seen: for the things which are seen are temporal; but the things which are not seen are eternal.'"

Mother Susannah opened her eyes and tilted her head to the side. Perhaps, I was becoming more than white, more than the little girl she didn't want him to marry. I took a deep breath at her gesture, thankful for air.

I was grateful for the love and protection of my husband and his clan. No matter how strange the customs and appearance of the Cherokee might be, they were interconnected to me in ways beyond my earthly understanding. I could give this to John and his mother. Weddings are the same, just spoken here with words unfamiliar. I thanked God with a prayerful heart for His reminder. Though the custom and costumes differ, we are all, '… fearfully and wonderfully made,' and that, 'my soul knows right well.' Psalms.

Honey entered our sanctuary and hesitated, feeling her presence might be an interruption. At her appearance, I realized another gift

God gave today. Honey spoke English and Cherokee. I touched her arm, asking, "Honey, could you tell Mother Susannah I said *yes*, with all my heart." At that, she lifted her head and found herself a part, not apart. She bounded to us with a new, unaccustomed task, as linkster, a translator.

I wiped my face and stood, wrapping an arm around Honey's shoulders. "Also, please tell her Buck is staying for dinner."

I did not wait to hear Honey's reply but squeezed Mother Susannah's hand and ran home, leaving the door open at my exit.

I heard John and Elias in the next room with filtered words, 'clans,' and 'children.' Their discussion seemed important. Returning to my desk and pulling a sheet from the drawer, I dipped my quill and wiped ink from its tip. Looking out the window, what could I say, in the fewest words? Then, remembering.

John,

I will never leave this land without you.

Yours,
Sarah

I folded the paper like official correspondence and wrote his noble name on the front, placing the note inside the book on top of the stack. It was the one I plucked from the floor, *Letters from Clarinda*, by Robert Burns. I took the book up the stairs to our bedroom and placed the book on John's pillow. He would find it soon enough.

As I descended, I read my mother's words. Sitting back at my desk to respond, I dipped my quill.

February 1824

Dear Mother,

I have worry over you and Father. I am grateful to know you both are safe. I praise God our family has faced no further violence.

I have to say I am surprised by the commentary of the ladies in the church choir. Let me assure you, most fervently, that I am not an 'Indian Princess.' The thought of such makes me laugh. Although, if you will forgive me, I will not tell John how they have coroneted he and me. He still holds such vitriol over our departure as his feelings remain the same shared with you and me in the carriage. I wonder why Cornwall changed its mind.

John says Cherokee ways are as ours, only called names strange to my ears. From among the Cherokee people I have met, it seems true. On the outskirts of Ridge land, there are poorer homes than the community in Cornwall, yet, their occupants seem content in their lives and happy with their children's successes. Many here are learning to read and accepting Christ as their Savior. Mother Susannah and I have attended Missionary Daniel Buttrick's services. Overjoyed at knowing the hymns by heart, we sing in both English and in Cherokee. Reverend Buttrick is a man of God and letters, as he seeks to translate the Bible into the Cherokee syllabary (a new written form of these people's mother tongue). We pray before meals and worship by serving others. It is such a blessing to see faith in deed, to act as God's hand.

Our apartment has a splendid fireplace' although, I have little need to use it for anything but warmth. We share our meals each day with John's parents. There is a parlor with new furnishings of pale blue where we read together. I doubt it will surprise you, but John has a study with papers in organized stacks on the floor. Cousin Elias is here often, talking and laughing with us both. Today, he brought so many books.

To answer your inquiry, we do not yet have a chiming clock. It is something I miss. However, if I ask, John tells me the time by the sun's position from the light in the room. We have laughed at his accuracy. He does not need his watch.

Mother Susannah and I sew in the evenings as you and I have done together many times. We are both working on a piece made from deer hide dried last fall and bleached in the sun. I have contributed to many of its parts, although I have not seen them sewn together. It assures to be quite an astonishing costume, once completed. Its pieces carry shells seen as adornments to bring luck. True or not, it is a stunning piece to touch.

While we sew, Major Ridge and John read newspapers from cities across the United States and speak for quite some time. I am sure they are preparing to make their case soon enough. John told me he drafts parts of a Cherokee Constitution. What an undertaking.

I have learned some Cherokee words, but John translates to me what I need to hear. I'd learn faster if he didn't. But I won't tell him that. He shares with me a great deal, and I am grateful for his confidence. Some things I must learn for myself.

Please send my love and prayers to all near you, so many miles from here. I pray for your health, contentment, and happiness. Please tell Jane all is well, so she will not fuss and upset you. Tell her I made a new friend. Her name is Honey, with blooms in her hair.

Please do not worry about me. My husband cares for me; the land is rich and soil fertile; I am welcome and safe at home. It is all, they are all, we are all so 'fearfully and wonderfully made.'

Our love to all,
Sarah

CHAPTER 20

I Left Mine to Beat in You

Sarah and John Ridge

March 1824

Cherokee Nation Territory

Sarah

I looked into a sky of emerging light. Sun rose behind breaking clouds, lighting them from underneath as they separated in dense horizontal passels. Gray-ridged crests highlighted in the white of shimmering sunlight bounding upwards. Underneath, illuminating clouds against reflected sunlight from the pale, blue sky, the opposite to dusk. Trees lined the mountains in the distance, casting a shadowed curve along the horizon, protecting the sun in the last moments of the night. Day began.

John returned to bed after I was dreaming. This morning, the book nestled on his pillow as if he'd never slept. From inside it, a note rested in my hand.

Dh Ani,

Elias and I left before sunrise with quiver and bow. Today, do not feed the fire in the hearth. Soon, we will relight from the one built together under the full moon. Took your heart with me and left mine to beat in you.

Until tonight,
John

Sounds of wheels and horses alerted me before I saw them, and I stood in the doorway to watch the procession announced with the squeaks of wheels. There were open wagons full of women and children, driven by attentive fathers. Warriors mounted muscled steeds, armed with weapons strapped to their backs and hips. Men dismounted their horses along the front grasses, elegant and dressed like white men with large medallions hanging from their necks. Feathers of varied colors and design stood proud above their heads. Younger men had no shirt at all. Instead, their chests were covered with white and black stripes in finger-width lines, horizontal from their faces extending down shoulders and arms. Many of their heads were bare except for patches of black hair from the crown of their heads extending the length of their backs. Older men wore elaborate sashes in bright patterns of blues and greens of woven intricacies.

Women wore calico tops made with flouncing sleeves, buttoned at the neck, and tucked into wrapped, buckskin skirts that extended to moccasin-covered feet. Children dressed as miniature versions of their parents: girls in garments in the same cloth their mothers wore, boys ready for stickball games, wearing little to slow their speed. Children ran in circles from under their mother's petticoats and aprons, chasing one another, scurrying over a ball. More noticeable than the children's attire were their smiles. They laughed high-pitched squeals repeating but unsustainable by one breath alone. I stood apart as they passed Ridge land for New Town and the New Moon of Spring. I could not help but return their gaze. It was I who was the outsider.

Major Ridge rode behind a crowd of those on foot and reined in Priest near our door, dismounting with a raised eyebrow. He dressed in traditional buckskin pants and moccasin boots rising to his knees. He wore a long-sleeved, fringed shirt adorned with red beads sewn at the seam extending his arms' length. Hawk feathers adorned his head, some split or had the ends removed, creating sharper angles. A larger feather framed his portrait at the center, once belonging to an eagle, the Chief of birds. Major Ridge was a Chief of men, of fathers, in attitude and accomplishment. From my experience, one enabled the other.

I was stoic with his awe. He stretched his hand to me, an invitation. Pockets, hidden through slits in my dress, held John's note as I closed our door and followed. Priest began his communion for the day, pulling fresh grass into his mouth. Major escorted me to the horse and gestured for me to mount.

"No, I couldn't. Priest belongs to you," I said.

He repeated his gesture in insistence.

With trust, I put my foot in the stirrup to swing my leg over Priest's broad back. Major laced the reins around the horse's ears and walked us both, winding the trail away from the parade, stepping to the pace of river water's travels. He sang the entire way, a tune without words in repeated melody. I found the third and hummed once I could expect the next note's pitch and the end of each subsequent phrase. When he stopped, Mother Susannah stood upon a steep slope beside the river, waiting. She looked across the riverbank, her back to him, wrapped in what must have been her bedclothes. Her hair stretched free and long, black-streaked with white. Honey sat beside Susannah's feet and rose at our approach.

Major Ridge stood in her line, lost in the sight of her. Susannah stood free on the ancient land of her mother's. He gazed at her, the wife of his heart and mother of his children. After a pause, he shook himself free of the vision and helped me to dismount, returning to his natural state atop his Priest. His face was proud and fierce, not in anger but identity, layering deep brown eyes under his stern forehead. He turned with pressure from his legs and rode away without a returning look to us, continuing earlier harmonies with a solo tune.

We were alone, hidden behind the trees of the forest-guarded banks of providing waters. Mother spoke as I slipped gingerly down the steep bank to attend her ritual.

"When the grass grew, and the trees sent out their pale fresh leaves, elders believed the Great One planted the first corn stalk. From it,

Selu was born. When she sprang, full-grown from the corn, she took two ears with golden tassels from her birth plant and ascended to take Kanati's hand, to be his wife."

Beside me, Honey's voice recanted Susannah's story as I watched her form disappear into the water and face the sun's rise, submerging and reemerging from below the rim between air and water. She surfaced and turned to me.

"Say ge, a-taw-asti-yi." She held out her dripping hand and encouraged me to follow her. I trusted her.

I was timid to undress, looking for others around me, but modesty paled compared to the holiness of this. She transfixed me with her command, compelling me to obey. Honey continued repeating Susannah's words as she undid the ties of my apron and skirts.

"Kanati was proud and boastful of his many animal hides and had a full stomach from his success as a hunter. Selu would be his wife and make him a better man, less boastful, less proud, more cautious, and grateful."

I waded into the water, colder than expected. Gooseflesh appeared on my legs and arms. I shivered, but when I took her hand, we submerged under the surface, and I rose without further shock from the cold.

We turned north.

"*In a brief time, they had a red son, kind and smart. One day, he met a boy in the forest who looked like his twin, one Cherokee, and one trickster. Selu and Kanati raised both boys as their own. In time, Selu gave birth to two daughters. Their home was full of corn, meat, and laughter: contentment."*

After I understood the legend, I followed Susannah's example; we cracked the water's surface again, dousing in falling drops.

We turned west.

"The boys followed their father to see where he gained his plentiful harvest of turkey and deer, elk and buffalo. They hid and watched as Kanati rolled away a stone from a cave and closed it behind him.

Kanati was out of sight for a time, and when the stone rolled free again, a deer draped his shoulders. He rolled closed the stone again, guarding the cave with his strength."

"After the father left the cave to return to Selu and the family, the boys crept from their hiding place. With might in will and strength of body, they rolled the stone from the cave to see. Once open, animals fled, leaping past them to take up homes in the forest, hidden amongst leaves, camouflaged from the eyes of boys and men forever."

Together, we bent to cover our heads and broke the water's surface again.

We turned south.

Honey continued to translate Susannah's words. *"Later, the boys wondered where their mother gathered the corn for their meals. They followed her to a small cabin and peered through the door. Selu rubbed her stomach and hips while filling an abundant basket with ears of corn. She placed the basket atop her head and left the cabin. Amazed, the scared boys watched their mother perform this magic and thought her a witch."*

Standing in the waist-high waters, we again covered ourselves in water, returning to the direction of the sunrise. We emerged, facing one another. We bound our hands together, hers underneath mine. My footing slipped on the slippery rocks; her hands kept me upright and grounded.

"Their father met the boys on their way home and told them he knew what they had done. He told them he must die and gave them quiver and arrows as their inheritance. The boys would now have to hunt their own meat."

As Honey recanted Selu's story of loss from the bank, Mother Susannah stepped closer to her, and I waded behind. She bent and reached for silt and sand from the shore and began rubbing the mixture on her arms, legs, across her chest, and through her hair. I mirrored her motions, lost in the story. Holy amongst the reeds, I felt baptized. After covering our bodies in the sand, we stretched back to the water's depth, returning the soil downstream to find freshwater. She left me and waded through to the bank, seeking fresh white flowers on a long stalk. The top towering buds were closed, but three rungs on the stem's bottom were open, lifting their faces to the sun. She pulled the flowers and leaves, dipped the buds in water, and rubbed her hands together. Bubbles formed the smell, a fresh and sweet floral. We rubbed our hair and face and body with the white suds, vanishing to the river's rush, and submerged three more times.

"When the boys returned home, they feared their mother and wanted to kill her, for she held power they misunderstood. Upon their return, she knew she would die. She told them, after they killed her, to drip her blood along the ground. Where blood spilled, corn would sprout. She said they must make their own meals. Their sisters would have to bake the family's bread. They must save seed to replant each year."

We robed and walked up the hill in silence, entering the house, sitting in the wooden chairs beside the fire. Susannah combed through her hair, and Honey pulled a comb through mine. Content, we dried and warmed in last winter's fire. My hair sprung in waves and curled; Susannah's hair fell straight and thick. Two inverses of one another, my youth to her age, my pale to her red, but we stared transfixed as a mother to a daughter with a forming bond.

She spoke of herself. Honey's child voice said the words.

"I've had two children die. Wallie died young, not yet walking. Nancy, my daughter, died giving birth the same year John left for the Foreign Mission School. Her child, a daughter, did not survive long. I mourned a great while. With John and my other daughter, Sollee, at school, my life felt absent of little ones and held no purpose. Once our children cease to need us, our lives leave us, and we become the winter corn stalk, barren, waiting. Honey has filled my empty breast."

Shocked, I looked at Honey. "Please tell her I did not know."

Honey translated my thoughts, and Mother Susannah smiled briefly, overtaken with remembered sadness.

"John does not speak of Nancy as she is gone. We will speak her name aloud during the full moon and remember. You, daughter, do not rush time and let me teach. Having you near reminded me."

She stood and walked from the room, crossing up the stairs. Honey watched as she passed and waited to speak until Mother Susannah stepped up the staircase's first rung. "She's goin' to get yous dress to marry Mr. John."

Astonished and stuttering, I repeated, "I did not know."

"It is the one yous been sewin' on for a month," Honey said. "Yous have to help make it to wears it."

The costume's design was open at the neck, and its diamond shape paralleled down my back, with bright blue shells and pearls outlining the design. Sleeves of bleached skins met a seam of long fringe extending like angel's wings when I raised my arms. A tapered waist held a belt, and the skirt stretched straight to my ankles. At the knees, the blue pattern of adorned tassels mirroring the diamond-shaped bodice. It was stunning. I had leather slippers to cover my feet in the color's inverse, blue-accented in white.

After dressing, Honey pulled a strip from the bouquet on top of her head and pulled my hair in a loose bind, building my gift, a blossom of blue.

Mother Susannah told me to carry the basket of corn in honor of Selu to give to John. She told me of the water vase we would share. She told me of the blankets tied around John and me during the ceremony: blue, a symbol of our childhood lives we left behind, and white, signifying our married lives as one person.

Honey helped Susannah dress in her costume of brown and blue sashes. After teaching me the wedding ritual, Mother Susannah turned wistful and looked out the window. Entranced, seeing something transparent to us, she spoke in far away, mystical tones, telling me of the children John and I would have together.

"First a daughter, born of the moon, to know medicine, to use her hands, and be Blessed."

She said I would bear more children from John's seed, and she would again listen to laughter running along the river. She told me of my sons, their children, and their children's children who would sing the same songs under the first full moon of spring. She foretold generations, dancing among green corn on this land. Her smoky voice smelled of saged wisdom through the clear air. She voiced hope, embodying what I knew to be God's Holy Spirit.

John

Leaving our horses to graze nearby, Elias and I stalked the deer on foot, seeking where bucks would find food, near the edges of tilled cornfields uplifted with clods of soil. I, with my bow, Elias with his knife, together, our four eyes ensured our harvest. However, it is a miraculous wonder the incoming buck did not hear us. Elias whispered questions of Harriet the entire day.

"I've told you, Elias. You must be smart. Sneak into town under cover of night. Samuel led a mob, nearly burning the house. Sarah said the town had forgiven us. Some Golds are different, as you well know. I showed you the paper, the Eagle?"

He leaned his back against me, eyes scanning across the field, thinking with a rare silence. He had seen the editorial then and was trying to rationalize his love of Harriet with fear of her punishment—one from which he was unable to protect her. I understood.

"You have to decide, as does she, whether your lives united can endure what might result. Have you asked her?"

"My mother said 'yes.' Does that count? We've been so busy reviewing Ross' Constitution, and I haven't asked Colonel Gold. I want to bring her home to New Town once the house is ready. Once we're ready." He thought for a few moments more. *"How did you ask Sarah?"*

"I'm not telling you that." Sarcasm and astonishment mixed in my face. Talk of Sarah brought my English.

"Come. You're the wordsmith. Tell me everything you said to convince her," he pleaded.

A rider's shape atop a horse stopped on the ridge and interrupted Elias' jest. Others traveling for the ceremony packed in groups, and families sought straighter roads with easier wagon passage. This rider was alone. His shining metal headdress reflected the sun's rays; plumes crowned his form. He stared south of the ridge, even though from that distance, he could not discern us as anything more than a brown splotch of earth. He began his descent on the path, turning beside the river, presumably to my father, who would not be there. However, Mother and Sarah would be.

"Do you see him?" Elias flattened his body on the ground.

"The stranger coming from the ridge? Muskogee Creek." After McIntosh's failed attempt at bribery, it would be difficult to know whether this stranger might come in kindness or anger. The stranger slipped behind the trees. We would need to intercept him before he reached the house.

Elias said, *"No, the buck."*

The deer walked out and nodded his head near the edge of the cornfield at the seam of grass and rust-colored, plowed soil turned to air before planting. The distance was further than thirty yards. I raised on my knees, turned the bow sideways to nock and draw. Aiming higher, gauged against the horizon, the arrow flew. It landed behind the buck's shoulder with a thump as he kicked his back legs, leaped, forcing a short-lived fearful run back into tangling vines.

We would need to track him as well as the Creek stranger coming down the crest of the hill.

"We need to go, Elias."

Buck and I rode with haste into New Town with the deer on the back of my horse, strapped behind the saddle. It took an afternoon of travel to arrive, passing through thirty miles of hills and riverbed. We had a message to deliver and needed to find my father.

Warriors had yet to light the fire but would do so at dusk. Drums had not yet begun. Warriors sat in circles with black woven wool blankets over their shoulders. In their hands lay stripping tools to remove the bark of white and black oaks from saplings. Torches would carry the fire longer distances to Cherokee; villages would pass the flame to another.

Women carried baskets on their heads to prepare a feast with the bushels from last year's harvest. Children played stickball nearby, screamed loudly with success. It was the same cry of men gambling wages, whether they won or lost.

I took the deer to a nearby tree and hung it from a rope in my saddlebag. Elias cut the hamstrings and the tongue to give to the fire tonight. We dressed the deer, pulling the hide away from the meat as I cut near the spine for the tenderloin. It would be my gift to Sarah.

The stranger's shadow wrapped around me still.

Father's smoke greeted me before I saw him, and I heard his whistling, that same tune of love and whiskey.

"Successful, I see." His voice found me, still armed with bow and quiver slicing across my back in a diagonal line. It had been too long since my first tools rested there.

Elias grinned as he always does. *"The arrow found the buck."* His tone shifted to one as anxious as my mood. *"We have a message for you, one from the southwest in Tuckabatchee."*

"Come." Father walked past us, past the crowds to his horse, retrieving parcels from his saddlebags. I lagged behind them both, looking towards the road. My thoughts burrowed deep with suspicion of the message's handler.

We wove through woods for twenty minutes, finally making our way to the embankment of Coosawattee's waters. Father dropped his parcels at his feet and leaned against a pine trunk.

"What do you two have to tell me?" Our expressions revealed that

we had words he would not want to be said, not today.

"Opothle Yoholo met us on the path near the mountain," I said. It was Yoholo's timing, I questioned. The Creeks had a similar ceremony to ours this night. Yoholo delivered this word instead of attending his own Spring Moon Ceremony. He rode to Cherokee land instead of forgiving grievances to ensure a fitting harvest for Creek crops.

"Yoholo sits on the Upper Creek Council." Father recognized the man as chief of Creek Nation, trusting his words.

"He invited you to attend Creek's council in Tuckabatchee. He wants you to understand what the Upper Creek Council has to say to the Lower Creek Chiefs," Elias delivered Yoholo's invitation.

"Did Yoholo say whether Governor Troupe would be present?" Father inquired with a raised eyebrow before crossing his arms across his chest.

"Troup is McIntosh's cousin; it is irrelevant whether he attends," I continued to speak of dividing allies and the repercussions of such.

"I will not go," Father declared with sternness and shook his head.

"I understand. McIntosh will only ..." I spoke my concerns fast, here amongst those I trusted.

Father interrupted me, *"You will. Take David Vann with you. Build trust of your own. Mine has waned with them. Be wary, be cautious, but listen."*

I would not argue, and I could not protest. I would go.

"Not a day for anxiousness, though. Your hunt, successful. Tonight, you marry."

Elias and I undressed to go to water. The river lay straight and full, gray from the silt among the drops. From his parcel, Father threw the dried Yucca soap to me. With the last of the day's sun at my back, I submerged and held my breath, enjoying the amplified sounds in my ears. I reached the bottom, pulling a handful of the silt that seeped through my fist, leaving less than half of my original grasp. When I rose, I ground the silt into my skin, on my face, and through my hair. With eyes shut, I submerged again and turned south.

We broke the surface at near the same time, passing soap to rub our arms, hands, and chests. We were parallel, and our motions mimicked a dance done many times, together for many years back.

We counter-turned without a word, faced east, extending our arms along the water's surface with our palms upward. The water billowed over the muscles in my shoulder, flowing to my hand, surpassing my barricade. I turned my palms and watched the water fall over lines of muscle and bone. I had the power to control it. I thought, '*What a piece of work is a man?*'

East again, the sunrise's direction, whose next light would bring us many blessings. We submerged among silt and stone, twisting in the water to face north.

I rose, as did Elias, facing the last gold of sunlight streaming through the black bark of straight pines and curved hardwoods. I rolled my hips and legs through the clear water, diving to chase the last glistening light. Our boyhood swims in the river prepared us to hold our breath. Collected rain absolved our childhoods, as we stood now as providers, weighted with responsibility—the care and protection of our women—the land and tradition of our people. As long as he and I stood side by side, Elias and I would submerge and surface together.

Shaking our hair free of drops, we climbed the bank, and I felt freer. Father threw each of us a parcel. Elias had clean skins and dry shoes. My red shirt, buckskin pants with garters for my knees, belt, and moccasins were inside mine. What would Sarah say? She had never seen me wear such before. The fabrics were smooth and unrestricted, foreign to me after the accustomed tightness of white man's clothes.

Inside my shoe was my yellow feather tie to hold my hair away from my eyes. It was small for my head now, although to Mother, an utterly irrelevant observation. I would always be her mockingbird.

Father took the feathers from my hand to tie back my hair. He spun me with his familiar grasp on my shoulders.

"*Skahtlelohskee, my son ... you chose well. Temper your pride with her, listen to her, protect her, fight for her if you have to, but most importantly, love her as you love our people. Make her one of us, as you have become a part of her. She will bring you more than you know, not just children, but peace. Whether you are sick and ill, destroyed and poor, lost and alone, she will find you long after I am gone. She will fly by your side. This is true."*

He placed a black and gray feather beside the yellow one longer, stronger, and pronounced against the black of my hair. Cherokee believed black feathers reminded us we are never alone. He turned me to face him.

"*As far as the Creek's message, you shall listen for me; take my voice with you. But tonight, you shall become the husband to the Sun, Skahtlelohskee."*

The rhythm began in oral song, and the drums stomped their entrance, one strong, one softer, unceasing and predictable, primal and tribal, ritual and ancient. Recognizing the call to the flames, we found our threesome paced with the stressed beat, stepping on the same foot in parallel line as we returned to the throng surrounding the warrior's circle.

Two men sat near a pallet of hay. Small strips of hickory bark curled and frayed at the center, edged on one side by their knees and on the other, by dirty-bottomed, calloused feet. Upon a plank of wood, each spun shaved juniper twigs and horseweed stalks between their palms. Sticks twisted and ground against a dark, circular base to the rhythm of drums. With heat and spark, the tinder caught. It was their honor to begin the fire anew each spring, to welcome and to sanctify the growth of new corn and life, come again to our land.

Those around the fire crept forward, walking on their knees to protect the budding light from the smallest breeze. A glow began on the men's faces as more wood succumbed to the flame. With warmth established, the drums changed tones and rhythms altered to one more playful. Dancers began pantomimed actions of an imaginary harvest, men scooping their arms near the ground, and women collecting imaginary ears of corn in their aprons, held wide with the hope of great bounty. Inside the dancers' circle, others continued to feed heavier oak to the spark while light stretched to meet the upcoming moon.

Blinded by the fire's light, Sarah appeared in white on horseback. Mother's shadow leaned over and spoke to her while the moon's ascending beams illuminated her, and she glowed.

Mother dismounted and found Father and reached to embrace me. When I looked back for Sarah, she and her light disappeared.

Dancers finished with a loud cry. The drummer's beat changed to a more complicated rhythm, and the ascending beats were slower, filled with compelling counters. Fire builders framed the fire with thin logs in a triangle, resting on one another at its apex. When the fire builders stepped away, Sarah appeared in the escaping light across the blaze from me. She dressed in a deer's embrace. Embers darted against a black sky, extinguishing, becoming invisible. Above the drums' heartbeat, a new flute melody interceded, and then another entered the song to duel in harmonious polyphony. Sarah radiated. Each sound begged for her Moon's favor.

Musicians began again. Haunting fire stood between us. She mirrored me on the opposite side of the flames. I walked left; she countered right, piercing me with eyes ignited with night. Our paces paralleled and pulled. Drums set the pace under our feet as she shifted one direction, and I turned back. We danced two years of delay through distant miles, my chase, her retreat, her bold decision, and my unceasing resolve. Drums paced our hearts.

Blessed Man stepped forward, chanting prosperity, repeating vows with the drum's consistency. Her circle complete, she faced me seconds later. In her arms, she held last season's corn like a newborn. Mine held deer meat wrapped in hide. I laid my gift at her feet, still tense in our gaze, mocking the dimness of fire's orange light. She placed her gift beside mine, grown from the earth. Mother wrapped Sarah's shoulders with a symbol of her childhood spent and did the same to me. With tears running down her face, Mother handed us an earthen vase, open on both sides. We were to share the water inside, although little could quench my thirst but Sarah.

As soon as the blankets warmed, the Blessed Man removed them both to produce a single blanket of white, blessed it, and tied it around us both. Flutes began again in harmony as the restless drums pulsed.

If Sarah ordered me into the fire, I would have heeded her command. Our spirits talked all the while. My soul told her of her radiance; hers said I gave her symmetry. The Blessed Man turned us to face him, but our eyes remained unchanged, still souls conversing with muted words.

We departed through the parting crowd, compelled backward forced by her light. I feared breaking passion's spell. Still not speaking aloud, I kissed her with open eyes. Her hair ignited in incandescent moonlight, and my strength meager to pull from her draw. There were no words.

We crept away. Folding the blanket under my arm, I took Sarah's hand, walked her to my unsaddled horse, and hoisted her leg to help her mount. I took my seat behind her and kicked forward.

The ride was not far, following the same path Father, Elias, and I journeyed this afternoon. Moonlight streamed against the pulse of rolling waters. We could still hear the drums. I swung my leg free, and she held her arms for me to guide her fall. She vined around me, sliding to the ground. Pulled again, I threw myself in her aura. Touching her lips, I succumbed willfully into the soul of her.

She reached for me, pulled the shirt from my chest, and dropped it to unaccustomed earth. She stretched her hands across my chest and pulled me to her. This passion rolled, flamed, hardened—molten red from the new fire. Earth was recreated.

She knelt to undo the gartered ribbons tied at my knees.

"Take me wherever you go, *Dh Ani*," I said between her kisses as she rose and held my face between her hands. She reached behind her waist to undo the belt to her dress. I stretched to pull from the hem and remove it over her head. In her nakedness, she undammed restrained beams.

She walked back into the water, carrying the light with her, stepping slowly down the slope, gripping silt between her toes.

Her voice, deeper, claimed, "I never left." Her outstretched hands gathered me, and she kissed my heart. "It is my heart beating in your chest. You took my own and left yours to beat in me."

Through the valley between her breasts, she guided me. I listened to the drum of our synchronized pulses—eternal, predictable, and known.

CHAPTER 21

House Divided House Full

John Ridge

Summer 1824

Tuckabatchee, Creek Territory

and Ridge Land, Cherokee Nation Territory

Once entering Tuckabatchee, down the Tallapoosa River, Vann and I reined back, slowing our horses in anxious measure. We entered the public circle surrounded by Creek's primitive homes. Deerskin tarps stretched against oblong frames, sealed in mud and grass. One two-room, dog-trot council house appeared, spear-heading the circle. From the approaching road, we were prudent not to alarm anyone. Meager mothers, defeated fathers, purposeless warriors parted in an aisle, biding idle time with caution and superstition.

Similarly, we inspected the Creek with vigilance, failing to advance with any speed. Yoholo invited Cherokee here, although the supposed guest was a King, not two Princes with invisible feathers. Apparently, these people were not only wary but uninformed.

"Marvelous place, affectionate people," Vann spoke in easy English with sarcastic litotes as he watched wary-handed warriors trace us with scowling eyes behind overlong hair.

"That they are. Suggests the injury from the last Cherokee council has not yet healed." Infection seeped from wounds of dignity, crossing from hut to hut, elevated by revenge and jealousy. No one walked forward to our horses.

At the twelve-o-clock position, the single log structure housed the Creek Council from the town's inner circle. A stone fireplace occupied its center. Speakers elevated on a wooden box found protection from disagreement by a single and empty podium. Sixteen Creek chiefs assembled on backless wooden benches. Once we took our seats, Opothle Yoholo rose and stood, focusing his wrinkled forehead to match the expression of the weapon-clad men, who straightened as he rose above their heads. Elders, Big Warrior and Little Prince, held positions of strength on the bench behind Yoholo, adorned with metal crowns holding feathers that bent against the wall behind them. Advanced age did not deter their resolve; it rooted them deeper. Noticeably absent from the council was McIntosh, although his presence persisted in more palpable ways than his bold tartan and boastful voice.

The meeting opened with Yoholo's customary honors to the "greatest warriors," claiming, "*Never was a nation more equal to the Creek in war.*"

My father told me the story of Horseshoe Bend many times. Since that battle, this 'glorious tribe' suffered continual losses. As reparation, warrior chiefs seceded land and suffered reduced hunting tracts. Deer and turkey ceased to thrive on mismanaged Creek land, shrinking further to its core with every futile aggression sought to recover the loss. Land rooted power. White Georgians would not return it to the Creek people unless forced by ink or blood. More efficient gunpowder and lead outnumbered Creek tomahawks.

Another defeat might prove a conclusion to their hostile legacy. Many Creek refused advancement and assimilation, while Cherokee sought progression, preservation, and fusion. Fate already knew, recorded the victor on some future battleground. For a brief time, the fight would be bloodless, with semantic weapons between adversaries. Creek pride volleyed against arrogant white ears with papered declarations, threatening war.

Vann whisper in confidential English, "They will have to seed a great deal more land than we have seen." Those seated next to me understood his tone if not his words. Vann had one of those faces where his intent lay on his surface, and his tone could not bluff. I acknowledged the truthfulness in his remark with a slight nod, keeping my attention on Yoholo. Here, people ate as frequently as their labors produced, but uncultivated soil would yield little for a long winter. These villages might sustain but would not flourish from untilled and weeded fields.

Yoholo continued, nodding to Vann and myself. Whether from acknowledgment or scolding because Vann had spoken, *"On deep and solemn reflection, we have, with one voice, followed the pattern of the Cherokee, and on no account whatsoever will we agree to sell 'one more foot of land,' neither by exchange nor otherwise. This is our law."*

To my surprise, the Upper Creeks heeded my father's adamant belief. It was McIntosh's leadership of the Lower Creek Nation that might very well drive the Creek into starvation and desperation. Verses copied in my youth from the book of Mark came to mind: "If a kingdom is divided against itself, it cannot stand." Mark's philosophy held magnitude.

Little Prince and Big Warrior wanted their decree in writing so their desires would last long past their advancing ages. Last, yes, they would. Followed by all the Creek chiefs? Of that, I was less confident.

Then, Yoholo transcended from plain speaking into increased volume and fervor. He smashed his hand upon the podium and spoke through clenched teeth. *"We have guns and ropes: and if any of our people should break these laws, those guns and ropes are to be their end."*

The man who needed Yoholo's reminder was absent, McIntosh. Agent Meriwether and Georgia's Agent Campbell would know of this decree soon enough to their dismay. I expected no amount of paper would divert them from their malicious intent to defraud and dispossess the Creek from their homeland. If Meriwether and Campbell had their way, all Creek land would be signed away, X'ed by hands of Lower Creek chiefs under McIntosh's pliable leadership. It mattered not to Georgia's government that McIntosh was only one of many Creek leaders.

Amidst murmurs and whispers, the meeting adjourned for dinner. Men trailed outside in single file, following the elders in procession. In the open circle, men found their friends and brothers from their mother's clans, shook hands, and leaned into one another to speak with confidentiality. To honor Creek Council, we left last. Stepping into the light, Yoholo came in haste to speak to us.

"Your father sent you instead." He remembered our previous meeting on the path near the Oostanaula.

"He did," I replied. *"I hope our presence is not a disturbance. I am to be his ears and return with words from your great Council. He leaves soon with Ross for Washington to appeal to Congress to redress Cherokee concerns. Your council's concerns are the same."*

"I feared your father turned his back on all of us, not only those who attempted to bribe Ross. That is not the case, I see." Opothle Yoholo appreciated the severity of Father's condemnation of McIntosh.

"It is not the Creek people my father shunned. Only the man who chose manipulation over integrity." I did not want to speak McIntosh's name for fear my tone might betray my abhorrence of the man.

"No. Honestly, I am glad you came. I have a request from the two of you."

We walked across the square to his camp and sat beside him as he circled his campfire and lit his pipe with hay. He drew long on the tobacco before continuing, inhaling in his nose, and exhaling smoke from his mouth. It rose around his eyes, masking his uncertain countenance. Although, he seemed calmer and continued.

"We have a few among us with the education each of you received," Yoholo said.

"It is something the Cherokee value," Vann spoke from remembered lessons at our schoolhouses in Brainerd and Spring Place Mission, bored to misbehavior.

"It is something the Creek can no longer afford." He looked back to us over his shoulder, saddened.

"I understand." I scanned through decades of written lessons, feeling avarice for more.

"Ridge, Vann, would each of you consider transcribing our decree in the white man's way, in white man's talk? It needs to be phrased in such a way to give weight to the words, weight their reputations deserve." He pointed with his pipe's end to Little Prince and Big Warrior. *"Before their age limited them, their lives were spent in unwavering service."* Shaking him from history, he returned to speak of his present dilemma. *"Our words need to be firm, speaking of the loss before these people—before all of us now."*

His body followed his pipe's smoke into the wind and faced the Creek masses with a father's care and a soldier's caution. He took a monumental risk in asking us to write his words. Honest tones and the sincerity of the Creek threat must pervade.

I looked to Vann, who shrugged his shoulders. He consented, as the document would not be long. Vann never minded any task asked of him, especially one he considered an evening's work. I, however, hoped we could articulate the consternation arising from the smoky head standing before us. After acknowledging Vann's agreement, I stood to address Opothle Yoholo's request and the depth of trust assigned to us.

"It would be our honor to provide this for your people." As the warriors before, I felt a kinship to their struggle but feared the futility of its resolve. Grateful in the tribute, we would construct its means. I hoped for a positive outcome.

In successive council days, no words resounded as powerfully as the speech Yoholo made on the initial. Vann and I wrote notes of their arguments, asking Yoholo to repeat phrasing iterated by Little Prince.

Clarity of connotation was my priority. Big Warrior added a last desire for the draft, *"Ask whites for justice."*

I thought about the word's meaning, perhaps differing from sender to receiver; however, I employed the word with the Creek connotation. Fundamentally, the Creeks sought their entitlement as they occupied the land and appreciated its nature in blood. Opposed, the minds of the whites received the land as victor's reward, bought and paid for with colonial blood, spilled to secure independence from the British. In irony, both were 'justice' indeed.

Yoholo and I translated the strict value of the expressions and sought the nineteen chiefs' signatures present. Yoholo handed the quill to Big Warrior and Little Prince to mark their Xs. Yoholo exclaimed his own name aloud as he etched his mark. The agreement was unanimous. As each passed our table, they gave us looks of commendation and gratitude, as two outsiders looking in on their critical history. The declaration sought justice; Yoholo's threat dared the same.

Handing the documents to Yoholo, I could not help but question, although it was not my place to do so. Suspicion overpowered me, and rather than assume, I inquired, *"Who will receive the second copy?"*

Gravely, he looked at me and bent his head low, but his eyes never left mine. *"Chief McIntosh at his home, Lochau Talofau. I ride southeast tomorrow."*

I responded to him with only a nod in support of his purpose. *"Thank you, Gentlemen. Send my regards to your father. Tell him I hope to see him at my fire."* We mounted.

"As you are welcome at ours, Opothle Yoholo."

Facts remained—if the Creek lost their territory, Georgia land would border the Cherokee Nation. The Creeks and their hopeful successes would be the only barrier keeping Meriwether and Campbell at bay. Vann and I focused on success; however, it felt poisoned with unjust venom. History taught me America's public officials' experience with occupation was a lesson held briefly in their memories because now, they sought to occupy Creek and Cherokee Nation Territory.

Half-way home, we released our horses to graze. At the riverbank, we stopped to wash, change clothes, and eat. Summer peaked, and air radiated heat ascending from the ground and the sky. It had not rained in weeks. Surrounding trees afforded some respite from the strength of the sunlight. We endured more buzz than bite from annoying mosquitoes.

We needed rest and distraction from our thoughts. Water would be our conduit into our peace of mind.

"Watch for snakes." I smiled as Vann disrobed and dived.

Surfacing and shaking his hair, he said, *"You watch for snakes; take care of yourself, Skahtlelohskee. I carry the venom inside of me. Remember? I am impervious."*

"You are not." Vann did not wait for my retort as he dove again.

When he rose, he carried two enormous stones.

"Come in. Find more. I'm hungry for fish."

I followed him into the muddy water and sought more rocks to build a V-shaped dam in the shallows to trap a small dinner.

We splashed one another, pretending we were much younger.

"So, you married her?" he said as we stacked the barricade.

"Twice." I forced myself to focus on the spiritual second rather than the violent first.

Not one for the formality insisted upon by his family. He said, *"I'm sorry I missed that, twice. Really, I am. I arrived at the ceremony on the second day. Where had you two gone?"*

I only grinned at him, choosing not to speak. My wife knew my whereabouts. At the time, that was all that mattered. Distanced by this trip, I hope Sarah fared well. Her voice from memory was ill-matched to the one heard in her presence.

"Don't tell me. I know anyway." He laughed in good humor at the happiness of a brother and friend. Vann understood desire.

"How is Jennie?" I inquired, as he did not say.

"She is the same as she's always been—bossy and right. She puts up with none of my boastings, and I love her for it. She's as big as the house now; I hope to miss the birth."

"Why would you say such a thing?"

"Because she will yell at me when her pains come. She will tell me to get away from her yet get angry when I do. Birthing children is women's work."

"Obviously." My sarcasm earned me another wave of water to the face.

He held his arms above him and looked at the Great Spirit in sincere prayer. *"I hope it is a boy."*

He shook as he exited the bank in front of me and sought his saddlebags for dry and more comfortable riding attire.

I chuckled and cut across to the opposite side of the river's bank. The sun tightened the skin on my back, evaporating drops of water dripping from my hair. In my hand, I snapped several saplings from the bank, stripping them to set a point, finding vines to leash the thin branches as one. Sharp they were not, but in my hand, many lay strong. I made my way to the center of the flow to observe our pool for trout. One would be enough meat to ease our hunger.

Twigs snapped as Vann stacked kindling for a fire as I waded and waited. Persistence never bothered me, required for trapping fish. There were separate matters in my life where required patience magnified my temper with acuteness.

I found a yucca plant, pushed its root ball free, and rinsed it. "Catch."

Vann reacted. He took his knife to the root and skinned the brown from the white bulb. He chopped and squeezed medicine from the pulp. From the bank, he dripped it into the shallow barrier between two trout trapped between the rocks. The plant's serum would stun the unlucky fish.

Vann had established a much larger fire by the time our food found us. I handed him two speared gray trout, and he fileted them on an adjacent rock with practiced swipes of his long blade. Once doing so, he tossed cornmeal on the meat and flung them in the waiting pan. Vann never traveled without his fish-frying pan.

The time our own, we talked through our lives spent apart as though the time were non-existent. Trout sizzled and crackled as I sought dry clothes, smoother and cooler than those I left Tuckabatchee wearing.

"It seems Yoholo already knows what will happen." Vann knew, wary of the same fears I contemplated. He shook his head.

"I imagine so. Whether it already has, I do not know. McIntosh would sell the land from under those people with no warning if it meant his pants had heavier pockets."

We sat on our heels, muzzled again. Vann rose to take up the white fish, deciding it had cooked long enough. We ate our fill in half the time taken to gig our catch, and without care for manners, we finished by licking our fingers.

"We learned that lesson long ago, didn't we?"

I could not follow his thought. *"Which?"*

"When the snake bit me, you saved my life. You kept us together, united. No matter the prize, even if it was a mighty buck with an arrow through his back."

"Yes, we did, didn't we?" Laughing, I hoped there would never be a time when Cherokee found division; strength lay on the same path, seeking the same end, all of the same mind.

We rode for home, arriving late in the afternoon. Sarah could meet my brother and friend. She would laugh at his sarcasm and banter like the rest of us.

Father rode the corn crop's outskirts on Priest, monitoring the dry spell by gaging the dust. A rainy spring led to a torrid June, and he worried for the young ears' future. Vann saw him before I did, wandering in concentration among the waist-high stalks stacked in rows. Even with this rainless month, sparse Creek fields contrasted to the fledgling plants before us.

Father acknowledged us both, saluting with an ear shucked in his hand, shaking his head.

"We need rain, although I imagine the sun hastened your trip home," Father observed.

"*We used the time wisely to remember each other's voices.*" Vann knew not to quip with my father when his forehead looked like it did now.

Vann and Father mounted again, and we all began a trot, side-by-side, and headed to familiar pastureland.

With the sun at our backs, I reported, "*We left a declaration from the Creeks: one whose insinuation on paper reflects similar attitudes to Cherokee leaders. Opothle Yoholo delivers the decree himself to those who seek coin instead of corn.*"

"Osda ... Osda ... Osda," Father whispered to the listening Great Spirit. If the Lower Creeks bargained a treaty against the Upper Creeks' preferences, Father's greatest fear would be another Creek war. Then, Campbell and Meriwether would ride fast to negotiate with Ross and the Council. Emblazoned with Creek defeat, they would scorch our southern border. Cherokee hoped the Creek injunction would stand.

We reached home and steered the horses to the stable for their well-deserved rest. I sought my bride. Not home, I met Vann again on my search. He smoked with Father, walking among the rainbow of four o'clock blooms on the border of the house.

"Has she left you already?" Vann smirked in English.

"Where could she go?" I returned his sarcasm, and he ran to follow me on my quest.

We stepped through the orchard, and I saw her near Honey and Old Saul's cabin, stooped to peer underneath its stone foundation. Sarah's apron was covered in dusty-red earth, like flour, while her hair dropped in long, red beams, escaping her white cap. Her arms were absent of accustomed garden implements or cut flowers.

"What is she carrying?" Vann asked as if I saw something he could not.

She leaned down to Honey, who was wiggling out from underneath the cabin's foundation. Honey's blue cotton and soles of black boots were buried under her house.

Sarah's arms overflowed in squirming browns and blacks. Honey's blooms were now all the same tint, rusty in dirt from waterless swimming. When Honey shook, a puff billowed around her. Honey held one pup by the scruff of the neck and stuffed Sarah's arms full. Honey re-submerged, only to stand briefly and swim through the dirt anew.

"Sarah!" I waved at her.

Vann remarked under his breath, "This is Sarah?"

"You're home!" Sarah split her attention from me to the insistent rooting fur in her arms.

She handed me two puppies and Vann one, without waiting for introductions. Sarah refocused on Honey's feet, wiggling out again with two more whimpering bundles in her hands.

"There are nine in the litter." Sarah beamed, excited about the new lives she held.

Honey couldn't contain her pride in finding the pups. "Old Babe hasn't been round in t'ree whole days. I looks and looks for her in all da normal spots and not finds her at all. Den, Mz Sarah and me was walking to da honeysuckles, and we's heard the littlest whimpers. We's jus' follows da sounds. Babe had dem puppies right where I started lookin' for her days ago. Dey's so widdle with der eyes shut agin' da sun."

Just then, the mother hound came, crouching from beneath the floor, and sat beside Sarah's feet, waiting patiently for her babies' return.

"Sarah, this is David Vann. He and I have been friends since …" I thought to tell her years, but standing there holding hound puppies, made me think of our ages when we romped through the grass together, probably the same age as these puppies. I looked at him and laughed, but his attention centered on the closed-eyed, round-bellied pup in his arms.

"Very nice to meet you, Mr. Vann. Here, I'll take that one from you."

Vann did not return his delicate bundle.

"Shall we find someplace to reunite this family?" I requested.

Leading our crowd over to the stable, the four of us walked with our heads facing arms full of sleepy-eyed squeaks. Babe, with teats full, ambled along the ground with wide paws. I took them all to the stable and used an empty stall to place the puppies near their mother in fresh hay.

Vann, Honey, and I stepped back, admiring nature at its fullest. Sarah knelt. Without the benefit of sight, the puppies smelled their way to their mother, flopping over one another to sit at her table. With a quiet and embarrassed curtsy, Honey left. David excused himself to dinner and my mother. Sarah did not rise and stayed beside Babe, rubbing the dog's long ears. She did not want to leave.

"What will we call them? They all look so similar. It isn't like we could name them for their size or coloring," Sarah said.

"If that were the case, we'd have to call them all *Digaleni,*" I laughed.

"What does that mean?" I knew she'd ask.

"Ears."

Sarah shook her head and looked at me. "How was the council meeting?"

I knelt to sit on my heels beside her and took her face in my hands, brushing tendrils away from her lips. "Resolute and threatening. How are you, my *Dh Ani*?"

"We missed you." Her tenderness was resplendent on my lips. She took my hand and placed it on her belly.

"Let's hope there aren't nine." I held my hand for her to stand and wrapped my arms around her, swaying together with utter joy.

CHAPTER 22

Uktena, Pale Snake

John Ridge

June 1824

Cherokee Nation Territory

Sunshine brought drought. Corn turned brown and shriveled, crushed dry with penetrating sunlight. People transported water from little creek beds to sustain their crops to no avail. The ground cracked with wounds, incapable of scab or healing. Dinner tables fell inadequate as bodies collapsed from deprivation and ill-health from the lack of sustenance. Those who settled themselves near rivers had tables more abundant while Cherokee on distant farms did not. Families were in critical need. People gathered to their clans, combining means and efforts. Profuse crops from early seeding and spring rains became crisp and worthless in this summer's unrelenting heat. Tempers flared in men's hungry bellies. Sickness spread in close quarters.

My family still produced and sold cotton, and the price at market remained significant. The income allowed us to share our bounty. My parent's home housed visitors in every room, accommodating some on the floor. The women, including Sarah, devoted days to kneading dough, scrubbing clothes, and tending to other mothers' children. It troubled me to see her tired from standing so long and carrying so many burdens, but she reassured me it felt good to help supply for my people's needs and continued. Father, the slaves, and I transported irrigation water in relentless trips from the Oostanaula to crops. A feudal attempt.

Parlors lay full of pallets and bodies. I stepped over them to a chair to collect Sarah home. She sat with her neck at an awkward angle, dozing with a lap of darned socks, her forehead damp and glistening. Even at eight in the evening, the kitchen remained warmer than the remaining rooms. She stirred at my touch.

We crossed the empty streambed to our apartment's porch, remaining, waiting for a gust of warm air. "The heat makes a vicious adversary through this incessant war of summer; it is inescapable." I stood and went inside to bring her some water.

"Ross is here," Sarah announced. It was late. He rode hard, passed us, dismounting in front of my parent's door, leaving his horse to wander. I gave Sarah the glass but watched Ross. We trailed through the cloud kicked up from his horse.

His shirt carried black smudges on his elbows and collar. *"There's fire,"* he panted, *"... near Spring Place. Set by Cherokee there. Streams dried out. River too far."*

Sarah offered him the drink in her hand. She could smell the smoke perspiring from his body. She managed to understand without any need for my translated account.

Father rallied, "*We must go now. We can shuttle from the Coosawattee by wagon. The fire will increase. Every leaf is kindling.*"

Strangers and recent friends inside chose action and immediately stood and tracked out of the door, ready to help as they could. I hesitated in the doorway, passed by warriors and farmers alike. "Sarah, Mother, remain close to the house. I will tell Old Saul to remain behind." Sarah nodded for them both.

Sarah grabbed Mother's arm as I followed the others, watching us as far as their eyes could trace us in the oncoming dark. Father and I mounted our horses and followed the caravan. Ross led in the wagon, stacked with the heads, with Old Saul running behind him into the road. We rode hard to the west.

It took us three hours. The night sky lit from the bottom as we turned to head north into the fire's light. Sweat dripped into our eyes, and I could not tell whether my visual distortion was from our bodies' exertions or the increasing density of the smoke that billowed and blocked the night from view. We knew the road by heart; although, the closer we came, the less we could see.

Elias met us and covered his mouth and nose with his shirt collar. *"I'll ride for Rich Joe Vann's and meet you in New Town."*

Father pulled the wagon into the chaos of Cherokee men gathering water in anything that would hold it. Canoes filled from the river transported larger amounts to douse the blaze. It required ten men to lift and load the canoe onto a waiting wagon. Based on the amount of smoke, the fire would consume acre after acre from the Federal Road to New Town.

"John," Father coughed through the smoke, *"Get in the water. Gather as many men as you can reach. Fill gourd, basket, pot, and load each man as they appear."* He ushered incoming wagons into a line of men, satiating thirsty casks only to empty them again on the fire line.

Absent of idle men for the labor ahead of us, I gathered children and women from the trails and woods who stood idle. I stared across the outbreak, coughing, fearful for these children's fathers who disappeared, charging into the gray smoke. Water would protect the young, and they could help. Collecting baskets and kettles, we created a vast chain. Father led the encircling wagons and warriors, returning to pass iron pots, baskets, and canoes with enough grease to seal them against losing their water. I waded into the river water. A year before, its depth exceeded my rib cage. Now, the Coosawattee barely reached my hips and remained stagnant. The river reacted kindly to our invasion and granted what remaining water she held.

Among the black-sooty faces reporting to refill wagons was Elias' younger brother, Stand. Ash covered his face, as black as his hair, a seamless countenance until it reached deerskin leather binding across his nose and mouth. He was unrecognizable until he opened his eyes and moved. He shrieked to me from the wagon line.

"*Skahtlelohskee, we're digging a firebreak around the school. That will halt the spread. Keep the water coming?*"

"*Where's Sollee?*" I shouted over the splashing.

"*What?*" He echoed.

"*Where's Sollee, my sister?*" Her unknown whereabouts hung heavy on me.

"*She's safe at Vann's house.*"

I could breathe. Our family lost Nancy in childbirth so many seasons ago. I could not comprehend my mother's pain if her baby were to burn in a fire. Ten years younger than I, Sollee attended school at Spring Place. Father had trouble enrolling her in a school she wanted that also wanted her. While here, she was closer to home. Many alternative schools would not be available to her—not in Baltimore, not in Boston.

Faces returning from the front line appeared like continuous images of the same man, streaked from streams of perspiration carved through black smudges as dark as boot polish. Many reported the fire danced over one break into a remote stretch of crispness on the forest floor. We could not save acre after acre with water, merely protect structures from smoldering into crumbling ground. The land would regenerate, but it would take a generation. We could only try to defend New Town on this side of the river and hold the flames from our capital. Further north, we must protect the school at Spring Place.

A movement drew my eyes from the line of shadowed bodies operating with pattern purpose. Upriver, a galloping horse ran southward through the water, pursued by leaping deer—gunshots blast around us from the west; birds few out of the smoke. Vann appeared on the bank, shooting as many deer as passed over the river, hoping to retreat to the woods for safety. Vann shot to fill empty stomachs with meat during the recovery from this fire.

From the bank, Father stood by Elias, who yelled, *"John, come."* I handed my basket to a daughter beside me and pulled my legs high to ascend to the shallows.

Panting and choking, Elias skirted up the bank on his hands and heels. *"Uktena,"* he shrieked. Father followed Elias' eyes to a considerable, diamond-backed snake with horns and sequenced, crystalline scales that withdrew from the water, whirling silt and sparking mica within the muddy water. Children shrieked and dashed into deeper water behind my outstretched arms. All action suspended, and stifling stillness wrapped our lot in endless rope, binding us to the river's bed. Father could not stray more than inches without inviting the snake's further draw to his legs, remaining in the serpent's slithering path. He held his palm out to Elias, who passed a waiting shovel into my father's grip. Cherokee would take a snake's life to safeguard self and clan—superstitious but unavoidable.

Father flipped the trowel to manage the blade downward. The snake raised its head with teeth-barring vengeance and coiled its body, bracing to spring from the ground. The snake followed Father's sequence of movement with side-eyes, pacing itself with what it regarded as prey. Its head darted left, then oscillated right, tongue enraged by the water's turmoil and the audacity of man to stand in its path. *Uktena* stretched forward with a wide jaw, striking only the wood of the shovel's handle. Then, the snake retreated to recoil for a repeat attack. Father had nowhere to escape; the bank rose behind him, and the water stretched in front. He raised the shovel's handle with his arms and exhaled in force. The crunching sound of the metal on scales and cartilage left the reptile's head divided from his lengthy full body.

Through our quiet anxiety, Father recited his prayer.

"I call on the spirit of Snake. I call upon the primordial forces you carry. I call upon your instinct and your heightened senses. Help me remain pressed tight to the present so that I may encounter this existence directly. Make me mindful of intricacy and open to change. Sensual spirit, I ask you for transformation. Help me shed what I have

outgrown. Clear my eyes so I might slide clear of the past into a newly-formed now. Coil your power, speed, and precision within me, so I might reconcile with the unseen and ingest the intelligence I crave."

Father accepted the animal's spirit within him. Then, he reached to the ground twice, once for the body and another for the head, removing the sight of the snake's corpse from the children's eyes. However, it would preserve in their detailed recollection. Its body lay concealed among brown brush and twigs, delivered back to Hell's parched briars.

Just before dawn, I crawled the bank and collapsed from weakness. Weary, many Cherokee lay among needles and overturned leaves, covered in soot and desperation.

"What started it? Who started it?" Elias asked, squatting beside me, pulling the kerchief off his mouth.

Ross walked beside him and spoke first but held a deep breath before doing so. *"They were hungry, trying to survive on chestnuts. It took too long to find them in the dry brush under the trees. They lit fires to scorch the brush aside. It got out of hand. At least, we protected the Capital."*

"Why did they not ask for help?" I understood the answer but asked the question, so others would realize we would support them. Elias stood and offered his hand to help me rise. I looked at him, and he threw my arm over his shoulder to help me step. Pain in my leg and hip renewed.

Later, men around us skinned deer and dried the meat, stretching hides along the timberline near the river. Smells of wet soot mixed with roasted fat in a sickening combination. People appeared in droves back from the destruction, gathering meat to nourish weakened children. We blanketed New Town in makeshift tents whose openings spilled of weary feet, bodies hidden from view.

Bare-chested with shoulder blades sticking out of their backs, children surged ahead of a multitude of women coughing through the vaporous field across from the newer buildings. Each woman held the edges of an extensive blanket holding another woman, who contorted into herself and shook. Once crossing the black barrier onto the protected ground, powerless to carry the corner any longer, the women fell in a hunched mass, weak.

"Snake." The young Cherokee woman led the group and shrieked the word aloud to all who could hear her, shouting above the surrounding women's weighted breathing and misery.

Elias and I listened. The woman's scream cut through the remaining smoke.

Elias said, *"How could she realize? How could she have known?"*

She lifted her hands high in the air, away from the malady at her feet, and stopped our increasing pace. Her hair dangled in clumps of muck and mud, matted against her face; her dress of skins hung off her rail-thin frame; her eyes sunken but, in contrast, fierce. *"Medicine Man told us sickness comes from creatures with no legs or arms. Uktena slithered and spanned the waters to return fire and death."* Disoriented, her spirit moved within her wild body. Fever overcame her as imagination blanketed her vision. Her rational mind steered away from the Christian God and into the hands of her own upbringing, superstition absent of logic and science.

Father walked calmly to her, and she altered her hands from the Great Spirit to push an unseen force against him. *"You,"* she declared with an accusation. *"You met his eyes. You sought to be his friend."*

"No. I killed him," Father spoke in gentle undertones as he stepped forward, hands ahead of him, *"Let us help you, let us help her."* He signaled to the mass of glares from the huddled women on the ground.

Father attempted to get closer to the woman, and she stopped him with her eyes. He towered over her in height but equaled her in will. When she could face him no longer, she collapsed, and Father caught her before her head hit the ground. He scooped her in his arms. The woman on the quilt was sick, with puss pockets on her face, neck, and chest. Fever high, sweat careened off her forehead. Other women helped them all to the river, to water, to cool the anger in their hearts and disillusionment in their minds. No medicine would cure festering wounds of the spirit while trying to heal those of the body.

No sooner after the attention concentrated on the suffering women, my sister came down the slope, along with one of the Vann slaves, and rode into town on a horse, jumping over a smoking log in the road. She sat erect, commanding esteem descending from her heritage but ignoring the red souls she passed. She lingered above Elias and me, waiting for one of us to settle her impatience and assist her down. She looked around her as though the carnage did not exist. Any regard she held from others, she inherited. None had been earned.

"Sollee, what are you doing here?" I asked, taking my arm from Elias' shoulder.

"I arrived to see," she expressed in English, not Cherokee.

"You should not have come. There's disease and danger."

"Why is it because I am female I am told to stand aside from the excitement?"

"That isn't the word I would use to characterize what has fallen here in the last two days, Sollee."

"It suggests so to me. Where's Father?"

"He's with some women who may have the pox, Sollee. You cannot see him now."

"You will not tell me when I can and cannot see my own Father, John."

"There is a woman with puss pockets. Those who brought her here looked fevered. It is smallpox, Sollee." I stopped her progression to the river with my body. "You will not follow. I am bone weak and tired, but you will not go down there. Go back to Vann's. Father and I will come see you when we can."

"Where's your wife?" she asked, changing the subject.

"At home with our Mother. She is with child."

"Humph," was her only voiced expression. Did Sollee think I would bring Sarah here and put her in danger?

She strode back to her horse, clicked her throat, mounted, and left the same way she came.

After she was unable to hear us any longer, Elias asked, "How can two people behave so differently growing up in the same house?"

"Because she never has to work for much, and I imagine she'll have to learn a great deal before she changes." She was a charmer and a beauty but selfish beyond her years.

Father quarantined the women in the council secretary's cabin. Women brought clean blankets; Elias and Vann brought food and water to the door, but no one dared open it.

During that moonless night, those who hadn't eaten much in weeks were fitful but full. I couldn't eat for waiting, prayerful in the quiet, anticipating another storm of twisted fire as punishment from the Great Spirit for unconfessed sins.

Father emerged and carried the woman from the council house, limp and chalky. She did not stir. He set her beside the fire burning in the center of tents and proceeded towards the river, staring at his own hands. I grabbed my blanket and walked behind him, taking one look at the body. It was not the old woman that succumbed to the pox, but the younger one who spoke from her ferocious anger. Panic stole her life, fear of the *Uktena.*

Father must have assumed the firestorm was Uktena's retribution. Without speaking, he took off his shirt and walked to water, submerging without prelude, trying to wash her death from him. His memory of this diseased night might travel downstream as well, no matter the implausibility. I left the blanket for him. I knew he would stay to quarantine and serve others. Now, he wanted to be alone.

I tried to sleep on a bench, roofed only by the open pavilion of the council house. Each time I closed my eyes, I heard the woman's voice repeat, *"... Uktena, pale snake."* It was dead.

I closed my eyes to the hours. Raindrops blew on the breeze into my face and into the cracks in the dirt beneath me. Awakening, the sky opened its eyes and wept for our loss. I stood and held my palms cupped, filled with water's healing.

CHAPTER 23

Columbines

Sarah Bird Northrup Ridge

September 1824

Cherokee Nation Territory

John came home a month before his father. He remained until he found recovery sufficient to return. Renewed rains spurred the cherry trees to blossom again a second time as a concession. Even after the fire, Ross spoke with determination to continue with the council session in October. With all their preparation, John and I spent considerable time around home walking in concentric circles. We had the same rudimentary point but revolved around one another instead of traveling in the same location at the same time. Today, my circle took me to the field near the wood's line, shaded by bordering oaks. Under my straw hat, guarding my eyes against the sun's rays, I discovered a perch for Honey's instruction in written English.

Honey was late, so I sat alone, rubbing the denser spot on my belly. Among the leaves, I picked up those newly fallen from around the blanket and waited. Honey's chores must have taken her longer than expected, or instead, she delayed of her choosing. I should not have shared with her my punishments, forced to write lines. She must worry that if she knows how to write, others might force her hand as punishment. However, I merely planned to teach her to make the letters in her name. Hope for her appearance dwindled.

Then, Honey ran from the path by the house, carrying something in her hand. I had ink, quill, paper; we required nothing further. She darted through the amber grasses with her blooms lit in the sunlight and her calico shoulders and arms tucked into her sides. Not examining her route, she ran fast, oscillating as she overcame the fields between the house and me. She whirled at the border and followed the path leading between the crops of grain and the bare berry patch.

"Mz Sarah!" She breathed heavily and placed her palms on her knees to rest when she reached my blanket.

"Slow down, Honey. What's wrong?"

"Nuthin's wrong. Only, I has sumefin' for you from Mr. John."

"All right. You could have walked. Why did you not come to write with me?"

She raised, though still panting. "Sit here a few minutes, Honey. Drink this," I said, handing her a gourd from my basket.

"This is what Mr. John say to bring you." We exchanged water for a book. He told me to say, and she remembered his puzzling message and said, "dat he's 'got 'nuthin' else to do.'" Her sentences broke with her breathing. "Aldough, I gots no idea what dat means. He seem busy studyin' whens I left him."

Honey handed me *Letters to Clarinda*, the book Elias delivered from Spring Place. Intrigued, I read to myself as Honey feasted on the contents of my basket beside her. John marked a passage with a ribbon of green. The author dated the page December 28, 1787.

'When dear matchless Clarinda fair,
First struck Sylvander's raptured view,
He gaz'd, he listened to despair,
Alas, 'was all he dared to do.'

The poem continued as if this admirer, Sylvander, dared not seek more than friendship with this woman, Clarinda, hailing her as his muse.

'The chill behest, disarm'd his muse,

Till passion, all impatient, grew.
He wrote, and hinted for excuse,
'Twas cause 'he'd nothing else to do.'

I grinned and leaned back against the tree behind me, thinking of Connecticut.

Honey said, "What's it say? Is it important?"

"Well, not exactly important, but meaningful to me. It was a message of sorts."

"Why did he not just tell me to tell you sumfin'?"

"Because he only wanted me to know."

"Well, dat seem silly."

"How so?" I laughed at Honey's dismay.

"Cause grownups alls da time are talking in secrets when they should just says what they means." Honey delivered more than John's words; I was to sample Honey's philosophy.

"I imagine that could discourage a person, not knowing what people are saying."

"Yous da one dat don' know. Yous frustrated? I understands everything dey say out loud and some of what deys don't."

"I know, Honey. You have a keen ear," I said. "Listen, you teach me something in Cherokee, and I'll show you how to write your name."

"Whys would I want to do dat?"

"So, you can tell secrets of your own someday. Maybe they would just be secrets to yourself or to someone you love."

"Can I's go first?"

"You can. What are you going to teach me?"

She stewed, tearing oak leaves into tiny shreds, running through a dictionary in her mind. When she decided, she plucked two blades of grass and held them close in the palms of her hands to whistle, blowing through them.

"*Osdi*, that's what's growing in yous belly." She intoned each syllable so that I would understand the sounds of the word. She held her head with pride at her choice.

"I did not know you knew. I guess it is not a secret any longer."

"Missus Susannah told me 'bout a month ago, and she say for me to watch you careful and don't ties yous up so tight anymo'."

"I appreciate that. *Osdi?* That is how you say, baby?"

"*Os—di*," she repeated.

"*Osdi*," I repeated. John said the word quite often; I concluded its meaning. "Okay. My turn then." I handed her the quill dipped in ink, but she didn't know how to grip it in her hand. Ink dripped on the sheet in front of her, and she gawked at it, returning the quill to me.

"I just mess it up. I don't wants to write." Her voice unwound like a top.

"Hmm." I had an idea. "Do you like to draw?"

"Likes in the dirt? Yesum, I scratch da flowers."

I knew a way she might feel more comfortable learning. I stood and walked under the trees to seek a long stick, one long enough to reach the ground when I stood. She followed behind me. I drew two lines connected in the middle. I handed her the stick.

She imitated the shape, larger beside mine, bracing the stick in the grip of both hands, one atop the other.

"That's an H. It makes the first sound in your name," I explained.

"Hu …" She made the sound. She beamed and announced, "Hhhhoney hhhhas hhhhands to hhhhhelp," exaggerating.

"Yes, she does." I laughed. It seemed as if paper and ink were unnecessary at Nature's school.

I drew a circle to the right of the H along with the letter n.

She took our long wooden pencil and copied my drawing.

"This is an o and sounds like o in the word '*osdi*.' I stretched the o longer than it should have been, as she did with her leading letter.

"The last shape is an n, and it makes the sound when you blow air out of your nose and put your tongue on the roof of your mouth. Like noise and nuisance."

"Pap calls me a nnnnnuisance." She mumbled, conscious of the admission.

"Why ever would he say such a thing?"

"He tells me alls da time hows I suppose to bees a Cherokee woman. He say Momma was Cherokee, and I's looks just likes her, but that I has to works da rest of my life, and not have no big house to lives in. If I was dat kind of woman, we would be free."

"Did you know your momma, Honey?"

"She die when I was *osdi.*" Honey took the stick from me, drew connecting channels from our H, around the o, through to the n, and encircled the three letters connecting them all within her circle's frame. She drew petals outside of the circle and a stem, walking around me as she did so. From the stem, she drew a leaf encompassing my feet. If I were to step outside the lines, I thought I might disturb her art. I stood stationary.

"Dat looks like dem daisies up on da ridge dat bust through the cracks in da rocks."

"Yes, it looks like a daisy. Honey made the flower and didn't need any help from the bees."

"You's funny, Mz Sarah." Honey interrupted her thought. "I has to get back. Momma Susannah baking bean bread, and I gots to grind da beans." She handed me the stick and ran back to the house.

I called after her. "Soon, we will do more lessons?"

"Yes, Mz Sarah. We can doos it soon."

I stopped her escape before she turned toward the house.

"Honey, can you come back a moment?"

"Yes, Missus?"

She stooped to me, and I pulled the green ribbon John used to mark the place, tying it around one bouquet atop her head.

"Thank you for bringing me this and for the charming drawing."

Honey's smile was abundant gratitude. I carefully stepped from the stem and went back to my seat beside ink and quill, unnecessary in Honey's hand. I copied Honey's drawing using the ink spot, starting and ending the same way but making three bound daisies, two larger and one small. Under the daisies, I stole a stanza from Burns' poem:

'Oh, could the Fates but name the price
Would bless me with your charms and you
With frantic joy, I'd pay it thrice,
If human art and power could do.'

I folded the parchment where the green ribbon had been and placed the book in my pocket. Grabbing my blanket and basket, I made my way back to the house, a more graceful trip than Honey just concluded.

I found my husband in his parent's dining room with an enormous paper map, which appeared to be a drawing of Georgia territory, Creek land, and Cherokee land upon a single glance. Ross and Major Ridge hunched beside John, who sat between them. Their heads bent with serious concerns I could not read, defined in words I would not understand. I merely passed through this room to the door on the other side for one minor task. John glanced at me while his father and Ross continued their research. I set the book on the edge of the table, and his eyes smiled. Without waiting, I walked to the opposing door to approach our apartment. Perhaps I could take a nap with my afternoon suddenly free of a waiting task.

Our bedroom window darkened in the afternoon sunshine, and the air caressed as warm as if ovens were beside our bed. I settled my head on my pillow, perusing the run-away sun. Before I could forge a thought, my eyes sealed, not recalling any cross-over into sleep.

Distant light turned golden when I untangled my eyelashes; I propped myself and swung my legs over the side of the bed and shifted something to the floor. John returned *Letters to Clarinda*. My note peeked between the pages as I plucked it from the floor.

Under my sketch and note, his font was narrower. He stole another fragment of prose from the page underneath:

'You are by this time fast asleep, Clarinda; may
good angels attend and guard you as constantly
and as faithfully as my good wishes do.

Beauty, whether waking or asleep,
Shot forth particular graces.'

Before memorizing his lingering addition, the knock and squeak of hinges alerted me. Assuming it was John, I rose. Surprising me at the bottom of the stairs was John's father. He extended his hand, and I ascended to take his arm, slipping *Letters from Clarinda* in my pocket. He and Ross were to leave before sunrise tomorrow for New Town, and this must be my goodbye from him for a season. I did not want to see him go. Things here felt assured when he was riding Priest in the dawn and dusk, always waiting for success or trouble, whichever dared to come upon him. He prepared for either or both.

We wandered together through the sunspots under the peach orchard trees, pursued by bees singing in chorus. Major Ridge plucked a lofty peach and passed it to me, like hard candy from a forbidden bowl on a top-cupboard. Plump and sunny, the peach's fuzz tickled, soft as yellow velvet ribbons. My handkerchief dabbed the dripping nectar released from the peach's pulp.

He stopped our walk to speak, but butterflies of burnt orange and black prevented his thought's completion. Two as ample as my palm darted between us. One settled on my hand, and another made me giggle while it found favor in my hair. He stepped back as I studied the wings' extension and contraction. Immovable, I held my apprehension and breath, waiting for their inevitable flight. With tiny antennae crossed, the butterfly tasted my skin as it stretched its wings.

"Whisper to it." John's voice was behind me, although he did not approach us. "Tell it a wish, and let it fly."

I cupped my free hand and whispered to the listening insect and blew, sharing my air to lift his wings. Both butterflies soared and darted together, landing to hover on nearby fruit. Major Ridge sought the butterfly's permission. He took my hands and talked to them instead of my face. He examined my slight frame and a growing belly, making me feel powerful. I do not know what it was about my new Father, but his presence of health, loaned to me, escorted me into a vastness I could not manage alone.

"This new life inside you will become the best part of me. Susannah was right. This baby will be Blessed." He used the butterfly's breath to intone his thought.

"He said the baby is Blessed, but not in the way you think. He and Mother believe the child will become a healer of body and spirit. "The butterflies …" John moved from behind me, diverting me from the mesmerizing pull of Major Ridge, who placed my husband's hands in mine. He placed his own behind his back and stepped to the house. Before he entered, he changed his thoughtful countenance to smile over his shoulder, taking any cloudy shadows with him. The butterflies remained with us, darting under the bower, in and out of the sun's encompassing beams.

"'It has spoiled my peace for this day. To be so near to my charming Clarinda, to miss her look while she was searching for me.'" John switched me to his left side to support him, walking with a less staggering gait and knit my arm through his as we chatted. We strolled along the path beside the river, heading upstream and skyward.

"You have spoiled me today with these bits of verse and notes."

"I wished you to know my thoughts. We've not talked much."

"We are fine," I tumbled on a buried tree root, and John narrowed his clutch on my arm, "… just sleepy and clumsy." I recovered my balance.

His mood became one of genuine inquiry. "Are you concerned your mother will not be here?" John asked me more than I had considered yet. "Would you like me to send for her when your time nears?"

He would if I asked, no matter the expense.

"No," I admitted. "I've written her. I had not considered the birth too much yet. Now I will worry. Thank you for that." I hoped the seed he just planted would not grow into a weeping willow.

"Mother will help you. Trust her."

"You will help me. I desire no other."

"That would send both of our mothers into hysterical fits." He laughed and kidnapped the peach from my hand, taking a bite.

"Why?" I asked, handing him my handkerchief.

"Superstition riddles traditional ways of childbirth; however, I suspect your Dr. Gold would not have allowed me near you when the child is born. Here, children, firstborn under the trees, are taken to water by their grandmothers, even before their fathers meet them. Although, you will do what you think is best."

He interrupted our stride and signaled to the rolling waters beside us. "They are named soon after. Although, the name usually changes."

"Why would it change?" I could not fathom changing a child's name once we had baptized him or her.

"If the child shows an aptitude to one thing or another, later their name changes along with the display of their talents."

"What about you? Has your name always been what your mother calls you now?"

"Yes. I've always been a mockingbird."

"Hmm." I stole his pitch.

"She told me I babbled from the moment I could speak and haven't stopped talking since."

So, it would be young and playful John talking to me; he was my choice of John's many faces and attitudes.

We could no longer see the house as we progressed along the flat banks near the river; a sharper bend reached upward away from the riverbed into the trees. I had not ventured this deep into the woods and was not confident I could manage it now.

"Which do you hope for? Son or a daughter?" he asked, rounding to bolster me up a steep step on the path. He passed his question to me and felt lighter by the exchange, bounding up the slope with no limp at all.

"I hope whoever grows inside me is healthy." I took a deep sigh before stepping.

"All mothers say that. Tell me." He shifted back to me at his thought's conclusion and proceeded as the passage became narrower.

John lifted me in the spirit of the butterflies, and we darted higher and higher, his stride lengthier than mine. With his anticipation, he was two feet ahead if we were not hand-in-hand or arm-in-arm.

"You tell me. Which would you prefer?" I summoned him back, stopping to grant more distance between us. This line of questioning would ensure his reveal—thoughts as rich as the moss-covered rocks on our incline.

"She and I are acquaintances. I dreamt of her." He grinned from the corner of his mouth and winked and lifted me on the path.

I seized his sticky hand. "How could you know? Do you have some God-given talent for prophecy, Mr. Ridge?"

"Perhaps, Mrs. Ridge. Last night, she laughed on my shoulders as I held onto her feet. I can see her." He shifted his gaze to a branch below us riding on the water, maneuvering smooth river rocks. "I am glad you feel well. I could not leave if you did not, and I need to attend this council meeting. Especially now, with her to arrive."

"When do you leave?"

"Sunday." He cleared his throat and allowed me to catch up to him, with my skirts in my hands, pulled up so seeing the ground was easier. It was becoming more problematic to look at my feet.

I winked. "We will miss you. I leaned against the rock face to settle for a time. "I will pray for you."

"I will return as soon as I am able."

Taking my hand to keep me upright, he did not defer his previous questions and rubbed his free hand up my arm.

"What will her name be? Will she be beautiful and smart like you or boastful and arrogant like me? Will she be a quiet beauty I must deliver to New Haven to avoid persistent suitors?"

He placed me in front with my back to him to propel me. Greenery became dark, and colors snuck across the gray rocky landscape. Crooked limbs of sourwood trees guarded mossy dogwood trunks. Jewelweed, whose flowers looked like orange impatiens, sprung through flecked tines of green ferns. Blue and white columbines burst through discarded fall leaves, highlighted against white daisy petals opening their yellow eyes, and maroon Sweet Beth arched toward the sun. Closed moonflower blooms and vines climbed around large pines topping higher than I could know. I halted, astounded at our God's garden. I inhaled the combination of color, fevered with jealousy of Heaven.

John's voice accompanied my silent reverence, "In this wood, we touch the Nightland."

"We must return at night when these are visible." I traced the moonflowers.

He removed my hand. "Don't touch those; they cause hallucinations. Something this elegant should never be as lethal as it is." He ushered me into a clearing, where ticklish grass laughed at the last remaining hour of sunlight. Here, the flowering audience heard the verse, iambs of whippoorwills and trochees of rusty-colored thrashers.

He picked a single columbine bursting through the rocky ground. He invited me to sit with the blossom instead of speaking his request.

"Will SHE run along these paths as I did with hound dogs barking ahead of her, tracking rabbits?"

"Will HE be lean and write elegant correspondence and poetry?" I answered as he settled down in the red sun's glow beside me.

With arms crossed on his chest, he lifted his head and quoted Sylvander with one open eye. *"'It isn't poetry, Clarinda; it is prose run mad.'"*

I passed the book from my pocket, settling it on his chest.

He dreamt then, "Will SHE ride tall and sing like Heaven's angels?"

I followed, "Will HE stand beside you and argue for Cherokee Nation?"

"Before the Revolution, Thomas Paine persuaded men to fight, so their sons would not have to do so."

"And that, my love, is why you must leave. Why your Father must go, and Ross. So, this child can inherit this land, this place. I have faith, and when all is said and done, the land will never be in danger again." This conversation dampened one of our last evenings together for the next month. I sparked his smile again. "See, I listen when you talk."

"I know you do. It is just when you say so little back, it worries me."

"You know how much I love you. That is all you need to know."

He opened his eyes to me and rolled on his side. "You do not say all I want to know. Tell me what you are thinking."

Among the flowers, my thoughts ran counterclockwise. "This instant? I am thinking of the day you first read to me about sad Ophelia, who lost her mind in grief. I told you what the flowers meant."

"You shocked me. I will never forget the violets." He took my hand and spun the moon ring around my finger. "What did the columbines mean?"

"Faithfulness." He raised to kiss me and laid his head in my lap, alongside the child he dreamt into existence. "I also think Clarinda sounds like a name for a smart poetess who has an affinity for languages and an uncanny ability to grow flowers. The best of both of us."

He talked through me to the child growing inside. "Clarinda. Daughter." Angling his head up to me, he added, "And, if she is a he, not Sylvander, please. John, again?"

"It will be more confusing than it already is if everyone has two names, and some of those names are the same for two different people." I could not help but smile in willing resignation. We would baptize this child with his name if he insisted. "Do you remember when you asked me to be your wife? The first time?" I qualified.

"I knew you would say 'absolutely not,' and never speak to me again. Even though I would have broken had you refused me."

I looked at him, astonished he ever thought such a thing. "I would never have gone to the river if I anticipated saying no to anything you proposed. I waited a whole month for you to light that candle."

He relaxed then, smiling out of one side of his mouth.

"We were beside rolling waters then …" I reminded him.

"Yes, they roared. I felt like I was shouting at you. Tell me what you are thinking."

I hesitated, feared he would think me too romantic, but I spoke regardless. "John Rollin Ridge, and call him Rollin?"

He closed his eyes, thinking, and spoke the name aloud to my belly. "Hmmm. Rollin. Son. Sounds like a diplomat or a president."

"Or a handsome horse-riding poet?" I questioned.

"Or a handsome horse-riding poet," he indulged me.

The following days escaped me, unable to unwind time. John mounted his horse in the early hours of dawn on Sunday morning, and we said goodbye with a lingering kiss. He handed me *Letters to Clarinda* with a new blue ribbon down the page. He smiled and kicked his horse north for New Town.

I opened the page, dated only as 'Sunday evening,' and the faithful columbine fell to my hand, pressed between the pages.

> *'You are an angel, Clarinda: you are surely no mortal that 'the earth owns.' To kiss your hand, to live on your smile, is to me, far more exquisite bliss than any of the dearest favors that the fairest of the sex, yourself excepted, can bestow.'*

CHAPTER 24

Hickory Nuts

Sarah Bird Northrup Ridge

November 1824

Cherokee Nation, Ridge Land

Daylight shortened. In autumn's afternoon dim, Honey and I faced the squirrels for hickory nuts to make *kenuche*. Many nuts filled a broad basket, a result of avid pursuit. We sought more. Once reaching the barren fruit trees beside the riverbed, Honey stripped her boots and knotted the laces together to drape them around her neck. I strolled behind as she tilted forward, now barefoot, to survey the ground with eyes keener than mine. Our sight was practically useless. Dropping leaves masked the nuts, which spanned wide like a man's broad palm. Deep rugs of speckled brown stretched to our ankles. Honey barked, "Ouch," and reached under her toes to clutch one or two for her effort, depositing them in the basket I held.

Honey sang a song with no words, pitched higher than I could sing, pursuing her jaunt under the trees. When she hummed, the crunching under her was predictable percussion. When she quit, leaves swooshing underfoot continued the music hovering around her.

"What is that song, Honey?"

"I's dunno. Just sumefin' I heard from some people in da woods when I's collecting nuts before."

"You went without me?" I inquired.

"When you and Mother Susannah was at church last Sundy … Papa told me to gits outside and not to come back in on his day ta rest. I knews we is gonna make Kenuche, and it takes 400 nuts to dos it right for more dan twos peoples." Honey revealed more than I asked.

"Mr. John mentioned you rarely say much, but you express yourself with little effort to me. Why is that?" I appealed. I hope she would not avoid singing on this topic.

"Papa don't wanna hears me. I figures few man-folk cares what I's gots to say, so I don' talks much round them. I listen, dough. Hear more with my mouth shut, anyway."

"Why does your Papa not want you to talk with him?"

"I's done talking about him, Mz Sarah." She rambled with her head yielding to the wooded floor and eyes downcast. "Ouch," finding her treasure trove, her exclamation echoed from tree trunks.

"Where did you meet those men who taught you the song?"

"Not far from here, up the path about an hour's wandering. But, deys not Cherokee; deys white traders. Deys in skins, like old Cherokee, not in coats with der necks all tied up in da black sashes like Mr. John wear."

"I see." I snickered. Men's fashion saw fit to cinch one up to the chin.

She cracked her cadence and kicked around the leaves surrounding an old hickory tree behind the massive trunk. I followed as she danced. Honey hid behind its years, aged through the ground, protruding with ribs of massive roots.

"I can't feels or sees no more here."

"Then, I guess it's time we go home. We will have to shell these plus the others we've collected in these last weeks."

Shoeless, Honey laughed and skipped ahead of me down the quieter ground of the brown, dirt trail. When I braced the basket on my hip, the child inside me pressed against my belly hard, and I paused a moment.

"You all righ', Mz Sarah?" Honey shouted back to me.

"Yes. Just surprised is all."

"What you stopping fo'?"

"The baby moved. Come here."

When she rushed back, I held her hand and settled it on my growing belly, and either a hand or a foot reached out and brushed her back.

She jerked her hand, "Dat scare me, Mz Sarah. It's gots to hurt."

"No. It does not hurt at all. Whoever is there grows just fine." I exhaled and patted where the baby had just been. It was a modest push, but the baby, most assuredly, wanted its existence noticed.

Honey reacted with timidity, placing her palm back where it rested before.

"Da *osdi* must just be trying to find a good sleeping spot. Doins da circles like Old Babe, mys hound dog, do 'fore she go to sleep." We began our walk back through the trees, but this time, Honey did not bounce ahead; she stayed beside me, taking the basket and resting it on her head. "Maybe she be lookin' for da cool spot? I flips my pillow over and over to find de cool side. Must bees da same thing." Honey smiled at me, proud that she solved the world's grandest mystery.

When we reached the house, I learned *Kenuche* was prepared from both the shells and paste from hickory nuts, and with added hominy, made a hearty soup. Susannah wanted to form the *Kenuche* ball now with the hope to prepare the soup once Major Ridge and John returned from the Council meeting in New Town. Susannah wrapped a handful of nuts in a towel and shattered the nuts into chunks with a hammer. Then, we all ground them, crushing them into mush. It was a struggle. After mashing only a handful, I relaxed back in my chair, stretched my right hand to rub the rigidity from my forearm.

"Shouldn't we separate the shells?" I asked Honey. Neither she nor Susannah seemed to worry about it, but to me, it was disconcerting to crush them. I experienced no other recipe where the shell cooked alongside the nutmeat, not to mention the arduous task of grinding the shells into a pulp.

"Nos. We will run it through a basket before wes puts in da hominy and get the big bits out. It won't hurt nuthin' to leaves them in there now." Honey translated my question to Susannah, who chuckled at my desire to shell each nut, thinking it more work and perceiving the difficulty from experience.

As we proceeded through the basket, Susannah held them in her palm and threw others in the fireplace. The longer we ground, the more she fired.

"Why is she wasting those?" I asked Honey.

"Des rotten," Honey said with casualness.

Now, counting an imperceptible number, I estimated how many rotten nuts I ground previously, perhaps ruining the entire ball of pulp. I murmured my own harsh judgment, and Susannah smiled from her pot and pestle. Susannah communicated to Honey, who reported she had worked through the ones I ground, appreciating I could not tell the difference. Susannah passed me one she was about to burn and encouraged me to hold one from my bundle and the other in each palm. I did so, contrasted, and understood what she knew. The rotten ones were lighter.

After an hour, we halted for cider, and Mother Susannah spoke a request to Honey. Honey bounced out the door in customary fashion, leaving dusky light and brisk air in at her flight. From the sunlight, I recognized the hour near 4:00. I sighed, knowing, by this time, John would not arrive home today.

I rose and lit the candles at the center of the table as we returned to our task, but Honey had not yet returned. Unable to know what errand Susannah assigned her, and with Susannah's repeated looks out the window and at the closed door, I imagined Susannah intended Honey's task to be brief. We broke the last of the nuts in the basket, and Susannah rolled the compact balls of nutmeat and shells together in a vast ball, extending in girth past her rolling palms. She slathered it in pork grease, picked up a basket that could accommodate its size, topped it with skins, and set it outside near the door to preserve.

We ate chicken stew and lingered. I scrubbed the dishes, watching the approaching darkness, feeling the chill of the evening. Susannah moved to the doorway, snatched her shawl, and spanned the green to Old Saul's shelter near the stables. An animated exchange began between the two as I blotted water from the last of our dishes. He shoved lighter palms into the air in frustrated vehemence. Afterward, she crossed up the trail where Honey and I walked this afternoon. Did she send Honey after more hickory nuts? Susannah knew these woods; she would find Honey in no time.

I drew my shawl and passed through the field to our apartment. With a last glance across the orchard, I freed the door and lit my evening candle. I recited one final prayer this day, '*For the son of man came to seek and to save the lost.*'

Dawn struck with a gray light permeating through rain showers. Fire vanished in the night, and the room became frigid to any extremity passing beyond the nest of warmth under the covers. I donned my wool stockings first. Honey never arrived. Dressed, I spanned the field to Susannah's home. A Cherokee rode up to the residence and secured his horse to the post near the stables. He crossed perpendicular to me. Both of us would reach the gate simultaneously, maintaining our current paces.

He wore buckskin trousers and a coat. His head was crimson, and his hair rolled under a turban. His brown tunic, copper at the collar, closed with a green sash knotted around his waist. Curious, I wondered whether he spoke English.

"Can I help?" His expression faltered and then covered the shock at my appearance. He was a newcomer.

"Yes, ma'am." He bowed at the waist, tucking his hands behind his back. His English was reluctant but not new.

"My name is John Arch. I travel with Missionary Buttrick from Brainerd, Tennessee, come to see whether Major Ridge has returned from the council meeting."

"Sadly, no. Neither men have returned. Would you like to speak to Mrs. Ridge?"

"Yes, please. Forgive my ignorance. Who are you?"

"I'm Sarah Ridge, John's wife. Let us go inside where we can talk—not remain here shivering. We can cook breakfast while attending to your news."

He masked dismay with courtesy, and his expression was one I was altogether familiar. Once looking at him, Mother Susannah embraced Mr. Arch as he entered the kitchen. She knew him in full measure, a boy's face embedded in the man. Their talk volleyed back and forth as she sat him down, touching his shoulders. Across from me at the table, we fixed plates with floured biscuits, dusty with brown tops. Inside were two broad strips of bacon, fat dripping from lengthy pieces extending outside the bread's constraints. We ate together before any other remarks were directed to me. Mr. Arch was hungry, as was I.

"I went to school with your husband, Mrs. Ridge, at Brainerd," he said.

"Have you continued your studies, Mr. Arch?"

"Yes. I am a missionary now, seeking to transform Cherokee souls into lives committed to our Savior. How did you and John meet?"

"In Connecticut, my father was the steward at the Foreign Mission School he attended. He took ill and stayed with us for a year so that we could care for him."

"John took ill when he was at Brainerd when we were younger. His coughing became fierce, and he tired easily. I remember when his parents arrived to bring him home."

"His hip scrofula still pains him, although his limp is small."

"I am pleased he is well. Susannah said one of your slaves seems to have strayed too far from home." Susannah refilled his cup.

"You could not find her?" I stood and stammered with shock, "She didn't come home last night?" I said to Susannah, knowing she would not understand.

"Since I must wait for Major, I would be happy to assist in the search for her."

"I will go with you." I pushed my chair aside, determined. Mr.

Arch hesitated but translated my sentence; I assumed with his additional opinion on the matter to Mother Susannah. She raised a disconcerted gesture with both palms. Hands seized my small but growing belly while her head swayed in protest.

I urged them both, pointlessly in English, "Honey spent one night away; we must find her. I will go. Old Saul is here. John and Major Ridge will be home soon."

Mr. Arch stood, "Perhaps, in your condition ..."

"I will be fine, Mr. Arch. Honey is a timid girl. She will not recognize you and will not speak with you. You'll require me to recover her."

He translated my plea, and Mother Susannah nodded, but her hands remained on her future grandchild, who touched her back through my skin. It seemed as if they both felt one another, understanding today's task: Honey. Susannah left the kitchen, climbed the staircase, and returned with a buckskin jacket, bordered with sheep's fleece and a red sash, wrapping each around me. Mr. Arch finished his coffee while we packed a knapsack with cornbread sliced through with the remaining bacon from breakfast kept warm inside and some cheese. She handed him two flasks to fill with water. Although she made no contention of approval, she accepted my heartfelt obligation.

"We will return before sundown." I followed Mr. Arch to the stable and called back my farewell.

"*Heyatahesdi,*" was Susannah's cautionary advice.

Mr. Arch replied that he would ensure our safety, and we would return as soon as we could. I hoped he was right. This day began in broken shards without Honey, partial in pattern with seams unmendable.

My transfixed eyes surveyed the path as we assumed a comfortable pace, I, on foot, and Mr. Arch ahead on his horse. Signs—a footprint, a broken limb—nothing seemed out of the ordinary. Our direction lay past the hickory grove, and the rolling waters rushed into my ears as the wind cut some of my hair from my hat; it would be a brisk day, colder than the last.

"What does she look like?" He turned his head to inquire from the sauntering sways of his horse.

"Who?" Absentminded, I focused my eyes on the ground.

"Honey, the slave girl we're searching for…" He retorted, astonished with my misunderstanding.

"I'm sorry. I am so preoccupied. I should have explained. Honey wore a blue cotton dress. Her hair is in spindles all over her head with multicolored ribbons tied around each one."

"Color will make her easier to find. How old is she?"

"She is ten, or so she believes. To me, she is Heaven sent. I owe her a great deal."

"Mrs. Ridge, let me assure you if she is within five miles of this farm, we will find her."

"I sincerely pray so, Mr. Arch."

A rocky incline guarded my left, and the steep riverbank descended on my right. The horse carrying Mr. Arch walked ahead of me. I could see his turban and brown jacket and shoulders above the half-leaved tree skirts of yellow and red. The incline caused me to slow, as did my constant survey of the ground, searching for anything not belonging. Jagged terrain bolstered me on the ascending trail. I cut the palm of my hand on a shrewd bit of stone that jutted out from the rock face.

My voice caused Mr. Arch to twist. He dismounted and lifted my palm to study where blood appeared and dripped off my palm. Surprised at seeing my blood, my energy drained where I stood. Helpless, I sat with my bleeding hand cradled in my lap. I took out my handkerchief to bind the wound. It stung but would be much sorer tomorrow. If I used the hand much, I would continually reopen the cut.

"Remain here," he urged and drifted down the steep bank adjacent to the river. I could not see him fully. He searched.

Dizzy, I sealed my eyes. When he surfaced from the depth, he climbed with hands and feet back up the bank carrying the stalk of a plant. Peeling the handkerchief from my wound, he placed the only green remaining on the brown yarrow against the blood and wrapped it anew.

"This will stop the bleeding. Well, it works when the buds are open." I was unsurprised by his knowledge of healing plants. "Can you continue?" he asked.

I assured him I could. He held his hand to assist my rise. Cradling my injury, I gripped his outstretched hand with an upside-down grasp. We propelled forward with thoughts of Honey. Mr. Arch walked beside me and held his horse's reins, whipping them on his thigh as we wandered.

Fresh horse's shoe prints darted across the earth under my feet in surfaced indentations, where few had been before. An intersecting path extended down from the wood perpendicular and joined this one. Near the intersection, where a pine tree trunk collapsed over in one storm's blast or another, we found black boots tied together slung into the brush.

"She has been here," I exclaimed.

"Why would she take off her boots?" Arch inquired.

"Grasping hickory nuts with her toes, although I doubt she lost the shoes intentionally." With newly gained knowledge, I distressed with the unthinkable.

"The brush is flat here, but no hickory tree grows nearby," Mr. Arch remarked and tromped up the hill, shouting Honey's name.

He stood above me. "I see nothing else out of the ordinary, Mrs. Ridge."

"Sure?" I asked.

"Nothing," he mumbled with foreboding at the absence of any other marker.

"We must continue." I was undaunted, even as I sought to catch my breath. "She walked this path."

"Yes, ma'am. That may be true." He hid the same suspicion I avoided.

The wind sliced through us, aimed against our faces. The light of day shadowed into dusk. Holding Honey's shoes in one hand and my white handkerchief in the other, my worry became heavier than anything I carried.

Mr. Arch sensed my slowing pace and found an insignificant spot in the timbers where flat ground allowed us to build a fire. He secured his horse to a nearby persimmon and began gathering kindling. I rolled out the blanket Susannah packed and rested atop one and exhaled, thinking of my broken promise to return tonight. My swollen feet squeezed in my boots. Proper or not, my shoes had to come off, albeit troublesome to accomplish with one hand.

"Let me help you." Arch stood at my feet and yanked off my boots after undoing the laces. My woolen feet retreated under my dress in modesty.

"Thank you, sir. I appreciate it. I just need a few minutes, and we can begin again."

"No, Mrs. Ridge. It is best if we halt for the night."

I untied the makeshift bandage on my hand, and the bleeding stopped. I unpacked the rations I carried, handing cornbread to Mr. Arch.

"Thanks be to God." After the brief prayer, he ate the slice and drained his canteen.

"Amen." I filled the quiet. "Thanks likewise to God for your generosity in escorting me. Other duties must occupy your time. I'm sure you did not set out to eat cornbread in the woods, searching for Honey."

"No, ma'am. I had no other task other than to find Major Ridge and wait for Missionary Buttrick." He smiled at me. "I'm pleased to be of service to you." He bowed in emphasis.

Turning on his heels, he lit the fire with gathered kindling. "I grew up in these mountains, north of here. Now that I am in service to God, there is little time spent among His creation. I study and try to bring salvation to the Cherokee people. I have not been home since the spring."

"That is a shame, Mr. Arch, to be inside so much. I love to be outside. If I could find a seed, I could grow God's garden. I've always had dirt under my nails and good at that, if not at other things."

"I'm sure that is not true, *Say ge*." I do not know whether he meant familiarity or whether it was an accident. He waited for my response.

"I'm called that here." I could only reply with the truth, although it felt too informal for this man I had known only a single day.

"You must call me John."

His smile made his hope obvious.

"No, I couldn't do that." I turned away. I appreciated his help.

"As you please."

Under the frame of fall leaves, what moonlight showed through was hampered more. It would take several more storms and wind to bare the trees for winter. We ate in silence, tempered by the popping of pine on the fire. Before I knew it, darkness encircled us. I could not find my way home alone.

"I will find more wood for the fire. Say … Mrs. Ridge." He stood above me and made his adjustment back to the minister's manners and proper Methodist decorum.

He leaned back against the sycamore trunk and sat underneath it. "It was a tree like this that smoked when the Thunderers lit the first fire. Has John shared the legend?"

"No, he hasn't." Similarities between Cherokee myth and Christian stories fascinated me.

"The brothers of Thunder sent lightning to fire a sycamore when the world was cold. Bear led a council to decide which animal was best to bring the fire across the water. Raven's feathers were once like the rainbow—translucent, but when sent to retrieve the fire, he flew over the sycamore, and they singed black. He could not bring the fire.

"James and John asked the Lord, 'Do you want us to call fire down from Heaven?'

"An owl tried to provide warmth for the council animals, but fire seared his eyes, now white around orange irises. A snake tried and also failed to return the fire. He darts, backtracking like he's still confined.

"'If I am a man of God, may fire come down from heaven and consume you and your fifty men.' Elijah."

"The last animal attempting to bring fire to warm the animals was a water spider. She was small but could swim. She spun a bowl onto her back, skirted across the water, and transported an ember from the blazing tree. Hot coals warm us today because of the bravery of the small water spider.

"John answered them all, 'I will baptize you with water. But one who is more powerful than I will come, the straps of whose sandals I am not worthy to untie. He will baptize you with the Holy Spirit and fire.'"

"Even the weak have strength we often overlook." He paused in thought. "This one night in the woods, and then, I fear, I must escort you home. It isn't safe."

"I understand," I said, needing to do as much as I was able. "We can search again in the morning, and with God's guidance, find her, but we will turn back at noon if we cannot do so."

"Agreed." Changing the subject, he asked with his back to the fire, undoing his blanket from the saddle, "When is your baby due to arrive?"

"February, I think. First children are often late, or so I am told."

"I am the oldest of my siblings." He handed me a blanket from his saddlebags. "And often late."

Guilty for accepting his gift of extra warmth, I fell into an uncomfortable sleep. I dreamt of singed feathers on raven wings and red stripes on the backs of courageous water spiders.

At dawn, I roused suddenly from sleep, hearing a sound not belonging to any animal. Mr. Arch lay across the fire from me, curled into a ball, his turban unraveled to reveal long black raven hair. I rose to complete my necessaries, spreading his blanket across his slumbering form, and sought my privacy. As I paddled through the scrub and noisy leaves, I heard a moan. I stopped my feet's clamoring and took notice.

The sound was high-pitched and echoed, like sound trapped in a jar. It continued, but words were indiscernible. It increased, and suddenly, another voice was masked—a male's voice—distant and heavier, answering the earlier wail in harsher tones.

I returned and woke Mr. Arch, notifying him of my discovery.

"Show me where you were."

He followed me to the spot, and we both listened. With the rock face and topography, Mr. Arch assumed the voice came from our right. It was where the noise would have flown the straightest distance.

"Let's continue the course and pay as much attention with our ears as with our eyes."

I was hesitant to withdraw. The trail encircled the woodland where we passed the night. I prayed to hear the voice again, Honey's voice.

Fresh boot prints darted in the road, with streaks, as if toes were dragged. Voices around a blind bend caused a commotion into the forest, although their words were still indiscernible. Mr. Arch kicked ahead to force our introduction to the men.

"Remain here, Mrs. Ridge," he instructed.

"If Honey is there, I need to go. She will not know you. She won't talk to you."

"But these men might. Give me a few minutes. I'll break with them and come to get you if she's there. Stay here."

Begrudging, I followed his directions. I paced with my palms on my back, stretching my coat tighter around my growing waistline, staring at the swollen red cut on my hand.

Another man on horseback approached, packed with pans that clanked together on his saddlebags. There was nowhere to hide between the steep rock face and the deep slope of the embankment. Forced, I followed where Arch's tracks led, my intent not to meet the incoming stranger alone.

Arch had dismounted and was speaking to three white men. Honey sat behind them, blooms undone, gagged, with her hands and feet bound. The men remained around their weak fire with liquor bottles beside them, more than I could count with a transitory look. Tattered and shapeless hats corralled long, dirty hair, disguising their dirt-smeared faces. One man rose from the ground only to crouch, arching his back in what seemed an accustomed posture, but would bring pain to most.

Arch gestured to Honey with reins in his hands. “We sent her on an errand days ago, and she must have lost her way this far from home.” Arch put his arm around me, feigning to be my husband. Reassured by the lie, I dared not speak. The clanking of pans behind us drew closer.

The crouching man answered, clawing at his chest, renewing a hole in his shirt produced by a similar itch. Behind us appeared the pan man, who tied his horse after his feet slapped the earth. He gazed at us, attempting to read our intent. His eyes tracked back to the others. The third man remained behind his hat, curled across the ground, reluctant.

His hat spoke from near the smoking fire, “Well, she’s ours now. Can get close to two hundred fer a Cherokee-speaking slave.” After making his intentions known, he reached for the whisky bottle beside him and angled it to his mouth. After finding only drops, he swung his legs to stand. He was shorter than I assumed when reaching full height, uncoiling from his bed on the dirt.

Arch said, “She’s ours. Please untie her, and we will leave you in peace.”

The Man in the Hat said, “Not likely.” His voice was like impenetrable, hypnotic smoke. I was nauseous at his breathing.

We had nothing of value to exchange for Honey’s life. The crouching man agreed with a grunt, as did the pan man, who closed in behind us.

The pan man pulled Arch’s hand from around my back, and I stepped aside with the intrusion. “This Cherokee ain’t your husband. No white woman would have no Cherokee man, no woman worth anything, and you look worth somethin’. He holding you against your will? Force himself on you and make you have his baby?” He called out each subsequent question, and by the last, he howled.

Arch found no words, nor did I. When I turned around, the two men stood in front of us, and the stench doubled.

Their inference was inaccurate. Although, nothing I might say would be deprived enough to convince them to understand. Nothing would contradict their present assumptions and desires. I could not argue at all.

Arch interrupted my reticence. "You can have my horse. Should yield you close to a hundred if you sell her." He must have talked before thinking, as his horse must have been his grandest possession in the world. He did not know Honey or me much either.

The Man with the Hat took it off and rubbed his skull under greasy blond hair. He favored Archibald Cooper in skin tone and attitude, but he looked whiter, paler, if such a thing could exist, with pearly blue eyes, unaccustomed to the light. "What kind of man would I be to leave behind this woman with you, Cherokee? I'll trade you the mare for the slave, but it is my Christian obligation to take this white woman. She don't belong with you." He seized my arm and thrust me behind him.

The pan man behind Arch unsheathed a blade from his waistline and gripped it between Arch and himself at eye level. He snickered at his upper hand, strode over to Honey, knelt, and positioned the knife between her eyes. Barefoot and terrified, she froze, eyes bulging red. He reached around her and slid the blade between the rope crisscrossed between her hands and cut the other, tied around her ankles. He left the gag in her mouth, and she scurried backward away into a nearby tree trunk, stopping her escape a few feet from the knife-wielder.

"Honey, come; this man will carry you home." Honey skirted the circle of the camp to the path. She and Arch retreated, keeping a wary eye on the men. Her last look to me was painful. Arch shook his head, rejecting my resolution. But, I made the choice nonetheless.

"I am the water spider," I said while Arch and Honey faded down the bank to the river. They left the water spider alone, swimming across treacherous waters with the world's warmth on my back.

CHAPTER 25

Shoe Boots

John Ridge

November 1824

New Town and Ridge Land

He entered wearing tall boots with tassels on each outer side, like Hessian mercenaries enlisted by the British during the American Revolution. Adorned in what he perceived as formal attire, his open military coat shouldered epaulets over an old hunting shirt. White hair on his chest peered beneath his open collar, covering Shoe Boots' taut and leathery skin. After entering, he raised his head, displaying his wrinkled face, masking suspicious eyes with forehead creases deep, aged by tribulation. The heavily armed man carried two horse pistols and a commanding knife at his side. Tall and trim, he wore a towering hat from 1812, with an immense red plume. He crouched to cross the doorway to preserve the hat's salute atop his head.

"Major, old friend. We find each other on different sides. You talk instead of fight, and I stand where I always have."

"Captain."

Shoe Boots cleared his throat and quietly addressed Ross at the podium in the front of the room.

"I seek citizenship for my wife, Doll, and our three children.

Doll was my slave, and now she is my wife. I fought for Cherokee my entire life. I stand with the people now. I oversee a farm of many acres and fund Cherokee education. I encourage missionaries to teach the Christian God. This, I ask. I want them all to be free citizens of Cherokee Nation. What property I have, how can I think of them having bone of my bone and flesh of my flesh and still called property?"

Father told stories of how Shoe Boots killed a man because he would not sing for him, how his tomahawk was red with Cherokee anger, how his captives suffered, even eaten. However, he was a staunch warrior, feared by his enemy, and yet a friend to the Gambolds at Brainerd and Spring Place Missionary School.

Ross recited the recent legislation regarding intermarriage between Cherokee and slave, prohibited, punishable by fifty-nine lashes and a fine.

"I have other children lost. Married twice before. Once to a Cherokee woman who died. Once to white woman, Clarinda, my captive, and at last to Doll, my slave. No children grew in Cherokee woman. Three children left with white woman back to Kentucky and will not return. Doll's children are mine. Heirs to my estate and farm. Only children that remain."

The name made me look up from the parchment in front of me. While Shoe Boots spoke, Elias tore a sheet of paper and wrote a single word across the scrap: "Sarah." I understood his intention and worry. Without more exact specifications, the law would consider children from our union by their lowest common denominator. It would not be their white heritage that dictated their opportunities; it would be their Cherokee ancestry, my culture. Would they be inferior to the whites, perceived savage, as I was in Connecticut, or valued because of their white mother?

He said his white wife took their three children back to American soil and refused to return. Would Sarah do the same? If she found the Cherokee too violent, and would she become too fearful to remain among us? Would she leave me? My thoughts ran to the greatest of fears.

Father interrupted and stood as speaker to address Shoe Boots, his friend, eye to eye. "*Shoe Boots, I know you as you do me. We will consider your request. Give the council a moment to discuss what questions we may have for you and to speak together before we vote.*"

Ross concurred and offered a recess to the representatives present from each designated district, although no one followed Shoe Boots outside. With Shoe Boots' request, our decision would immediately test the law. Could it stand, hold itself firm? Would we hold this man accountable for a decision made in another time? Again, we would reconsider, replaying the argument against the same walls: blood, heritage, ancestral rights, and white perception.

Behind Shoe Boots, a protracted silence sustained. One man cleared his throat; another lit a pipe and shouldered the window. No one left the room during the recess except the man asking us to display weakness in our judicial obligations to uphold the law and give value to slaves where whites held little.

I stood, placing my hands upon the gray table, gathering papers in front of me. *"I do not know whether I can speak to this any longer. I need to recuse myself from this conversation entirely. Let the council do what it believes to be right."* I stood then, handing Elias' scrap of paper to Father, and tried to exit the courthouse.

Ross stopped me in English, insisting I stay. "The question is whether Cherokee Nation will continue its tradition of matriarchal lineage or whether we adjust to the ways of the whites and have a patriarchal line of ownership for wealth and property."

"Slaves are property and not persons." Rich Joe Vann spoke from his family's vast wealth and his father's notable indiscretions. His own drunken father's affairs with slaves and their violent abuse were widely known. Perhaps Vann had more kin on his plantation than he knew. The practice was more common than one might suspect. Rich Joe Vann's father was the first to transfer money and property to his son rather than his wives. At twelve years old, Rich Joe inherited his nickname.

Ross interjected. "Property that can bear more property … Shoe Boots means to make these half-slave, half-Cherokee children equal citizens."

"Shoe Boots' wealth supports Missionary School efforts. Can we afford not to grant his children citizenship? If denied, what if he pulls financial support for the schools?" Father's intuition hinted that Shoe Boots would do precisely this if his requests were denied. In Father's opinion, Shoe Boots sought payment for debts owed for a lifetime of warrior's sacrifices.

Elias stood to present his opinion on the claim. *"What would the Cherokee Nation look like to whites if we granted freedom and citizenship to slaves? Whites might disrespect us even more than they do now. If half-Cherokee, half-slave children can own property, what might stop the massive immigration of runaway slaves from American land to immigrate to Cherokee Nation, seeking freedom? Georgia would abolish our law and overtake us if that were to occur."*

Ross then spoke, "If we grant this, we establish a precedent contradictory to our law."

I turned around, standing with my hand on the brass knob, and faced Ross, my friend and our elected leader. *"The law did not exist when he entered into this 'marriage' with his slave woman, Doll. If we punish all those who committed acts prior to our written laws, we impose a punishment before they knew it wrong to commit the transgression. Do we punish polygamists? Do we call back those who sold our land against our better judgment and restrain them to a tree for lashings? We cannot hold the man accountable for the broken law—one he did not understand when he entered this common marriage with her. Neither is she to blame; she did what her master commanded of her. Do we punish the children for the sins of the father?"*

Mumbles ran through the crowd. Father stood between his protégé, Ross, and his nephew and son, torn between setting an example and upholding his vote. Father's debate continued, considering Shoe Boots' funding of Cherokee education and his unborn grandchildren's citizenship. Justice's scales tilted and would balance or falter, based upon the decision today.

Hicks spoke, *"This council meeting has extended past six weeks already. These characterizations require more thought; however, I also believe that we cannot hold a man accountable for new laws."* My father nodded, seeking a similar compromise.

"*Agreed*, agreed," reverberated voices bounced in two languages among these new, upstanding walls.

Ross spoke above the crowd's noise of indiscernible mumbles of assertion and denials. "If we set this criterion for dissolving the matriarchal line of inheritance, then we are adopting a pattern that may give us more influence with whites commissioners sent to negotiate with us. It may likewise prevent whites from marriage into Cherokee clans in hopes of stealing the land from its daughters. Although, our women will protest this change."

Vann spoke, knowing of my marriage to Sarah and Elias' plans to marry a white woman as well. *"What about white women's intermarriage to Cherokee men?"*

Elias replied, *"What would they stand to gain in the minds of their own people?"*

"Mockery, insult, reproach, and cruelty." It outraged me to say so, but Sarah experienced it because of her devotion to me. Harriet and Elias would likely see worse treatment.

Ross walked down from the platform and stood among the representatives to arrange the vote and speak its verdict. He invited Shoe Boots to re-enter. There were only six of us standing in the room: Father, Ross, and I, Elias, Vann, and Shoe Boots, six points on a star, deciding its trajectory, one to soar or fall. Winning the majority, we exempted Shoe Boots from the law, his children gaining immunity. Therefore, here rest a precedent that Cherokee children, although only half Cherokee, could be accorded citizenship. However, we now differentiated between children of black mothers and white mothers.

At the conclusion of the day, council business was done. Elias returned home with Father and me. It rained, making the three-hour ride from New Town much longer. Horseshoes sank into puddles making deeper indentations on the road. Our black coats did not repel the water as buckskins would. Elias said little, considering another obstacle between him and Harriet, one he would likely share in a letter this very evening. Father sought comfort, knowing that he stood right by his old friend, Shoe Boots. But, I worried. Our child's future would be limited by its skin color, bound within Cherokee Nation's geographical lines. It was another reason to fight harder for sovereignty.

Once we turned south, I could no longer ride at the sluggish pace our thoughts dictated. Contemplative and contentious, my thoughts argued their particular agenda, opposing each one that came before it. Some thoughts turned more progressive with the Cherokee Nation's reputation and our sovereignty. Allowing slaves onto Cherokee land to marry and seek freedom for their children would be humane and Christian. However, by doing so, we might squander our growing reputation with the whites, emphasizing their distaste and doubt inherent in the whites' minds already.

However, we wrote a law, signed a law: Slaves were not free on Cherokee land, and future children bred between slaves and Indians would not be free either. We followed the guidance of the White Fathers, although I questioned which wolf they fed.

During Jefferson's political years, he wanted white and Native peoples to merge, to develop into one. Would he have not also pursued liberation for generations of his slaves? Could he not realize the paradox of philosophy in his declaration that "all men are created equal"? I assume he undertook one battle at a time, first freedom for America, then freedom for all who walked on its land. Could Jefferson condemn mixed-blood children created but disregarded, as whites viewed the Cherokee?

We must protect Jefferson's ideal and the innocents, a product of a blended people. However, I could not guarantee my child's future in the world of whites. There were too many unknowns and too many old perceptions growing like wild vines at the wide base of ancient trees in this new America.

We could protect them, my children, on Cherokee land, with Cherokee sovereignty. With my resolution made and a year to draft the law, I would propose that children of white mothers and Cherokee fathers would become Cherokee citizens. With our sovereignty, the law regarding half-slave and half-Cherokee could be overturned, based on Shoe Boots' precedent. With compromise set in my mind, I kicked into a run and left Elias and Father to breathe in the rain. I needed to talk to my wife. She had to know, although this navigated tumultuous waters between us.

I arrived home to find our apartment dark, so I rode on to the stables to shelter my horse and walked across the orchard's border to my parent's home. I stood in the entryway, dripping from November's chill, meeting concerned faces. Honey hung her head low, wrapped in Mother's arms. Angry heads leaned against the mantle by the parlor's fireplace. Reverend Buttrick held a hand on a stranger's shoulder with comforting consolation. The scene's hush brought my apprehension, as did Sarah's missing presence.

Mother left Honey's side to remove my wet coat. She held her stiff hands against my cheeks.

"Skahtlelohskee, come warm yourself, and I will tell you what has happened."

"Tell me now," I demanded.

"It is a long tale. Come sit by the fire." She gestured to the chair near the orange blaze.

"Where's Sarah?" I insisted.

"Skahtlelohskee, this is Arch. Do you remember him from Brainerd? He has been a friend to us these last days." I nodded at a faint remembrance of John Arch. Ages had passed since I attended Brainerd. Why was he here? Mother escorted me to greet him. Her

tone brought an unknown fear, one I expected to grieve soon enough.

"Mother, where is Sarah?"

"White squatters took her, my son."

I could not form words.

Honey came to stand between my dripping feet in her shift and robe.

She pulled my hand down, asking me to sit by the fire. I looked into her eyes as she spoke in tearful hiccups. "It bees my fault, sir. I's the one who stays out too late getting the hickory nuts. I's the one who did not runs away. I tooks my shoes off. I's the one that let dems gets to me."

"Who are you talking of, Honey?"

"Dem white men. Mz Sarah and Mista Arch comes to find me, and dey did. Mista Arch trade da horse for Mz Sarah and me, but they think Mz Sarah not want to bes with no Indian, so deys keeps her and gives me back. Mr. Arch, he gave dem his horse as swaps fer me."

I held her by both arms to steady myself and curbed her wandering feet. "Who were these men, Honey?"

"Dems white traders. I's meet dem up de road a patch 'bouts a week or so ago. Deys singing songs about luvin' women wid the blacks hair, and I follows da songs. Dey all smells like whiskey. Dey is mean, mean as snakes and just as full of poisons." Honey cried, and Mother wrapped her in the calico of her skirt. Mother looked at me, unmasking the alarm she shielded from this child.

"Honey, what did they do before Sarah and Arch found you?" I did not want to ask her to recall the memory, but I had to know my enemy.

"Dey drug me behinds a horse on da rope and talk about goins to sell whiskey to da Creeks."

"Is that all they did? Tie you up to take you with them?" I asked too quickly, too harshly.

"Day say dat dey gonna use me up and sell me. Don' wants to say no mo'."

"I need to know to help find Ms. Sarah, Honey. No one is angry with you. None of this is your fault." I spoke calmer, an act against my spirit.

"Da Man with the Hat hurts me bad. Da pulls up my dress, sos I couldn't see. I cries and cries, screams, and, no one hears. I is so sorry, Mr. John. I loves Mz Sarah. I dos." Tears ran in ashy streaks down her face.

Buttrick took hold of Honey and prayed over her hair, spiraling and curling over her bent head.

"John, the Lord will judge them," Reverend Buttrick warned.

"She is my life. Mine to love, mine to protect. 'To me, belongeth vengeance, and recompense; their foot shall slide in due time: for the day of their calamity is at hand, and the things that shall come upon them make haste.'"

"Where's your father?" Mother asked in quiet tones.

"He and Elias will be here soon. They were right behind me."

"I'm going now. Send them after me when they arrive." I stood to find my way back into the rain.

"*Wait for them. Eat. Change clothes. Fill your quiver. Prepare."* Mother knew what I might have to do, and her reminder was her consent.

"I'm going with you. I'll take you to where they were. They won't be there now." Arch knew they'd take Sarah from Cherokee land.

I nodded. I forced myself up the stairs, gripping indentations on the wood of the stair rail. Numb, my heart beat a forgotten song, one of painted faces and war parties: a history we could not leave behind, as it was still necessary. I screamed and shook the windows. Savage.

I changed clothes and returned, stripping away my education and white customs. My knowledge of the forest, Uncle Wattie's stories, and Father's lessons flooded me back to my childhood senses. The rain stopped while I waited for Father and Elias to arrive.

When I stepped into the kitchen, Reverend Buttrick sat in silent prayer at the kitchen table. Father and Elias arrived, and Mother told them their night was not through. Elias stuttered, but with my rage apparent, as Father put his hand on Elias' lapel to stop his talking. I didn't want to hear one word of patience. Justice was the only English word I knew.

"Are you coming with me?" I asked.

No one answered but left the room with a purpose, change clothes and arming themselves.

Mother had three bowls in front of her. With a pestle, she ground bear grease into bark and berry, praying her ancient prayer. The black paint was for Father, proven in battle. She painted his palms and fingers with the color, and he covered his mouth with his hands, transferring the print on his face. Father had won monumental victories with gun, bow, tomahawk, and hands. Elias and Arch painted green diagonal lines across their foreheads to endure the road ahead, watchful. Mother covered my eyelids, across the bridge of my nose, from temple to temple in red.

Father spoke, *"As a warrior, I will stand tall, as this has become my destiny."*

Arch followed, *"I hear the cries of the ancient ones, calling me to protect all that is sacred."*

Then Elias said, *"I will share the truth, what is right to remain forever free."*

"On this red road laid before me, I will keep my head to the sky if I must die."

We left, armed by the Great Spirit, and rode bareback on fresh horses, following Arch up the ridge, disappearing among the trees.

What would come followed what had been.

CHAPTER 26

The Bluff

Sarah Bird Northrup Ridge

November 1824

Cherokee Nation Territory, West of Ridge Land

After Honey and Arch were out of my sight, the three white squatters began packing their encampment. I remained still, remembering where I was but watching them. A sapling, bent and off-centered, stood as a weak sentry to their campfire beside a great river rock soaking heat from the sunlight. Behind them stood an oak whose protruding and outstretched limbs spread apart from the woodland by feet. Damaged and marred from some disease or creature, the tree was weak and shunned. Limbs held three horses' reins.

The men threw glass bottles into the thicket after coiling their gray blankets. Whitmore, the name the squatters called him, wore breeches too small for his robust belly. Exposing a rim of hairy skin, his stomach protruded from beneath his shirt. He tugged up his trousers from the middle of his rear and groaned each time he stooped to grab a blanket or a bottle. A yellow stripe of military trousers stressed the second man's height. This man did not utter any words but snickered with an airy, artificial laugh to mask his awkwardness. The last man, the one in the hat, seemed to hide his eyes. White blond hair jutted out from the brim on the sides, sheltering his profile from my sight. He rose last, and facing his horse, assisted the others only by breathing.

I did not know whether I could recognize this place again. The forest's picture changed with the chilled winds of fall. Leaves masked the ground and crinkled, crushing under their boot soles. My hand plunged into my pocket. I still had the bloodied handkerchief from the gash made yesterday on the rock face. I could leave it here; leave myself some sign to find the path home. John remained at the council meeting. He would not learn of my capture for days. Arch must bring him here. The anxiety of not delivering our baby at home made me short of breath, and I coughed to cover anxious wheezing bought on by the thought.

At my sound, the Man with the Hat turned and stepped towards me, halting short of the fire between us. His smirk was visible as he undid the buttons on his pants. I hastily turned my back, hearing him urinating on the fire to extinguish it. He snickered at my modesty.

"You've seen a man naked before, based on your condition. I have more to show you than that Cherokee who had you." His voice was satin and slippery, tenor and tenacious.

"What are you going to do with me?" I whispered. I do not know whether he heard me, as it took him three or four of my steamy breaths to answer.

"I don't rightly know yet. But, I gather you're more valuable alive than dead, so rest easy on that assurance." His sarcasm was rancorous, devoid of any Godly consciousness.

"You can turn around now." I did so without my sight reaching his feet. He wandered to Arch's horse, still next to me. He scoured through the newly-gained saddlebags. Based on what I saw of their camp, I assumed he sought liquor or money. All he found was Arch's blanket and his Bible. One he tossed to me, and the other, he thrust to the ground.

"Don't take no stock in the book where God blesses the slave and shuns the master." He spit and moved across the camp to his horse, stepping through the steaming coals from their campfire. My body was stoic and immobile, even though all I wanted to do was run. He gathered a rope from his horse's saddlebags while I blanketed my shoulders with shaking hands and looped the ends through the tie around the waist of my jacket. Before I could secure it well, he strode back to reach for my arm. With his touch, my spirit separated, stood beside my body, a witness to crimes yet committed. These sins would be against my body; my eyes refused to watch. My spirit must witness it for me.

"I won't run; I can't." I pleaded with a younger voice, one more scared with his grip tightly around my arm. My heart pounded in my breast, making my speech meek. He let his fingers slide down my coat sleeve, only to yank my wrists together and bind them. He unleashed the remaining rope coiled between our feet. I watched it slip and twist as he tied and knotted, estimating the rope's stretch and limits in my mind.

"Now," he countered, testing his knot-work, glaring at me with a cocked head, "I know you won't."

Courage lifted my eyes, watching him walk away. With a backward, assured stride, the Man in the Hat squinted his eyes as he extended the slack of rope, attaching the other end to the pommel of his saddle.

The man in the striped pants came to take Auld's horse's reins, and I thought he would assist me in mounting. Once beside me, he snickered. Sound and air simultaneously escaped through his nose while he pulled Auld's horse to where the other two mounted. I would walk.

Whitmore lead, the man in striped pants followed, and last, looking over his shoulder at me, the Man in the Hat kicked his horse. With the tightening slack in the rope, the tension compelled me to trudge behind them. We moved west. Morning sun was at our backs. Splinters of rope bit into my wrists like thorny shackles.

We trekked for more than an hour with sunlight nearing midday, at its highest point. The sun's rays pushed through the clouds from yesterday's rainstorm. God illuminated me, and I took hope from His gift. Without their eyes on me, I clenched and slackened my fists, spreading the rope but penetrating the flesh of my wrists. I tugged and wrenched, but the slight movement I gained did not free my hands. In front of me, the Man in the Hat whistled. Horses paused, and he dismounted, following the rope back to me. I do not know what made him stop. By the expressions of the others, nor did they. My eyes tracked his uncertain pace and let my hands drop to ease the growing pain in my shoulders.

He unscrewed and lifted a filthy canteen to my mouth. I coughed more water than I swallowed.

"We aren't camping here. We've got to pass over into Creek land. Don't want a hundred Cherokee Injuns on our tail looking for you. Once we get there, no one will be looking." His smug smirk displayed the amusement the plan brought him.

"Have you been to Creek land?" My voice sounded foreign in my ears, as I had been silent for so long.

"Once, recently. Lower Creeks pay better than Upper Creeks for women and whiskey."

I choked on the water as he tilted the canteen again to my mouth. "Do they buy women," I stuttered, "like me?"

"One might—McIntosh, a Creek Chief. You should feel right at home." Unprovoked, he gently undid the tie of my bonnet and tossed it aside to the ground. He gripped my cap, grabbing my hair with it as he threw it. I shook my head away from his grip. His breath was too close, rancid like rotting meat. He stroked my hair with his greasy hand, slipping film and filth over my ear, and hissed. "I haven't decided if I'm giving you up yet. I knew you was red like an apple." His tongue darted from his mouth, stretching spittle from my jaw to the side of my eye.

I pulled away from him, shuttering—indignant and repulsed. He reacted with a blow to my face, causing me to collapse to my knees. For the first time, my witness cried. If tears fell from me now, I would lose my ability to think. For the sake of the baby growing inside me,

I could not afford to be meek. I stood again, with my bound wrists in front of my rounding belly. He touched himself through his pants and shouted back to the unobservant others, "Whitmore, give me that whiskey you bought from Lavender." One side of my face felt numb with cold as if anesthetized with poison, the other heated with the swelling of Hell's branding.

My witness turned her head at Lavender's name, a name we both recognized. George Lavender ran the trading post, granted permission to do so by John's father. Whiskey bought and consumed was a crime on Cherokee land, not that the law would curb any desires of these three. They did not honor Cherokee law or God's laws. The rope's slack tightened as the Man in the Hat stumbled and grabbed the rope to steady himself. He pulled me towards him, laughed, and mounted. I jerked forward behind the pull from the horses.

We plodded onward, up rockier terrain, as the sun shifted to midafternoon. The horse jolted upward, and I stumbled again, trying to climb at the pace the horses set. The rope tightened and snapped, causing me to stumble and fall. My spirit drained with the jolt, but I had to remain conscious. Anticipation fueled each new alert; fear delivered me further. I must stand again.

I concentrated on twisting my hands. My wrists stretched the rough twine, tugging it at right angles. Raw and bleeding, the pain gave way to persistence. Holding my breath and chewing on my lip, one thumb escaped the bindings. Silently exhilarated at the small feat, I cupped my palm, attempting to slide the rest of my hand through the knots and twists. My knuckles were too wide. I glanced up as the men's backs, swinging with the slow swags of their horse's tails, passing a bottle between the three of them at the same tempo. Whitmore and the man in the striped pants kept their eyes on the trail ahead, while the Man in the Hat glared with desire back at me.

I pulled my eyes away from his undressing stare and surveyed the unfamiliar terrain surrounded me, realizing the dangers here were from both man and nature. I desperately wanted to stop moving, even if only for a few moments, but the rope remained tight on my knuckles. Blood dripped down my hand, not only from the rope bindings but from the reopened cut on my palm. Pain reminded me to stay alert, awake. The sun melted beside me, slipping behind pine-topped ridges. Oncoming night brought further jeopardy from the darkness. The Man in the Hat ensured it.

The Man with the Hat laughed and punched striped pants in the arm. He swayed, righting himself with an accompanying snicker. Gray clouds gathered and dropped the temperature faster than the setting sun. My legs shook, weary from tiredness, swollen and numb. Blood from my wrists collected near the rope across my hands, soaking into the hemp and running down my fingers. I watched two more drops fall and flatten on the ground. I wedged my thumb back into the ropes and wriggled my wrist, cutting the skin more. As blood dripped from the open wounds, I smeared it along the rope's lines. I found it easier to move my thumb in and out of the rope's binding with the moisture. I rubbed my wrists together, smearing blood across my hands as much as possible. The blood enabled me to free my thumb and move the rope past my knuckles. With one hand free, I kept my wrists together, so my captors remained ignorant of my attempts to free myself.

My mind wandered with each step; flashes of memory struck me like poses in oil paintings: John speaking in front of the congregation at the church in Cornwall, his gift of the lily bulbs in the canvas sack, how he signed his name, our wedding, forced to hide in the root cellar.

The root cellar… When the mob surrounded our house, we hid and waited for them to search for us elsewhere. With one hand free, I scanned the terrain for some place, any place, to disguise myself, granting me one last choice this day. The Man in the Hat assured me of having no other.

Above us was an outcropping of rock stretching high along the trail, twisting upward. Sounds of the river ran beneath us, falling briskly from the recent rain. My eyes followed dark roots, slinking into embedded earth beside me. The roots masked themselves beneath the brush. Where did they go? Did they find a cave where water might pool?

The men belched and laughed, passing the bottle back and forth. If the squatters kept this pace, they might not notice if I was missing from the end of the rope. I smeared dripping blood from one wrist onto the other, wriggling my still-bound hand to free it. With a spontaneous decision, I released the rope and dashed to slide, feet first, following the roots below.

The drop was further than I expected, and I toppled to my knees, propelled forward when my feet splashed in yesterday's rain. Bleeding hands stopped my fall. I soaked them in the pool of water at my feet and pulled the already bloody handkerchief from my pocket to bind the torn skin of one wrist. My stockings scraped to bloody my shins. I had not thought of the drop. I had not thought about the fall. I had not thought about the dark.

Inside, the air was damp and cold, like frozen frost. The tips of my fingers could still reach the cave's opening, but the last day's light was insufficient to light my path any further than a few steps. My hand grazed the rock face behind my back, and I sat amidst the puddles. I struggled to inhale, to settle where I was, mute, expecting the dreaded eyes and otherworldly voice of Man with the Hat. Tears spilled down my cheeks, in pain from the drop. For now, I was hidden, outside of his reach.

I cupped water from the puddle and patted it on my face, down my neck. Invisible to my captors, my witness joined me, and I became whole. I would wait in this pit of earth and listen. A whippoorwill called the sundown; an owl hooted with melancholy and tender empathy; their sounds echoed off the rock walls. I warmed with their companionship.

I tried to occupy my mind and close my eyes, trying to forgive myself for burying us in this cave. I forced myself to breathe slowly and think about what Arch and Honey would do at home. Arch would be a day's passage behind me. That was the best I could hope. The worst would be to perish from starvation alone in this cave. No. There was a worse outcome: raped, abandoned, found dead. My hands and feet tingled. My breath was too loud. I prayed, *Jesus, please light my way to safety for the innocent baby.* In this moment of prayer, the child inside me spread a hand to mirror mine, laying atop my belly.

Feet darted above me, and I wriggled, pushing my back against the cavern wall and pulling my feet close to my chest. The Man with the Hat never asked my name, and I never offered it. Therefore, he had nothing to call, nothing to yell. Recognizing his oversight, he kicked leaves around the cave opening where I hid. I preferred to starve than to answer him. He did not care who I was, only what color I was and how much whiskey he could carry from trading me to McIntosh. His evil came from what he would take from me, what he wanted to force me to do. Here in the dark, sound gave away the enemy.

He shouted. "Red … You'll show out when you're hungry enough. We'll camp right here. I ain't going nowhere."

His volume varied, as if he walked in circles, sending his snide voice in differing directions. As he spoke, the tone of bustle above me did not cease. Men's voices and horses' whinnies became more distinct as they threw logs, tossed them to make a fire. I smelled salt pork slung on an iron pan, the same one that clanked in front of me as we walked. I salivated and listened to their exchange.

"She ain't gone far. She just hiding." The Man in the Hat's voice.

"I can't find her. Can you?" Whitmore gave a sarcastic reply.

Striped pants laughed.

"Not yet, but I will." The Man in the Hat spoke and swore. Leaves crunched under his boots near the bluff's opening; his legs darted to block the fire's light. His hand came through the void. I covered my mouth to block the sound of my rapid breathing.

"We still got the extra horse," Whitmore said, "even if she's up and climbed a tree."

The comment made him turn and remove his hand from the opening. "She's pregnant. She ain't up no tree, you drunk bastard," he cursed again with the anger my absence ensured.

I could see my hands as long as their fire burned. I prayed with gratitude, trying to focus on the flame's intermittent light on the cave wall and the smell of warmth. I dug my hand into my bag for the last remaining cheese. I only swallowed a bite, hoping the little food would keep my belly quiet for the perpetual night ahead.

Suffocating darkness closed around me. I heard sizzles from the pats of rain. Light dimmed. Enclosed, and with nowhere to flee, the puddle deepened. When the fire's light ceased, I found myself in absolute obscurity.

Startled to consciousness by grunts and dread above, three successive swooping sounds sunk in deeper tones; they came from weapons, not voices. Cursing screams followed from the scuffles of men. Moans of pain swelled in force; leaves and earth fell on my head and in my eyes. A warrior howled while gasps and groans of life left bodies. Then, I heard flapping wings, sparrows taking flight out of the pines into the breaking daylight; blessed dawn arrived.

Arch shouted my name into the trees, coming closer. His voice became more distinct and less distant. Then, it shifted in a single moment. My three white captors fled or—I had no room in this hole for that thought.

"I'm here," and stretched my hand as far as it would reach to the opening, with my fingertips extended. My voice crackled. It was not Arch's hand that reached for me, though; it was John's ringed hand I saw, blood and rain speckling his uncut knuckles. I reached for him.

"I've got her," he shouted confirmation to the others above.

"Are you all right? How did you get in there?" he asked.

"I slid, but I can't get out the way I came. Don't let me go," I begged him.

"Never." It was a single word but assured and decisive.

He must have laid down beside the hole; timid daylight shifted back to darkness. He extended more of his arm, holding out a canteen of water.

I reached further to take it and saw blood extending up to his forearm.

"Are you hurt?" I needed to know. "Are they gone?"

"They are. I am not hurt."

I breathed deeply in the frost and exhaled steam.

John's father's voice sang through the air, chanting an unrelenting melody, absent of rhythm. With a raw fierceness, John joined the song, still holding my hand. What followed was noiseless. Moon-eyed spirits hushed the birds' prayers of grateful retribution.

"Hold on to me; we will get you out. Talk to me," John whispered.

"I'm scared." My breath became thick. With John's touch, one trauma escaped me merely to reinstate within the confines of this space. I managed, "The baby," breath, "is safe," exhale.

He breathed after me with reassured weariness. Major spoke down to him, and John answered back to him in Cherokee. They were devising some kind of plan. One man offered a solution, the other altered it, and an arrangement settled between them.

"I need to let you go." As he did, I stepped forward into the light in his absence to see what I wish I had avoided. The man's hat lay absent its blonde hair. Red spread in a line, seeping around its brim.

"Arch, hold Sarah's hand. I'm going downriver to the larger cave opening and coming in after her." John's feet emerged, kicking the man's empty hat aside.

He crouched to the opening. "Sarah, I know these caverns. It opens larger downhill. There is a slender passage, but only one of us can fit through it. Can you walk? *Dh Ani*, you can do this. Follow my voice."

"Yes, but I can't see," I said, trying to help them understand.

"We will send you down a torch once I enter on the downhill side."

"John ..." I tried to oppose him. His balance was not that of his father's, although not his fault.

"I'm coming after you." There would be no discussion, and I had no other solution to offer.

John let go, and Arch's hand replaced his own.

"Mrs. Ridge," Arch questioned.

"Thank you for returning with my family. Call me *Say ge*," I said upward towards his shadow.

He chuckled. "I'll call you Little Spider, carrying fire to the world." He squeezed my hand.

"What is happening?" I asked.

"This is the top of the cave. Water enters here to hollow the weaker rock and feed the river. John is coming through the other side. His torch just disappeared behind the rocky opening."

That sent another sudden burst of fear traveling down my blood-stream, through each arm, and down each leg. I tingled in its aftermath. Arch had to sense the change in my breathing. I relaxed my grip and sat down again.

"I don't like," gasp, "small spaces," gasp, "unlit spaces." Before, I wanted to escape. With John in danger, my distress renewed.

"Let us pray then. Breathe, *Say ge*, breathe deep and slow." His words tripled against the cave's walls.

"Heavenly Father, Son, and Spirit, in the gloom, you are the light. You taught us to believe in you. '… whatever is true, whatever is noble, whatever is right, whatever is pure, whatever is lovely, whatever is admirable—if anything is excellent or praiseworthy—think about such things. Whatever you have learned or received from me or seen in me—put it into practice. And the God of peace will be with you.' Amen."

His hand lengthened, and I rose and took hold. Courage followed. Through frozen winter ground, the purples of spring are dormant until warmth brings them green, bursting forth through melting soil.

Major's voice commanded, and Arch answered as he passed down a lit pine knot with fire wrapping around its end.

"Little Spider, if the torch dims, you have little air. Be sure your fire stays lit. Walk forward to the right; stay to the right. This cave is not vast. John will meet you on the other side. It will not take long. He is moving to you as you progress to him."

"I can't move." My vision dimmed behind the blur of unceasing tears.

"Yes, you can, Little Spider. You must, for the baby growing inside you. You must."

I held the torch, seeing what I had been unable to the preceding night. The walls were much ampler than I imagined. While small at first, the air-holding cavern was taller than I. Moisture dripped from walls striped with rust and black in patterns. I focused my eyes forward, seeking oncoming torchlight, and meticulously placed my boot, proceeding downward with measured steps.

Sweat seeped from the walls and grew in speed and volume, dripping in continuous runs to the ground, swelling in cold ponds that stretched to the top of my boots. My steps led to an invisible bottom. My skirts became heavy, soaked in water to my knees. With one hand cupping my belly and the other with the torch, I strode blindly into cold water. I gasped and stopped—closed my eyes and walked deeper into the increasingly connecting ponds cascading from one to another.

"John!" I shouted, but my echo sent only my voice back to me. I stepped on smooth rocks. I braced my back to the wall for more assured balance. Ponds ran simultaneously, cresting as they fell downhill. The water rose to my thighs. Cold and harsh, I had to exhale. I must continue; John waited for me.

The passage narrowed, and water thickened.

"Sarah!" He called me.

"John!" I cried to hear his voice again.

Water angled into a taller but narrower passage from where John's voice traveled. In the narrowness, I panicked. My boots slipped. Holding the torch as high as I could, water swept me from my feet and tousled me in the cold, flowing current. I had to recover some control, grab ahold of something to stop myself in the water's chaos. Everything I touched slid from my slippery and numb fingers with water's force. Fire's light revealed a narrower passage ahead. In last glimpses, I caught my breath and passed through, wet to the bone. I closed my eyes in relief as the water carried me through. I reached out my hand, the other still aloft with the pine torch.

Water thinned as the passage opened up further. My feet pushed against the opening where waters gushed past. I stood and put my back to the wall. Water fell three feet beneath me. John was underneath, soaked in the waterfall's spray.

"You must leap. I will catch you. I promise." He flicked wet hair away from his eyes.

I hesitated.

In one second, I saw him with revealing detail. His face was swathed in red paint. Blood washed away from his brown arms. Shadows revealed his cheekbones deeper, starker against the highlights of his cheeks brought on by the cold. His arm's reach was broad. His feet braced in brown moccasin buckskin boots against the slate-colored stones. His long bowstring stretched across his coat, with the ends diagonally appearing behind his back, parallel to his empty quiver. He was still my husband, golden-eyed, but changed before my eyes, an Indian. He was so cultured, so intelligent. That had not changed. It was not the costume or the paint, but his demeanor and fearlessness. It was the same as his father's, now becoming his own.

The last step was steep. I leaped and touched the ground. He caught me fast, taking the dripping torch from my hand. He wiped wet hair from my eyes, cupped my face, and placed it on his chest. He wrapped his shoulders around me. My arms fell to my sides with weariness. We did not speak; we leaned into one another, among the droplets of sunlight through open-air, framed by the cave's open mouth. Together, but separated in our minds, we prayed a most honest prayer to God with two names.

CHAPTER 27

From Grave to Cradle

John Ridge

November 1824–February 1825

Ridge Land

Outside, moonlight peeked through winter clouds. I awoke with Sarah's hand curling and uncurling on my head. She fell asleep on the horse carrying us home. I stripped her damp and still sleeping form, covered her in blankets, and tried to warm the room where she slept. I sat beside our bed, and in my exhaustion, rested my head beside her. My body ached with pain, but I could not disturb her rest, lying beside her, so restless. After the rush of anger in my blood, the only conclusion was a dreamless sleep, one that would not clear my mind.

Her voice woke me. "Come," she said with her body curled into where I sat. Hushed, her voice sounded deeper with her request.

My body rejected the movement as I tried to stand. I was stiff and swollen from exertion.

"Come," she said again and held open the blankets to me, sliding over to allow me room.

I answered her invitation and lay by her side, facing her. Our foreheads touched; our hands wound at our chests. She was warm and alive. I, cold and embittered, fury still iced my blood. I could not thaw until I knew.

"Your cheek is purple at the bone; your wrists seared with fire. What else, Sarah? Tell me." I murmured, kissing her nestled forehead. I had to know what she endured. No matter her confession to the men's sins, they faced their punishment, executed for the worst of them.

It took her an age to answer, and I thought she'd fallen asleep. I waited.

"He was the devil himself—the blonde one. I pulled free, hid, as we had done before. It was all I could think to do."

"Did he touch you? Force himself on you?" I was not sure I could hear her answer.

"No." She nestled closer to my chest, and I breathed deeper.

She took my hand, placed it next to her hip, overlapped her hand on mine, and pressed. It was a firmer spot, warmer than the surrounding skin.

"Our child is right here," she murmured.

After her words, the tension on her belly lifted, the baby shifting. Movements between our still bodies lay cradled and safe under our hands. My blood rushed under my skin and flushed into a summer's afternoon.

"You've never been more beautiful to me, my *Dh Ani*."

She did not answer but slid my hand around her, and I felt the child stretch and move again.

Sarah looked at my face. Her red hair spilled and pooled behind her like swirls under the waterfall. "I am not, John, but he will be."

"I left my heart to beat in you," I said, remembering. Comforted and reassured, we slept for hours and hours.

Time passed. Leaves emptied the trees. The wind blew in the cold as snow dusted, falling in wet flakes remaining only a single day. Sarah's wounds healed. She never asked for more details of the men's deaths, and I was afraid to ask her for more. She did not broach the days of her captivity. In my weakness, I could not force her to speak of it.

We walked every day down by the river where the ground was flat.

"I need to wash your hands and feet," I said to her hand in mine.

"Why?" She would not understand this cautionary tradition.

"In preparation." It was to keep her well, to show her how I would always care for her.

"John, it's freezing." She protested as I helped her to sit by the bank and began removing her boots. She tried to pull her feet away, but her further protestations only allowed me to remove her stockings easier.

"Yes. Then, I get to warm you again. A well thought out plan, if you ask me." She stuck her bare feet in the water and pulled back. Rather than suffer a slow cold, she doused both feet at once. The shiver ran through her, but she left her feet in the water.

"Hurry." She laughed through a cringe. "I can tell that they are in the water, but I can't see them." At this moment, she was here, with me.

I rubbed silt and sand from the riverbank onto her feet, and she pulled them away, squealing. She rinsed them again, and I tried to redress them.

"Believe it or not, that helped. I know they are fat and swollen." She kept laughing and pulling her feet away from me. "Give me that," at her request, I held her stocking out of her reach. She gave in and handed her frozen toes back to me.

"I'm just a son doing exactly as his mother commands."

"It is the same, isn't it?" she said as I laced her boots. "Only called different names."

We both knelt together at the water's edge to wash our hands.

"Yes, it is the same." I kissed her and helped her stand.

Our baby grew as Sarah and I walked each day, although the distances we traveled gradually became shorter. January turned to February. While she seemed fine, I found myself waiting for something else, her full voice to return. Often, she sat staring out the window with her lap covered in yarn, clicking needles in her hands, waiting too. Her soul hid behind her eyes, a deeper blue in concentrated color.

I interrupted her thoughts.

"I bought you something. Well, it isn't really for you."

"What is it?" she asked me, showing momentary excitement.

I went outside to pick up the cradle and reentered to set it beside her. I knelt at her feet.

Made of walnut wood, honey-colored, with iron legs in incomplete circles, arcs used to rock. It sat low to the ground so Sarah could place our child inside and ease him without having to stand. Mother had woven a basket, oblong with handles that rested inside, so Sarah could carry the child from room to room or outside without having to disturb the baby's slumber. Here, old ways bound in new wood.

"It is beautiful, John. Where did you get it?" She smiled in surprise.

"I ordered it from Lavender last month. Do you like it?"

Her smile fell, and she stood and walked across the room. I watched as she opened the door to our apartment and stood in its frame in the cold night air, breathing deeply, her hands on her back. Then she crumbled, bent at the waist, held her head in her hands, and screamed.

"Sarah?" I stood with the sound's rippling and watched her walk out into the night.

She shouted from the yard, "It was Lavender. He sold them the whiskey. The Man with the Hat."

"What are you saying?" I put my hands in front of me, trying to walk to her, but she retreated, and I stopped.

Father came to his doorway with his pipe in his mouth to ascertain the disturbance. He set the pipe on the porch table and began running up behind Sarah without her knowing.

Her voice broke, along with a shattering behind her eyes.

"I heard them, John." Her sobs interceded into her speech, "Lavender knew they were there. Lavender knew they had Honey. He sold them the liquor."

My father stopped running a few feet behind her. Sarah's admission stopped him.

"I couldn't stop them from hurting Honey. I couldn't get there fast enough. The Man, he licked me. I could smell the whiskey." She tried to touch the side of her face but could not make contact. Her hands shook against an unseen force pushing from inside her, propelling her hand away as magnets charged with the same energy. She wanted to show me and could not. She shook in her sorrow and collapsed to the ground in billows of purple.

She cried, mixing through screams and wails. She clenched her fists in front of her, pushing out the cold air trapped in her skirts, pounding her hands into the ground. Father moved to her, reaching from behind her to stop her arms, wrapping his own around her. Her lament continued as he pulled her to him. He looked to me for a solution, one I did not know.

"*Tell her. She knows already, but she needs to hear it from you.*" He spoke over her head to me.

"We killed them all. Shot them with arrows. Father and I took their scalps. They will never assault anyone again, Sarah."

Sarah's small body crumpled in on itself, held encased in Father's arms. He looked at me, but her eyes sought my honesty as I knelt beside them both.

She peeked and spoke, muted by his arms. "Lavender will know you took their lives. They are white men, John. He will know and will kill you for it."

"He will not know, Sarah. He will not know. We burnt the bodies in the cave. They were trespassers on Cherokee land. They stole what I love most. No earthly punishment would ease my spirit, except their death." I nodded to Father, who passed my wife back to me.

Over her head, I said to Father, *"Burn the cradle. Take it from the parlor and burn it."* His warrior's pride reignited from the ground with the task. Father walked with the wood in his arms and down below the barn, determined to ease his daughter in whatever way he could.

She curled into herself even more, but her cries changed. They were replaced by something different, a surprised moan escaping from deep inside her. Water seeped from under her skirt and soaked the ground at our knees. We were in the water all over again.

"Sarah, Are you all right?" I asked.

"I don't know." She stopped crying and wrapped her arms around our child. Her tone changed, her mind focused on her body's sensations.

"God reminded me what is important. I'm sorry; I know you did what you had to do. You saved us both." With this change, her voice returned. I felt absolved.

I helped her stand. I wiped her face and held her head in my hands. I was desperate to close the door on this; we could not live trembling. Not now. "Don't let your spirit leave me."

"Never," she cringed and closed her eyes as the word seeped from her. Then, she could not keep still. I put my hand on her back and held her right hand with my left. We walked in the cold darkness in small circles first that extended outwards. She led our way.

Every few minutes, she stopped and hunched her back.

"Breathe, *Dh Ani*." She remembered with my command. Mother and Honey came out with a shawl and a cup, walking behind us. Seeing Honey, Sarah stopped.

"Honey, I'm so sorry I couldn't stop them." Sarah held her arms to Honey, who ran to cover the remaining ground between them. Their embrace lasted until another of Sarah's pains interrupted.

"*Drink this; it is cherry bark. Will speed the baby's arrival and ease your pain. Let's get you inside.*" Mother remarked to me at our last stop, both of us crouched, talking around Sarah's bent back.

Sarah strained but trusted my mother and drank. "Not yet. I need to walk." I translated my wife's words back to my mother. Helplessness rose in me unlike any, drawing on patience I exhausted hours ago.

Sarah sensed it and said, "Breathe, John." She groaned as she rose again to propel us forward. Mother went back into the house, bringing blankets and a knife onto the porch, and Honey stayed with us. Our eyes met across the distance: us walking in circles, Mother, a fixed point. We shared a look of concern, but also one of joy. Dawn could not come fast enough. Mother knew.

In the darkest moment of the night, Sarah allowed me to take her home. Honey helped her change from her dress into her shift. She rose, paced to the table in the kitchen. Trying to help her, Sarah asked that I knead her back with my fists as she rested her head on the table between the tightness and calm. Her breath rushed through her as she relaxed. Then, a few moments later, she would pace again. All repeated at intervals. Her hands wrapped around our child. I did not know if she was trying to keep the baby growing inside her or welcome the child into her arms instantaneously. I do not know whether she could have articulated her want at that point either.

She breathed out and said, "Something is different." She spoke. Her head hung down between her arms while she began to shake. I turned her around to me and saw it in her eyes.

"Honey, go get Mother."

Honey sprinted across the yard.

"Take me with you?" Sarah asked.

I grabbed the coat from beside the door and wrapped it across her arched back. We stepped out again into the February night. Sarah stopped every two steps or so, trying to get her arms in the sleeves. My worry anticipated not making it to their door.

"*Utsi!*" I called from the border of the orchard. Mother appeared with a candle in hand. Honey ran and picked up the blankets and knife from the porch. They returned across the yard to us, lighting the darkness.

Sarah stopped again, and a sound burst from her body, alarming me. She could not stop shaking.

"Go inside with your father," Mother said. *"We will be fine."*

Sarah looked at me with eyes saying all she could not. Honey took my place. Before I stepped away, Sarah breathed deep and fast, "Taking your heart." She forced the air from her lungs to inhale again. I kissed her forehead and transferred her weight.

When I reached the doorway, Father turned his face to the side to look at me from under his forearms, leaning against the mantle, arching his back. Firelight lit his front before he turned to warm his back. Father sought his pipe from his chair on the side of the room. I walked to where he had been, finding the pose he recently abandoned.

"She will not break," Father commanded.

"Will I?" I asked.

My question pierced through the air, as did Sarah's yell from the yard. I paced, stopping each time I heard her. The clock on the mantle ticked. Fire popped. My shoe taps made sounds on the floor. I paced to the fireplace. I leaned against the table. I lit more candles. I put water in the iron pot suspended on the kitchen fire. My heart could not stand this.

Mother chanted, and the sound came in through closed windows. Sarah screamed as if she were splitting in half. Father stood by the door, so I would not leave.

"I need to be with her." I must.

"No. You will not go. Your mother will tell us."

I repeated the same pattern each minute for the last fifteen. The night's curse broke with a cry wrapped in arms under the trees.

From the window, Mother's silhouette held a child in the moon's beam. She sang of ancient souls born anew from the Great Spirit, sent to heal and guide the living. She left Honey with Sarah for a moment, crossed down to the riverbank, and submerged the child, increasing the volume of the child's song of cries. She swaddled it and held it close, returning our baby to Sarah.

Mother left the three of them and walked slowly to the door where we stood, waiting.

She was smiling and crying herself, all at the same time. *"Sarah is strong."*

"Rollin, is he?" I had to know.

"Rollin is Clarinda, Skahtlelohskee. The daughter of the sun born under the moon." She touched my father's face, kissed him, and called him *'enisi.'* Grandfather.

"*Aluli*," I whispered to myself. "She is a mother."

Our lives no longer belonged to each other, nor were they any longer our own. Our hearts now beat in Clarinda's chest, in drum beats familiar.

CHAPTER 28

Honey

Clarinda Ridge

October 1856

Near Rome, Georgia

Honey was half-Cherokee and half-African, but family. She'd say she was born hushed but lived loud. When I was born, she and her father belonged to Grandpa. In his attempt to acclimate to white culture, Grandpa adopted many habits, some of which were neither admirable nor Christian. My Grandpa's plantation was expansive, too vast for him to seed and harvest alone, even with Grandma's help. He grew orchards of fruit, cultivated corn and wheat and cotton fields, owned cattle and hogs, bred and trained horses. He ran a prosperous ferry across the Oostanaula and oversaw George Lavender's trading post. To do so, he owned slaves.

Some were indentured Cherokee, choosing to sell their labor for room and board. Some descended from slaves sold to Grandpa by Rich Joe Vann. Some slaves Grandpa received as payment or traded with Shoe Boots' in exchange for livestock. Honey's parents were different; they sought refuge on Grandpa's farm.

As far back as I can recall, Honey's door was always open near Grandma's kitchen. Bonding with my mother as her translator, Honey became my constant companion, caring for me like an older sister, laughing beside me as my most faithful friend. We spoke the same language. I loved her more than I could say and felt her death as profoundly as Papa's and Momma's. Every slave that comes to my door, I treat as I would my Honey.

When Papa built our house near Grandpa's in 1828, she moved with us to help Momma with the never-ceasing chores of running our new estate, Rolling Waters. She made bread for all of us. Even after Miss Sophie came to teach our school, Honey was more like Momma's sister. Honey married Peter, Papa's groomsman, although they had no children of their own. She joked, said Momma and Papa had seven babies, and she did not have time to care for any more. She kept the pain of her barrenness locked away, only turning the key once to tell me the white Man in the Hat broke her. When I was fifteen, a year after we lost Honey, Momma told me the story, one of hickory nuts and caves. After listening, I understood the reason for Honey's reluctance to turn the key.

Honey and Peter followed my parents and siblings with a wagon of their belongings. On the journey, the Mississippi River separated our families. Honey and Peter's wagon wheel broke, and rushing water pulled them downstream as they attempted to cross. Peter swam to shore. We never found Honey.

My family searched for them then and mourned them after. In 1836, alone, Peter arrived on foot at our new house on Cherokee land in Oklahoma. Ragged and torn from travel and grief, he had a child wrapped in a threadbare Cherokee blanket. It was my brother, Waccoli, found in the woods near the Arkansas border. Paul knew what Honey would have done and took Waccoli into his arms.

To honor Honey's memory and keep her with us, Momma named our new home Honey Creek and cared and loved Waccoli as Honey had done for us all.

CHAPTER 29

Weeds in the Wheat

John Ridge

March and April 1825

Cherokee Nation Territory and

Lower Creek Land near the Chattahoochee River

Sarah sat in the afternoon stillness with sleeping Clarinda on her breast. Golden sunlight spread in diagonal rays through the panes of window glass. The white calico of Sarah's bodice and Clarinda's blanket absorbed the light, glowing, as if light emanated from them and reflected inside the glass. I closed the door in silent inches, not clicking the latch, and trod lightly to them. Placing my hat on the letters beside her, I stole Clarinda from her mother's sunshine and curled her into me. She still was slight enough to hold with one hand and forearm. She grew every day.

My daughter's face charmed with brown eyes open or closed. Still dreaming, the baby did not shudder, did not startle. Sarah bundled her so tight, the blanket bound and comforted her tiny fists. Clarinda cried little, as she was seldom without someone's arms wrapping around her or someone cooing over her dusting of red hair. If Father was home, he held Clarinda.

Sarah woke when I placed Clarinda in the basket but managed not to make a sound herself. In this last month, I learned new mothers wake in a startled instant; with a hungry infant, there was little time for sighs or slipping back into sleep. Without words, I requested my wife to rise, my hand outstretched, and her slender fingers reached for mine. "Close your eyes," I mouthed.

Not looking behind me, I angled her through the parlor to the open door and escorted her outside. I retrieved the parcel wrapped in brown paper from the step and placed the box in her hands. She opened her eyes. Without opening it, she leaned to kiss me from the tread above.

I whispered, "You don't know what it is yet."

"You still deserve my kiss."

She sat on the step and unwrapped the paper covering. It was a walnut box, six inches wide, with a small, hand-painted blue flower in the lid's center.

She looked at me in surprise and studied the box in her lap. "Open it," I said. New hinges made no noise as she did so.

Inside was an embellished, dotted, golden cylinder, with tabs of steel teeth behind. I handed her the key. She wound the mechanism, and it sprung to life, plucking out pitches of an unfamiliar melody.

"I ordered it from New Town months ago, hoping it would be here the day Clarinda was born." I offered her my hand, "Mrs. Ridge, would you do me the honor?"

"Here?" She looked for witnesses to prevent accepting my hand. Embarrassment hindered her, a fault of her upbringing.

"We've never waltzed together before." She gave reason to say no, knowing she'd say yes.

I yielded to her ear, "I'm struggling to amend that fact."

Finding no one watching, she resigned with a gratifying smile, "Then, it would be my pleasure, Mr. Ridge," and she set the open box on the step and gave me her hand.

I walked to the open ground in front of our apartment and bowed before she curtsied. I held my arms, and she stepped to me, placing a familiar hand on my shoulder and her other in mine. We waltzed to a song powered by mechanical gear and spring, a symphony in threes, plucked notes from steel tines.

"Hmm, I must confess a sin," I said. Sarah grinned and angled her head with curiosity.

She followed where I led. "Where did you commit this transgression, Mr. Ridge?" inquiring, permitting me to tease her more.

"In Washington City." It was no lie.

"I expect that was quite some while ago." She remembered everything. "Out with it. Confess."

"I danced with a white woman." I hung my head in mocking shame.

Sarah laughed and, once regaining breath, remarked, "Seems you have sinned again. How shameful. I will pray for your soul." She stepped back, but I tightened my grip on her hand and her back to keep her close.

"You should. She was blonde, tied up in bows with a waist the diameter of a sapling. Daughter to a Virginia politician. Powerful parents."

"Were you in love, Mr. Ridge?" Sarah inquired with her coy voice; she was not afraid.

"I considered it. She was tempting," I lied.

Sarah's smile burst with laughter. She thought aloud without consideration, "That must make you a rascal then, Mr. Ridge."

I retorted, "What causes you to say so, Mrs. Ridge?"

"Because you left Washington to come to Connecticut to marry me."

"That I did, Mrs. Ridge. A trip I would make a thousand times more."

The song wound and slowed, but we carried on, continuing to step and glide to the tune in our ears, attending the earlier cadence and refrain.

"Happy Anniversary, *Dh Ani*. My words are dull in English. In Cherokee, the sentiment means more, *Gvgeyuhi.* You will eat if I do not. I will protect you, even if that means I put myself in danger. It means I hold your life dearer with every breath."

She wound her arms up to my back and kissed me again, "*Osda*

… good," she replied. "*Gvgeyuhi, Skahtlelohskee. Wado.* I love you, John. Thank you for the music box. I am grateful." From the open door, Clarinda stirred. We both left the ballroom made of dirt and stone to hold our daughter again.

Vann arrived before dinner, hammering on our door. I came from my study to discover him standing behind Sarah, who held Clarinda over her shoulder. They all stood by the fireplace, red light dancing across their faces from the flames. Sarah's hand ran in little circles on Clarinda's back.

Vann spoke to Clarinda's open eyes, who gazed over to Sarah's left. "Every time I meet you, you have your arms full, Mrs. Ridge."

Sarah grinned. "That is true, Mr. Vann. Please call me Sarah or Say ge, either or both."

"Then, you must call me David or Vann, or both."

"Fair." Sarah smiled at Vann's informality while Clarinda burped.

He chuckled and turned to me. His pleasant expression fell from his face. He spoke in Cherokee, "*I have had a fistfight with myself over whether to tell you this. But you must know.*"

I walked to him as Sarah took Clarinda up the stairs. I placed my hands on his shoulders.

"Who won, brother?" I asked, not falling for Vann's dramatics.

"Troublesome news from Indian Springs. Seven Lower Creeks, under McIntosh's direction, signed a treaty with Campbell and Meriwether. Yoholo arrived in New Town yesterday on his way to Tuckabatchee to tell Big Warrior and Little Prince. He stopped to share his story and give us a warning."

"When?" I walked away from him to the window, seeing only the framed and destitute Creek in my imagination. *"All those people ..."*

"February 12. Agents Meriwether and Campbell must already be close to Washington to ratify the treaty in Congress."

"How much money?"

"Four hundred thousand. Although, I imagine less than half of the sum will find its way to the people of Creek Nation."

"I agree." My pacing began.

"Yoholo went to stop him. Made a speech, standing on one of the river rocks near McIntosh's tavern. Yesterday, he said that he reminded McIntosh of the law again, the one we wrote for them. He screamed at McIntosh through a window, 'I have told you your fate if you sign that paper. Beware.' McIntosh's traitors violated the law we transcribed. None of Yoholo's speech mattered. None of it mattered." Vann coughed to fill the void made by my reluctance. There was nothing more to say. *"Campbell and Meriwether will knock on our door next."*

Without a knock, Father strode into the parlor. Rather than greet Vann or me, he glided with three enormous steps to the end of the stairs as Sarah returned with his granddaughter. He rubbed the child's head and held his arms open for Sarah to let him have the baby.

"Come. Eat." With his arms full, he talked to us but looked at the blanketed babe. Sarah took his arm as they left, both shadowed by his massive frame as they stretched into the colorful dusk.

"Does he know?" I asked.

"Yes," Vann said, bracing the door open with his back.

Honey held Clarinda in the next room so Sarah could hear them both. Honey rocked in the chair and sang to the child, shadowed in the spilling candlelight from the dining room. My mother tried to induce conversation at the table, but Vann was the only one to answer her. Dinner lacked dialogue, only clinking glasses and cutlery, and Honey's child voice hummed. Sarah and I looked at one another. Mother gazed at Father, and Vann tried speaking pleasantries to lessen the hidden outrage, tangible around the table.

Sarah leaned over to my ear, asking, "What is wrong?"

Before I could answer, Father pointed his fork and said, *"Go. See if we can do anything to stop it. Ride to Tuckabatchee tomorrow."*

He had been speculating all this while, analyzing options to decide. He resolved, not conferring with me prior, assuming I would do as he suggested. Just because I could speak English did not mean I carried the authority demanded to intervene in a Creek war faction.

I was not at all confident that I preferred to arbitrate. Let Yoholo do what he must. Creek found it challenging to talk first. They sought answers in angry arrows and musket balls flying into the hearts of their adversaries.

I thrust my chair away from the table; legs scraped across the floor, and I left my plate full of food touched but unconsumed. Eyes prickled on my back as I limped through the open door. All must have watched me go, except one. As far as I could observe, Father's white hair did not move.

Weak from this evening's news, my mind walked in a straight line with bodily anger that my mind did not expect. Because of the eight signatories' violations, the Creek Nation would suffer and surrender all they cultivated, their ancestors' graves, and home. My friend, Opothle Yoholo, must be infuriated with grief at this immense loss, one outside of his command and control. Anxious with exceeding apprehension for his people's future, he would seek allies—Menawa, Creek's fiercest warrior.

I encircled the house first, finding myself reciting the same views again as my feet stepped onto the wheat field. Weeds grew from the crumbling of earth, supported on spring's first winds, green amongst the buds fresh from sowing. In the rising dark, little grew of any quality. In my frustration, I pulled seeding sprouts and invading weeds. I tugged, overwhelmed by their number. Like my conclusions, the weeds sprawled differently down deepening roads of ceaseless turns, leading to an identical destination. In particular, one weed had stronger roots, and as I pulled, it would not budge. I tried both hands in earnestness to yank the intruder, but its roots were complex. All I accomplished was to remove the sticky stock aside, separating it from the massive white root underneath the ground.

Sarah arrived from behind me and watched my task. With her arms crossed, she scrutinized me from the edge of the field. I watched her from the corner of my eye. In my fervor, I threw the weed's stem back into a further bed, riddled with its own kind.

"Let them be." She walked to me. "Vann told me; now, you tell me. What are you thinking?"

"McIntosh will die. As much as I resent the man, I do not prefer that kind of death for him and his household. However, with my next breath, I feel so angry, so swollen with fury that I need to be the one to shoot him myself. Are my desires only from selfishness? We should ally the Creek to Cherokee, fighting the same conflict, linked in the same resolution to stand. But McIntosh is a renegade; he twisted his back against his tribe, back-stabbing them with knives made from his grandiose view of his self-worth."

I snatched another handful of weeds and tossed them from my grip. "Nothing will stop Georgia now. Nothing will restrain the intentions of the government from seizing this ground." All my conclusions suggested the same outcome. I remained and propped my elbows on my knees, bending my heavy head between them.

"You must hold them back or try at least. You and Vann, Elias and Ross, and your father. So do what your father says. Go to the Creek. Go to Washington. Renegotiate, if you are able."

"I can't engage in their feuds for them on either front. I am a representative of the Cherokee Legislative Council. I cannot argue for the Creek. My people do not live there. My interests conflict with that purpose. Cherokee will pay for this in actions we cannot yet divine."

Sarah sat beside me, knowing there was something I could do, but neither of us guessed what that might be. We both watched out onto the earth at nothing, in particular, feeling our bodies dampening from rising dew. Sarah spoke first, and I twisted to her question in the dark at the wonder of its piercing note.

"Who planted the weeds, John?" Her pitch firm, a surprising strength from her. What an unbelievable point to question.

"The curve of the wind. Uncontrollable," was my impatient answer. Why was she saying this? It was late March; we had only recently planted. She of all women should appreciate the overwhelming force of weeds.

"What will grow here?" She already knew the answer.

"Wheat," I answered with a quick response. What was she saying?

"Will someone pull these weeds, so they don't entangle in the crop?"

"I imagine so. But they will remove as many culm leaves as weeds and diminish the wheat."

"What would result from letting the weeds grow beside the wheat, and when the harvest arrives, remove the green weeds first and leave the rest of the grain?"

"Weeds would be obvious to detect then. No one would break their backs to tear them from the ground."

"That would be the sense of it. And a road around it, too."

She rose beside me, stooping to kiss the top of my forehead. "That was Jesus' understanding, not mine." She walked back into the house with her arms behind her.

Sarah quoted Matthew's version of Jesus' parable of the weeds. McIntosh was a deep-seated weed—entirely, and his conspirators would extend from his roots. However, if Yoholo pulled him now, McIntosh's followers would endure to advance, watered, and fertilized with white's temptation of gold and ground. Was it better to delay so that the renegades would reveal themselves? Was I about to ask Yoholo to spare McIntosh's life? Perhaps if Yoholo spared him, whites would recognize the McIntosh faction's words as a waste; nothing but weeds among the grain. My answer sprouted from Cherokee ground.

Vann and I left at daybreak. I held Sarah's hand and kissed its pale back. She had such belief in me.

"Clarinda will be bigger when you return home," she said.

"I don't want to leave either of you." It was the truth.

"Use words, John. Tell Yoholo. Wait to pull the weeds right before the wheat." She kissed my cheek as we embraced and whispered in my ear, "'Love your enemies, bless those who curse you, do good to those who hate you, and pray for those who spitefully use you and persecute you.'"

"I will try." We traveled west.

Along with the reins, I held McIntosh's trial in my mind and argued for the defense and the prosecution. I disputed my hypocrisy. How could I slay those who hurt me privately but try to save the life of one who signed away an entire nation? My left side argued with my right. What was moral and what was true were right, both in the same season? I would not apologize for taking the men's souls who risked Sarah's life and the life of my child. Now in the underworld, they wasted their time on Earth in evil and drunken selfishness. Great Spirit, what they could have done to her. Their sole motive was to bring harm for self-gain. Was McIntosh's motive so far from the same? He did not kill with liquor and rape; he did so with black ink and brown parchment and red deception. Is violence the only crime? No. "The only crime is pride," I spoke aloud to myself.

Mixed blood, two-faced McIntosh was a powerful rook to the Creeks but a pawn to the Whites. He could do so much good for his people if only he could see beyond his greed. Could I rationalize his choice? Was it better to treat with compromised terms or to have mandates forced upon an unwilling people? McIntosh's real intent was one I doubted ever hearing from his mouth.

Yoholo could not reason with him; I could not either. He must believe moving west would save his people; he had to believe that. Should he die for what he thought was right? Perhaps his determination was misunderstood. His avarice and pride manipulated his conclusions and guided all of his transactions, although he remained confident in his opinion, made evident by his script on the treaty. He thought what he was doing was right.

We never made it to Tuckabatchee. Over three hundred Creek warriors, walking and riding in the opposite direction, intercepted us on the road. The multitude of men swerved around us on both sides, parting and inhibiting our progression forward as a rock does a stream.

Painted red for battle, their faces spoke not, focused only ahead to seek bloody retribution. Armed with tomahawks, bows, full quivers, and hipped pistols, they were to begin the slaughter of those who took their peace, took their land. Warriors purged and fasted, their chests stretched tautly, bare and thin, slick with sweat from the angry fire, burned in veins running through the blood—a never-ending fuel. Menawa rode fast beside the crowd of fierce warriors motivated only in righteous violence. Yoholo followed Menawa's great feathers, head heavy with the weight of his thoughts.

"Listen, Yoholo," I addressed him, trying to get him to stop.

His eyes pierced me beyond the black paint surrounding his eyes.

"It is the law," were his only words. He kicked his horse forward, only looking at Vann and me in the eye a single time.

We wove behind him and met the tempo of his horse's gait. I spoke to his back.

"What if there are others? Others beyond those that signed who will continue McIntosh's agenda? Let time ease the pain and travel with Vann and me to Washington. Use your gifts of speech to oppose the treaty. Do not bloody this sacred ground again. It is what we fight to keep. Whites will see this as tribal violence, no more."

He did not answer but kicked his horse to a run to catch Menawa's steed, hunching his head forward. Nor did he speak to us further but allowed our presence behind the radiating fury of Creek warriors. *Witnesses*, I thought.

For many miles, we traveled behind, angling south down the edge of Cherokee country and then east into the center of Creek land. Yoholo knew we were there, our presence reminding him of the Cherokee: a nation who would no longer have the geographic distance to the Georgian politicians if the Creek were no longer our friends. I considered his mind—determined; I preferred him to listen, become pliant. He had to bend, not break. In his mind, the law and McIntosh's choice left him no alternative. I understood and knew there would be no more talking.

Amidst a humid night, April 30th, Vann and I drove our horses around the backs of warriors, stalking and climbing trees around the dogtrot dwelling. We sat atop a steep, rocky outcropping bordered on one side by the rising Chattahoochee River, staring at *Lochau Talofau*, Acorn Bluff, McIntosh's home. Creek men set it aflame, crashing torches through the expensive glass. His Cherokee wife cried and ran in fear while his stubborn Creek wife watched from the yard. Her people betrayed her husband yet followed their law. Children dashed for the false security of circling pines and oaks. Shots fired from the upstairs window down upon McIntosh's mother's cousins and clan allies. We watched the illiterate son, Chilly McIntosh, costumed as a woman, dive into the brown river with a folded document in his mouth. It was the Treaty of Indian Springs, made weak with water and clay.

Vann inquired, "Should we kill him?"

"We should not interfere. Yoholo made that abundantly clear."

McIntosh and another man fired at Creek warriors from the upper level in volleys, but the smoke below rose considerably; coughing sounded through the open windows. McIntosh made his last stand on his front porch, firing his last shot into the backs of men, once brother and son. Creek warriors drug him by the arms and legs, stabbing him with blades on the very ground now belonging to Georgia, sold by McIntosh's signature. Blood oozed from the holes, signing and sealing another treaty with the ground, murdered but just. Still defiant unto death, he sat up to speak. *What could he say?* I thought to myself. Then, he collapsed under the weight of his selfishness and lead. They riddled his body with fifty more pistol shots.

On the hill, surrounded by outcrops of granite, emergent lilies sprouted from between the rocks like white flags asking for peace. We attended the war cries resounding from the rising flames and received each roar, resonating through to our skulls. Vann and I jolted with each new whoop sucked from the air. It was the same song the land recalled from memory, generations past: a song twisted in thickly woven vines of betrayal and murder, avenging no one, in all truthfulness. With the

Creek warriors' quest complete, the earth lay mute. It understood the Creek no longer. While its brother, the river held his cries under the surface as snakes swam north against the current, undisturbed.

CHAPTER 30

Voices We Cannot Hear

Sarah Northrup Ridge

Summer 1825

Cherokee Nation Territory

Major Ridge knocked with abruptness, like surprising thunder from a still distant storm. I woke, accustomed to shallow sleep in John's absence and rising to change and feed the baby. Hearing the commotion, I checked on Clarinda, who did not stir; her arms were stretched back, and her hands relaxed beside her head. I stretched out my palm on her heart, touching her to feel her breathe. I gripped the candle, lit it from the banked fire, and rushed down the stairs. I answered the door, tense with anticipation of troublesome words. Little good arrived from knocked doors late into the night.

He escorted Honey into my waiting arms. She hugged my waist with a fierce hold, her face dripping, striped in tears, and remaining breath from abandoned sobs. I bound one arm around her and held the candle aloft to study their faces.

She whispered, her face to my side, "Sumfin' happen to my Papa, Mz Sarah. I's supposing to stay with you while Momma Susannah and da Major looks in after him." He bowed his head and walked to their cabin's light near the stables.

I shushed her, as I did Clarinda when I could not determine her needs. I gripped Honey's shoulders and led her to rest beside me on the sofa. I set the candle down on my desk and leaned back to wrap both of my arms around her. Her tears fell. She would have to endure the images anew, to repeat them aloud.

"What happened?" She stretched along with me, both of us in our shifts, like two doves sitting beside one another on a branch, cooing to calm.

"I wokes up cause I's hears him gaspin' for breaths. His eyes were wide, but he just stared at da roof. He didn't recognize me at alls. His hands were at his sides, but his legs were stretching and wouldn' stops da steps. His quilt was on da floor."

I hugged her stronger and settled my head atop her matted blooms. No child should have to watch their father in pain, to relive it for the rest of their days. Throughout my sympathy, I kept seeing my father in place of hers. The imagery made her story sharper, fiercer, piercing in my imagination.

"Mother Susannah and Major Ridge are with him, now. They will help him, Honey."

"I is empty." She pointed to her chest. "I knows he don' like me, but he's alls I got. He's my bear, even though all he do is growl."

"I'm here, Honey. You know, my sweet girl, I will not leave you." I rocked her in my arms; although, she found little comfort.

She was a timid child again, in many respects, curling up in her nightdress on my lap. Hiccups came and withdrew. She summoned her will and spoke what I asked to learn all this time, unsure my palms were wide enough to hold what she would give.

"My Papa say dat he loves my momma fierce. He see her da first time and could only sees her afters. He dids not thinks what to say to dis Cherokee woman. She so pretty, he woul' say, skin lighter than his, olive dat matched da grass. He walks down the rows of corn or wheat or beans and just keeps his eyes on her. One day, in da morning fog, she let her hair down low, an' she walk to him to speak.

"He dids not understan' what she saying tho. But hes took her hand and tried to speak in da Cherokee. He say some words he'd heard others say, but he dids not learn what dey mean. He speak wrong, and she laugh and laugh. From den ons, de try to talks each day. He teachin' her more words and songs in English, and she teachin' him more words and songs in Cherokee. Dey loves to do da talks." She grabbed my hand and pulled it around to her chest. No one had comforted this child in such a long span; she trusted few other than Mother Susannah and myself. Since the Man in the Hat took her, I doubted she thought anywhere safe.

"Da womens of her clan, the deer clan, dey say no. She cannots marry him, cause she's gots da farm, and no slave can takes it 'way.'"

Honey peered to me, needed me to learn her story, now that it might end. "But I's coming alreadys. So, Momma and Papa runs away, an' da Major, he find dems an' he say dey to stay here and works for him. Papa say dey was happy fors a time. I shows up, and she name me Honey. But, den her sickness came, and she could not makes da bread for Mother Susannah no mo. She could not eats even herself. She turn da pale colors, and her heart stop thumpin'. Papa say she quiet after I's come. Dat I's da one dat tooks der talks away. Now, he sing no song. Grumbles like da thunder, so loud whe' he push me out da door."

She crumpled her face, and tears welled deep. Her self-worth a shallow pond, told so by the wounded man she called her Papa. I understood never being enough.

"I's can talks da Cherokees too. Why he not sings with me?" Her question welled my tears.

There was nothing I could will myself to say to ease her renewed grief from blame she might always know—no words anyone might utter to lessen this child's losses, former and present. So, I said nothing and held her tight. She slept in moments, only to wake again and listen for approaching but imaginary feet outside. Discovering nothing, she would drift to sleep again. I did not sleep but watched candle wax drip to rest in a pool, turn solid again, harden and lighten. Damp wax was shiny. Once dried, the sheen muted.

When I was a child, my Papa seemed larger than life. He carried me in his arms, as an extension of himself, dipping through doorways with me aloft and once on the ground, crawling with me under tabletops to hide from Mother. He'd repaint the wooden faces of my dolls, chipped and smeared from holding and tossing, crying smeared faces changed to ones holding demure, closed-mouth smiles. However, as time passed and the Cornwall Academy opened, I found him no longer, too busy above the tabletops where I hid and pulled impatiently on his trouser legs. He no longer repaired crying faces. My voice was too quiet to deter him. When I turned ten, Mother's voice bristled and scorned. My father and I lost the ability to hide together, and it was my face, like a doll, who no longer had red painted lips, losing their definition.

Clarinda did not wake one time in the darkness before sunrise. She must have known I needed to hold Honey. When Major and Susannah returned, Honey's belongings were in a basket in Susannah's arms, dresses folded with a cornhusk doll bearing no face atop her faded clothing. He smelled of fire from a pyre; the burning clung to his hair, skin, and clothes. He torched their cabin with Old Saul's body inside, fearing unknown illness or disease. There was no longer any need for candlelight; the sun rose white, translucent, dimming the flames to smoke.

In the doorway, Mother Susannah held her arms open to Honey, and she became a grandmother again. Honey rose to meet a family, one that would never harm her or tell her she was unworthy. Honey's family would sing with her in two languages. Wax hardened, made an unfamiliar shape from its melting, but one moldable and unique.

In the months that followed, Honey's blooms changed into pink-striped lilies. Her innocence restored, free of fault for being born, freer in every way. She found her voice again with the smallest Ridge, Clarinda, who sat and smiled and waved her hands, reaching for Honey's fresh flowers atop her hair. Honey sang Clarinda a new song, one she composed herself. As she would say, 'the talks began again.'

In July, Major Ridge handed Clarinda a wooden horse from the porch, and he put it in her hand as we passed. He rubbed her hair and kissed her head. She grabbed him in return and held fast. With laughter, he unwound her hand, sticky and wet from its regular place in her mouth. I never grew tired of seeing them together. God meant them to seek and find one another. She recognized love the same way as I did. Clarinda's grandpa preferred her above all others, as it should be.

We sat on a blanket in the grass near the house, and I held the galloping horse just outside of Clarinda's reach, calling to her. She looked at my face and rocked back and forth on her little pudgy legs to reach it. She collapsed on her belly with her efforts and kicked her arms and legs out to the side with dismay and frustration.

"I know, my Moonbeam, he's just out of reach, isn't he? If you wait, he just might find you." And I trotted the wooden horse to her waiting grasp and helped her to her back, so she could use both hands to see her pony.

We both focused on the horse she held. Wild horses galloped together across vast expanses of grasses uninhabited by man. High on hills and deep in valleys, they followed one another, pack animals; yet, at the will of one, they shifted, turned, and fled, afraid of dangers only the leader saw, yet the others followed the panic of one.

John wrote last month, recalling what he tried to stop and its result. He rode back to Tuckabatchee with Yoholo, intending to devise some plan, some intervention, that might save the land and Creek Nation. Vann rode for home, but John remained. I understood. I did not expect him home this week. I could not stop him, would not stop him. There were words to say and negotiations to make to hold the ground where we sat—no one could stop him. To love him would mean watching him ride away. I knew this when he read the letter to President Monroe.

Clarinda's focus changed as she rolled again to her tummy. Distracted from the galloping horse, she turned her head to the distance from me and pushed her head up. I followed her eyes and traced John around the last bend in the road from New Town. Clarinda and I both forgot the horse we held, so we could go to greet her Papa, who dismounted near the stable door. I lifted her in my arms. We met him in half the time it would take him to cross to us.

"He's early, Moonbeam." I kissed her cheek before holding hers to my own.

We stopped when we were close to one another. John left in March, and now it was July. In a flash, he memorized his daughter over again, who changed so from his last memory. He squinted in the sunlight behind us. Surprised, he looked at me and freed a fierce love I closed in an empty drawer in his absence. I handed Clarinda to him, so I could wrap my arms around his waist to open it.

"*Dh Ani, Svnoyi Agalisgv* ..." As if she recognized her name, she stared at his face and grabbed his hat, hanging on to it with a tight and slobbery fist. He laughed, kissed my forehead, and cooed at his daughter's bright golden eyes. Her eyelashes stretched into the sky.

"Clarinda says it is time for her Papa to hang his hat at her house; her mother agrees," I said.

"I am here, my Moonbeam," he chuckled and tossed her high, and her smile lifted in the delight of flight, something she didn't know she could do. Fly.

After dinner, John delivered Elias' invitation. He requested we come to New Town to receive his friend, Samuel Worcester, and listen to his sermon. Elias befriended him from his time spent studying at Andover Theology Seminary. Mr. Worcester was a missionary sent by the American Board of Foreign Missions and expected a permanent appointment in New Town by the end of the summer. John said that Mrs. Ann Orr Worcester, his wife, was from New Hampshire. Elias assumed my presence might make her heart feel welcome.

John rested his hands on my chair top to escort me from the dinner table and whispered, "Father has Clarinda. Take a walk with me? I have things to tell you."

We stepped to the door. Mother Susannah did not look up from her sewing but waved. Clarinda and her Grandpa were both asleep in the rocking chair.

John offered me his hand, and we stepped into the warm summer's evening. A choir of frogs and night birds delighted in the oaks bordering the Oostanaula and hid mosquitos behind damp and humidity-curled leaves. Fireflies lit in intermittent strobes, like candles blowing in a gentle breeze, unextinguished.

"See the owl?" John pointed to woods.

"No, where is he?" I followed his pointing finger beyond the river into the forest beyond. I focused, looking for movement among the vines and trunks, but witnessed nothing other than flickering light, pulling my attention from the wooded darkness.

He hesitated, considering. "Why are owls always male? There must be girl owls."

I laughed. "It's true." He increased his speed, so our hands stretched as far apart, extending but still kept our fingers together. "Where are you taking me?" I asked.

"Someplace dark." His smile lit with moonlight's reflection.

"It is night. Everywhere is dark." He did not find my retort witty enough to stop pulling me toward the stables.

"One day, a woman decided that it was time for her daughter to choose a husband. Many suitors came to the door. One man, in particular, brought only small rodents as gifts to propose marriage. Although his gift was small, he was handsome and kind and very protective." With every two or three sentences, he checked whether I was still listening.

"… and smart and spoke three languages … I understand."

That stopped him and allowed me to catch up. "No! That's me, not him. I can read Latin, so that makes four."

"All right," I said. "I'm listening."

He continued the story forward in motion. "Therefore, this precocious daughter wanted him above all the other hunters who brought much better feasts. Mother had reservations, but she agreed to the marriage since the man promised to the daughter that she would never go hungry."

We walked through the dark stable to its other side. Through the tunnel of horse whinnies and smells of damp hay, he walked to the moonlight open on the other side. Once in his familiar beam, he turned and took my face in both hands. Walking forward and pushing me back, I found the barn's outside wall and knew I could not step any further.

John summarized the remaining story, between blue-hazed kisses. "The husband moved onto the wife's land. The man brought small fish and small animals for his wife to eat, but never deer. I have missed you. This trip only put me in a horrible temper from the moment I left until I rode home and found you both sitting on the blanket in the sun."

He kissed me like the hunter.

I breathed deeply through my nose, inhaling him. "Did she take his tools and put them outside the door?"

"No. Worse. She followed him into the woods on his next hunt and watched him transform into an owl. Once she realized his secret, she was so angry when he arrived back home, shaped, formed like a man, she released him from his vows and sent him away. So, now, the owl stays awake all night watching her and hoots, seeking her forgiveness."

"That is the best and worst part of that story," I said.

He turned and slid his back down the side of the barn and pulled me beside him, holding my hand.

I laid across his lap until he whispered, "I have some news from Connecticut."

I sat up. "What is it? My parents have been well. Since their last letter."

"It is not your parents, but Harriet and hers. Elias proposed marriage to her shortly after Clarinda was born. Before you interrupt me with questions, she consented. He did not tell me until I stopped in New Town on my journey home from Tuckabatchee yesterday."

"That is wonderful news," I spoke in quiet tones and exalted feelings for Elias and Harriet. However, John's tone was not one of joy.

"Does it not seem so to you?" I sensed mystery behind his words.

"Her father *denied them*. Even after he helped us, he still said no. He witnessed what we endured and did not want the same or worse for his daughter. She begged him, but they locked her in the upstairs room of a neighbor's house while the town lost all sensibility. She has been ill, Sarah. Her father agreed to the marriage to save her life. She recovers at home."

I stood, walking a scant distance away from the news, holding my hand to my mouth, imagining the harsh judgment of my friend and Elias powerless here, so far away. "How is Elias?"

"He is frustrated and scared for her. Even though her father agreed, she cannot write to him anymore, and he fears writing again to her."

He got up too, and his shadow reached mine. I stopped my pacing. He sighed; there was more to say. He comforted me, rubbing his hands down my arms, but avoided my eyes and looked beyond, over my head. "Her brother-in-law is a minister, and he is making public statements in opposition to their union. Harriet is facing far more ridicule than you did. The church choir wore black armbands, Sarah. They made dolls depicting them, dressed them up, and burned them beneath her bedroom window."

"Cornwall will blame the school," I assumed. The thought was incredulous. "Your school will close." Anger rose at my parents, resenting all the things Mother had not told me in these last months. I doubt they were trying to protect me from anything; I am nine hundred miles away. It was their blindness to all this and perhaps some vain responsibility. "My parents?"

"Someone wrote to them, said I struck you. During the ride home, I reasoned through who might have said such a thing. Perhaps someone followed you after … I assumed—it doesn't matter." He ran his hand through his hair. John's tell revealed his frustration. "Now, I hold more certainty that it was someone from Cornwall trying to inject fuel into an already ignited flame. Realize they are talking about us, using you as evidence against Elias and Harriet's marriage."

I was so lost, hearing the words he said but listening only with half ears. We had not been to Cornwall for more than a year. "Could anyone who knew you ever expect you'd do such a thing?" I asked.

"They know it isn't true. I asked Minister Buttrick to write to them and tell them how often he sees you and how happy you seem. He sent it yesterday. They are trying to prevent Harriet's marriage by proving how poor your marriage became. Are you unhappily married, Mrs. Ridge?" He let the air out of his lungs in relief that he did not have to hold the information to himself any longer.

"The town must expect … I don't care what the town assumes." Furious, I clenched my fists. More than that, my empathy for Elias overcame my anger. "What does Elias plan to do?"

"He leaves next month to go to her. That is one reason he wants to visit us all before he departs. After the wedding, he and Harriet will travel the long way home, doing lectures along the way to raise additional funds for his printing press. Sarah, he is building her a beautiful house in New Town, along with the print shop. All to keep him busy while he waits for her."

I sat on a stump in my dismay. "John, what have we done? Why do I ache with guilt and responsibility?"

"Because you love Harriet, and you love Elias and your parents. You'd blame yourself if harm came to any of them. None of this is our fault. He will be careful."

I rose. "I need to go home to write Harriet and my parents."

He took my hand to stop me from walking away. "Sarah, there is nothing you can say. Talk to Elias on Sunday. Write to Harriet tomorrow." He pulled me back to him and wrapped me in his arms. "Tonight, just be here with me." We stood still, holding an advancing storm at bay that slipped in front of the moon. He took his time to look at me. "Tell me about Clarinda. Is she crawling?"

His distraction worked. "We were studying very hard on that when you came home. John, she is just beautiful. She has your eyes. She is impatient, like you too. She sleeps so well. Nothing wakes her, not slamming doors or loud voices."

"What? Isn't that unusual?" He smiled with suspect surprise. "Does she make noises?"

"She cries, if that is what you mean, but only on rare occasions. No one gives her reason to do so. We all anticipate her needs. Your mother has not had a baby to hold for quite a while; she is smitten. She speaks to Clarinda in Cherokee all the time, as does your father. She loves him the most. Clarinda imitates the expressions we all make at her. Honey sings to her. I sing to her. She is my heart when you are away; she beats for me."

"Does she like the music box?" he asked.

"She hasn't noticed it," I replied, watching moonlight find his face, looking toward the house.

He let me go and walked past me to take a shorter route to his parent's door. I followed but ran to stay with him. "What is it, John?" His pace was urgent, and he did not answer. What more could be wrong?

He limped the steps, traveled straight into the back kitchen, and grabbed a wooden spoon and an iron pot. I followed him and stepped aside when he returned to the parlor, trying not to topple in the wind that he stirred with his heated tempo. Mother stood because of his urgency. Major Ridge stirred and opened his eyes, still holding Clarinda close. None of us found any reason to rationalize John's actions. We were lost.

"Is Clarinda still asleep?" John asked in hushed tones.

Father responded with a solitary nod.

"Hold her, Father. Try not to startle her."

John banged a spoon to the pot, but Clarinda's eyes did not flutter. She did not stir or cry. She breathed her accustomed pattern and rhythm. Galloping horses could not wake her.

John dropped the trumpery on the wooden floor, clanging and bashing with separation as loud as when he beat them together. His face revealed a singular purpose, one he did not voice. He went into the parlor and took down a powder horn and a flintlock pistol from a tall shelf, slung open a drawer to grab something small that fit in his hand. He loaded it while he walked outside, irrational and fighting against emotions he didn't share. He was not my John who reasoned through everything he did, many times from both sides.

I had to calm him. "Put it back, John."

"Bring her!" he ordered, terse.

Major handed our sleeping daughter to me, and we followed John to the yard in single file, hoping to slow his wild intention. Powerless, I could not fathom what John was trying to prove.

"Son, what is this? What are you doing?" His father's question did not deter John from his task.

He held the loaded gun aloft at the guilty moon.

"John, no," I shouted. Still, Clarinda did not wake.

"Is she mute, Sarah? Can she hear you?" He would have his answer tonight.

With the gun above his head, he fired. Birds flew from the trees behind the house in a flurry and settled again as gun smoke drifted and blocked Clarinda's father from my sight. It hung in the humid air, sulfurous. I stared into my baby's closed eyes, hoping to gather her wail against my chest. We cringed at the gun's retort and echo, but Clarinda did not move. She was as comforted in my arms as she had always been. All our eyes rested upon her closed ones, waiting for her to scream, but she remained taciturn and peaceful.

John let the gun drop to the ground. Sinking to his knees, John collapsed, defeated. He spoke to himself more than us, "*How can I have a daughter that cannot hear? A daughter I cannot talk to?"* He looked at me, at his parents, and held his hand to his heart. He screamed, "I speak three languages; how can I have a daughter that I cannot talk to?" John broke.

I flipped through moments since her birth, searching in my mind for memory to challenge his suspicion. I took Clarinda inside, opened her blanket, and rubbed her arms and legs to wake her. She made a brief sound when cooler air blew onto her skin. She stuck her hand in her mouth and looked up at me, scrunching her eyes together, curious why I seemed upset. I picked her up from under her arms and bounced her to the doorway.

John spoke in bursts of fragmented Cherokee and English I only understood in pieces. "… feeble-minded." Susannah cried her son's tears. *"She won't ever go to school. She won't have friends."* Major Ridge shrunk to cave into his porch chair. His eyes stared at the painted wood, repainting it in salty water. He reached for his wife's shaking hand, never questioning whether he might not find it.

John opened his hands from the ground to hold Clarinda. I couldn't hesitate. He held her away from him, looking into her face. She reached her arms to him to brush his face. With love and fear, he pulled her close to his chest. John spoke to Clarinda, to me, to his parents, to the owl, to God, "We will never hear her voice." He wrapped her in his wings.

My mind pulled forth a memory, one from my childhood, falling from the tree, blood on the ground, the last time I climbed. My vision blurred and distorted again, for me, for John, because Clarinda did not cry. We all fell.

CHAPTER 31

Fly

Clarinda Ridge

October 1856

Near Rome, Georgia

I am fluent in the language of herbs. If Grandma knew of someone who had illness or injury, she took Momma and me with her to the sick person's cabin. I watched her, knew it was her intention for me to do so as she signed what she said aloud. She placed her hand on the ill person's forehead, examined their palms, the soles of their feet. She smelled them. Grandma Susannah put her hands on their belly and checked their chests for rash or paleness. Then, she would use my language to say, "*Clarinda, I know which plant we need.*"

She knew her patient's Cherokee names, the clan of their mothers. When we sought medicine, she described the leaves' shape, and Momma drew them for me: stalk and vine, the shape and color of the blooms. As we walked home, I pointed out many of the plants she described, questioning her. Grandma would shake her head no and continued home down the beaten river path, often straying to examine beyond the dusty green edges for the plant sought. She floated with the breeze. When she saw the desired plant, shaped like the one I pointed to earlier, she chanted the name of the sick and their clan. I watched her lips move. Wind shook the plant's stem, or bees hovered above a blossom's color. I would hold her smoking pipe while she dug the plant and root from the ground, watched as she peered with open palms and closed eyes, nodding with affirmation.

"Yes, Clarinda. This is the one." Memorizing the symptoms and the treatment together was how I learned Grandma's skill. The Great Spirit, God, led me to the plant, sure to ease the pain or close the wound. I was born without sound or voice, but healing grew in my hands.

They raised me with four languages, studied by sight and touch. I signed with my family, although only they understood what I said. I can write in Cherokee and English and read Latin. When Papa wrote editorials for the Cherokee Phoenix for Uncle Elias, he would sign the article not with any of his names but called himself the philosopher, "Socrates." When I complained about learning, Papa said it was my inheritance.

My education came in questions, just like the philosopher's name he borrowed. When I was six years old, Papa asked me, "What is your name?" And once I wrote my name's letters in Mother's English, he'd ask the same question again, but write it in the right-sided loops and crosses of Sequoyah's syllabary, "Who are you?" He found a question like that one, and its answer, far more revealing. *"Svnoyi Agalisgv"* was my answer, "Moonbeam."

He wrote his last question to me on one of his last nights, although we did not know so at the time. He coughed from a disease that settled in his chest, and he was hot to the touch. Momma made him a bed of blankets near the fire. Grandma and I gave him milkweed oil and pleurisy root tea. He coughed more than he spoke and wrote with me as I sat with him on the floor. He wrote, *"Moonbeam, when we leave the Earth, what dreams will come?"* I did not consider the question for long before my thirteen-year-old mind dipped the quill to write, *"I do not know for sure, Papa, but in the dreams, I hope we fly."*

He wrote, *"Soar, my Moonbeam. You've always had the strength to fly."*

He flew to the Nightland on June 22, 1839. Twenty-five men came in the early morning, drug my father from his pallet on the floor, and pulled him outside. Momma ran to the door, but men wielding rifles held her on the porch. Our hysterical tears did not deter the assassins. Ross' men stabbed Papa in the chest and limbs twenty-five times, and once more, the twenty-sixth, across his throat. At his end, Papa rose as if he would speak, and instead of words, blood bubbled from his lips. His white night clothes seeped red, and then, the color stopped moving. Each man walked across his bloodied body before riding to steal Grandpa's life. Uncle Elias' died last. Cherokee blamed our family for all the lives lost on the trail to Oklahoma. It was that day, the day Papa, Uncle Elias, and Grandpa signed the Treaty of Echota, that our family became enemies to our nation who could not see, not hear.

CHAPTER 32

Blindfolded in the Woods

John Ridge

October 1826–December 1826

New Echota and Washington City

For a Cherokee boy to become a man, he must challenge his terror and learn to listen. Blindfolded, elders leave him alone in the woods for a single night to suffer the elements without the benefit of all his senses. He must stay awake and tune his ears to discern what is dangerous and what it is not. He must remain in that state for the entirety of the night, kept in isolation. Only after sunrise is he permitted to remove the blindfold and look with renewed splendor again at the forest and see the creatures whose sounds frightened him the night through. Instead, the boy must force dread away from him and listen with a man's courage to interpret the unknown.

I did so when I was twelve. Sleep was impossible. My mind intercepted each noise's origin from its pace, its weight. My mind processed each noise with renewed attention. I was wary and weary, not from the lack of sleep but from the intense focus required of me. Great interminable stretches pushed rational thoughts to the back of my mind, and my imagination took hold. Everything I sensed was dangerous. I released the distress, attempting to surmount the ever-changing visions in my mind. Without sight, I lost the ability to predict and anticipate. With listening forced on me, survival became dependent upon my audible interpretation of each singular moment.

After the sustained night, birds chirped from wakefulness and hunger. I refused to move. Boots pounded the earth, ones whose presence was unknown throughout the night. Long strides and muffled leather struck the ground and destroyed leaves underfoot. Sound came so close, increasing in volume as it neared. Hands touched my face, and I flinched at the unbidden intrusion in irrational fear. Once my night's companion revealed himself, I squinted and raised my head to follow his height: knees to hands, hands to shoulders, ending with Father's approving gaze. He watched me, protected me through the night. I felt alone but never was.

This I vowed to Clarinda. Sarah and I would be her ears and teach her to listen with her other senses. She would learn the world by sight instead of sound. With the syllabary, I would teach her Cherokee. Her mother and I would teach her English. We would travel this stormy night through beside our daughter. Her mother and I would never fail to keep watch until she listened for herself, in her way.

Council made many great laws asking my Cherokee family to listen, remove their blindfolds, and witness the impending white world. The council knew the transition must be gradual, so Cherokee eyes could adjust and act accordingly. With whites interacting with our people more and more, there was little time to protect and shelter our people like the men described in Plato's *Allegory of the Cave*. The Cherokee—Cave people—saw whites in front of a fire, painted in shadows on walls. It was time to turn them around, to visualize reality, the immediacy, the inevitability of the white's encroachment. It had been behind them all their lives.

Substantial business was accomplished during the two months spent in debate with other chiefs from the eight districts. We renamed New Town, New Echota, after the beloved Cherokee cluster of towns north in the mountains with the same name. We agreed to survey land for one hundred new homesteads in the surrounding territory. We established laws for those who traveled our grounds and interacted with our people. Whites who married Cherokee women could no longer practice polygamy; a clerk would now approve marriages, and the couple must pay a small fine. Foundational procedures for witnesses, bonds, justice, and punishment were established. We would honor probated wills in court, following the patriarchal line. We established property rights. I wrote a law against rape, where punishments for multiple offenses meant death.

Agent Meriwether arrived from Washington City. Ross invited him so he could witness our legislative processes. Ross held one particular mandate until Meriwether's arrival.

Ross declared, "White Men seeking to sell their wares on our land must pay a tax."

We had discussed it. By doing so, Cherokee agents would know which white peddlers were here and deter those who would not pay. Meriwether stood, crossing his hands over his chest, disagreeing with the proposal. He believed white merchants should be welcomed and uncharged. He said, affronted by the proposal, and addressed the council, "It is their right to do so, sir." Recognizing his misdeed, he deterred his embarrassment with consolation, "With these goods, Cherokee will improve—advance." His argument retreated backward like a startled crawfish.

Meriwether's argument was sly, one crafted from the Cherokee Legislative Council's desire to ensure a better life for those we represented. However, Ross' counterclaim was logical and irrefutable. He referred Meriwether to the abominable Stamp Act and Tea Act. The Crown forced taxes upon the colonists to pay British military debts from the Seven Year's War. Jefferson and Franklin argued against it in the Declaration of Independence, forcing the world to recognize King George's many transgressions: "He has levied taxes on us without our consent." In 1776, Franklin and Jefferson's slogan, 'No taxation without representation,' belted from backroom meetings with men drunk on rum, headlined from tabloid print, nailed to trees in towns across the Eastern Coast. Ross argued the same precedent now.

Ross stood above the council at the wooden podium and addressed the still standing Meriwether. “We are placed precisely, sir, on the same footing with foreign nations and several states … and have not the several states exercised the rights of taxing merchants and peddlers? Could Congress regulate Great Britain’s trade or France’s internal trade? In the name of common sense and equal justice, why was the right of the Cherokee Nation disputed? The American government, we believe, has never advocated the doctrine that taxes can be imposed where the people taxed are underrepresented. We, sir, are not represented in Congress at all.”

Time had come for America to recognize the Cherokee Nation as a state or an independent Indian sovereign. Through Ross’ claim, by remaining a “foreign nation,” Cherokee Nation could choose not to allow white immigration to our country. It was not a stretch to ascertain Meriwether’s intent, whether to trade or to marry; whites sought what Cherokee possessed: the ground where we stood.

Whites entering freely would continue to wreak havoc and bring danger to our people. Whites would break Cherokee law in favor of Georgia’s contradictory laws and their assumed superiority granted by the United States. It was the inevitable end. This point of contention separated Ross and me.

During an adjournment, Ross and I walked across the valley land in private conversation. We stood together under a saw-leafed oak with its leaves turning brown, falling with the season. “My vision for the future of Cherokee Nation rests in its sovereignty,” I said.

“It is a vision we all desire, John. But the land, to remain here, must be our priority.” He lit his pipe and looked at the ground, kicking the leaves with omniscience.

“Consider this. As a foreign nation, whites must obey our laws and system of government within our boundary lines. If the United States government refuses our representation, they also must concede we are an independent nation. In our sovereignty, we keep both—land and law." I borrowed from his infallible argument.

"You read Meriwether. His voice reaches those who would like nothing more than to dissolve Cherokee's claim to both, as you say, law and land." Ross smoked, reeling through more thoughts of mind than he had words to give them merit.

I continued, "Yes, but he cannot, would not, argue with Jefferson, nor with the precedent set through his nation's rebellion against tyranny. Ross, we are a Nation under the Great Spirit," I needlessly reminded him. "Do not doubt, Ross. Lead and know. United."

Meriwether did not approach the subject again, and the tax passed. The funds, held in the Treasury, would go to support education and to build structures higher than the Council House. With our defiance and our rights, we rose.

On one of the last days, I brought additional business. After the Shoe Boots decision made by the previous year's council, now was the time to readdress the subject. The council accepted my position: As long as the Cherokee husband was living or that his white wife bore half-Cherokee children, then the children of that union, no matter the clan, would be accepted and given all rights of Cherokee citizenship. His widow would also be protected and given an equal portion of an estate in his property and assets. On November 10th, 1826, the vote unanimously accepted my argument regarding a Cherokee man's marriage rights to a White woman. Cherokee sovereignty on our land protected any present and future children from Elias' marriage to Harriet or from my union. Clarinda was safe, as well as her brother or sister now growing inside Sarah.

Father stood and asked Vann and me to recall, for the benefit of the council, the murder of Chief McIntosh. Opothle Yoholo's intervention and plan for reversal of the Indian Springs' treaty concessions interested the delegates.

I spoke only of Cherokee's involvement in the situation. "The Lower Creek Nation, Little Prince and Opothle Yoholo, have requested Vann's and my presence at the Creek's appeal in Washington to annul

McIntosh's false treaty signed in Indian Springs. General Gaines has agreed to a preliminary treaty with Yoholo. Each faction will present their version of the Indian Springs Treaty to Thomas McKenney, an Indian Affairs agent and a Quaker, as well as President-Elect Adams who will reconsider the situation."

Ross said, "John, you sit on the Cherokee Council. McKenney and President-elect Adams may very well think you speak for Cherokee Nation—by representation." Ross seemed tired today and bitter at my request. I understood his reservations. To send me to act as Secretary to the Creeks could mean his voice might sound softer to the whites.

Sarah and I discussed this, and regrettably, I knew my course.

"I understand the Council's reservations. The opportunity to negotiate on behalf of the Muscogee Creek Nation is an honor. Opothle Yoholo is also a friend and brother in great distress for his people. One does not turn away from those in need. If I can help him keep Creek land from greedy Georgians or negotiate a larger sum for the Creek Nation if their delegation decides to emigrate, I am obligated to do so. We must keep Georgia from progressing further north to seek Cherokee land. With Chief McIntosh's signature, Creek land is gone."

Murmurs in the crowd suggested a division in the council's decision. I spoke over them, especially to Meriwether, who sat on the last pew by the door, anticipating leaving first.

"General Gaines has made a preliminary treaty; he adhered to Yoholo's words. Gaines agreed McIntosh created the treaty under a cloud, and the U.S. government must act under a clear sky. According to the Treaty at Indian Springs, Creeks must relinquish all land east of the Chattahoochee. Yoholo has agreed to allow Chilly McIntosh and his faction reparations for their losses and allow them to emigrate west of the Mississippi. Yoholo has asked Vann and me to seek an annulment to the treaty and to link for him to help save his Nation."

After I defended Creek land, Meriwether exited the council house, assumedly to write to McKenney and others before our departure to Washington.

Success in Washington would repel white intruders on one side of Cherokee Nation. McIntosh's treaty threatened the other three. Father knew, as did Ross and I, of Georgia's relentlessness, their sway in the Congress, their threats to deny support to President-Elect Adams, should he side rightly with Yoholo and Creek Nation. We were backed into the Northwest corner of Georgia, intensely determined not to falter our ground.

I addressed the apprehensive blindness in the room. "What can we do, but try to help them keep the soil of their ancestors, and, in turn, hope to save our own? Therefore, if I must, I resign my position on this council to attend to the needs of my friend."

Vann spoke for himself, "I also will resign if the council sees a conflict to Cherokee interests."

Conversation among the council ceased.

Ross said, "Go then, and with English words, argue for Creek Nation."

Seventeen in our party entered Washington City on horseback in full Indian regalia. Yoholo insisted, and I could not blame his intent. There would be no pretense in Washington, none other than Indians claiming what remained of Creek-occupied territory. I did not speak my concerns aloud to the delegation but worried that we competed with deeply established perceptions of Indians already without accentuating the situation with skins and feathers. If we fought this battle for Cherokee rather than Creek, I would not have conceded to this intimidation attempt. It reminded white congressmen of their history instead of propelling the Cherokee Nation into the future with respect and dignity.

We stayed at the Indian Queen Hotel while our newly-arrived opposition, the McIntosh faction, stayed at the Tennyson. Chilly McIntosh was here. This would not be a two-way debate with only the United States, but a three-way debate with McIntosh's weeds. At one point of the triangle stood McIntosh's heir, Creek justice stood at another, and the President and Congress' judgment reached the peak, like the recently constructed Capital cupola.

McKenney stood unwavering and non-negotiable. He acted on behalf of Georgia's Governor Troup, who wanted all Creek gone from Georgia land. He sought it relentlessly. He coveted the very ground Yoholo could not give—the land east of the Chattahoochee. Yoholo tried firm and respectful denial; he tried passive resistance. Negotiations were stiff and unpliable on both sides.

Vann and I put Yoholo's passion into a letter explaining further to ward away protests from Barbour, the Secretary of War.

"Further concessions cannot be made and after the reason first assigned, more you cannot demand. We now appeal to the magnanimity of the United States. We have traveled a long road to perform this duty. It is ordained by the Great Creator that we are so reduced as to be dependent on your power and mercy: and if the hugeness of Strength you determine to decide by power and not by right, we shall return to our friends and live there, until you take possession of our country. Then shall we beg Bread from the whites and live the life of vagabonds on the soil of our progenitors? We shall not touch a cent of money for our Lands thus forced from our hands, and not a drop of white man's blood will spill. And as fast as we are knocked in the head—the throats of our wives and children are cut, by the first tide of the population that knows not law, we will then afford the United States a Spectacle of Emigration, which we hope may be to a Country prepared by the Great Spirit for honest and Unfortunate Indians."

Negotiations continued and ceased in relentlessness. In January, I dined in my room. Letters from home remained unread and unanswered, and I needed respite from the relentless imperceptibility of obtuse and stubborn men, white and red alike. Blind conversations could not draw straight lines. Before I could begin the meal or letters, there was a knocking at my door, a messenger delivering a letter from McKenney. It urged compromise again.

My plate would be cold, and letters would remain unread tonight.

My knock on Yoholo's nearby door went unanswered. I heard the unmistakable sound of shattering glass. Fearing an altercation or injury to one party or both, I opened the door uninvited. I found only one man kneeling in front of a fire with a knife to his chest and broken glass on the stone hearth.

"Do not do this." Like a drought of words, no command more profound grew from me. I was shocked and knew not what to say.

"Go home. You and Vann can articulate our pleas no other way. I have dishonored my people. Being a skilled speaker means nothing if I cannot convince them to change their minds."

"I know." I closed the door behind me and sat beside him on the floor, facing a dwindling flame and sparse heat.

"I cannot fathom any way through, where Creek survive on their present land." Yoholo's head was too weak to rise, so I put my hand on the blade's handle to take it from him. In utter defeat, he murmured, *"I am dishonorable if I compromise."*

I thought of McKenney's request in my coat pocket. *"We are at a stalemate."*

I took the knife from his hand; it was the only thing holding his chest upright, and he heaved forward when I placed it out of his reach. I was honest with him but speaking to myself as well. *"Enemies surround us, attack and divert, shift, and sting. A clear and compromised resolution may not exist when both sides have no equal ground."* He shook his head to agree.

I coughed, stood, helped him from the ground, leaving his knife on the floor. I held him by the arms and spoke through a set jaw. *"If you must bend, sell it to them and charge them well for it, Yoholo. Use the money to build Creek Nation wherever you lead your people to go."* His failure would also be mine. Barbour's vice grip yielded only when Creek sold.

At the end of the month, in Barbour's office, the Secretary of War, the Creek party signed away the remaining land in Georgia. In return, they received McIntosh’s initial settlement along with $217,600 in immediate payment and a perpetual annuity of $20,000. The Creek fought a six-month battle with the government and lost more than they gained, again. Governor Troupe of Georgia won, and nothing ever changed.

When we left Washington for home, Vann and I took a separate carriage from the Creek delegation. They needed time to voice their fears freely and discuss plans.

When the country opened and the sky became uncluttered with the white man’s culture, green nature resurfaced. I told Vann of Clarinda. Until now, I protected her with my silence. In actuality, I denied his friendship and goodwill by choosing this quieter route. I justified it by saying we had little time, and we had obligations, which we did. I should have made time. Long talks of disappointment to the Creeks stole my attention, built my frustration. Now, as we faced southern skies, guilt made time.

“Clarinda is mute.” No consolation would be enough. He might think less of me because of Clarinda’s inabilities.

His usual sarcasm and wit left his body with a single exhale. He looked out of the window and studied the barren, winter landscape before saying, *“... and you have a limp, and your Sarah has red hair.”*

“It is different.” He must recognize. I sat amazed at his equivocation to the three of us.

“I do not realize how.” His eyes were sincere, unmasked, and filled the hollow space inside my heart with hope. Hope that others would view each of our inabilities or gifts in the same manner. Whites viewed our differences. Cherokee, like my friend David Vann, recognized our similarities. One perspective seemed more Christian than the other.

Are we not all mute in one way or another? Whites in Washington, McKenney, and Barbour found it unfathomable to hear Yoholo. The President refused to adhere, anxious of political reprisal. McIntosh refuted Yoholo’s words, or more likely, McIntosh refused to be advised from Yoholo's podium on rocks. Clarinda's mind could not process voices. Sarah could not understand all my parents say. Her parents say little unpleasant, choosing muteness over acceptance. A time arrived when each of us spoke but remained mute to the ones we needed to hear us most. I nodded at him, understanding; my voice humbled in deft gratitude of his simple mastery, his Christianity against my complexity, entwined in imaginary braids of wild moonflower vines.

"Amazing Grace" entered my mind. Sarah's soprano voice bound off the carriage frame of my memory, "I was blind, but now I see …" I did not need to look at her to sense her light. From miles far away, she reminded me. In emotional distress, blindfolds cover our ears and leave us our eyes to seek solace for our needs by faith alone.

CHAPTER 33

Signs

Sarah Bird Northrup Ridge

March 1827

Cherokee Nation Territory

From our lengthy passage, I knew arrival dates uncertain. Near midnight, John had not reached home. I expected him days ago, and his continuing absence burdened me with additional weight in worry. With the new child to come soon, I needed sleep. Tonight, my daughter whimpered and protested, tense in every regard. Restless, Clarinda's teeth appeared, forcing her nose to run and jaw to ache. She slept poorly, and I held her restlessness, swinging her through the light of the high, waxing moon, ornamented with twinkling dots from this opaque night.

On nights such as these, it became a habit to open John's gift, the music box, when Clarinda woke. Only I could hear the pluck of tines, but the music stirred John in my mind with each measure. I cleared the lid, showed Clarinda the key, and wound the barrel. When sound emerged, she stretched her fist and touched the box. I gasped.

"No, Clarinda. You might pull it to the floor."

When she touched it, her restlessness ceased. The distraction interested her. She reached again, and I let her hand remain. She smiled, rocked her head to the waltz in the same rhythm and time. It was the moment I learned how perfect she was, and we listened together.

"Moonbeam, Momma will wind it again." She lay her hand atop my own, two in miniature, mirroring the other. Her head swayed from side to side. She blundered from my arms, and I set her feet to the floor. John had been in Washington when she walked the first time.

Playing with Clarinda this late at night meant we both would be awake for hours longer. But, with her discovery, time did not count. I sat on the settee, and she came to me. Once the melody halted, I put her hand to my throat so that she could feel my voice. Like the waltz from the music box, I sang,

> *"Softly now, the light of day, Fades upon my sight away.*
> *Free from care and labor free. Lord,*
> *I would commune with thee."*

I saw her laugh with an open mouth and gasp with wide eyes. She met my song, and I rocked her close. We stood and danced a waltz of our own, drifting around furniture, flowing with naked toes on the rug, dressed in imaginary gowns, our hands hidden behind long white gloves. On this wood floor, a strange symphony composed only for Clarinda was attended by its first listener.

His limp drug his shoe taps on the stairs. He freed the door and settled his hat upon the entry table. He discovered us in the candlelight, spinning in circles, our shadows elongated upon the wall. Clarinda's head turned to look at him. I followed her eyes. He remained, bewildered, staring at the two of us.

"Let me memorize you both," he murmured, leaning on the open door's frame, with his blue coat draped across his arm.

The distance between us was insignificant, but we both paused. Our familiarity was lost, and we were embarrassed, younger, not realizing which tune might trim the distance. I put Clarinda on the floor, and she toddled across instead of squealing spoken words. Her mind misplaced him, but this was her realm where no one arrived who was suspect. He knelt to draw her up and rose when she reached for his face.

Clarinda touched her Father's voice. He needed to study her, but she nestled into his chin and turned her head to his throat. We'd spent the last hour learning this together.

I whispered, "Let her stay. Talk to her, in Cherokee."

"My moonbeam," he said, and she heard. She lifted and grinned sparse teeth at him. With golden eyes, the same as his, she greeted him with smiles. There was no desire to interpret or interrupt. Clarinda stretched to the fireplace, reaching her torso towards the mantle, her arms outstretched. I sat to watch them solve this puzzle together: her wish and his understanding.

He cranked the music box. Clarinda laid her palm out to receive the vibrations radiating sound, ones she discerned by magic. We hummed the same tune, needing no words. I'd lost my waltzing partner to our beautiful Clarinda.

Spring light was like no other. It produced not the intensity of summer heat nor the faint gray light from harvest but was pure warm. We slept later than we ordinarily would. The plantation began spring planting while the animals rose long before us. I dressed before he woke and took Clarinda to Honey to prepare a picnic basket for lunch. The Wisteria was thriving. Clarinda loved to reach the vines to make the purple blooms fall.

With Clarinda's hand in mine and my other loaded with our basket and blanket, we strode back into the glow of day. I spun around to the kitchen where Honey remained.

"Come with us," I said.

"No, missus. Mr. John been gone a whiles. You threes go togethers." She shrugged her shoulders and stepped into the darkness of the kitchen. Light framed her, just behind the open door.

"Honey, please? Help me chase Clarinda. I'm too pregnant now to keep up with her."

"She's fast, Mz Sarah," Honey was not wrong.

"I know, Honey." Honey took the basket from my hand and passed us, still standing on the stairs.

We divided the grassy yard. Clarinda and Honey seamed through the grass, opposing John, who was speaking with his father. It would take them both time to interpret all that developed and the repercussions to Cherokee from the Creek trials in Washington. Many conferences of defeat and frustrations would spin between them, with questions and answers I couldn't discern. John watched us pass, and his father swept a gesture, a sign in our direction. Today, John was ours, free of quill and parchment, translation or argument.

Clarinda preferred to walk on her own, even though I was constantly afraid she'd fall. Once her shoes reached the pasture, she was ahead of my strides. Honey pretended to chase her to the Wisteria vines, and I laughed behind them. Honey faked a run, as I had witnessed her sprint many times. Clarinda peeked over her shoulder and smirked, and turned to dart in a different direction. When we landed in the purple shadows, I flipped the blanket in front of me, soaring it into the wind. It was a patchwork quilt of my design, multicolored strips of Cherokee blankets, and patches of new dresses. Some variety Clarinda wore, brown cotton sprinkled with crimson flowers. It was something I created, finished by myself.

John's red shirt was open, his gait relaxed, and his limp, unnoticeable. The surrounding meadow shaped his shadow as it drew closer and broad. In the sunshine, he glowed golden, skin soaking in the light. He held his boots in his hand.

"No shoes today, ladies." My favorite John arrived—the one with the wide grin and charming expressions. Written or spoken, certainly, he knew what to say to me.

"I ain't gots mine on no how," Honey interjected. She rarely had any desire to wear them, especially on a day like today.

He scooped Clarinda around her running waist and placed her on the blanket next to me. Clarinda's feet wiggled and kicked as he removed her shoes and socks. He whistled on her feet, and she wrinkled her nose. She pulled her legs away, and he pulled them back, just to do it all over. She paid him for his efforts in smiles and belly-shaking toothy grins. Honey took Clarinda's hand, and they brushed their way through green shadows to sunlight, weaving dirt through their toes.

Then, John perched on his heels in front of me and slapped his thigh.

"The last time we did this, it was colder." He smirked, so I did what he proposed.

"It was." He unlaced and hoisted one of my boots aside.

"And, you were unable to look to your feet." He unlaced the second.

"I can't now." He tossed the second boot free, lost in a haze of green grass beside us.

I scampered back in surprise at his hands reaching for my leg. Unwinding the stocking, inside out, he rose, reaching the other leg with an expression I'd forgotten with his absence. He took his shoes off too and flung them beside mine, hidden in among the long blades and dandelions.

"How has my heart been while I've been elsewhere?" he asked, remaining beside me, staring at our similar toes.

"Temperamental and prone to bouts of arresting and starting over without my consent," I said.

His reply was not sarcastic. "You do not understand how true that is."

"Tell me what happened? The outcome?" I asked, unsure if I'd endure the consequences of his answer.

"More men speaking to one another, and none heard the other. The Creek treasury is full, at least. They have a year to remove west. They cannot linger on Georgia's new territory any longer."

"And my heart," I requested, "Did it serve you well?"

"It was consistent, faithful, and resolute. It kept me alive and sane," he said.

"I missed you every day," I touched his cheek and kissed him.

"And I you, *Dh Ani*." He mirrored my touch.

We watched Clarinda and Honey facing one another, divided through the blades of grass. Honey put dandelions in Clarinda's hair, wispy red tied with a ribbon of remaining fabric from the dress she wore. Honey talked to Clarinda, and she studied Honey's face. They were inverses of one another. Honey made a gesture with her hands, and Clarinda responded. I looked twice at what I was seeing.

Honey scooped Clarinda in both arms and began striding towards us. Clarinda's legs lifted high from tickling grass. I stood.

"What's wrong, Sarah? Sit with me." John did not see.

"Is she hurt?" He stood, expecting some danger to prompt my rise.

"Clarinda is hungry is all, Mz Sarah." Honey and Clarinda stepped into the tree's shade.

I was emphatic. "How do you know, Honey? Tell me how you know."

"She tell me so with her fingers." Honey shrugged her shoulders and spoke aloud those words as if they meant nothing.

John searched his child's face, looked at her hands and feet. He looked to Clarinda's face, examining it for what Honey understood.

"She touch her fingers to her mouth. She do dat alls day. She tell me what she wish."

John said, "Show me what she did with her hands." Honey did so.

John made the same gesture to his mouth that Honey showed him but moving in front of his daughter. Clarinda imitated and wiggled to reach me. I set her down, and she shuffled to the basket lifting the lid herself and nearly falling inside.

John turned to Honey and urged her, "Does she do anything else? Make any further movements with her hands that tell you what she wishes to say?"

"She tell me when she wan' Mz Sarah cause she sleepy or finicky. She sticks her thumb on her chin like she just missed her mouth wid it."

"Like this?" and he knelt to Clarinda and did the same gesture

Honey described. Clarinda looked up at me. I handed her a piece of bread from the basket and stretched to take her in my arms. All this time, I watched her face, waiting for sounds that would never arrive. She'd spoken to me every day, and I was mute.

"What does she do when she wants you?" John was loud and spoke to Honey with a frenzy to learn the language of Clarinda's hands.

"She touch her chin agin, but she wipe it, like the honey has dripped there. I thought of dat and teaches her like Mz Sarah teach me the letters and da words. Yous gots to show me one time, and I's knows it. Clarinda little. She smart, though. She catch on pretty quick."

I made the gesture this time, one that meant Honey. Clarinda scrutinized my face.

"Like this?" I touched my bottom lip with three fingers and let them slide down to my chin. Clarinda's eyes looked at Honey in the same instant.

John was more than excited. He picked up our daughter and kissed both cheeks and her eyelids. I hugged Honey with fierceness, so tight she squirmed away.

"Honey, I owe you more than I could ever repay."

"No, Mz Sarah. Yous saved me." Her smile was gratitude enough for anything I ever did or could do for her. Nevertheless, what she has given to our family, her love, was the most fragrant bloom Honey ever created.

John interrogated Honey further. She managed not to falter but demonstrated hand signs of her invention, teaching Clarinda's parents to talk to their daughter. Clarinda sat in John's lap, and Honey and I across from them. Honey taught us all, and we received the lessons like new children ourselves.

"She does this all the time, Honey. Do you know what that might mean?" I put my fingers together in a point, using both hands, and touched and untouched the left tips to the right.

"Dat mean she want more of whatevers you givin' hers."

Epiphanies of the day and having John near amplified the afternoon sun. His presence was like this land after a storm, like rain puddles remain in the grass, limbs fall and break, but then, blue sky returns. Perhaps the Cherokee had a word for that kind of peace; English did not.

Honey ran back to the house to help Mother Susannah, and John and I remained with Clarinda pointing to bugs and flowers in her line of sight, trying to give them a movement, a gesture, an image. With time and repetition, she would remember and show us what she wanted to say.

He put his hands on the tree trunk wrapped in waving purple. Then, he made the ground with his forearm and held the alternative arm to the side perpendicular, wiggling that hand's fingers. He spoke to her, "*itlugv.*" Repeatedly, he touched the tree and made a tree's shape with his arms.

I said to her, "Tree." She followed his hands and face and repeated the word with her arms. Her ground was slanted, and her leaves did not wiggle like her father's, but the sign's roots were there.

She settled her head on my lap, facing my toes. "I think that one is clear enough," I said.

He laid beside me with his head facing her, taking care of her, pulling the flower crown she wore away from her wispy red hair.

"Today will never leave me, *Dh Ani*. As long as I live, as many losses as we may face, today alone will root deep."

I brushed his hair out of his eyes.

Dinner was a celebration, not only of John's homecoming but also of Clarinda's words. She was tired and fussy and only wanted her grandpa. When she saw him, she put her thumb to her forehead and repeated the gesture until he picked her up.

"I recognize that one," Grandpa said, kissing Clarinda's cheeks before placing her on his shoulders. This was Clarinda's favorite game, to parade around the house, high on the Ridge. He held her feet, looked under tables and chairs, up the stairs and down, pretending he had lost her. Most of the time, she would cover his eyes with her hands

from her throne above, holding tight. He would have to move one of her hands to not topple from surprising darkness.

Mother Susannah was weepy. *"I will teach her hands the plants that grow and the healing they bring. I will teach her to weave. I will sign with her to tell the stories."* John translated the beautiful promises to me. I would be listening. Mother Susannah embraced me, and in the quiet, I heard more with her arms than if she had spoken in Cherokee. I recalled my first night here. We sewed together. With signs, Grandmother would teach, Clarinda would learn, and we would find a way.

John stayed beside his mother while Honey pulled me down the hallway to her room. She brought Clarinda's nightclothes there and made her a bundle of blankets on the floor with pillows on all sides.

"I keeps Clarinda tonigh' so you and Mr. John can go talks."

"Are you sure, Honey? You can come to get me if she needs me. I could use a full night's sleep."

She nodded in affirmation. I turned back as I entered her doorway to ask, "Did Mr. John ask you to do this?"

"No," she said, but she swayed her head in affirmation. "He say I'm not supposin' to tell you, Mz Sarah."

"I'll pretend like I don't know."

In the parlor, Grandma Susannah sat Clarinda on her lap. Clarinda yawned, and she put Clarinda's arm behind her own back and cradled her across her lap. Clarinda's other hand raised on its own to Susannah's throat as she spoke.

"Selu is our mother, born from the corn ..."

Clarinda would be asleep soon.

John disappeared from the house. I passed outside and scanned the horizon of sunset oranges and roses of sunset, but he'd vanished. I waddled to our apartment. There was a candle in the window, a single blaze of lighting in his study's window. Surely, he would not be working tonight, not arriving home only yesterday.

Opening and closing the door, I shouted, "Please work tomorrow, not tonight."

There was no answer.

I opened his study door. He was not there. I rested in his chair, staring at the candle. Then, it occurred to me, not in a note this time, but in his voice repeating the words from his note years before,

"… wait for the candle. Meet me by the river."

I rose, left the door open, and walked through the orchard to the Oostanaula.

If only I were a poet. He sat alone in red. His frame, slender and tall, sat upon a stump near the water's edge. He viewed his river as it crested across broken limbs and rocks. Highlighted by the spectrum of spring, lush green and yellow predicted new growth. Smells of fish in the water drew mockingbirds, thrashers, and robins nesting above him, singing a repeated phrase, interrupted by the solo hoot of an owl. They sang verses John knew, songs he heard, ones he sang himself.

He sensed me, and I paused at his gaze from a distance across the rolling waters. I approached him, saying nothing. He reached his hands through my red strands. We found one another's eyes, as we always would, and put our hands on one another's heart to hold the rhythm, familiar, predictable, and known.

CHAPTER 34

In Melody

Clarinda Ridge

Nightland

The wind stirs my still form, and my soul ascends from my poisoned body. I turn away and rise to fly into the Nightland. Above me, the owl swoops. His wings guide me as I trail behind in his unused breeze. I caress the passing stars with outstretched hands, spreading stardust with my fingertips. We travel together, searing through the audible wind. I touch my ears, hearing constant rushing while we leave the Earth behind.

The owl glides away while I descend into a great forest, gripping the warm ground with bare toes. Sounds of hidden katydids, croaks of bullfrogs, and cricket chirps do not frighten me. The insect's names spear in the forefront of my mind. Voices call to me, speak my name. I hear what I've known by sight: my name, *"Clarinda."* Following a familiar rhythm, drums beat and pace my bare feet. Popping sounds of burning pinewood reveal a great fire.

Deep-voiced warriors chant and sing, wearing headdresses of feathers earned in battle, weighing their heads low. Mothers and children dance and stomp in opposing circles and repeat the song with endless breath. I hear my people. Cherokee voices extend for miles, all warmed by this inextinguishable blaze. In their joyous dance, there are no more rivers of tears.

Silhouetted bodies separate from the fire's light and walk towards me. I recognized their strides, a formidable man and his tiny woman. Grandma and Grandpa open their arms to me in a grateful embrace and speak words I know. I hear their voices, muted before but always familiar.

Rich, like fertile soil, Grandpa's deep voice forms Cherokee words, *"I found you, my Clarinda."* He lifts me from the ground, and his arms feel powerful again.

Grandma signs and speaks, "*My Blessed, I am so proud of you.*" I held her hands again. In my memory, her fingers are aged, spots mask crevices in wrinkled skin. Here they are firm, like the crust of freshly made bread. Unable to see one another clearly from tears, our voices crest with laughter, searching one another's face from volumes of recollections.

"*I am here with you.*" My voice speaks the words. Sounds that rest inside me speak. My voice resonates in my ears, unique, familiar, and mine.

My grandparents escort me, one on either side, to the fire where warriors raise dust underfoot. Above the blaze, embers never cease to glow and fly infinitely higher. Wind swoops the owl from the forest's hickories and into fire's reaching light. His mighty talons shrink into flint-tipped arrows that fill the quiver appearing on his back. His broad wings collapse into wide shoulders. Brown and white downy feathers sear solid into breechcloth, leggings, and tunic. His eyes never change eyes that match my own. *Skili* hovers before me, above the ground.

"Speak to me," *Skili* says, touching the ground with human feet.

"I never stopped." I kiss him fiercely.

Taking my hand, he leads me to dance among the spirits of my Cherokee ancestors. We join the circle around the fire, moving counterclockwise, to wind back the earthly time spent apart.

From the shadows, seven warriors emerge and stand as sentry

beside the forest's border. Long sourwood limbs rest in their hands, holding them like stakes, rooting the seven to the rock-less ground. Their hair hangs overlong and masks their faces. Each time *Skili* and I pass, a warrior swipes his limb on my legs, knocking me to my knees. I feel no pain, only the force of the blow. I am the only one to see them. *Skili* brings me to my feet and spins us again.

On the seventh swipe, I fall to the ground. The Seven converge and swarm, steal me from the fire. Holding me above them, they run into darkness. I pry their grips that bind my arms, but there are too many hands. I cry aloud, scream for my grandparents, for *Skili*, my owl. Beyond the fire's light, I am lost. The Seven force my spirit into a wooden box and use their stakes to slide through openings, lifting me inside from the ground, from the Nightland.

Inside and alone, I scream, "Free me from this darkness." The Seven do not answer.

"Stop. I am hungry," I call outside my cage.

They do not open the box and travel onward.

"I am thirsty. Give me drink," I scream.

They do not answer and do not free me.

For seven days, they travel back to Earth, back to time. Confined in midnight, I wail and bang my hands inside my cage.

"I am smothering; there is no more air." Weak and weary, I whisper. No one hears me.

Movement stops. They lower me to solid ground. I hear their words, English words I know. "We must return the daughter to her mother, the sun. If we open the box, she will return to the Nightland. We will remain in darkness. We have no sunlight while the mother grieves."

The Seven debate whether to open the box, whether to allow me air. Arguments seep from their mouths like poison; fear drips from their words like water seeping through the wood. Yet, still, they fear releasing the lid of my box, my prison.

I feel a tug, and then another. Unseen hands touch my body, pull and twist my hair around my neck, down my arms. Long hair binds my arms back, and invisible hands tuck my legs beneath my body. A chant begins, one I've heard, one known from the time before I was born. The Great Spirit transforms me.

The Seven decide and slide their poles free to release the lid. Out I fly, a great horned owl, feathers of brown and white, instead of Momma's red hair. Mute, I make no sound. I hide from the Seven, among the deep-green and heart-shaped leaves, behind the open white blooms and twisted vines. I mask myself behind the moonflowers. My thoughts run backward to my last night when I sewed the moonflower into existence. Its presence hides my spirit.

The Seven curse and squawk, speak in a language I no longer understand. They use man's voice, and now, I am an owl. They close the box and walk ahead, holding the frame higher without my weight. Resolved to face their fate, the Seven leave in shame. They free me, the Daughter of the Sun, knowing their suffering will continue on Earth for this transgression.

My cries begin—mourning the loss of my grandparents, Momma, Papa—mourning my earthly passing. Through a night of grief and cold, I ruffle my feathers and stick my head beside my wing, keeping my breath warm, lost and alone.

Skili, my owl, swoops from above, eyes alert, open to me in the freshest dawn. He wraps his talons around a towering oak limb. Faithfully, still on guard, his eyes find me.

I tried my Owl voice, *"Speak to me,"* I say.

Skili hoots in return, *"I never stopped."*

Dust closes the day. *Skili* flies north. In his absence, sundown brings a familiar waltz, a song in chirps. Beside me sits a brown cardinal with a honeyed breast and a tail of red. I recognize her and her song.

"Follows me home, Moonbeam. I sings da whole way."

We travel throughout the night, never needing sleep and never growing hungry. We soar over forested mountaintops in a blue haze, while underneath us, a straight and ancient river guides our turns. Following Honey, I glide lower, bringing the landscape closer and clearer. Orange streaks bring sky's dawn. Honey's feathers extend to swoop above a dark green strawberry field with white flowers of newly sprung buds, like constellations under instead of above.

Sustaining wind glides us to land, and we rest on the full branches of a nearby laurel tree. A radiant hummingbird sits with a breast of red on the limb above me, framed by flight feathers of transparent gray hiding their shimmer of blue. She is *wa-le-la,* Momma. Beside her echoes the mockingbird song, *Skahtlelohskee*, Papa, tall and proud in feathers of gray-tipped black. Above us, *Skili*'s owl wings stretch in gyrating circles, spanning the blue sky.

In eternal chords of melody, harmonious, the choir sings.

AUTHOR ACKNOWLEDGEMENTS

Writing a book is challenging and more rewarding than I could have ever imagined. It is the art of hearing voices: believing and transcribing what characters through history provide.

For me, this story began in a special collections library at the University of West Georgia, in a researched fiction course, where I found a family for 'the medicine woman' alone in the woods. The Ridge family's successes, struggles, and loss became one that I felt compelled to put on the page. Their losses were significant, their tragedy, one of an entire people. However, their intentions were noble and forthright, seeing the inevitable emigration of the Cherokee Nation. Their intent was to put Cherokee Nation's people above the land. No one foresaw the horrific tragedy of the Trail of Tears.

None of this would have been possible without my husband and best friend, Jon. He listened, plotted, brainstormed, and listened again during every draft.

I'm eternally grateful to my daughter, Emma, who envisioned "Laundry" and planted the seeds for Honey. I'm also grateful to my sons, who keep telling me, "I'll read it when it's finished."

I'd like to thank my mentor, Claudia Best, the most well-read person I know. Also, I'd like to express my gratitude to my fellow English teacher, Carla Read, and, not least in importance, Penny Lewis, author. Even in original draft form, this trio read every scene and encouraged me through every blunder, never judging my grammar, although they noticed every flaw. Every writer deserves a Claudia, a Carla, and a Penny.

Through this process, I've made new friends: Norma LeAnn Gruschow Gambini, Michelle Mitchell, LaNae Barton Marier, Gabrielle Burkhart, and Leslie Stalfort Simmons. Also, my friends for years who had no fear in telling me something "needed revision," Jennifer Miller, Dana Cheshire, and Bethany Dowda. Each shared their critical eye and support. I thank God for your friendship and your advice.

Thank you to AP Literature, Class of 2020 at Alexander High School who taught the teacher.

With honor and respect, I'd like to thank Ridge family descendants Nancy Brown, Dorothy Horner, and Paul and Dottie Ridenour for the answers their genealogical research provided. Their kindness to strangers is something I hope to one day emulate.

To Heather Shores, museum director at Major Ridge's Home/ Chieftain's Museum, and Dee Dee Lamb, friend to the Fayetteville Historical Society, the "Sarah expert," thank you so much. I'd also like to extend my gratitude to David Marion Wilkinson, author of *Oblivion's Altar*, who said, "Major Ridge was the greatest Native American leader, totally forgotten to history." He reminded me that I had every right to tell their story, "to focus on their human relationships." Thank you, sir.

I'd also like to acknowledge Charles Frazier and Tommy Wildcat, who I was honored to hear speak and perform in October of 2019 at a Chieftain's Museum event. Both spoke of the importance of preserving the Cherokee language and how critical it was to preserving Cherokee culture. Their encouragement prompted me to continue writing after hearing their commentary on Cherokee culture and heritage in preserving Native culture, integral to our united, American story.

To the authors and scholars whose research informed so many of my choices: Diane Glancy's *Pushing The Bear*, Charles Frazier's *Thirteen Moons* and *Cold Mountain*, Theresa Strouth Gaul's edits of *To Marry an Indian: Harriet Gold Boudinot's Letters 1823-1839*, Daniel Blake Smith's *An American Betrayal: Cherokee Patriots and the Trail of Tears*, James Parins' *John Rollin Ridge*, Theda Purdue's *Cherokee Women*, and Thurman Wilkins' *Cherokee Tragedy: The Ridge Family and the Decimation of a People*.

Heather Siler and Defiance Press have held my hand through publication. Thank you. I'd also like to thank the contributions of cover art designers and editors who contributed their talents to this project. I hope one day to return their kindness and expertise to another new author. Thank you.

Made in the USA
Columbia, SC
18 September 2021